SAMARITAN

RICHARD PRICE

SAMARITAN

ALFRED A. KNOPF   NEW YORK   2003

THIS IS A BORZOI BOOK
PUBLISHED BY ALFRED A. KNOPF

Copyright © 2003 by Richard Price

All rights reserved under International and Pan-American
Copyright Conventions. Published in the United States
by Alfred A. Knopf, a division of Random House, Inc.,
New York and simultaneously in Canada by
Random House of Canada Limited, Toronto.
Distributed by Random House, Inc., New York.
www.aaknopf.com

Knopf, Borzoi Books, and the colophon are registered
trademarks of Random House, Inc.

Library of Congress Cataloging-in-Publication Data
Price, Richard.
Samaritan / Richard Price. — 1st ed.
p.   cm.
ISBN 0-375-41115-1
1. Police — New Jersey — Fiction. 2. Victims of violent crimes —
Fiction. 3. High school teachers — Fiction. 4. Policewomen —
Fiction. 5. New Jersey — Fiction. I. Title.

PS3566.R544 A78 2003
813'.54 — dc21   2002069378

Manufactured in the United States of America
First Edition

ACKNOWLEDGMENTS

This book could not have been written without the help of the following people: Larry Mullane, Nicky Luster, Jack Smith, Jeff Naiditch, Cassandra Wiggins, Robin Desser, Genevieve Hudson-Price, and especially, Denise Davis.

For Judy, Annie and Gen,
with love

And for Archie A.—in memory

SAMARITAN

Take heed that ye do not your alms before men, to be seen of them: otherwise ye have no reward of your Father which is in heaven.

Therefore when thou doest thine alms, do not sound a trumpet before thee, as the hypocrites do in the synagogues and in the streets, that they may have glory of men. Verily I say unto you, They have their reward.

But when thou doest alms, let not thy left hand know what thy right hand doeth.

—Matthew 6:1–3

Prologue

OUT OF TIME

Ray—January 10

Ray Mitchell, white, forty-three, and his thirteen-year-old daughter, Ruby, sat perched on the top slat of a playground bench in the heart of the Hopewell Houses, a twenty-four-tower low-income housing project in the city of Dempsy, New Jersey.

It was just after sundown: a clear winter's night, the sky still holding on to that last tinge of electric blue. Directly above their heads, sneaker-fruit and snagged plastic bags dangled from bare tree limbs; above that, an encircling ring of fourteen-story buildings; hundreds of aluminum-framed eyes twitching TV-light silver, and above all, the stars, faintly panting, like dogs at rest.

They were alone, but Ray wasn't too concerned about it—he had grown up in these houses; eighteen years ending in college, and naive or not he just couldn't quite regard Hopewell as an alien nation. Besides, a foot and a half of snow had fallen in the last two days and that kind of drama tended to put a hush on things, herd most of the worrisome stuff indoors.

Not that it was even all that cold—they were reasonably comfortable sitting there under the yellow glow of sodium lights, looking out over the pristine crust under which, half-buried, were geodesic monkey bars, two concrete crawl-through barrels and three cement seals, only their snouts and eyes visible above the snow line, as if they were truly at sea.

Two Hispanic teenaged girls cocooned inside puffy coats and speaking through their scarves walked past the playground, talking to each other about various boys' hair. Ray attempted to catch his daughter's eye to see if she had overheard any of that but Ruby, embarrassed about being here, about not belonging here, studied her boots.

As the girls walked out of earshot, the snowy silence returned, a phenom-enal silence for a place so huge, the only sounds the fitful rustling of the plastic bags skewered on the branches overhead, the sporadic buzzing of front-door security locks in the buildings behind them and the occasional crunching tread of tenants making their way along the snowpacked foot-paths.

"Dad?" Ruby said in a soft high voice. "When you were a child, did Grandma and Grandpa like living here?"

"When I was a child?" Ray touched by her formality. "I guess. I mean, here was here, you know what I'm saying? People lived where they lived. At least, back then they did."

At the low end of the projects, along Rocker Drive, an elevated PATH train shot past the Houses, briefly visible to them through a gap in the buildings.

"Tell me another one," Ruby said, her breath curling in the air.

"Another story?"

"Yeah."

"About Prince and Dub?"

"Tell me some more names."

"More?" He had already rattled off at least a dozen. "Jesus, okay, hang on . . . There was Butchie, Big Chief, Psycho, Hercules, Little Psycho—no relation to regular Psycho—Cookie, Tweetie . . ."

"Tell me a story about Tweetie."

"About Tweetie? OK. Oh. How about one with Tweetie and Dub?"

"Sure."

"OK. When I was twelve? Dub's thirteen, we're playing stickball on the sidewalk in front of the building, about eight guys. You know what stickball is?"

"Yes."

"How do you . . ."

"Just go."

"OK. We're playing on the sidewalk. Dub's standing there at the plate, got the bat . . ."

Ray slipped off the bench, struck a pose.

"Ball comes in . . ." He took a full swing. "And behind him is this girl Tweetie, she's just like, daydreaming or whatever, and the stick, on the back-swing, like, clips her right over the eye like, zzzip . . . Slices off half of her eyebrow, the skin, the flesh—"

"Stop." Ruby hissed, jiggling her knees.

"Dub, he doesn't even know he did it. But she's standing there, and you know, like Dub she was black, Tweetie, very dark-skinned, and it's like all of a sudden over her eye there's this deep bright pink gash, totally dry, she says, 'Oh Dub,' in a shock voice, not mad, more like upset, or scared. And, I remember what was freaky to me, was that from the waist up she was calm, but below? Her legs were running in place. And in the next second, that dry pink gash? It just fills up with blood. And now Dub sees what he did, everybody sees it, and I remember, she says, 'Oh Dub,' again, in this fluty voice and then the blood just . . . spills, comes down over that side of her face like someone had turned on a faucet, and everybody just freaks, just . . . We're all twelve, thirteen years old, Tweetie is like, ten, but when we saw all that blood? People, the guys, everybody freaked and most of them, they ran away, they just ran, except me, I'm standing there, and Dub. Dub is still holding the stickbat and he has this angry look on his face like, it's not, it's more like he's stunned, he knows he's in trouble, he knows he should do something, apologize, explain why it's not his fault, but he can't, he can't even move, you know, the blood, and now she's crying, Tweetie, and me, I'm as freaked as anybody but I just wound up going robot on it. What I do is, I pull off my sweaty T-shirt, a white T-shirt, roll it up in a ball and I go over and put it on her eyebrow, like a compress. I'm holding it there with one hand, and I put my arm around her shoulder, she was a short little pudgy kid, a butterball, and I steer her to the curb and we sit on the curb rib to rib. I'm holding my T-shirt to that gash, I got my arm around her, and we just sit there. I have no idea what to do, what I'm doing, she's crying, and Dub, he's still standing there with the stickbat. He looks fierce, like he wants to punch somebody, but he is stone paralyzed . . .

"We're sitting there maybe three minutes, me and Tweetie, I think I got the blood stopped, Dub's playing statue, and all of a sudden I look at him and his eyes go, Pop! Buggin'. And he's, someone's coming from the other direction and just like that he drops the stickbat and hauls ass out of there. And he could run, Dub, but this wasn't running, this was freight-training, he was pumping so hard he could've gone through a wall.

"So I turn to see what made him go off? It's Eddie Paris, his dad. Eddie doesn't chase him or anything. He just crouches down in front of me and Tweetie on the curb, you know, like squatting on the balls of his feet? And he's calm, got a cigarette hanging from his lips, got his hair all processed, you know, marcelled back and I'm like, finally we got a grownup there, thank God, but instantly Tweetie starts saying, 'Mr. Paris, it's not Dub's fault, he didn't see me, it's my fault,' because she, I mean, everybody knew *how Eddie lit into his kids when they screwed up and it was— I guess she was a nice enough person, a kid, I didn't really know her but . . .*

"She says all this stuff to get Dub off the hook, but Eddie, it's like he's not even paying attention to her. He just puts his hand on my hand holding that T-shirt, I mean that thing was a big red sponge by this point, and he tells me to let go and he starts trying to tease the shirt off the gash to see the damage? But he can't. The cotton has meshed with the wound and was like stuck to it so he takes my hand, puts it back on the T-shirt, says, 'Just sit tight.' And that's what we did . . ."

"Where was Tweetie's dad?"

"I don't think she had one. Her family, her mother was some kind of wino or something, had this crackly voice, dragged herself around in a housedress . . ."

"A what?"

"Bathrobe. And she had two older brothers, Tweetie, one was like this ghetto-style drag queen, Antoine, he'd go around in flip-flops and a hair net. He'd like, camel-walk like . . ."

Ray got up again and took a few steps in a languid undulating mime, his eyes both sleepy and predatory. "You know, hung around the boys' room at school, tell you you were standing too close to the urinal, make you take a step back to see what . . ." Ray broke it off. "Anyways, Antoine, he stabbed someone, went to reform school, came out, stabbed someone else, went to jail. And she had this other brother Butchie, in and out of jail, real hard-core tough guy, stickups, guns, drugs, no sense of humor . . ."

"What do you mean no sense . . ."

"I'm, it's a joke."

Ruby stared at him, the story getting away from her.

"OK. Five minutes after he left us, Eddie Paris pulls up to the curb in his station wagon and he puts me and Tweetie in the backseat. We're like Siamese twins connected by a T-shirt.

"He drives us to the Dempsy Medical Center, I'm still with no shirt on and I'm wearing white dungarees."

"Dungarees?"

"Jeans. They just started selling white ones that summer. White, so you can imagine what they looked like with all that blood.

"We go into the emergency room. I'm topless, sitting there with her a half hour on the benches until she gets called. The doctor finally takes over on the T-shirt-holding job, they give me a hospital smock to wear and they *let me watch as they kind of wash the T-shirt away from her eyebrow, little by little; then they sew her up, guy looked like he was lacing a boot.*

"Eddie drives us back home, not saying a word, and little Tweetie, she just keeps up this line of 'Mr. Paris, Dub didn't see me, it's not his fault, it was an accident,' which is pretty amazing that a ten-year-old could have that awareness of other people, the trouble they were in, you know what I'm saying?"

"Go on."

"Eddie just keeps driving, doesn't say a word, takes us back to Hopewell and that was it."

"Did she say thank you?"

"To who."

"To you."

"Nope."

"Why not?"

"I don't know. She was a little kid."

"But she talked about Dub."

"Dub was in trouble, I wasn't. Ruby, she was in fifth grade. 'Thank you' is like Latin to a fifth-grader."

"I would have said thank you."

"And I would have said you're welcome, whatever."

"What happened to Dub?"

"Somebody said that he slept on the roof of our building that night, came home the next afternoon once his dad went off to work. But I don't really know."

"What happened to Tweetie?"

"I'm not sure. Something not good, I think. The last thing I remember with her was about three, four years later, when she was a teenager. She got caught spray-painting 'White Bitch' on the wall of Eleven Building, caught by the housing cops right in the act. And, I remember, that day, being on the basketball courts, all of a sudden everybody's running to the fence and there's Tweetie between these two cops and she's not exactly crying but there's, like, leakage, coming down her face and they just march her off to the management office on the other side of the projects, a whole bunch of kids kind of following them, making jokes and whatever. I mean, I hate to say this, Ruby, but kids can be real shits."

"Did you make any jokes?"

"I don't remember. I hope not."

"Did Dub make any jokes?"

"I don't think he was there."

"Did Dub ever apologize?"

"For the, to Tweetie? My guess is not."

"I would have apologized."

"I don't doubt it."

Another train shot past down on Rocker, distance giving it the scale of a Christmas toy.

"Go on," Ruby said.

"Go on where . . ."

"Tell me another one."

Part I

CONTRECOUP

< Chapter 1

Ray — January 4

Entering Paulus Hook High School for only the second time since graduation twenty-five years earlier, Ray approached the security desk, a rickety
card table set up beneath a blue-and-gold Christmas/Kwanza/Hanukkah
banner, which still hung from the ceiling in the darkly varnished lobby
four days into the New Year.

The uniformed guard standing behind the sign-in book was a grand-
motherly black woman: short, bespectacled, wearing an odd homemade
uniform of fuzzy knit watch cap, gray slacks and a commando sweater, a
khaki ribbed pullover with a saddle-shaped leather patch straddling the
left shoulder.

"You got a visitor's pass?" she asked Ray as he hunched over the sign-in
sheet.

"Me? I'm here to guest-teach a class."

"They give you a teacher's ID?"

"A what?" Then, "No . . ."

Straightening up, he was struck with a humid waft of boiled hot dogs
and some kind of furry bean-based soup that threw him right back into
tenth grade. "Today's my first day."

. . .

With all regulation classrooms booked at this hour, Ray had been offered the faculty lounge to conduct his volunteer writers' workshop, but in his anxiety for this thing to come off he had shown up too early, walking in on four real teachers brown-bagging it around a long conference table that centered the room.

Despite his stranger status, not one of them even looked his way, and after standing inside the doorway for an awkward moment, he quietly maneuvered himself behind a large scuffed desk wedged into a corner and just sat there waiting for the period-ending bell.

The teachers, all men, seemed to be working their way through a hit list of rotten apples.

"Rosario?"

"Out."

"Jenkins?"

"Out."

"Fanshaw?"

"Out. I talked with his mother and I think he's out of the house, too."

"Maldonado?"

"Out. I just told him. I swear, that kid does 'Bewildered' better than anybody on two feet. 'Mr. Rosen, what I do? Suspended! Why?' Because you're on your own fuckin' planet, Edgardo . . ."

"How about Templeton . . ."

"I'm giving him one last chance."

"Aw, he got to you with that smile, huh?"

"Nah, nah nah, I just said, 'Hey Curtis, there's a new statute on the books—Consorting with Known Morons. I see you with Dukey, Ghost, or any of that crew? I don't care if it's a country mile from school property. You're vaporized.'"

"Vaporized?"

"Don't worry, he understood me loud and clear."

They were either ignoring him or simply letting him be, Ray scanning the walls, taking in the student artwork; mostly crude cut-felt mosaics featuring idyllic tableaus of urban positivism: a black family eating dinner together, multicolored neighbors planting a community garden, big brown kids reading to little brown kids.

When the bell finally rang, the teachers at the table groaned to their feet, as reluctant to go back to the classrooms as any of the students.

Three of them filed out of the lounge without ever acknowledging him, but the last one made a stop at the desk, leaning forward on his knuckles to offer a confidence.

"I would rate ninety-six percent of the kids in this school from OK to Great; the other four percent are just stone fucking assholes taking up space and there's nothing we can do about it."

Alone now, Ray took in the disembodied sound track of the students out in the halls, a steady murmurous stream of agitation, punctuated by squawks, bird caws and bellows.

Five minutes went by, the muffled hullabaloo gradually fading away out there, yet he found himself still facing an empty room.

To conceal how awkward and vaguely embarrassed he was beginning to feel, he began fiddling with his cell phone; checking for messages, calling the sports hotline, the 970 weather forecast; played with his datebook; then scribbled down a few introductory notes for his phantom students; coming off busy as hell, yet when the school's principal, Bill or Bob Egan, knocked on the open door of the empty lounge, Ray almost shot to his feet with relief.

Despite his office, the principal, whom Ray vaguely remembered coming in as a new English teacher way back when, struck him as a knockabout guy: knobby-faced, silver-haired, sporting an inexpensive suit and a broad blue tie patterned with New York Giants football helmets.

Swinging around one of the chairs from the conference table, Egan sat facing Ray across the catercorner desk.

"So I understand you're from Hopewell Houses originally," he said, hauling one leg up across the other, the weak afternoon sun hitting his exposed shin, making the fish-white skin there gleam like marble.

"Originally," Ray said, waiting for more.

"I'm from the Howard Houses myself. Used to be half-Irish back then. It was never a picnic but it wasn't like it is now."

"No kidding," still waiting.

"And you graduated from here, what . . . the late seventies?"

"Seventy-eight."

"Seventy-eight. That's great, just great. And for how long were you a writer on that show?"

"Three years," Ray said, understanding now that all this Q and A was nothing but a preamble to an apology.

"Three years," Egan mused. "Out in LA?"

"Yup."

"I spent some time in San Diego when I was in the navy, but I never made it over to LA. Got any new projects in the works?"

"Not really," that question always weighing a ton. "Just kind of recharging my batteries for now." Then, to speed things along, "Other than, you know, teaching this class here." He gestured to the empty conference table.

Egan looked at his wristwatch; winced. "You know I told my Language Arts people, 'Get your kids to the workshop, it's an incredible resource. Make sure you get them . . .' You try to delegate responsibility around here. You try . . ." He winced. "Look, the truth of it is, getting a dozen kids in this building to commit and see through on a voluntary class? It's like pushing a rope. But I know they want to do it. You want to shoot for tomorrow? Same time, same station. And I will personally, physically, get them in here."

"Sure," Ray said, the day now like chalk in his mouth.

Egan got up, shook his hand.

"Hey, we have Wall Street guys coming in here seven, seven-thirty in the morning to tutor? I call the kids at home the night before. 'Yeah, Mr. Egan, I'll be there, I'll be there.'" He shrugged. "Like pushing a rope." He shook Ray's hand again.

"I thank you for your patience with us."

Chapter 2 >

Nerese — February 9

Entering the Hook for the first time since graduation twenty-two years earlier, Detective Nerese Ammons, lugging two slide carousels featuring a
freak show of murdered bodies, confiscated weapons and various drug still
lifes, approached the security desk on shaky pins.

The uniformed guard, tilting back in her folding chair as she watched
Nerese coming on, was Tutsi-tall and sharp as flint, the set of her eyes and
mouth exquisitely unforgiving, eight silver rings dangling in a crescent
along the outer shell of her right ear.

"You got a visitor's permit?" It was more of a throw-down challenge
than a question.

"A what?" Nerese half-snapped, the impersonal hostility combined
with the psychic disorientation of being back in this building working on
her nerves.

The guard just stared at her.

"I'm here for a special assembly," Nerese said more evenly.

"Do you have, a visitor's permit," the guard said a little more loudly, a
little more slowly, Nerese wondering if perhaps at some point over the
years, she had locked up a member of this bitch's family.

. . .

"Let me ask you something!" Nerese near shouted as she prowled the stage of the auditorium, mike in hand. "Let me ask you"—addressing the fistful of hyped yet surly At-Risk students who made up her audience— "who do you think, remember we're talking the police now, who do you think, is the more dangerous of the species. Male? Or female . . ."

"Male!" the boys howled, hooted, spreading their tail feathers, but not really listening.

"Male, huh?" She laughed, the detective's shield clipped to the waist of her dark blue skirt suit winking gold in the mahogany-stained hall. "Male, OK, male."

Having blown off the entertaining yet useless slides after the first tray, the "Be a Leader, Not a Follower" speech altogether, Nerese was winging it this afternoon, almost free-associating.

Trailing mike cord, she walked off the stage to stand before the students in the front row.

"You." She pointed at a big lunk slouched so low in his seat he seemed to be melting, the kid shave-headed with small turned-down ears. "Come on up here . . ."

That was enough to make the others cut loose with another twist-and-shout session, the boy tentatively rising to his feet half-smiling and fake-limping down to the police in front.

She had picked a giant; six-four, -five, towering over her self-consciously, muttering "Shut up" to his classmates in the seats.

"What's your name . . ." She had to rear back to make eye contact.

"Jamiel."

"Shamiel?"

"Jamiel," then, "Shut up," again to the seats.

"OK now," holding Jamiel by the elbow as she addressed the others. "I'm on patrol, I come up on Jamiel here in an alley and he's up to no good. But it's just me and him . . . All things being equal, who do you think's gonna come out that alley like nothing happened. Who . . ."

Some of the kids got all thinky and quiet, trying to suss it out as if it were a trick question, others spinning out to new heights, Nerese ignoring the ruckus. "Who . . ."

"You?" one girl said cautiously, the others tentatively agreeing, the alternative way too obvious.

"All things being equal, you think *me*?" She curled a hand against her chest. "*Hell*, no. Look at this ol' boy! He can kick my behind up one side of the block and down the other . . ."

Jamiel started rocking, a hand covering his face.

"Look at him! What do you think, they teach us some supersecret karate moves? Do I look like Jackie Chan to you?"

The kids turned into popcorn.

"Look at him, and look at me. But now, and this is why I'm telling you the female is the far deadlier of the species . . . Because all things are *not* equal, and if it's just me and him in that alley? I'm gonna do whatever I have to do to survive. If I got the time? I'll get on my radio, call out the troops. But if I don't? I'm goin' right for Baby Huey," patting the holstered Glock on her belt. "See, a male cop, he might be all macho, thinking, Yeah, I'll take this kid down with my bare hands, and all that. But me? Unh-uh. I can't take him like that. And I *will* survive . . . The female, boys and girls, is the far more deadlier of the species . . ."

The PA speakers affixed to the balcony booped loudly, signaling the end of the period, and the kids began to file out of the auditorium, not one of them even looking back at her over their shoulders.

"You're welcome," she said out loud but not really put out, seized as she was by the irresponsibility of her own crackpot lecture, once again proving to herself that you could say anything you wanted in this school system—in this city, most likely—because no one ever really listened anyhow.

She had never considered herself a sour or even pessimistic individual before, and she hoped after retirement she would come back up to the light, but these last few months of endgame assignments were just straight up kicking her ass.

Coming off the stage with her Crime Doesn't Pay slide show in a Waldbaum's shopping bag, she noticed a gray-haired gent in a shiny suit sitting by himself toward the rear of the auditorium, and as she made her way up the aisle he rose to greet her.

"Detective Ammons?" The guy offered his hand, Nerese faltering as she stripped the gray from his hair, filled in a few facial creases.

"Mr. Egan?"

"Yeah," cocking his head. "Do we know each other?"

"Mr. Egan." Nerese brightened. "I was in your English class like twenty-odd years ago. Nerese Ammons?"

"Nerese?" he said tentatively, not remembering her.

"I *loved* that class. I'll never forget, you read us parts of *Grendel* in Old English."

"*Beowulf?*" he gently corrected.

"What did I say," Nerese flushed, praying that he hadn't sat through her Looney Tunes lecture.

"So you're a detective," he beamed. "That's great, just great."

"I also had two years of college," she blurted, embarrassing herself further. "You still teaching English?"

"Well, these days I'm the principal, actually," he said, almost apologetically.

"Hey, there you go." Nerese smiled, but just wanting to get the hell out of there now.

"Listen," Egan took her hand in both of his. "These kids, I can't tell you how grateful we are for you coming in like this."

"No problem." Her hand slid free as she headed once again for the doors.

"Listen, Denise . . ."

"Nerese," she listlessly corrected him, just like she had to correct every third or fourth person who addressed her by name every day of her life.

"Nerese. Sorry." He perched on the arm of a chair. "Can I talk to you about something?"

She dropped into the hinged seat directly across the aisle from him, the two of them dwarfed by the oceanic emptiness of the hall.

"Which district do you work out of?"

"The Bow and Arrow district," she said.

"Come again?"

"I'm ten weeks from retirement. When you have less than a half-year to go they take you out of the field, give you stuff like this." She flapped a hand toward the stage.

"Oh yeah? Why's that?"

"It's a long story." Nerese sinking, sinking.

"The reason I'm asking, Nerese, is that we had a teacher here, a volunteer no less, local guy, terrific guy, was a very successful television writer out in California, came back to town, came to us, offered to teach a writing class off the cuff, got stood up by the kids three four times in a row before I could make it happen. The guy was patient, never complained, just kept showing up until we finally got the thing airborne. Taught here for a month, like I said, a great guy, an incredible resource for us . . ." Egan took a breath, hauled one leg up across the other.

Nerese stole a peek at her watch: 2:15.

"Anyways, two days ago, the guy was assaulted, got his head bashed in pretty good. He's laid up in Dempsy Medical. And, I made some inquiries, they don't know what happened, who did it, but the poor bastard almost died."

"This was in school?"

"No no no. In his apartment. Now, I know a few detectives, made some calls, but my guys, turns out they're retired, on vacation, one guy's under indictment apparently. The thing is, whoever did this? They're still out there and for whatever reason there doesn't seem to be much of an investigation going on, and you know, Jesus Christ, I'd like to see someone nail that sonofabitch."

"No, I hear you," Nerese said softly, thinking, Not my table.

"I mean, I feel like I owe this guy for what he did for the kids here, you know?"

"You think it was any of them?"

"His students? Nah. I mean who the hell knows these days, but no. Not really. Anyways, I'm just wondering if I could impose on you, you know, see if you could look into it, light a fire under somebody's ass, because . . ."

"I'll look into it," Nerese said, just to say something, as she cautiously rose from her seat.

"That's great, just great." Egan offered his hand again, Nerese having to put down her shopping bag to shake.

"By the way," she said. "Your security guard?" She nodded to the lobby. "Has got a real attitude problem."

"Hey," he shrugged, "she's a security guard."

"Nice to see you again, Mr. Egan." And once again she began to make her way up the aisle to the doors.

"Nerese?"

She turned.

"You want the guy's name?"

She just caught herself before asking him, What guy.

"Ray Mitchell," he said.

"Ray Mitchell." She nodded, embarrassed yet again; lethargy tending to perpetrate itself.

She headed for the rear doors again, stopped, turned back. "Ray Mitchell?"

He nodded.

"From Dempsy?"

"Originally," he answered cautiously.

"How old's this guy . . ."

"How old? I don't know. Forty? Early forties?"

"Early forties?" Nerese put down the Waldbaum's bag. "And you're saying he was assaulted?"

Nerese read Egan's awkward silence as a yes, and for the first time in months she felt within herself something akin to joy.

Chapter 3 >

Hospital — February 10

Contrecoup contrecoup contrecoup—the word leaden and tasteless, a gray mantra that braided its way through Ray's open-eyed dreams, the dreams themselves going on and on, stretching like putty and always involving his daughter, Ruby—Ruby in a crowded elevator, someone lecturing her, "They don't give out trophies for trying, and they don't give out trophies for crying"—Ruby building a house out of ice bricks for herself, cheerily rejecting Ray's entreaties to put on a hat and make some friends—Ruby and her dead grandmother in bed, Ray setting up TVs for them to watch; a dozen in a tight horseshoe around the mattress.

Ray clawed his way back into the world with a tooth-grinding hypnagogic lurch; then lay there in the hospital bed, balloon-brained, trying to remember what had happened to him. He slipped back into dreams, then fought his way out again and again and again, each time resurfacing with another detail, another crummy piece of the puzzle.

All the beds in the monitored-care ward were separated from each other by Plexiglas partitions and open at the foot facing the nurses' station, so that the only way he could get any privacy was to keep his eyes shut; the problem with that was the brilliant juddering sparks that went off against the darkness every time he lowered his lids.

Catching his reflection in a stainless-steel pitcher on the night table, he discovered that the whites of his eyes had turned cherry red, the surrounding skin from forehead to cheekbone now slick and purple as a braised onion. And then, with a sleepwalker's detachment, he took in the shaved patch, the circumference of a wineglass, on the left slope of his skull, bristling with blood-blackened stitches.

A nurse entered and adjusted his IV drip.

"Your wife and daughter's out there, do you want them to come in?"

He could tell from the set of her mouth that it was taking him too long to process the question.

"No," he finally, drunkenly blurted, his head paper-thin and pulsing. "No," saying it more calmly, trying to seize control of himself, but no way would Ruby get to see him like this.

"No problem," she shrugged.

He noticed that the pinky on his left hand was thickly taped, the dressing extending down across his palm and terminating in a mooring bind around his wrist.

"Contrecoup," he said.

"Come again?"

"Contrecoup. What's contrecoup."

"That's the fourth time you asked me that today."

Ray waited.

"It's a shift in the brain mass," she said easily. "You take a good enough whack up here?" She suspended the heel of her palm between his eyes, the mere thought of contact nauseating him. "The brain gets bounced to the opposite side of the cranial cavity, then rebounds back to the center. It's like whiplash of the gray matter. Contrecoup. Maybe I should write it down for you."

There was no way he could judge if this last comment of hers was sarcastic, and he couldn't marshal his wits to ask if that was what had happened to him, although why else would that be the new word for today. Or yesterday. Or the day before that . . .

Sighting from the open foot of his bed straight through the glass exterior wall that separated the monitored-care ward from the main hallway, he caught a slice of his ex-wife and their daughter seated on a couch out by the elevator bank, Ruby's eyes wet, mouth pursed, his ex with an arm around her shoulder, looking self-contained yet braced: a crisis goalie.

But before he could organize a coherent reaction to the sight of them, a short heavyset black woman wearing a stocking cap and a North Face coat, a grocery bag in either hand, came barreling into his stall with the proprietary air of a nurse coming on duty.

"Hey, Ray! How you doing?" near-shouting as if to be heard over loud music, the hip-length puffy coat making her as round as a ball.

She put down the bags, which were brimming with videos; Ray now thinking that she was some kind of civilian candy striper, a recreation aide.

"Do you know who I am?" She briskly rubbed her hands as if she were still outside, then unzipped her coat to reveal the detective's shield clipped to the breast pocket of a lumberjack shirt.

"A cop?" he said distractedly, desperately trying to put together a response to Ruby and her mother out in the lobby.

"But who *am* I," going all playful on him like it was a game.

She brought herself to the edge of the bed, Ray reading "N. Ammons" off her shield.

"I don't believe this," she said with theatrical exasperation.

"N. Ammons," he said, a little frightened of her now; all this bizarre familiarity. "N. Ammons, N. Ammons . . ."

"Ray," she cut him off. "Up here."

She touched the remains of her left eyebrow, more than half of it a whitish plug of scar tissue, all the more livid for being set against the deep brown of her skin.

"Tweetie," he said flatly.

"Tweetie . . ." She laughed deep and gravelly like a man, took off her coat and dropped heavily into the visitors' chair next to his bed. "Nobody's called me that since the Flood."

"Tweetie Ammons," he said, his eyes flitting back and forth between the elevator banks and this woman who might or might not actually be here. "And you're a cop."

"Going on twenty years. So you remember this, huh?"

"The stickbat. With Dub."

"With Dub. He's a cop too now, a sergeant over in Jersey City."

"Your brothers are Antoine and Butchie and your mother is Olive."

"That's right," she said in a more sober tone, sizing him up now.

"So how are they?" Ray trying so hard but sounding to himself like a cordial robot.

"Nah nah nah," she growled. "Don't get me goin' there. How's yours? How's your folks?"

"My mother's dead, my father's down in Mississippi."

"Aw, I liked your moms, Ray. She was like a movie star."

"Yeah," he said. "She thought so, too."

"Man, I hate this hospital . . ." Nerese hunkered in, her voice dropping to a confidential drawl. "Can I tell you what happened to me here one time?"

Ray's ex-wife finally got up from the couch and pushed the elevator button, refueling his struggle over how to greet them.

"Ray, you got to hear this . . . *Ray.*" Nerese touched his hand to bring him around. "Last December, right before Christmas? Me and my partner, Willy Soto, we caught a job up in the Heights, some old Irish lady, her live-at-home son had broke her nose, right? So we bring her here, but we can't find the son. Turns out the guy was an ex-cop about forty years old, a juicer, OK? So, all right, we get an order of protection for her, a warrant for him. Now, I went back to the building and interviewed this woman's neighbors, found out that the guy, when he got his load on? He used his mother like a regular punching bag but she never once complained, called 911, asked him to move out, nothing. And, you know, when I heard that, I knew she was gonna protect her little baby no matter what, right? So, back in the hospital I go to the lady in the next bed, give her my card, tell her if your roommate's red-nosed Sonny Boy shows up, you page me."

"Huh," Ray declared, trying to fall into the story, but at the same time becoming aware of a vague sense of shame starting to creep up on him, curling in wisps around his heart.

"Anyways, the next day, I get the page, the eagle has landed. Me and Willy, bang, we race down here, catch him in the room hanging over his mother's hospital bed, yelling in her face, something about money. So we drag him out to the hallway, you know, trying to cuff him up?

"All of a sudden the nurses, the doctors, the visitors, everybody starts yellin' at us, 'Hey! Hey! What are you doing to him! We're calling Security! Somebody call Security!' You know, because Willy's black too, so all they saw was two thugs pounding on a white man, read us as some kind of middle-aged gangbangers, crackheads, or whatever. Then Sonny Boy starts screaming, 'Get this fat black bitch off me!' At which point I'm like, Fuck the handcuffs, and I just start whaling on him because Ray, I am not that fat. But in any event, here comes Security, me and Willy, we got our hands full with this guy, neither one of us can get to our shields, next thing we know we're fighting with Security too! It took fif-teen minutes for them to get it through their thick racist-ass skulls that we were cops. And that sonofabitch almost got away from us again, can you believe that?"

"Yes."

"Sure you can. And after that? I came here every day to visit that nice old lady to try and drill it into her head that her son was a mortal danger to her. But don't you know soon as she went home she had him move right back in with her?

"And six months later, guess what happened . . ."

"He killed her," Ray said.

"Nah. She's fine." Nerese waved him off. "Him, on the other hand, he got good and oiled one night, wound up run over by a PATH train. Toot-toot. Peanut butter." Nerese laughed. "God is good, huh?"

"Tweetie," Ray said. "You're a cop."

"Yeah, but what's even better"—she leaned in closer, rubbing her hands—"right now I'm *your* cop. So what happened?"

And just like that, she lost him, his bloodred eyes sliding away from her in a sullen glaze.

The catching detective had told her that Ray wouldn't cooperate, which, in the always hopping city of Dempsy, New Jersey, automatically dropped the case into the Fuckit file.

"What happened, Ray," waiting out both his willful reticence and the typically slow reaction time of a concussed victim. "Can you remember what happened?"

Having interviewed countless blunt force trauma vics over the last two decades, Nerese had a reasonably good idea of what she was dealing with here, the lacerated scalp resting atop either a so far bloodless brain contusion or a small intracranial bleed; anything more dire, and the skull would have been burr-holed to clip the bleed and evacuate the overflow.

And although the monitor showed his BP at 110 over 70 and his heart rate holding steady at 75, the IV was pumping Decadron, a powerful steroid given to control swelling of the brain, which probably meant the poor bastard hadn't really slept since he'd been admitted and most likely immediately hooked up—no one slept on Decadron—which further meant that in addition to whatever disorientation he was experiencing, he was also probably on his way to a nice bout of sleep disorder psychosis, steroid psychosis, critical care unit psychosis, take your pick. He could also develop a subdural hematoma, the gap between the skull lining and the brain filling with expelled blood from the healing tissue, the doctors in that case, too, needing to go in drilling to relieve the pressure. Any and all of this meant she had to work fast, before he became either too estranged from reality or straight-out unconscious; any and all of this liable to happen in a blink, the emotional and medical status of brain-whack patients as treacherously unstable as the weather conditions around Mount Everest.

The problem with Nerese working fast, though, was that she was world famous for her tortoiselike pace—getting where she was going more often than not, but, as Willy Soto had once said, "Fast ain't your speed."

"Ray." She took his hand in hers. "You need to tell me what happened."

"Doorbell rings," he finally said. "I open the door, next thing I know some paramedic's asking me my date of birth."

"Doorbell rings," she nodded, reaching into one of the shopping bags and pulling out a notepad. "You got a doorman?"

"An intercom," he said grudgingly, Nerese taking his willful surliness as a good sign, at least biology-wise.

"An intercom. So, you've got to buzz people up, right?"

"He must've rung someone else's buzzer, got in the building that way."

"He?"

"I'm assuming."

"OK." She shrugged. "'He' rings your doorbell. You ask who's there? Or did you just open up the door?"

He took a long time answering, Nerese not sure if it was the head injury or Ray just trying to buy some time here.

"I don't remember. I must've asked who's there, I guess. I don't remember."

"Look through the peephole?"

"If I did, I don't remember."

"Don't remember. OK, so you open the door. Next thing you're in a rig heading for the hospital. So whoever did this, it's not like you invited them inside because you'd most definitely remember that, right?"

"Right."

"Ray . . . When you came to the door, were you carrying a big vase with you?"

"A what?" he said, then, "No."

"You got one in the house?"

"I guess."

"Where in the house?"

"Living room."

"Where in the living room?"

"In a corner, between the couches."

"See, Ray, I'm asking, because the medics told me, they come up to get you, you're laying there, someone had smashed a big vase over your head. Blood and plaster everywhere."

"Shit."

"They said you were seizing up, flopping around like a fish on a dock, had a sharp chunk of plaster in your fist?" She pointed with her pen to his bandaged pinkie, Ray staring at it as if he had never realized that there was a hand at the end of that particular arm. "Almost severed your own finger there."

He closed his eyes, winced as if pricked, opened them.

"So let me ask you this . . . When you opened the door, was this guy by any chance *carrying* a big vase? You know, like waiting for you, like, 'Surprise!'"

He didn't answer.

"OK . . . So you must've gotten clocked with that vase that was sitting in the corner between the two couches, huh?"

He started to turn away from her, reaching weakly behind him to close his open-backed smock, then gave up.

"So this guy had to have entered your apartment, looked around, spotted the vase, walked over to the corner between the two couches, picked up the vase, come back up to you and . . ." Nerese mimed raising that vase over his head, slowly bringing it down in front of his face.

"Why are you making me feel like I'm the criminal," he said without heat.

"Ray. Are you afraid of this guy?"

"What guy . . ."

"Ray." She sighed. "You invited the guy in, or he pushed his way in, or something, but there's no way you can tell me you have no memory of it."

Looking overwhelmingly dejected, he finally successfully rolled on his side away from her, delicately pulling the thin blanket up to his ribs to cover himself.

"Ray, you know this guy, don't you . . ."

He turned back to her.

"You know, you have used my name in front of everything you've said to me. That's a technique car salesmen use."

"Ray, are you afraid of him?"

"No," he said calmly, finally, as if not having the stamina for all this.

"You know him though, right?"

She was on the verge of repeating the question when he finally responded. "I don't want to press charges."

Nerese nodded, trying to read him, picking up not fear—more like embarrassment, shame; thinking, Maybe something sexual, man-man, hoping it wasn't man-boy, Ray just wanting it to go away at any price.

"You want me to press them for you? I can do that."

"No."

"How 'bout I just run him for outstanding warrants? Get him like that? You don't have to have nothing to do with it. Just give me a name."

"No. No. No." A weary, determined chant.

"Ray, please don't make me go out to the lounge and get all psychological on your pretty daughter out there. 'Did you ever see your dad have an argument with anybody. Did your dad ever seem worried about anybody. Can you think of anyone who'd want to hurt . . .' Because I tell you, Ray, I don't know about your wife . . ."

"Ex."

"Whatever, but I took one look at your daughter's sad little face out there? And I *know* she's got something for me."

His eyes reflexively shifted to the right of her, trying to see through the glass wall to the elevator banks. The girl and her mother must have left, because when he spoke again his voice was stronger. "What's with all the videotapes?" He nodded to the shopping bags at her feet.

"We had a homicide in a Burger King down on JFK. These are from the security cameras. Twenty-four hours of people eating themselves to death."

"Tweetie," he said in that flat tone of his. "Last time I saw you, you were getting snatched up for spray-painting 'White Bitch' on the side of Eleven Building. How are you a cop."

"C'mon, Ray," she said softly, "I was thirteen years old."

"How are you a cop."

"I'm gonna save that one for down the line with you," she said cleanly. "When I, re-know you better. Because that one there, is the story to end all stories. But I'll make you a deal . . ."

"What's the N. for," nodding to her shield.

"Nerese."

"Nerese," he repeated. "Where'd 'Tweetie' come from."

Nerese smiled; they were drifting way off subject; but if he needed to shoot the shit for a while, hear a story or two before he would give it up to her, she could do that.

"My grandmother had a cleft palate or something. That's how she said 'Sweetie.'"

"Sweetie," Ray tried it on for size. "Officer Sweetie."

"Actually, it's Detective Sweetie. At least for the next few months. Then I'm out."

"Out?"

"Retiring."

"Retiring . . . What are you, forty? Forty-one?"

"Something like that. See, you can retire after twenty years, go out with half pay for the rest of your life, and believe me, I am going. This job's for shit these days if you don't have a political hook, which I don't, so come this summer? I'm moving to Florida, like near Jacksonville? That's where my mother's people are from originally. My son's father's people, too. You ever been to Florida?"

"Tweetie, I'm a Jew," he said, and from the great effort he made to smile she guessed it was some kind of joke.

"Ray, I swear to God, every time I get off the plane down there? It all slows down. Air's all sweet . . . And, I tell my son Darren, he's almost eighteen, I tell him if he don't get accepted into a college with a scholarship attached, or have a real job come June? He's going into the army, 'cause Mommy has left the building. Not that he believes me or anything. He's just like his father, wherever he may be, a big baby, thinks I was put on this earth to stuff his face and clean his mess. But it's not just my son. I got a ton of people I'm carrying, and I more or less need to square them all away before I go."

She took a breather, checking Ray out, not wanting him to go south on her, his hobbled mind lagging too far behind what she was building for him here. He looked fairly sunk into himself but was still listening.

"See, I bought this house in Jersey City, about five years ago, right? I gave the upstairs to my mother, she's so preserved in alcohol I don't think she'll *ever* die, she's like seventy-five now and she's up there with her brother, my uncle, he's like seventy-eight, and downstairs it's me and my son, OK?

"Now, outside the house? I got my brother Antoine, you remember Antoine? Who, by the way, legally changed his name to Toni a few years back. Anyways, Antoine, Toni, he's got the Package now . . ."

"Unh," Ray softly grunted in sympathy, giving his face to her again.

"Yeah," bobbing her head in acknowledgment. "Sometimes he's in the hospital, sometimes he's in jail, sometimes he's on my couch. I'm trying to get him into this Christian Brothers hospice over in Bayonne, but he's not quite sick enough yet . . .

"And my brother Butchie, you remember him too, right? He's in jail. Again. But he'll be out soon. Again. I tell him he can't come around anymore, but he will. He likes to break in through the back door in the middle of the night. The way I find out about it is when I go down in the morning, see him dead asleep in the pantry, like to scare me half to death. He's lucky I haven't shot his ass . . . And you want to hear something else? I go down to Florida three months ago to see my cousins? And, as a courtesy I go visit my son's paternal grandfather because I had heard that he was mandated into a state home for the elderly. I go in there, he takes one look at me, sits up in bed, says, 'Flossie?' He always thinks I'm his dead daughter Flossie. Anyways, he's like, 'Flossie? If you leave me here, I'll *die* here . . .' So, what the hell, I go and bring him back up with me to New Jersey, get him checked out by my doctor? Doctor says he's got creeping dementia, it's an early warning sign of Alzheimer's. But Ray"—Nerese touched his arm again to keep him in this—"the man is ninety-seven years old. Ninety, seven. He ain't got time for early warning signs of *shit*. So, OK. I go and stick him upstairs with my mother and uncle, and it's like 'Hell Up in Harlem.'"

Ray sighed, a deep chest-lifting exhalation that ended in tears. "Tweetie, I'm so fucked," not looking at her.

She put her hand in his, and he took it.

"You want to tell me what's going on?"

"No," he said, "but keep talking."

She waited a beat, to see if he'd say anything else, then got back into it. "See, Ray, I think one of the reasons I became a police officer to begin with was to make my family keep its distance. 'You want to be a criminal, Antoine? Butchie? You too?' 'Well, you know you can't be near me no more. I'm not gonna waste time telling you shit is wrong. You just best stay away 'cause I'm on the Job and that's that.'

"But I tell you, Ray, praise to God, I have discovered over the years that I am blessed. I am truly blessed. And so now I'm like the man in the family, carrying everybody. But I don't know if I'm doing anybody any favors. They could probably learn to make it on their own, you know, most of them, which is good for me, because the truth be known? Yes, I am blessed, but I am also tired. I am as tired as I am blessed, and that's no lie.

"Like, OK. You want to hear a typical day off for me? A few weeks ago, that ninety-seven-year-old man I parked upstairs? He don't . . . He's crazy with that dementia thing. My mother's all like, 'Get that man out of my house!' *Her* house, right? But so, OK . . . I make some calls, cash in some favors, and I get him placed in Beth Abraham, a seniors' home something like five blocks from the house.

"So like, last Saturday I get Darren to pack him up, I take him over to the home, sign him in, take him up to his new room, unpack, and I see my son has done his usual expert job. The man's got no pajamas, no robe, no toothbrush, no . . . So I leave him there, go running to Caldor's over in Gannon, get him underwear, toothpaste, I don't even remember if the man's got *teeth*, underpants, socks, a belt, slippers; store's a Saturday mad-house, checkout line's a mile long . . . I run back to Beth Abraham, old man's sitting up in bed just like in Florida, 'Flossie,' he says, 'if you leave me here, I'll *die* here. You ain't even a *Christian* no more.'

"And I want to say, 'Oh yeah? How 'bout you save that "no Christian" shit for that forty-six-goin'-on-five-year-old poppa-was-a-rollin'-stone no-show son of yours, except, oh yeah, I don't see him around here for you to say that to . . . In fact, I haven't seen him around here for you to say that to since I brung your no-blood-relation-of-mine ass up from Florida three months ago.'

"See, but I don't say any of that. The man's old and scared, and God doesn't give us any more than he thinks we can handle and I am truly, truly blessed. However, that's a typical day off for me, Ray, so who broke that vase over your head, just give me the name so I can lock his ass up, go home, get in bed and watch *ER* like everybody else. What do you say, huh?" She touched her scarred eyebrow. "C'mon. I owe you one . . ."

‹ Chapter 4

Classroom — January 7

A moment after the eerie electronic *boop* that signaled the beginning of class, Principal Egan finally, finally, after three days of false starts, herded seven students into the faculty lounge, the kids all flat-faced, eyes averted, not a smile in the bunch. There were four girls, two black, one Latina, one who could've been either, all with hair shellacked into frozen flips and waves, all sporting huge gold earrings, two with crucifixes on chains, the girls looking good; and three boys, two black, both of them in long-sleeved white shirts, cuffs buttoned above bony wrists, their ties askew, and a chubby, prepubescent Latino kid with a short inarticulate haircut, this boy also sporting a crucifix, which on him Ray found both off-putting and reassuring.

Unable to look them in the eye as they scraped back their chairs before settling in at the long table, he directed his attention to the principal.

"Seven?" speaking over their heads as if they were refrigerators or air conditioners.

"Hey," Egan shrugged, "be thankful for that many."

"No no no, that's fine, that's fine."

"They're good kids." Egan turned to them. "Right?" Then left the room.

Ray sat there in this new silence, trying to smile, but it was a rictus grin, so he stopped, buried his nose in his one page of notes, then went at it again.

"How you doin'," his voice too Bowery Boy, but before he could reinvent himself, another blast from the PA invaded the room from the small loudspeaker mounted above the blackboard.

"Mr. Moffat, please come to the Resource Room, Mr. Moffat . . ." in a dead Dempsy drawl.

"What is this, the Medical Center?"

Nothing; two of the girls exchanging glances, playing with the stiff collars of their blouses; all the others fascinated by their own nails, the wood grain of the table; the air suffused with wariness.

"OK," he began again, and again was interrupted, this time by a stocky skirt-suited woman bustling into the lounge, black-eyed, black-haired, all manila folders and eyeglass chains, the students sagging with recognition.

"Hi," addressing Ray as she scraped up a seat. "I'm Mrs. Bondo and I'll be sitting in."

"For today?" Ray not liking this.

"For a while." Then, "Can you sit up, Rashaad?"

"OK." He finally plunged in. "My name is Ray Mitchell, this is the writers' workshop. Show up every week, do the requested work and I'll throw you an A."

"They're not receiving grades for this, just extra credit," Mrs. Bondo said.

"OK. Show up, do the work, I'll throw you twenty dollars."

Two of the girls exchanged "This man he crazy" looks; the long bony boy Rashaad saying, "Dag, I'll take it."

Ray wasn't displeased with this reaction until he checked out Mrs. Bondo; the woman smiling but not amused. Ray was becoming more and more focused on her and, losing some of his gun-shyness around the kids, he gave them his first clear-eyed look.

"You guys seem young for high school."

"They're all ninth-graders," Mrs. Bondo said.

"Ninth?" Ray repeated, then got it; none of these kids were from the bunch that had stood him up for the last three days running; Egan had most likely jettisoned that whole crew and shanghaied a batch of more malleable freshmen, those less savvy to the ways of the Hook, less sure of how to get out of things. Fine with him.

"Ninth grade. Great. So, OK. I'm going to tell you who I am, what I'm doing here, and then we'll go around the horn and give names, whatever else you want to say, OK?"

Nothing.

"First off. Everybody knows this class is creative writing, right?"

Two hands went up.

"Yes, you know, or . . ."

"I thought this was supposed to be a club," the Latino boy said. He wore gold-framed glasses and had a pretty good likeness of The Rock drawn in ballpoint on the cover of his three-ring binder.

"It's a class, it's a club. OK, it's a club. Next week I'll give out membership cards and teach you the secret handshake."

Unable to read this manic spritzing, the kids looked at him, then at each other, Ray telling himself, Slow down, slow down.

"In any event, my name is Ray Mitchell. I grew up across the street in Hopewell just like some of you."

"For real?" one of the girls drawled.

"For real. You heard of back in the day? I was there in back of in back in the day. Sixties, early seventies. I went to this school right here, not a great student, went to college, taught high school for a while, quit"—leaving out why—"and started driving a cab. And I drove that cab for a lot of reasons, not the least of which was because I wanted to be a writer and I figured that's where the stories were, in the backseats of taxis. But unfortunately that's not exactly how it works, so I must have put a million miles on that thing without ever really writing anything worth killing a tree for." That one went over everyone's head including Mrs. Bondo's, the "Mrs." already set in his mind as hard and fast as if he were a ninth-grader himself. "Then I became a . . . Does anybody here know what a polygraph is?"

"Algebra?" the chubby kid ventured.

"Not, no . . ." His voice hanging.

"Lie detector." One of the black girls, dark black with big Bo Diddly–framed eyeglasses, the lacquered waves of her hair arranged in a sequence of arches like the roof of the Sydney Opera House.

"Exactly. Thank you. I worked for a small outfit which gave lie detector tests to people looking for low-end jobs which required them to be around money or merchandise." Ray gave that girl a second look; the way she had calmly given the answer, no "Ooh-ooh" with her hand in the air.

"And let me tell you, if you're a big fan of weird in this life, tying people up with rubber tubing eight hours a day, then scaring them into ratting themselves out, is definitely a way to go."

Off-balance blankness all around the table. Ray wondered how he had ever done this full-time for five years without getting fired—recalled, then, that he sort of had . . .

"Anyways, after that I went back to driving a cab, and then through a series of circumstances, mostly embarrassing, I finally became a writer— but not the way I envisioned it. I got a writing *job*, wrote for a TV show, which is to say, I went from driving a hack, to being one."

Stares and more stares; Ray once again telling himself, Calm. Down.

"Well, in any event, I became one of the writers on *Brokedown High*."

"The TV show?" the Latina girl said, the table slightly coming to life.

"The TV show."

"You wrote that?"

"Myself and others."

"Whoa."

"Yes, I'd have to say, that was fairly phat of me."

Mrs. Bondo threw him another restrained smile that made him want to end this as quickly as possible; drop the one-fifth of an Emmy nomination altogether.

"In any event . . ."

There was another electronic shout-out. "Mr. Cromartie? Mr. Cromartie, please come to the principal's office. Mr. Cromartie?"

He restrained himself from another wisecrack, infinitesimally but with great effort attempting to close down his nightclub approach to education; every positive change in his life, every minute increment in character, acquired more or less through shame.

"OK, so, who are you guys?" Nodding to the chubby kid with the wrestler drawn on his binder.

"Efram," he said, sinking into his shirt collar.

"Efram . . ." Ray waiting.

"They know," he shrugged.

"Efram They Know."

"Last name too, Efram," Mrs. Bondo said.

"Bello."

"Efram Bello," Ray said. "OK, so if Mrs. Bondo married Efram Bello, her name would become Mrs. Bondo-Bello, right?"

Hands flew to mouths all around the table, stifled sniggers and gasps, the kids going all big-eyed, Ray thinking how odd it was that these projects kids, witness all their lives to such extremes in human behavior, would be so easily shocked by the slightest breach of teacher decorum. It didn't take a genius to explain this paradox, but he was way too percolated to think about it beyond his initial observation.

"OK, you there, young sir . . ."

"Rashaad," the boy said, then added, after glancing at Mrs. Bondo, "Macbeth."

"Rashaad Macbeth?"

The boy's long narrow face, high forehead, slightly bulging eyes and small startled mouth made Ray think of a newborn giraffe.

Then the other five: Dierdre, Felicia, Myra, Jamaal and Altagracia; each name given quietly, no tongue-clucking, no peripheral eyeballing, no playing for the back rows; Ray so far having braced himself for nothing. The sobriety of the roll call could have been due to the close quarters of the seminar table, the presence of Mrs. Bondo, the unknown subject, or more astonishingly to Ray, they could simply be a bunch of nice fourteen-year-old kids.

"OK. Let me ask you—this is creative writing. This is voluntary. Somebody tell me why you're here."

"'Cause I got stories," said Rashaad, his hand half-raised.

"Yes," Ray said almost gratefully. "'I got stories.' You all have stories, whether you know it or not. And here, right here, is where you're going to give them up."

He reached into the shopping bag at his feet, pulled out seven of the ten red-and-black writing journals he had bought for them across the river in Chinatown and dealt them out like playing cards.

"'But Officer, I don't *have* any stories.' 'Oh ho, indeed you do, my dear,'" Ray backsliding, doing voices once again, trying to get them to laugh, although he was too jazzed now to care if they did or didn't. "You have crazy mad stories, *all* of you. Everybody here, if I go around the table and squeeze you a little? Each and every one of you can give me six great stories. That's six times seven kids equals forty-two plus fourteen between me and Mrs. Bondo equals fifty-four . . ."

"Fifty-six," said Efram.

"Fifty-six, thank you, stories. They're about your friends, your neighbors, your families, most definitely your families . . . And these are very very important stories to you. Stories you've grown up with. The time my uncle got so angry that . . . The, the day my grandmother left her house thinking that . . . My parents, the first time they met, they . . . My brother, just 'cause that other kid dared him, I couldn't believe it when he . . . Oh man, my mother, I've never seen her like that when she . . .

"And all these stories, they're up here," touching his temple, "and in here," touching his heart, corny but what the hell. "And we love them, because they're ours. Because even if they're not true, and believe me, at least half of these stories are not, they've set up house in us, they're part of us, they *are* us . . .

"Yeah, OK," talking to himself now more than to them. "This is great. OK, this class? Forget it. OK? Don't even think of it as creative writing. It's just stories. The writing assignments? Stories, telling stories . . . Can somebody wake this guy up?"

One of the girls punched the boy Jamaal, whose forehead was resting on the table; Ray so happy now, stories his lifelong lifeline; to Ruby, to romance, to himself; stories the ballast, the crash cart, the air.

"And the thing is, what are you, Hopewell kids? Neighborhood kids? Oh man, nobody out there knows what you know . . . And what you may think of as, as, everyday? As boring? That's like . . . No. That's . . . Me? When I want to read something, a book, a story, a newspaper article, I'm thinking, Time is tight, why should I read this? What does this individual have to tell to me that I don't already know?"

Then checking himself, something off in the message.

"Not that what you write has to be a show-stopper, mind-boggling or, you know, 'Can you top this?' All I am saying, is, believe me, you're all so much more interesting, so much more special than you might think.

"So, every week, you're going to write me a few pages, doesn't have to have a beginning or an end, just some kind of snapshot, word picture, bring it in and read it to the class or I'll read it for you and we'll talk. Questions?"

Jamaal, the sleeper, raised his hand. "Does spelling count?"

The girl with the big-framed glasses, Myra, clucked her tongue in irritation.

"Spelling is good. It's good to have spelling." His disappointment in the question was neutralized by this Myra; something cooking there.

"Can we write in pencil?"

"Pencil, pen, blood, as long as I can decipher it."

"Do they have to be true?"

"Fool me. OK. You know what? What do we have left, twenty minutes? Does anybody want to kick it off and give up a story right now?"

The immediate reaction was unilateral silence, frowny and tense.

"Just verbal, any story." Then, "Anything. A dream, a joke . . ."

Not one of them would so much as meet his eye; Ray quickly coming to understand that he wouldn't be able to pry loose a volunteer from this crew right now with blasting caps.

"C'mon, one brave soul."

He gave it a perfunctory ten count, then flopped his hands onto the table. "OK, then," his voice heavy with surrender. "You leave me no choice but to give you one of my own."

Off the hook for now, the class settled into their spines.

And in this first moment of relaxed surrender to him, Ray learned something: Rashaad Macbeth loved Felicia Stevenson, the tall butter-scotch-colored girl who sat directly across the table from him, but sad to say, Ray positive about this, this love was a one-way deal.

Since the beginning of class the boy had been alternating deep scrutiny of his pen tip with throwing her quick furtive glances; thirty seconds for the pen, two seconds for Felicia; thirty and two, thirty and two, but the girl hadn't glanced his way even once.

"OK," Ray began. "Here we go. Growing up, I had a cousin Jackie, my grandmother's sister's son, about ten years older than me. Now Jackie's dad—his name was Stubby—was a really short guy, five-three, five-four, and Stubby had a very dark complexion and very dark eyes because he was half Russian Jew, half Guatemalan Indian, which is a whole other story in itself. Now Jackie's older brother, Benny? He looked just like Stubby—dark skin, eyes, five foot three. The problem was that Jackie had yellow-blond hair, and by the time he was eleven? Was very close to six feet tall, and, even though Jackie's mother was fair-skinned, Stubby had decided that the kid wasn't his, that his wife had gotten pregnant by some other man and, that was that. And the way he dealt with it, was to freeze Jackie out. He wouldn't talk to him, wouldn't touch him, wouldn't look at him; this little boy just didn't exist for him. I mean this, this Stubby, he was one of those angry shrimps who go into the Golden Gloves; mean pissed-off midgets, just want to punch out the world because they're so short. You know, the worst kind of bullies . . ."

"And to be honest, Jackie might *not* have been his. His mother, my great-aunt, I don't know, she was kind of there, not there, *did* have boyfriends, eventually flew the coop, so . . ."

Ray checked on Bondo, who seemed to be holding herself off.

"In any event, by the time Jackie was your age, younger even, he was a severely abused child, you know, psychologically.

"And, my grandmother, Jackie's mother's sister, her name was Ceil, she told me that when Jackie was little she'd hear him down in the street calling up, 'Aunt Ceil, Aunt Ceil,' you know, down there by himself, this was on Tonawanda Avenue back in the early fifties, my whole family, aunts, uncles, grandparents, they all lived in three, four different walk-ups on Tonawanda . . . Anyways, my grandmother, later on she'd tell me, 'Ray, I'm ashamed of myself to the day I die but whenever I'd hear Jackie down there calling up to me, I'd never go to the window, I'd never invite him to come up because I was afraid of Stubby.'"

"Guy's like five-three?" Rashaad reared back in disdain.

"I know, but sometimes rage has a way of blowing people up."

"Five-three." Rashaad shot a quick glance at Felicia.

"Anyways, Jackie, by the time he was thirteen, was pretty much an alley cat, a street kid, and by the time he was fifteen? He was shooting heroin."

Mrs. Bondo shifted like a mountain, exhaled heavily through her nose, and Ray froze: what the hell he was doing, telling this story—trying to establish his down credentials? Get over as an honorary hard-knock homie? But he was hip-deep in it, and thinking it would be pointless to stop right now, he forged on.

"To tell you the truth, I never really knew my cousin Jackie, there was too much of an age difference, but what I *think* I remember, was a very sweet guy, very friendly, kind of gabby, and big. *Huge.* I'm talking six-four, well over two hundred pounds, plus he was a weight lifter. I mean, from what I was told, if you didn't know that he was a drug addict, you could never have guessed it."

Ray faltered again, trying to figure out how to race through the rest; couldn't, and decided to continue at the pace he needed despite his fear of getting panned or reproached.

"Anyways, by the time Jackie was in his mid-twenties, he'd been struggling with his addiction close to ten years. His mom had split when he was sixteen, so it was just him, his brother Benny and Stubby. And, he'd be out there in the street running with the wolves—ripping people off, getting high, arrested, going to jail, ripping people off, getting high, arrested, going to jail . . . And, the closest thing he had to a guardian angel, a friend, a father figure back then was this guy who lived down the street,

Jack Zullo, who was a highly decorated and highly connected Dempsy detective. And unlike everybody in my hear-no-evil, see-no-evil family, Jack Zullo had seen and heard it all, every type of grief and human misery out there, and he always felt sorry for Jackie, hated Stubby and did what he could to help my cousin out, which pretty much boiled down to fixing it so that he would skate now and then when he came before a judge. Now, you have to remember that this was the early 1960s, and at that time, rehab, therapy, any kind of positive-oriented drug treatment was pretty much unheard of in this city. Basically drug addicts were seen as evil degenerate criminals."

"They are," Rashaad said imperiously, some of the other kids sucking wind, checking out Ray to see if he'd take that as an affront; but he was too busy racing the anxiety clock.

"Anyways, this cop did what he could until he ran into some trouble himself, legal trouble." Ray edited out the nine consecutive life sentences for contract murders on behalf of various New Jersey crime families.

"Nonetheless, by the time Jackie was twenty-five, he had been supposedly drug-free for over a year, he was engaged, had even reconciled with Stubby. In fact, Stubby had got him an apprentice card with the International Brotherhood of Electrical Workers, which meant very good money and solid job security back then. Still does, in fact . . .

"But the night before Jackie's wedding, April 23, 1965, a tragic mystery came about which at this point in time I can safely say will never be solved." Ray was back to enjoying himself.

"April twenty-third, three a.m. Jackie's brother Benny rings our doorbell, we were living in Hopewell by then, wakes up my parents.

"Apparently earlier in the day, Jackie had had an argument with Stubby, stormed out of the house and vanished.

"So around midnight Benny had been sent out to track his brother down, which basically meant hitting all the old dope spots, hunting down all of Jackie's allegedly ex-running buddies, and checking out all the emergency rooms. No Jackie anywhere. Finally he had called the county morgue at Dempsy Medical, described his brother over the phone, blond, six-four, two-thirty, the morgue said, 'Yeah, we got someone like that, come on down and make an ID.'

"And so Benny had come to our house, I couldn't have been more than five, six years old at the time, to ask, to beg my parents to go with him to the morgue because he just couldn't bear to see . . .

"Well, they all went, and yes, it was Jackie on the slab; an overdose.

"And then Benny turned to my parents again. 'I have to go home and tell my father. Could you please come with me.'

"So somewheres around sunrise they all go to Stubby's house to break the news. They walk in and the first thing they see is that all the hallway mirrors are covered with sheets. And when they come upon Stubby in the living room? He was barefoot and sitting on a wooden crate, had a skull-cap on his head, a yarmulke. He was sitting shivah, which is what Jews do when they're in mourning for a family member.

"They had come by to *break* the news, but Stubby was already set up. He looks at them, says, 'He's dead, right?' He just knew.

"Stubby lived another twenty years, but to the day he died he never told anyone what he and Jackie had argued about that made him so sure that this kid was going to go out and basically kill himself right before his wedding."

The class seemed drawn in, just one girl scowling at her nails.

Mrs. Bondo's face was an arrangement of downward-pointing arrow-heads, looking as if she was having an incredibly difficult time keeping her mouth shut.

"And so, for me, if I was in this class? What I would probably try to play around with, would be to imagine the conversation that took place . . ." And here Ray faltered, sensing in the pit of his gut how wildly inappropriate this "example" was, the whole saga so complex, lurid and melodramatic. "The, the conversation that took place between this mean little bastard . . ." The class flinched at his language, but Ray was too wretchedly embarrassed to care. He couldn't believe that Bondo hadn't shut him down halfway through this mess. "The conversation between this psychological child abuser, who after years and years of being hurtful and hateful to this poor overgrown kid growing up under his roof, was now finally, finally trying to do the right thing by him . . . and the kid himself, an emotionally screwed-up, con-man junkie jailbird hustler. What went wrong? Who said what to who that would make my cousin go and fall off the earth like that right before his wedding?"

"Maybe he didn't want to get married," Altagracia, the girl studying her nails, said.

Myra, the smart quiet one, raised her hand. "Well what do we write about if no one in our families has a drug problem?" Saying it with just the right balance of innocence and dryness to zing it right in there.

"It's just my family tree," he said lamely. "You know, one of the shakier branches."

Mrs. Bondo fleetingly smiled down at her folders and that minute, almost secretive smile gave him some insight into her discomfited restraint; she had made the difficult decision to let the students deal with him and his sprawling drug drama on their own, trusting that at least one of the kids would rise to the occasion and set him right.

He felt chastened but also fascinated; he couldn't imagine being in possession of such restraint himself.

Nonetheless he wanted a second shot at getting it right; *had* to get it right.

"OK, what do we have, ten minutes? Forget that story. It's too, it's too everything. Real quick—here's a snapshot from Hopewell back in the day, a real bite-size quickie, no beginning, no end.

"Growing up, there was a guy in my building, a black guy named Eddie Paris. Eddie was a motorman on the PATH train, and he had two girls, I forget their names, and two sons, Winston and Terrance, who everybody called Dub and Prince, don't ask me why. Prince, the oldest kid, was really something else. He went to Incarnation, the Catholic high school on Hurley Street, number one in his class, Honor Society, captain of the track team, which came in second in the state one year, captain of the fencing team, you know, competitive dueling, and on top of everything else? He could sing. And I mean sing—not hip-hop not headbanger not rock and roll but *sing* . . ." Drawing blanks.

"He would give concerts. Recitals. Anyways, a snapshot. 1976. I'm sixteen, high school junior right here at Paulus Hook. Prince is a senior at Incarnation. On this particular spring day I'm in my bedroom doing my homework, and I hear an argument down in the street. I look out my window and it's Prince and his dad, Eddie Paris, down there, lots of hand waving, lots of shouting, and Prince, this great, great kid is . . . He's got tears running down his face.

"And I hear Eddie shouting at him, 'If I could I would, Terrance, but I have *four* children, not just you so I *can't*.'

"At which point, Prince grabs his head, turns and, still crying, he just starts running blind up the Hopewell hill, this track star kid flying like a rocket, bawling his eyes out. And that's it. Just that . . ." Making them come to him.

But shy, incurious or simply too spaced out from the first story, they didn't take the bait, and it killed him.

"OK. Three minutes left. Your first assignment. Go home and find a photograph of someone in your family, Mom, Dad, Grandma, the cat, whoever. Except that the photo has to have been taken before you were born. And I want you to write me something involving that individual and what I want to know is, where did they go, what did they do right after the photographer said thank you. And don't ask. Make it up. Use what you heard about them from back in the day. OK?

"Two minutes. I have some good news, I have some bad news." And Ray brought up a number of paperbacks, spread them out across the table. "One to a customer, from me to you. That's the good news. Bad news is that you have to read them. No book report, just read it.

"And let me just say something about these particular books. They're mostly written by people who grew up without the advantages, some in cities, some rural—hard lives all around. And, the reason I chose them for you was because I feel that we read to learn new things, sure, absolutely, but more often than not, what we really get out of the good books we read is self-recognition. We read and discover stuff about life that we already knew, except that we didn't *know* we knew it until we read it in a particular book. And this self-recognition, this discovering ourselves in the writings of others can be very exciting, can make us feel a little less isolated inside our own thing and a little more connected to the larger world."

There was a uniform glaze out there, and, worried about boring them, Ray picked up the pace.

"OK. So what we have here is James Baldwin, *Go Tell It on the Mountain*. Harlem poor churchy hellfire kind of adolescence. Richard Wright, *Uncle Tom's Children*. Southern poor cracker-country racism, 1920s, '30s. John Steinbeck, *Of Mice and Men*. Great story, great writer, but mainly in there because us white guys got to represent. Sandra Cisneros, *The House on Mango Street*. Growing up Hispanic in Chicago. Poets. Lucille Clifton, Etheridge Knight. Afro-American. *El Bronx Remembered*. Growing up Hispanic in some outer borough of New York, I can't remember which, and last but not least, *Best Loved Horror Stories*, in there for whatever, OK? When I say three, everybody take a book. One, two . . ."

And on "three," six students lunged for *Best Loved Horror Stories*.

"Whoa." He removed it from circulation. "Again. One, two . . ."

And six books were gone, both Hispanic books taken by black kids, the girl Altagracia holding the copy of *Uncle Tom's Children* by the corner and glaring at Ray as if she had been unfairly bumped in the first round of musical chairs.

What was he supposed to do? Shrugging, he slid her the collection of horror stories.

Myra, the girl with the big glasses, was the only kid not to take a book. "Aren't you going to take any?"

"No thank you," she said almost inaudibly, holding up a paperback copy of *Spoon River Anthology*. "I'm already reading something."

"Good for you," Ray said mildly, this kid most definitely The One.

Out in the hallway, Ray walked with Mrs. Bondo, her heavy purse and armload of manila folders.

"I hope you didn't mind the Bondo-Bello crack. I just wanted to loosen everybody up."

"No problem," she said, looking straight ahead, navigating the hyped-up foot traffic coming in both directions.

"I'm sorry about that story with my cousin. I kind of got carried away."

"It's life."

"So . . . Was that OK?" Ray going fishing.

"Was what OK." She grabbed the back of some kid's shirt who tried sprinting past them. "Slow down, Malik."

"The class. Was the class OK . . ."

Mrs. Bondo took a long time answering. "So why was this Prince kid running up the hill?"

"God, I thought *nobody'd* ask," Ray said. "Terrance, Prince, he'd just gotten accepted to Dartmouth but they hadn't offered him a scholarship and his father was telling him that he couldn't afford the tuition, and that the poor kid would have to go to Rutgers-Dempsy and commute from home."

"That's where I went," Mrs. Bondo said. "Rutgers-Dempsy."

"Oh yeah?" Ray said brightly, his cheeks burning.

But then she added, "That has got to be one of the saddest stories I've heard all week."

"So was the class OK?" Ray asked again, and again she was a long time in answering.

"Well, I'll tell you," she began, then looked directly at him. "It might be helpful for you to understand that the kids are actually more afraid of you than you are of them."

Chapter 5 >

In the Field—February 11

Ever the gent, short and stocky Bobby Sugar emerged from the bathroom still knotting the drawstring of his sweatpants, a rolled Newark *Star-Ledger* between elbow and ribs.

"Let's get down to it," addressing Nerese waiting for him at the dining room table in his cheaply but newly built townhouse apartment. "Let's do it."

Although Nerese still thought that the fastest way to make some headway on finding out what had happened to Ray was to work on his daughter, before she committed herself on this one she just needed to make sure that his noncooperation wasn't masking something best left in the dark, that she wasn't about to go to bat for a drug dealer or a pedophile or someone with any number of other disqualifying occupations or enthusiasms.

And although she and Sugar had had their share of beefs in the past, in the three years since his retirement from the Dempsy PD he had become a first-rate gagger, one of a rarefied breed of PIs who, by creating dozens of false identities for themselves over the phone, could assemble a portfolio as thick as the Bible on anyone living or dead, without ever having to leave their apartment.

To various police departments around the country, to the IRS, to credit retrievers and to innumerable banks, he was an FBI agent doing a workup on a suspect. To the Central Insurance Bureau, he was a fraud investigator from Blue Cross needing a history of claims. Referencing the staff rosters of every public and private hospital from New York to California, he was an affiliated doctor compiling the medical history of a new patient; and to former employers he was either an executive headhunter needing off-the-record feedback on a potential recruit, or a political campaign manager doing a background check on a new volunteer.

The secret of his success, especially with the evening at-home calls to former employers and sometimes even neighbors and relatives, was that Sugar, like any halfway decent detective or journalist, knew that once you got people talking, the problem was to shut them up.

"So how's the kid," he asked, sliding into the chair across the table from her, an open box of Dunkin' Donuts and a plastic punch bowl filled with off-season candy canes between them.

"Darren?" Nerese shrugged, tore off half a doughnut. "Darren's Darren."

Looking out the window over Bobby's shoulder, she saw a Chinese restaurant cheek by jowl with a funeral home, four lanes of two-way traffic tearing up the blacktop down there like time was money.

"Neesy." Bobby leaned over the dinette table, chest hair sprouting from the V neck of his T-shirt. "The thing to remember with kids? Is that they tend to outgrow themselves."

She nodded as if in deep acceptance, although she had a hard time envisioning her son outgrowing anything save for his clothes. Nonetheless, in the last few years whenever Bobby Sugar had something to say about children Nerese always made a point of opening herself up to it.

This had not always been the case; in fact, when they had first worked out of the same detectives squad in the mid-nineties, whenever Sugar had occasion to open his mouth on anything, Nerese more often than not had been inclined to put her fist in it.

In October of '95, when the O.J. verdict came in, Sugar had gone apoplectic at Nerese's lack of outrage; Nerese dismissing his smokescreen tirade at the sorry state of American justice as what a friend of hers called soft bigotry. But when O.J. was finally nailed in civil court, they had actually wound up throwing punches in the squad room after she came in to work and found that he had plastered her desk and locker door with torn-out "Guilty" headlines from every newspaper in the New York–New Jersey area.

In response to her calling him a Ginny-assed redneck motherfucker that day as she was being dragged away by two other detectives in the squad, Sugar had pulled himself together, smoothed back his hair, readjusted the knot of his noose-yanked tie and said, "I'm not a racist. I'm an empiricist."

Because she was embarrassed that she had no idea what that word meant, his declaration went a long way in momentarily cooling her off; but after consulting the dictionary that night, she came in the next day saying, "Empiricist, my ass. Some people just see what they want to see."

After that, the two of them had barely made eye contact until the day, a year and a half later, when her then twelve-year-old son was rushed to the hospital with a ruptured appendix while she was stuck on an extradition assignment, picking up a fugitive rapist in California.

By the time she finally made it to the Dempsy Medical Center a full day and night after the surgery, she found Bobby Sugar at his bedside, the two of them watching a game show on the ceiling-mounted TV. Later, she'd found out that, knowing Nerese's mother was in the hospital herself at the time and that her brothers were not exactly go-to guys, Sugar had taken it upon himself to be her very frightened boy's stand-in parent, and had spent the better part of the last thirty-six hours pretty much holding Darren's hand.

And for that, he could have waltzed in from the john wearing a Klan hood and cracking a bullwhip and Nerese would have done nothing more than call him an asshole before going back to work on the assorted doughnuts.

"Ready?" Sugar asked, reaching for a manila folder on the windowsill. Nerese opened a reporter's pad.

"OK. Raymond Randolph Mitchell, born '60 married '91 divorced '95, one kid Ruby Draw-Mitchell born in '90. Last six addresses: 644 Broadway in New York, from '88 to '94—his ex and kid are still living there—10 Jones Street in Greenwich Village, from '95 to '98, then big move, 1330 La Cienega in West Hollywood, '98 to the fall of '01, then back to New York, the Gramercy Park Hotel mid-September to mid-October of the same year, then from there to current, residing in Little Venice at 44 Othello Way, right here in Dempsy. Questions? Comments?"

"Go ahead," Nerese said, her pen motionless, suspended above the pad.

"OK, criminal—nothing on the NCIC computer, but you know that.

And, checking in with One Police Plaza, with Hudson, Essex, Bergen, Dempsy County prosecutors offices and with the LAPD, there's nothing, no open complaints, nothing charged then dismissed. Also, there's no litigation, no torts, nothing in civil court and no tax liens.

"On medicals . . . No hospital admissions except for, you know, the present situation: no rehab clinics, no methadone maintenance, no psychiatric admissions, no HIV therapy and no lab work—blood tests, X rays, EEGs, EKGs, MRIs, CAT scans, nada.

"He doesn't see a shrink and it looks like the guy doesn't even have a regular doctor, which is none too bright once you hit forty. Questions?"

"Go ahead." Nerese broke off a section of doughnut, put it down, picked it up, put it down.

"OK. Employment. And this is somewhat interesting. From '87 to '90 he was a public school teacher, English, Fannie Lou Hamer High School in the Bronx. Then from '90 to '93 he was driving a cab for an outfit called Orion, then from '93 to '95, get this, he was a polygrapher for an outfit, also New York, called Truth and Justice, did mostly employment screens, then from '95 to '97 he was back driving a cab for two garages, first DMG then Scorpio."

"He went from teaching high school to driving a cab?" Nerese started doodling, a whirling stroke like a tornado.

"OK," Sugar flipped a page. "According to the Special Investigations office over at the New York Board of Ed? He was facing some kind of disciplinary hearing, so it could have been one of those you-can't-fire-me-I-quit deals."

"A hearing for what?"

"Apparently, back in '90 he took thirty kids and went AWOL on a class trip."

"How'd you . . . They never release that shit."

"Yeah, well, I was calling from the chancellor's office, so it was strictly in-house." Sugar patted himself on the head.

"Then drove a cab again after the polygraph gig?"

"Yeah, but then get this. From '98 to 2001 he worked out in LA for a company called Satchmo Productions, was a staff writer on that TV show *Brokedown High*? The guy starts pulling down four, count 'em, four grand a week. Left *that* gig, God knows why, and other than the volunteer teaching thing over at the Hook? Basically, he's been unemployed ever since. Or, given his financials, maybe a better word is 'retired.'"

Nerese kept doodling.

"You want the financials?"

"Sure."

"OK." He turned a page. "AmEx and MasterCard combined averages from seven to fifteen hundred a month, no distinct purchasing patterns to speak of, mostly restaurants, bookstores, music stores, the odd TV or microwave at P. C. Richard, Moviefone tickets here and there, a few clothing stores, no favorite bars, no masked charges, you know, dummy corporations for whores, lap dances, massages, any kind of sex or sex-related products.

"Has, at present, three hundred and four thousand dollars in a Pruden-tial-Bache money market account, down from an opening balance of three hundred seventy-seven, six months ago, no further deposits, so it's most likely what he could save from that high-priced writing job out in LA, living off it like his own trust-fund baby. No stocks, bonds, any kind of investments, shares or partnerships . . . OK. The mortgage on Othello Way runs him fourteen hundred and eighty bucks a month, lays out another thirteen hundred per in child support, has never missed a pay-ment on either one. OK," turning the page. "Withdraws, roughly another five thousand a month, deposits it into a checking account at First Dempsy for, I'm guessing cash machine access, you know, general out of pocket and to pay the smaller bills, cable, gas and whatnot, however, last month he transferred sixteen thousand, not five, could be to cover holiday expenses, could be something else, but that's the one thing I don't have yet, the canceled checks from the First Dempsy account. My guy in the proof department over there's on vacation, but I should have it for you in a few days."

Sugar nudged the Plexiglas bowl toward Nerese. "Candy cane?"

"So what do you think?" Nerese had filled the page with tornadoes, dollar signs and "Satchmo."

"Well, if it was me, what I'd like to know"—Sugar pulled his elbows back, a hollow pop emanating from his sternum—"is how you go from driving a cab to raking in four Gs a week writing a television show. And *then* I'd like to know, who in their right fucking mind walks out on that kind of cheddar, comes back to Dempsy fucking New Jersey with their hands in their pockets whistling Dixie."

"Anybody out there have anything to say about it?"

"Hard to get a straight answer." Sugar flipped some pages. "I talked to three people—two said he just quit, happens all the time, high burnout rate, guy's a good guy, everybody wishes him well. The third said, well, he wouldn't say straight out, but there might have been an incident, maybe not, of a, get this, a racial nature. Something said at a party, some kind of, of misunderstanding or misinterpretation or . . . I couldn't . . . Usually I got people talking till my ears bleed, but I don't know. I got all the names and numbers for you if you want to take a crack at it, but frankly I don't think anything out there followed him back to New Jersey just to go upside his head. If I were you? I'd stay local, canvass the neighbors, talk to the kids at the Hook, other teachers or, even more to the point, I'd just ask him what the hell happened and keep asking until he'll tell you just to fuckin' get rid of you. That's what I'd do."

Nerese looked down at her open pad, "racial" having joined "Satchmo," the doodles and the dollar signs.

"So," Sugar said, sliding the folder across the table, Nerese lost in thought until the silence caught her attention. Snapping to, she fished the check out of her purse: three hundred dollars, a third of Sugar's usual fee.

"So how's Darren doing?" he asked, palming the check.

"You asked me that already," Nerese responded with a little bit of an edge—despite the massive discount, three hundred dollars for anything not life and death was a painful amount of money. "How's your guy?"

"Taylor?" Sugar's face came alive. "Come here."

Rising from the dinette, Nerese followed him into the living room, a six-piece chocolate-brown velour sectional-and-easy-chair ensemble camouflaged atop a chocolate-brown wall-to-wall rug so new she could still smell the nap.

"Check it out." Sugar gestured to a large trophy nesting between Blockbuster video boxes on a shelf over his television: first place in an under-eighteen kick-boxing tournament at the Jersey City Boys Club.

"The kid's a monster." Sugar beamed.

Nerese's gaze strayed to a framed yearbook photo of Taylor Sugar; Nerese as always doing a double-take at rediscovering that Sugar, never married, and still more or less an urban redneck, had an adopted son who was either Asian or Hispanic, he'd never tell which.

"That's great, Bobby."

"Wait. Check it out . . ." And before she could stop him, Sugar turned sideways and pulled down his sweatpants to mid-thigh, revealing a brown-and-amber bruise which, despite a few days' worth of fading, still resembled a fully articulated human foot.

"Taylor was practicing in the kitchen, and me as usual with my head up my ass? I just come around the corner and walked right into it. Look . . . ," touching himself right below the hip. "You can still make out all five toes."

A luxury development built on reclaimed marshland abutting the Hudson River, Little Venice was politically part of Dempsy proper but geographically a long, lonesome mile from the nearest residential or commercial district of the city.

There was a security shack and a remote-controlled gate at the entrance to the development, the guard obliged to phone the tenants before allowing their visitors on the grounds. But given the vast and porous wasteland that enveloped this checkpoint it was too much to hope for that there should be a record of Ray receiving any guests the day of the assault, especially if they had come to do him dirt.

As Nerese came through the gates, manned today by a retired cop she knew by face but not by name, the air became redolent of a heady mix of river tang and churned earth, and she found herself on a fragile ribbon of asphalt hemmed in by hillocks of backhoed dirt, each mound posted as the future site of a pool, tennis court, health club or recreation center — each one a rest stop for the gulls, overrun with cracked clam shells, construction debris and its own random greenery — weeds, moss, Arms to Heaven and whatever else took root via neglect.

The houses themselves, which began a half-mile beyond the checkpoint, were a picturesque scrunch of vaguely Tudor four-story structures that brought to Nerese's mind the movie-set village terrorized by the Frankenstein monster, with a touch of Popeye waterfront thrown in to acknowledge their proximity to the river.

Standing before Ray's third-floor apartment with the key supplied by the management office already in the lock, she abruptly changed her mind about reading his place first, and opted instead for ringing the bell of his nearest neighbor, a Mrs. Kuben, who had discovered Ray sprawled and seizing just inside his own doorway and had made the call to 911.

The woman who eventually made it to the door was in her seventies, tall but crooked at a fifteen-degree angle from osteoporosis, her piled hair frosted and filigreed a brilliant rusty orange.

"Good morning." Nerese reflexively smiled and stepped back, her police ID alongside her face. "I'm Detective Ammons from the Dempsy PD? Can I speak to you about what happened next door?"

"You know, they tell you a place is safe," Mrs. Kuben said, nudging a cookie-covered plate an inch closer to Nerese, who was seated across from her at the dining table. "So you move in."

The apartment had that un-lived-in feel that Nerese sometimes encountered in old people's digs, the rooms spotless but reeking oppressively of camphor, her eyelids fluttering against the fumes.

"The catching detective says you made the call to 911 at a quarter past five in the evening. Does that sound about right?"

"If that's what they say," she shrugged.

"Well let me ask you, how'd it come about that you found him?"

"I went to take out the garbage, saw his door was half-open, and, believe me, I mind my own business, but I went to knock, because we live in the world we live in as I'm sure you know, and there he was"— she put a hand over her mouth and slowly shook her head—"lying in his blood, shaking like a leaf."

"Unh," Nerese grunted in sympathy. "OK. Let me ask . . . Before then, at any time that afternoon, did you hear or see anything out of the ordinary, you know, through the walls, out in the hallway, an argument, raised voices, a person, people that you hadn't ever seen before, or . . ."

The medics had said that Ray could have been lying there for as long as two hours before this woman had come upon him.

"Like I told you already," Mrs. Kuben said, "I mind my own business."

"No, I understand, I understand, but sometimes you just can't help it. A loud noise, an unfamiliar face, anything . . ."

"No," leaning back and folding her arms across her chest.

"How about your husband?"

"My husband?" Mrs. Kuben threw her a tight smile. "For forty-three years the man ran an empire. Now he has his name, address and phone number pinned to his shirt before he leaves the apartment."

"That's rough," Nerese said heavily, then leaned forward. "Tell me something I should know."

"Something you should know?" The older woman fought down a smile at the challenge as Nerese's eye strayed to the photo gallery lining the dinette walls: children, grandchildren, immigrant ancestors—the past, present and future all taken to the same framer and laminated diploma-style onto identically irregular slabs of heavily varnished wood.

"I'll tell you something you should know. His parents? He bought them that place three years ago. Two hundred and twenty-five thousand dollars. Paid the monthly maintenance, the utilities, everything, OK? In October, Jeanette, the mother . . . It happened quick. So, he comes back from California or New York, I don't know which, to bury, you know, and to be with his father."

Nerese heard a shuffling noise from the back bedroom, the dry whisk of slippers on a carpetless floor.

"Except his father, Artie, he can't wait to get the hell out of here. So the son winds up stuck with the apartment, and instead of putting it on the market he decides to move in, which"—giving the cookie plate a quarter-turn to re-entice Nerese—"I think was a mistake. This isn't any place for a young person to set up house."

"Artie," Nerese murmured, vaguely remembering Ray's father from Hopewell, glasses and a pompadour; a bus driver, a cab driver . . . "Where'd he go?" She took a bite of something else, the filling prune or fig, and almost spat it out into her palm.

"Where?" Mrs. Kuben crossed her arms over her chest. "Olive Branch, Mississippi. It's a snowbird setup like West Palm or DelRay, but a little cheaper, a little younger. And frankly I don't blame the man. His wife's not cold in the ground two minutes and the widows around here, they started lining up for him like he was the Early Bird Special. Came at him with everything they had—bank statements, plane tickets, summer homes. He told me this one individual, he wouldn't say who but I can guess, not one week after the funeral she comes and drags him over to her apartment, pulls him into the bedroom, throws open a walk-in closet and shows him all the clothes left over from the first mister—suits, jackets, silk shirts, cruise wear—tells him she can have everything altered, can you believe that?"

"Yeah, I can, actually," Nerese said mildly, leaving it at that.

"They wouldn't even give him the time to grieve."

"So what else should I know."

"What else?"

The backroom shuffle started up again, then abruptly succumbed to the sounds of a TV commercial.

"Did he ever bring anyone into the apartment?"

"I don't know if it's my place to say."

"It's definitely your place to say." Nerese reached across to touch the woman's wrist.

"Well." Mrs. Kuben gave the cookie plate another spin before getting back into it. "His daughter, of course. Ruby. A sweetheart, but why on earth a person would give their child the name of the woman who comes to clean your house is beyond me."

"Who else . . ."

Mrs. Kuben hesitated, then: "He brought around people. Certain people."

"Certain people?"

Mrs. Kuben looked pained now.

"What kind of people?"

"Different people at different times."

Nerese waited.

"Look, the residents here, we're mostly retired, we worked hard all our lives. My husband . . ."

"No no no. I understand, I understand." Nerese, assuming now she meant nonwhites, watched her twist in the wind.

"At this stage of the game we should be entitled to our privacy, to our, our peace of mind," the woman both angry and pleading.

Nerese shook her head like a horse, said, "Absolutely," then settled back into waiting—the two of them suddenly engaged in a silent struggle.

"Why are you making me say something I don't want to say," Mrs. Kuben finally blurted, so pissed off and embarrassed now that she yanked the cookie plate away.

"Hey, if I lived here?" Nerese leaned forward, hand on heart. "I'd feel the exact same way. Just tell me about the people."

"I don't know." Mrs. Kuben, defeated, looked away. "A couple of kids one time."

"Kids. White? Black?" Nerese helping her out of the tar pit.

"The second."

"Anybody else?"

"A young man. Not a kid, but young."

"Black? White?"

"The first."

"You see him more than once?"

"A few times."

"Catch his name?"

"No."

"How'd he seem to you?"

"To me?" She shrugged. "Civil. Neatly dressed, but for the street."

"How were they together?"

"I don't understand the question."

"How were they . . . How did Ray seem around this guy?"

"You know. Happy to see him, I guess. Friendly."

"Friendly," Nerese repeated. "Friendly like what, pals? More than pals?" Just tossing it in the water, see what floated to the surface.

"He has a daughter," Mrs. Kuben said coldly.

"Anybody else?" Nerese holding off on pressing for more details on the young man right now, this lady not going anywhere with her name-tagged husband.

"Well, actually, yeah. This one individual I saw him with the most. A woman . . ." Waiting for Nerese's white-black question.

"Black?"

"That or something else. You know, very light-skinned. Attractive. She'd come by with her kids, two boys. Sometimes one boy. Sometimes alone. Her I'd see the most."

Nerese grunted, thinking, With her kids.

"Did you catch her name?"

"No."

"When she came by alone, was it during the day? Night?" Nerese thinking, Where there's kids there's a father, at least a biological one.

"Day," Mrs. Kuben said. "Maybe night too, but like I said, come nine o'clock I'm dead as a doornail."

Nerese reached across the table for a cookie sculpted into a seashell, dark pink, the bottom half dipped in chocolate.

"You think they were seeing each other?"

"Socially?" Mrs. Kuben asked.

"Socially," wishing she could just ask, Was he fucking her.

"Could be," Mrs. Kuben shrugged.

"When they were together, how did they strike you, friendly, businesslike, affectionate . . ."

Mrs. Kuben gave this some thought, then said, "Quiet."

"Quiet?" Nerese was thrown.

"You know, well-behaved."

"Well-behaved . . ."

Mrs. Kuben finally looked her in the eye. "Like they were hiding something."

Skirting the brownish blood-spatter in the vestibule, the fingerprint powder–stippled shards of vase, the discarded rubber gloves, torn gauze wrappers and other detritus left by the EMS crew that worked on Ray before moving him, Nerese walked across the black-and-white tile floor of the sun-blasted living room and stepped out onto the cement-and-Astroturf terrace to gawk at the Statue of Liberty, gently hovering over its star-shaped base like a rocketship about to touch down.

Utterly jazzed, she just stood there, elbows on the rail, wondering if there was anyone in the world who couldn't be made happy by the sight of moving water, imagining herself waking up here, opening her eyes and there it would be, tossing up diamonds, slapping itself silly and making every day feel like Day One.

Then, reentering the apartment from the terrace, she gave the living room a fresh look. Minus the caustic reek of mothballs, and discounting the faint arcs of black fingerprint powder that still clung to the front door and the wall around it like the mysterious markings of a prehistoric civilization, the place had the same vaguely geriatric un-lived-in feel as Mrs. Kuben's digs next door; everything color-coordinated and spotless to the point of sterility, as if cleanliness itself were a school of style.

Giving Ray the benefit of the doubt, she imagined that he had simply left everything the way he found it when he moved in three months ago; the only two objects that caught her eye as probably coming in with him were an old-time full-length funhouse mirror mounted on a wall in a heavy wooden frame, the ancient silvering on its bulbous rolling surface peeled and browning in all four corners; and, at the opposite end of the man-toy spectrum, a fifty-four-inch flat-screen television, the whole of it no thicker than a hardcover book and so recently purchased that a few minute shreds of static-charged packing foam still clung to the gunmetal-gray frame.

Taking her time, looking for whatever, she began to roam the room as if she were in a museum, first checking out what hung on the walls. Three paintings: one, a hokey Paris street scene, all slanted umbrellas, quaint cafés and the base of the Eiffel Tower; two, a portrait of an aged Jew, gray-bearded, shawl-draped, an open prayer book in his gnarled hands; and last a stylized portrait of a wistful waif fondling a flower, the long-necked child so almond-eyed, almond-headed, that she seemed more alien than orphan.

The only thing that spoke of Ray on these walls was a certificate announcing his Emmy nomination for writing *Brokedown High*. Nerese had heard enough about the show by now, but in truth had never seen it save for a few minutes now and then while channel-surfing, although she could imagine easily enough what it was like.

Beneath this framed smidgen of prestige, on a low corner table that filled the square gap created by two couches positioned at right angles to each other, a modest accumulation of variously shaped vases sprouted like a miniature skyline; the original location of the one snatched up as a weapon indicated by a relatively dust-free circle.

The large TV centered a floor-to-ceiling wall unit that extended the length of the living room, Nerese perusing the shelves now: novels, biographies, no double-takes there; a few hundred CDs; fifty or so movies on tape, mainstream stuff—*Braveheart*, *West Side Story* and the like—Nerese popping a few from their boxes to see if the cassette inside was in fact what the packaging advertised; everything checking out, no secret porno stash; and then she came upon two framed photos nestling on a shelf, one of his daughter—Ruby, Mrs. Kuben had said—playing basketball for her school; a graceful lanky thing, caught here airborne and arched like a bow during the tip-off. Her opposite number was a black girl with flying hair extensions who matched Ruby's taut symmetry like they were twin folds of an inkblot, both kids wide-eyed, mouths agape, the basketball a pebbled moon inches above their extended fingertips.

The second photo was a head shot of Ray's ex-wife, blue-white skin, long reddish hair carelessly arranged and clear confident eyes, her mouth thin but with the slightest uptick at the corners as if she were politely listening to a long-winded joke she had heard before, Nerese intuiting by the combination of bone structure and facial expression that this woman had no ass on her whatsoever.

There were two possibilities here regarding this photo: either Ray was still hung up on his ex or he just wanted to give his daughter a little visual continuity while playing musical houses; Nerese hoped it was the latter.

Opening a cabinet beneath the television she came across the liquor stash: mostly kiddy shit, pimp shit—Amaretto, Boggs Cranberry Liqueur, Midori, retsina, whatever the hell that was—the only serious contender a quart of Seagrams, but it was three-quarters full, and dusty.

In an adjoining cabinet Nerese discovered a stack of unboxed videos, maybe two dozen, each cassette neatly labeled, *NYPD Blue*, *Law & Order*, *Oz*, *The Sopranos*, general title followed by the series number, episode title and airing date.

Running one through the VCR—that big flat-screen TV like visual morphine—she discovered that *Law & Order* was, in fact, *Law & Order*; Nerese both relieved and a little frustrated, this room not telling her shit.

Before moving on to the rear quarters of the apartment, she hunkered down over the remains of the vase, only thin splinters and powdery nuggets remaining, the larger pieces having been removed to a crime lab, dropped into a ten-gallon terrarium with a dollop of Krazy Glue and fumed overnight in order to raise fingerprints. The results had been unhelpful, just Ray and his parents. The vase had had a bulbous base and a long thin neck, the thing most likely swung like a bat by that neck, which, the crime lab had told her, was missing from the accumulated pieces, probably snapping off on impact, the doer most likely taking it with him.

Moving to the kitchen she found shrink-wrapped chicken parts and raw vegetables in the refrigerator—Ray actually cooking his own meals; some vitamins in there too, along with a half-full bottle of Heineken.

As she knocked off the rest of the beer for him, she noticed five twenty-dollar bills sticking out from beneath a blender on the kitchen counter, plain as day—so much for a robbery, although when things got out of hand people tended to bolt, so . . .

The bathroom was spotless, no hairs in the tub or sink, Ray starting to get on her nerves now.

The medicine cabinet contained Advil, Mylanta, Donnatal—an antispasmodic for the gut that her mother used—and Ventolin, an asthma inhalant. There were no condoms—Nerese thinking about Ray's light-skinned girlfriend—and, in keeping with Bobby Sugar's report, no medication for HIV or any other STD—no evidence of a life-altering, revenge-inspiring medical condition.

Above the toilet, matted vertically in the same elongated rectangular frame, were three taxi licenses: the top one, Usher Mittnacht looking out at her from 1935; the middle, Arthur Mitchell from 1958—Artie; Nerese had been dead-on in remembering the glasses and pompadour—and, holding up the other two, Raymond Mitchell, 1990, Ray looking a little fucked-up there, hollow-eyed and slack-mouthed—but who wouldn't feel that way posing for a hack permit, third generation in a row like evolution spinning its wheels.

This photo, however, given the tissue trauma he had sustained from the assault, offered to Nerese her first clean read of what Ray looked like as an adult. His face vaguely reminded her of an African mask, long and tapered with a small full mouth and slightly protruding heavy-lidded eyes — bedroom eyes, her mother would have called them. Yet despite their sleepy aspect, and despite the depressing circumstances behind the photo op, there was a distinct sense of almost too much alertness in his gaze, a constant monitoring quality that suggested to her that Ray hadn't had an unself-conscious moment in his life.

He had nice hair, though, dark and swirly, lying about his head in thick lazy piles like carelessly coiled ropes.

In the bedroom there were more hand-labeled videos piled around a second TV — all *Buffy the Vampire Slayer* and *Angel* — Nerese not even bothering to give them a test drive, and in a night table drawer she found two joints, one half-smoked, both withered and weightless with age, Nerese muttering out loud, "At least finish the fucking thing, Ray," and a small bottle of baby oil, which once again made her think of Ray's lady friend although, considering the petrified joints, maybe he just suffered from dry elbows.

In the closet, all of the clothes were mainstream retail — Gap, Levi's, Banana Republic — no whips, leather, garter belts or boas, but in one of the corners hung a square-cornered multi-hangered plastic clothes protector like a zippered tent, inside which were a dozen skirt suits and pantsuits, most of them cut from thick nubby material, couch material, the patterns and colors simultaneously garish and dull — the type of clothes respectable older women wore once sex was off the program; Nerese assumed these items had belonged to Ray's mother. And that, she declared to herself, was that.

But back in the living room, with the sunlight beaming in at a slightly different angle than before, Nerese noticed another bit of wall art that had eluded both her and the crime scene dusters: two greasy handprints, now highlighted by the rays, situated about ten feet to the left of the front door, flush to the surface, roughly five feet high and spaced approximately eighteen inches apart.

Facing the wall and letting her own hands hover over the rough outlines, she found that if she stepped back a little without moving her upper body, she was in a perfect stance to be frisked, and utterly vulnerable to a head shot coming from either side of the plate or from behind.

And if that blow were in fact coming up on the left side of the head, which was where Ray had caught it, the force and the direction of the impact would land her directly in the pile of medical and investigative debris on the floor.

A little spooked by her re-creation, and thinking that she had pretty much gotten all she could from an eyeball read of the scene for now, Nerese was granted one last discovery when she wound up skating on a sheet of paper that lay camouflaged on one of the large white floor tiles as she headed for the door.

With a bellyful of adrenaline from her near spill, she picked up the sheet and found on the flip side a masterfully drawn caricature, done in ballpoint ink, of a preadolescent homie, some ghetto Dondi, clothes comically oversize, the kid floppy as a puppy except that he was brandishing an enormous hand cannon—specifically, an anatomically correct Glock 19—aiming it directly at Nerese, the legend printed deco-style beneath his feet: "What's Mine Is Mine."

Pocketing the drawing, she finally left the apartment.

Outdoors again, she inhaled a low-tide stench, funky but evocative, coming off the conjunction of river and bay. And she thought about Ray, ex-cabbie, ex–TV show writer, up there in his apartment surrounded by seniors, watching endless taped TV shows, cooking dinner for himself and seeing his daughter, what . . . one night a week? Two weekends a month?

Then Ray the other way—inner-city public school volunteer with money to burn, hooking up with some other-tribe girlfriend, bringing her around, bringing around her other-tribe kids, "wild Indians," she guessed his half-crazed neighbors would call them; bringing around at least one young male street acquaintance who might or might not be the hard-core artist in her pocket, bringing around whoever and whoever and whoever had put him against that wall, intent on sending him into the black land.

Standing there under the drifting cry of the gulls, Nerese looked out across the Hudson to the skyline of lower New York. Then, turning around, she took in the Gothic spires of the Medical Center in downtown Dempsy. Little Venice was roughly equidistant from both—but despite the toney digs, the views, the peaceful primacy of bird caw and sun-dappled water, she experienced not so much a sense of exclusivity, as that of being stranded.

Chapter 6 >

Hospital — February 12

"Can you tell me where you are?" the neurologist asked in an impersonal singsong as he shined a light in Ray's left eye to see if the right pupil would sympathetically dilate—the consensual reflex, Nerese thought it was called.

"Our Lady of Perpetual Misery," Ray snapped, no real humor in his voice.

"Can you spell the word 'house' backwards?" slowly withdrawing the light to test for distance adjustment.

"Sure I can," Ray said, then defiantly clammed up.

"Can you do so, please?" In that same impervious lilt.

"E, S, O . . . E-S-U-O-H."

"OK. Can you tell me the name of the President?" The light gliding from far left to far right.

"President of *what* . . ."

"The United States?"

"Davy Crockett."

"Can you tell me the name of the President of the United States, please?"

"Oh give me a fucking break!" Ray brayed like a mule, his voice crackling with exasperation, dehydration and maybe a little something else—something not fully arrived yet.

Refraining from announcing her presence until the neurologist finished his bedside exam, Nerese was shocked at the change in Ray over the last twenty-four hours. The good news was that he was more alert; the bad, that he was nearly out of control with agitation.

His skin, merely sallow the day before, was now the color of air-hardened cheese, and even through the empurpled mask of ecchymosis that raccooned his eyes she could plainly pick up the hollow pockets of shadow deepening under his blood-drowned whites, the Decadron-induced sleeplessness, or once again, something as yet unannounced, starting to ferociously take its toll.

She was desperate for the neurologist to finish up so she could get to work here.

"Are you experiencing any headaches?" the doc murmured as he flipped up the bottom of the blanket to expose Ray's feet.

"You mean besides you?" Then, "Hey!" aimed at Nerese as he finally noticed her standing quietly beyond the pale.

"Hey, gorgeous." She gave him back a discreet wave, once again musing on the fact that because of the nature of his injuries she could stare at his face all day long and still not have any idea of what he normally looked like.

"Are we done yet?" Ray asked with a sprightly rage.

"Almost," the neurologist murmured, running a pencil-shaped metal rod up the sole of one foot.

"That's the Babinski test?" Nerese asked cautiously.

"Babinski reflex," running the other foot, Ray barely responding to the pressure.

If his toes had splayed and arched that would have been bad news, otherwise known as a positive or negative Babinski, she could never remember which.

"He's looking good, huh?" she ventured.

"So far," the guy not turning to her. "Hold your hands out directly in front of you and close your eyes, please?"

Ray thrust his arms forward, his hands bunched into fists.

"Close your eyes, please?"

Ray looked to Nerese in exasperation.

"Close your eyes, please?"

Ray finally did as he was told, looking now, with his stitched bashed and multicolored face, his lightly shut eyelids and his double straight-arm, like a caricature of the Frankenstein monster.

"Hold them steady, please?"

Ray stiffened slightly at the elbows to lock himself in as the doctor, sliding the flat of his hand between the extended fists, lightly batted them back and forth as if to widen the gap.

"Steady, please?"

Fuming ostentatiously, Ray complied as the doctor continued his fluttery assault.

"Steady . . ."

Nerese knew he was looking for one of the arms to involuntarily fall away from the other: pronator drift it was called, a sign of incipient paresis on the side of the body opposite the trauma site, the blinkered patient not even aware that he was flunking, but Ray seemed to be hanging in just fine.

"OK, then," the neurologist said, then simply walked away, Ray calling after him, "Don't I even get a fucking lollipop?"

Nerese waited a beat for this latest profanity to stop reverberating through the ward before she dropped her shoulder bag, shrugged off her coat and sat in what she already thought of as her chair.

"You always curse people out like that?"

"Like what," Ray said.

"How you feeling today."

"Me? Freaked. Bored. I can't read, I can't watch TV, I try to listen to books on tape but I can't, I can't . . . I go off somewheres, or I get hung up on some sentence or phrase, next thing I know I missed half a chapter," the words rattling out of him like rocks down a chute.

Nerese saw no evidence of a book, a television or a cassette player, didn't think the last two would even be permitted in a ward like this, and concluded that Ray had been either hallucinating or dreaming about these activities.

"You getting any visitors?"

"You."

"How 'bout your daughter?"

"No. I don't want her here. Are you kidding me? I look like fuckin' Linda Blair. I mean *look* at this." Tapping the shaved and sutured patch of scalp. "It's like a fuckin' helipad up there. So no. No Ruby. She'd completely flip."

"That's too bad," Nerese said gently.

"I mean, I talk to her on the phone, but, you know, that's not . . . She's thirteen, so it's, How's school. Good. How's Mom. Fine. How's tricks. Good. I don't think kids start using full sentences until they graduate college, and they're incapable of asking you about *your* motherfucking day until they're thirty-five. So, I know, it's like, I know she's very . . . She's, she's suffering over this, but I don't see how coming here . . ."

"What do you mean, she's suffering?" Nerese going to work.

" 'What do you mean, she's suffering?' " Ray mimicking her note for note. "And by the way, talking about kids? As soon as I'm presentable? I want you to bring your son in to see me. You know, because you were talking full-boat scholarship or the Army, right? It just so happens that I write *great* recommendations for college, been doing it since I was a high school teacher, so let me just talk to him, get a sense of where he's coming from, and I will do him right."

"Great," Nerese said, thinking, In a pig's ass.

"I think that's my true art form, the college recommendation, plus you know, with the cachet of the TV show under my feet? You know, the scholastic and secular? All's I need is a little face-to-face for inspiration, then forget about it, anywhere he wants to go. In like Flynn."

"OK then," Nerese dismissing all this self-trumpeting as Decadron-tongue.

But even if Ray's offer had been a sober one, Nerese would never have taken him up on it. Butchie, Antoine, her mother, her uncle and especially she herself, when appropriate, were all part of the arsenal of charm-and-disarm; Darren was off-limits. Using his name in the course of an investigation always gave her the creeps; made her feel like something bad was about to happen. Even the little she had semi-complained about him to Ray during her first visit to the hospital left her with a faint sense of dread, and now that she and Ray were officially reacquainted, Nerese doubted that she'd ever voluntarily bring up her son's name again.

"Anyways"—Nerese arched her back—"I got to tell you, your place, Ray?" She brought bunched fingertips to her lips and blew a kiss. "Out of sight."

"Thanks," he said with off-balance tentativeness, then, "What?"

"What do you mean, 'What.' " Nerese rolled up her sleeves.

"What were you doing in my place?"

"It's my crime scene."

"Oh no. No *way*."

"It's my catch."

"Tweetie," things moving a little too fast for him now. "What the fuck, don't you have anything better to do?"

"Actually, I don't." She leaned forward. "See, the department? Once you're down to six months and a wake-up—you know, getting ready to put in your papers? They automatically reclassify you as functionally insane and yank you from the rotation. Start assigning you shit like driving blood samples to the state lab in Sea Girt, or reorganizing the filing system for the gambling squad, because they don't want anybody out on the street who's distracted, you know, got one eye on the clock or going through some kind of midlife identity crisis. That's no good. That can be dangerous. And as far as my situation vis-à-vis the job right now? They have me mostly on this public school circuit, giving talks, like, the po-lice is your friend, watch out for peer pressure, don't be a dropout, drugs are bad for you . . . You know, like there's one kid left on the planet that hasn't heard this shit a million times before."

She was losing him to his discomfort, Ray licking his dry lips, eyes going wide left then wide right as if his optical stalks were hot-wired to a metronome.

"Anyways, my point being, you know, in regard to your being laid up like this? Because you don't want to cooperate, nobody really gives a shit what happened to you. In fact, the only reason this thing isn't dead and buried is that I personally asked to pursue it and the Job sees it as a harmless enough activity for a lame duck like me so, the answer is, No, I don't have anything better to do."

"They won't even give me so much as a chip of ice," he said, as if not having heard a word out of her mouth. "My tongue feels like the pad on a dog's paw."

"They usually don't give anything oral to head traumas until they're out of the woods," Nerese said. "Let me ask you something. Your next-door neighbor, Mrs. Kuben? Does her place always smell like that? It's like a five-room mothball in there."

"Oh man, that's nothing," he said jaggedly. "Did you pick up on her Ziploc fetish? Anything smaller than a piano she's got stashed in a Ziploc bag. She buys stuff in the supermarket, you know, pasta, dry cereal, sugar, takes it out of the box, throws the box away, transfers everything to labeled Baggies. My father told me he saw her sitting at her dining table tearing open little packets of Sweet'n Low, you know, however many packets come in a box? Tearing them open, and dumping them all together into a see-through sandwich bag."

"Can I ask you something personal? Why are you living there?"

"I don't know," Ray said. "When the Trade Center went down I came back from LA."

"Came back?"

"I wouldn't have, but I couldn't convince Claire to let Ruby come out west to me, so . . . Anyways, I'm back not even three weeks, living in a hotel in the city, bang, my mother dies.

"So I come across the river, move in with my dad, temporarily I'm thinking, make sure he's not alone, that he's OK . . . Two weeks after the funeral? Guess what. The guy books. He fucking books down south, and I'm standing there by myself in the middle of the living room, just standing there like an idiot. I mean, I was glad the guy had a game plan for himself, glad I didn't have to . . . But I was just standing there and then I figure, well, I own the place, paid for it, don't have any other address, I'm gigless, not sure what's next, you have to lay your head down *somewhere*, so . . ." He trailed off.

"Anyways," Nerese moving in. "That Mrs. Kuben? How do I say this . . . She says you got so many, let's call 'em people of color, marching through your doors? It's like a stop on the Underground Railroad."

Ray stared at her, processing, then, "Fuck her. They weren't bothering anybody."

"Who's 'they'?"

"Truly, truly, fuck her, that bougie-assed Ziploc-packing stick-your-nose-in-everybody's . . ."

"Actually, the one I'm interested in, Ray, is the hootchie."

"The what?" Ray needing another minute to integrate again, then, "And fuck you too."

Nerese took it in stride, but let her face cloud over like he had just lost a friend; Ray instantly losing his bluster.

"Sorry." He turned away, embarrassed.

"So who is she?"

"No." Shaking his head, shutting this down.

"You know I'm gonna find out anyhow."

"Why are you doing this, Nerese . . ."

Nerese, now.

"It's easy to make me stop."

"*Why*." Almost shouting it.

"Why?" Nerese got up and stepped back from the bed. She had been thinking nonstop about this since the moment Mr. Egan had told her of Ray's assault three days ago in the school auditorium, and now, right now she wanted to answer him as clearly as she could.

"Why, Ray, is because I believe in reciprocity, like I believe in God. I believe heart and soul in doing unto others as they do unto me, good *or* bad, and I make damn sure everybody around me knows it too, because let me tell you something: I have discovered that no matter what kind of shit I have to deal with, no matter what kind of animal behavior I have to contend with, it keeps me decent, it keeps the people *around* me decent, and these days, decency, simple human decency, is getting to be like hens' teeth, OK? So if you want, I can sit here all day listening to you going on about fuck this one, fuck that one, fuck Nerese, but, you know, whether you make it hard for me or easy, the fact of the matter, like I told you the last time, is that I owe you. Sorry."

"But I don't *want*—"

"Ray Ray Ray," drowning him out. "You don't *know* what you want. Nobody . . . Hey. I walk in here yesterday you looked like someone shoved your face in a blender. I walk in here yesterday you were like two heartbeats away from slitting your wrists. And to*day*? You look even worse. Plus now you're bouncing off the walls, motor-mouthing, cursing people out like you're on meth or something. I mean, whoever did this to you, it's like they drop-kicked your brain into the Twilight Zone, so . . ."

"Forget it," folding his arms across his chest like an Indian chief, like a child.

"Ray." Nerese took it down a peg. "That guy came into your home, lined you up against your own living room wall and tried to take you out like your head was a piñata."

"What?"

"How can you let someone get away with that. How can you let some-one violate you like that and not try to get yours back. If you don't stand up for yourself on this, it's gonna eat you alive. If you don't stand up for yourself on this, it's gonna give you *cancer*."

"Lined me up against the wall?" he said haltingly.

"Plus, Ray, it's not just about you. Guys like that? This is what they do and they keep on doin' it until they get snatched, so even if not for your own—"

"What did you mean 'lined me up against the wall' . . ."

"Ray," Nerese said heavily, as she assumed the position, her hands braced against the Plexiglas partition. She twisted her face toward him. "Ring a bell?"

At first he looked nonplussed, but then as the recognition came into his eyes, she thought he would vomit.

"Ray."

"No." Looking away from her, dull with dread.

"OK. OK," she said lightly, stepping away from the wall, afraid to push him any further on this right now.

Next to the pitcher on the night table she noticed a sheet of paper folded in the middle and propped into an A-frame.

Reaching across Ray's body, she picked it up and saw another armed and dangerous ghetto waif, once again the legend beneath the feet, "What's Mine Is Mine."

"It's a kid's," Ray said.

"This guy?" She produced the drawing from his apartment.

"You can just *take* shit?" Ray slowly coming back to himself, annoyed but not particularly nervous.

"Who is he?"

"Some old student."

"He visited you here?"

"Once."

"I thought you said nobody came but me."

"He came *once!*" Ray barked, starting to rev it up again.

"Old student . . ." Nerese said evenly, gingerly pushing for more.

"From like twelve years ago when I was teaching in the Bronx, we keep in touch. He's a good kid, Salim El-Amin, used to be Coley Rodgers."

The words came out of him in a jacked gobble, but despite his returning agitation he gave up the name without blinking and Nerese, not smelling anything worth immediately pursuing here, attempted to calm him down by retreating into history. "So you started out as a teacher, huh?"

"Got to eat."

"What, you didn't like it?" She slipped this second drawing into her pocket along with the first, that "What's Mine Is Mine" still bugging her a little.

"Not really."

"I understand you quit. Took a bunch of kids from a class trip and skipped town or something."

Ray stared at her. Nerese braced for another outburst.

"Let me tell you something," his jaw locked at a slant again. "What I got busted for? That was the only day I enjoyed being a teacher. I took a tenth-grade English class to Central Park to see *As You Like It*, you know, 'Hey nonny nonny.' They were fucking bored out of their minds. I had a feeling they would be, and because I hate the idea of a captive audience? For backup I snuck a football in my bag. Sure enough, by the middle of the second act? We're out of there. I took them over to the Sheep Meadow and we had a game, girls versus boys, I'm quarterbacking for the boys, and the kids, they were in heaven. It was like they couldn't believe I did this for them, cut them such a break.

"I mean, neither could the school. I was sent up for review, but by that point I was like, Fuck it I quit.

"I mean, it wasn't like I was a bad teacher or I didn't try, or I didn't care, or I took it out on my students. I just . . .

"I don't know. To me, the whole point of high school is to graduate, you know, hit it and quit it. And to go back there, voluntarily, and to deal with the department heads, the senior teachers, the principal, the audits, the evaluations, it was too much like still being a student worrying about your report card, you know? It was like the same type of pissy two-bit tyrants that ruled my life from kindergarten to twelfth grade as teachers were now my bosses. Thank you, no, so . . ."

"I don't know, Ray, me?" Nerese said easily, trying to slow him down again. "If I had to do it all over again? I'd've definitely been a teacher. I like working with kids, you know, as long as they don't follow me home."

"Yeah well, I think I'd've been a cop myself," Ray said. "You guys, you got a backstage pass to the greatest show on earth."

"No, well, you must be talking about some *other* cop. Do you know how I became a detective?" Feeling herself about to go off on a tear, Nerese tried to rein it in, but it was no use—this one always made her nuts. "I had to put in fifty-four months sitting behind a desk doing candidate evaluations for the police academy. Fifty-four months, that was the route offered to me for a gold shield.

"See, I wanted plainclothes narcotics, because that's only fourteen months, and it's for real, but they turned me down because of my brothers. They said, 'What are you gonna do if you hit a place and one of your brothers is in there shootin' up, pipin' up? What are you gonna do if you know three hours before it goes down that your squad's gonna hit some spot, some apartment, and there's every chance in the world that someone in your family is working there, or scoring there. Are you gonna warn them to stay away?'

"And I'm like, 'Hell no, nothing doing, live by the needle, die by the needle, that is strictly their own goddamn problem,' but they didn't want to take a chance with me so I got to ride a motherfucking desk for fifty-four months, put on an average of six pounds a year, got my gold shield, but everybody knew how I got it, what I did, didn't do for it. And to this day I get little or no respect from other detectives because of it, no matter, no matter what I've done on the Job since. I'm just some high-profile black female desk jockey got the shield to make the department look good, so fuck this greatest-show-on-earth bullshit . . ." Nerese gulped some air. "Did I mention to you I'm retiring in a few months?"

"Yeah, well, still . . . You know what I really hated about teaching?" Ray just getting back into his own thing. "I hated the idea of getting older every year while the students stayed the same age or, you know, when they graduated, they were like ships sailing off for adventure and there I am waving bye-bye, stuck on the dock . . ."

Despite her awareness of his altered state, Nerese felt surprisingly wounded by Ray's lack of response to her fifty-four-month sob story—wounded enough that she had to remind herself that what she was doing here, was working.

"Plus one other small thing?" he said. "Towards the end of my teaching career? Like, the last year or two? I was an up-and-coming cokehead. Not every day, not every night, but enough, and occasionally I'd go into class high, have a half-gram in my wallet, standing in front of thirty kids at a clip, I'm either skying or crashing, paranoid out of my ass, like, Why are they *looking* at me? Because you're the teacher, schmuck . . . And as embarrassing as it is to tell you this? Understand, Nerese, and this in no way exonerates me or mitigates what I did, but I was also very ashamed of myself. I mean I never got caught, but I never got away with it, either."

"But so, I don't understand," Nerese said. "If you hated teaching so much, why'd you go back and volunteer for more?"

"I had four really bad years on coke—teaching, driving a cab, doing polygraphs . . . I mean if someone had hooked me up to one of those machines when I was a polygrapher? The fucking stylus would have shot off into the wall. And I didn't really stop until I got the writing deal on that TV show; then I cleaned up for good. Then about two years ago, I got nominated for an Emmy. Well, one-fifth of an Emmy, since there were four other writers of that episode. And a week after that, I get this call from one of my old teachers at the Hook, Mr. Mufson, remember him? Asks me would I like to address the graduating class, you know, local boy makes good, comes home to talk, hail the conquering hero and, Tweetie, I swear I was such a nothing student at that school, so it's . . . How could I not?"

Tweetie again.

"So, I show up at the assembly, all the kids are in cap and gown, nine-tenths are like, 'Who the hell's *this* clown?' but the teachers knew, my old bitch-ass teachers and, I'm up on the podium, I look out and there's not one white face, you know Paulus Hook now, and because all I see are minority kids and because I'm haunted by my own drug history, I just toss my speech and go into this confessional thing about drugs, how they almost destroyed me, don't let them destroy you, you've got your whole life in front of, et cetera, the world's your oyster, et cetera. It was a pretty damn good speech, the only thing was, the school didn't have a drug problem. I mean yeah, there's always some kids who want to break bad, get cash money paid, but those kids are strictly interested in the business end of things. I mean, who sitting there wearing a cap and gown in that auditorium would be contemplating a career as a drug addict? These kids are graduating. Half are headed for college. My whole address was a class-action insult. But still, parents are coming up to me afterwards shaking my hand, asking me if I had written copies of what I said, my own parents are in the audience, Ruby, my old teachers, and there was something so, I don't know, intoxicating about the whole thing, so heady . . .

"And, you know, a year later, the Towers go down, I'm back, de-gigged, money's not a problem just then, but I need, I really need to do something with myself. And, I remembered how good, what a rush that was, that graduation-day thing, so I went and got something going for myself over there. And it was different than teaching in the Bronx because they weren't paying me, so all they could say to me was thanks, thank you, thank you so much . . ."

"Money's not a problem," Nerese murmured with hammy envy. "Which reminds me. My guy who did the background check on you? He wanted to know how somebody goes from driving a cab to writing a TV show."

Ray stared at her, absorbing "my guy," absorbing "background check."

"That's for some other time," he said flatly.

"Whatever . . . And he also asked me to ask you how the hell someone walks out on four bigs a week in order to come back to *this* toilet and work for nothing."

Ray took a moment with that, too; Nerese knowing everything but his shoe size. And his assailant.

"Also for another time," struggling to keep his voice on an even keel.

"Because, he had heard something about an incident, a misunderstanding . . . I can't believe this myself, Ray, so if you say bullshit, bullshit it is, but something about something *racial* out there?"

She saw the truth of it in his face, in the immensity of his nonreaction. "Another time," he managed to say.

Nerese gave it a minute, then began gathering herself, throwing out big deep sighs as she rose from her chair. "And no way you're giving me a name here."

Ray, as if lost in all his "some other times," looked right through her.

"You're just gonna make me bust my hump out there, old lady that I am . . ."

Nothing.

"Won't even give me the name of that cha-cha you were seen squiring around Little Venice with."

Carefully rolling on his side, he gave her his back.

"Well, this is intriguing, Ray, I'll give you that."

And having finally collected and organized herself, she turned to leave. "OK, then . . ."

"Hey Tweetie?" he said softly.

Sensing a prelude to revelation in the hesitant calling of her name, she turned expectantly.

"When I told you that was the only time I enjoyed being a teacher? You know, taking those kids AWOL? That wasn't exactly true."

Nerese waited.

"I pulled that AWOL shit with them every time we had a class trip. Year in, year out, my kids always counted on me for that." Ray coughed, shot her a half-smile. "That was just the only time I ever got caught."

Chapter 7

Classroom — January 10

"This is me and my friends at Six Flags amusement park," the girl Dierdre read to the class from her Chinese notebook as a Polaroid was passed around the table.

> "This was taken last year. We went by bus and it took so long to get there I was a old lady with six kids and eight grandchildren by the time we got there. If you want to go to Six Flags don't ever go by bus. Otherwise I had fun."

"OK," Ray said, smiling. "Thank you."

What else was there to say? She hadn't done what he'd asked: find a photo of family before the writer's birth and make up a story about the people in the picture — but he was grateful for the stab at humor, for her doing anything at all.

"Rashaad, what do you have . . ." nodding to the tall long-headed boy who pined for the oblivious Felicia.

"Yeah, I wrote something." He displayed his hands palms up. "But I forgot the book at home."

"No." Ray shrugged. "Class can't work that way. If you don't bring stuff in, we have nothing to do."

"Well, I can *tell* you it."

"No," Mrs. Bondo said, Ray about to say the same, resenting her butting in. "This class is a privilege," she added, making it sound like a prison perk. "If you abuse it, it'll be taken away."

"OK then," Ray said as lightly as he could. "Next victim."

Jamaal tentatively raised a hand, then passed around an eight-by-ten color photo of a corpse.

The boys got into this one, squinting open-mouthed, Efram asking the inevitable, "He's dead?"

The subject was a thirtyish black man laid out in a satin-lined casket, eyes lightly shut, lips infinitesimally parted, a rosary entwined in his clasped hands. Lilies peeked out from the top right corner of the frame.

Two of the girls unconsciously leaned into each other, the photo on the table between them.

When the picture was passed to Mrs. Bondo, she somehow managed to project both skeptical wariness and raw curiosity.

Once again Ray was suffused with gratitude. "Go ahead, Jamaal."

> "This is a picture of my uncle before he was buried. I never really knew him because he lived in Brooklyn but my mother told me that when he was in high school he was a starter on the basketball team and they won the city championship one year even though he was five-foot-eight. This gives me hope because even though I am five-foot-eight too next year I hope to start for Paulus Hook. Right now I'm on the JV and have the highest free-throw percentage of anybody."

Jamaal read in a halting monotone, as if the words were listed vertically, or the handwriting unfamiliar.

> "My uncle was also the class clown which I am too. It makes me sad that he died because I think he could have been a positive role model for me and a friend.
> "My uncle was shot although you can't see because it was in the back. He was minding his own business too."

Once again, not what he had asked for, but bringing in a body like that . . .

"What was your uncle's name?"

"Spoony."

A few kids tittered, but Jamaal didn't seem to mind.

"My boy died?" Rashaad said. "Got his head stuck in a elevator shaft with the elevator like smashing it into the wall? Had a close-coffin funeral."

"Oh," Altagracia popped. "That was Supreme, right?"

"Yeah, uh-huh . . ."

"Hang on, hang on," Ray said, then decided to step off.

"My pastor in church?" Rashaad continued, actually rolling his face on the table as he spoke. "There was this kid, right? He got his-self all shot up the night before in the church parking lot. You know, kilt? The pastor, he said, 'You think that boy woke up yes-tiday mornin' sat up on his bed said to himself, "Today's my day to *die*"? You best get right with Jesus 'cause you *never* know when your ticket's gonna get punched.'"

"He's right." Efram nodded soberly, nobody laughing or cracking wise, and Ray was taken by that.

"Rashaad, I'm not going to tell you again," Mrs. Bondo said. "Sit up."

"Tell me again? You din't tell me the first time."

"A few years ago, I was walking by an old graveyard downstate near Trenton," Ray said impulsively, "and I came across a woman's headstone had to be from the early nineteenth century, said,

> To my darling husband
> and children dear, I am not dead
> but sleeping here.
> As I am now
> you soon shall be.
> Prepare for death
> and follow me."

"That's nasty," Altagracia said.

Both Rashaad and Efram repeated the epitaph in half-whispers, as if committing it to memory.

"Who's next?"

Three of the four remaining students raised their hands, Myra, the *Spoon River Anthology* kid, his ace-in-the-hole kid, raising hers only slightly as if she knew she had the goods and could wait her turn.

"I'm sorry, what's your name again?" Ray asked a tall, berry-dark girl, his voice delicate with apology.

"Mercedes," she said. "I wasn't here last week."

"But you did the work anyhow?" Ray smiled. "Wow. Thank you. Please . . ." He gestured to her papers.

Her photo was of a thirtyish woman, morbidly obese, sitting on a bench in the Hopewell Houses, a cigarette in one hand, a can of Coke in the other. On one side of her sat Mercedes at half her present age, on the other side another little girl, both kids placidly resting their heads on the woman's broad thighs.

"This is my Aunt Kim. She was a waitress in Jersey City at a restaurant until her diabetes made it too hard for her to stand all the time. The other girl is Monique who is my best friend and cousin. She is Kim's daughter. Even though my Aunt Kim has diabetes everybody in the family makes sure she takes her shots and does what the doctor says for her to do in general.

"Besides her daughter Monique, Kim is my favorite person in my family, including my mother, her sister."

Ray made a reflective noise, stalling, wondering if these kids even heard themselves.

"How much does that lady weigh?" Efram ventured as politely as he could, provoking a cloud of reproachful clucks from the girls, Altagracia snapping back, "How much do *you* weigh?"

"No, I'm just asking." Efram hunched up, a mortified smile on his frozen mug.

"OK, stop," Ray said affably, what he hoped was affably.

"I don't want to talk about mine," Mercedes said evenly but emphatically.

"See what you did, stupid?" Altagracia said.

"Just *stop*," Ray barked, and they did; the momentary effectiveness of his spontaneous outburst taking him back, in not a great way, to his days as a paid teacher. "Mercedes, I would like to talk about it if, it's OK with you," he said placatingly, but just saying it, not really having anything on his mind.

"Unh-uh." Mercedes shut him down, but she didn't seem too banged up about it and he let it go.

"Felicia, right?"

The tall light-skinned girl nodded imperceptibly, shyness or fear reducing her mouth and eyes to slits as she slid a photo facedown toward him as if they were playing poker.

The black-and-white snap was of a tall well-built unsmiling black man in a double-breasted suit, standing in front of the lions' cage in the long-gone Dempsy County zoo.

"Gimme that thing," Rashaad said in a mock-brusque tone, snatching it away, putting on a show for his never-to-be girlfriend.

"Do you not want to be in this class, Rashaad?" Mrs. Bondo asked.

"This is my grandfather, Roy V. Smalley," Felicia murmured.

> "He is the first African-American fireman in Dempsy. He did it for one and a half year then quit because of the prejudice and work for the post office. He also was in the Army and had four kids who are my mother and uncles. This is 1948 and is in Dempsy."

Felicia's head seemed to retract into her high white blouse collar, the kid another vertical reader, another assignment-muffer, but the picture, the history . . . Ray pored over the photo, studying the man's dour expression, romantically reading into it rage, dignity, doggedness, then surrender.

"Is your grandfather still alive?"

Felicia shook her head no.

"The first black fireman . . ." Ray just lofting it out there. "You kids," he said earnestly, "you have so much to write about, you have . . ." Then, to Felicia, "What was he like?"

"Strict," she said, staring at the table.

"You knew him?"

"No. My mother said, though."

"Strict," Ray repeated greedily, turning the word over like a prism. "I'll bet."

"Can I read now?" Altagracia waved both hands like someone flagging down a rescue boat, then spun a yellowing color photo across the table.

The subject was a frail little girl, xylophone-ribbed, wearing nothing but underpants and leaning into what Ray thought might be a banyan tree. She had large dark fever-bright eyes, and her voluminous black hair fell around her shoulders like an opera cape.

"It's like a Gauguin," Ray said to Mrs. Bondo, who nodded in vague acknowledgment.

It's like a Gauguin, Ray repeated to himself mincingly. Jesus Christ. "Go ahead."

"This is my dad in Santo Domingo," Altagracia began.

> "He almost died because of disease until my grand-
> mother, his mother, took him to this man in the village who
> everybody said was a healer and was healed. He was healed
> by praying. That is why I love Jesus. My dad in this picture is
> seven years old and is leaning against the tree because the
> sickness was still a little bit in his legs."

"That's a boy?" Efram asked.

"Why was his hair so long?" Ray asked.

"Yeah, OK. My grandmother? When she prayed to Jesus? She said to him, 'If you let him live, I won't ever cut his hair again.'"

"Why?" Myra asked, the first word out of her all day.

"Because this way? Every time somebody sees him in the village, they look at all the hair and think about how Jesus saved him."

"There you go," Ray said happily.

So far not one kid had done what he'd asked. But he hadn't exactly delivered on his own end, either—hadn't made any comments worth a crap, no real feedback, criticism or even simple encouragement coming from him toward the kids, no teaching of any recognizable kind. But maybe, he thought, just for today it was enough to play show and tell. He'd be better in the next class.

"Efram."

"Yeah, OK." The chubby kid brought out a comic book cutout of Superman taped to a red piece of construction paper.

The class hung back until his opening salvo: "This is a self-portrait of me," then started barking with glee, Efram shrugging and plowing on.

> "This is a self-portrait of me which I drew and posed for at
> the same time. Of course I can do that because I can get in a
> pose then zoom to the easel so fast I can see my own pose.
>
> "My favorite sport is basketball. I once beat Allen Iverson
> in a game of one-on-one so bad he started to cry and begged

me never to play again so he could be the best player in the world. I felt sorry for him so I did it. I now put all my super-power energy into women."

The class completely fell apart, everyone shouting as if in a revival tent.

Unflappable, immune to the disoriented free-for-all of derision and joy he had provoked—even Mrs. Bondo laughed out loud—Efram turned to Ray. "That's it."

"What the hell am I supposed to say?" Ray said, too loudly.

"You don't have to say nothing. You can just enjoy it."

The kid looked about two years away from body hair, Ray entranced by his cool-jerk confidence, his serene aloofness.

The other students were falling all over themselves trying to come up with the ultimate retort, but they were unmanned by the fat boy going on the offensive like that, weren't quickwitted in that way, and the table gradually subsided into a sporadic roundelay of coos and haws, Efram bathing in it like a Buddha.

"OK, calm down, calm down," Mrs. Bondo said gently, still smiling, the kids equally getting off on how Efram had made her laugh.

"Let's just keep going," Ray said, feeling now like a talk show host with a hot guest list, nodding at long last to Myra.

The girl took a minute to find her photo, another color-drained Instamatic, this one time-stamped seventeen years earlier. It was a snap of a youngish black couple standing in front of a church, the neutral-faced woman resting a hand atop her ballooning stomach.

Because she read in a thin murmurous voice and because the class was still buzzing from Efram's Superman challenge, Myra was halfway through her recitation before anyone even noticed that she had started.

"Hang on, hang on." Ray held up a hand. "Can you start again, please? C'mon, let's be quiet, OK?"

"The baby is in her belly," Myra began in a minute monotone.

"But only I can see it in this picture.

"The baby has a full set of teeth already and is mad at me even though I won't be born for three more years.

"When I get inside my mother's stomach, the baby has left mousetraps in there from three years ago.

"When the baby is born it lays in the crib all day but when my parents go to sleep at night it sneaks out the window to go hunting.

"Sometimes it comes into my bed, puts its face right up against mine, shows me its teeth and I am so scared I can't move.

"The baby never grows up, it just gets bigger.

"The baby is dead."

Silence, everyone staring at her as she returned the photo to her journal.

"What do you mean, 'the baby's dead.' The baby's *dead?*" Efram asked.

Myra shrugged; it is what it is.

"That's like that old-time movie, *It's Alive*. Rashaad grinned then went into voice-over mode. "There's one thing wrong with the Robinson baby . . . It's ali-i-ive!"

"Damn," Altagracia snapped. "What does it take for you to shut up?"

The class then went back to watching Myra as she self-consciously fussed with her Chinese writing book; Ray thinking, The One.

In five teaching seasons there had been five kids—Sherman South, Esperanza Castro, Garcelle House, Caroline Yang and Hassan Pridgen— each kid invariably poker-faced but reached, stirred to the core by what Ray was offering. These were the kids who, in the midst of earth science, gym, algebra, cafeteria stench would manage to knock out a handwritten thirty-page story or a collection of poems, drop it on his desk at the end of class and split. There was always something furtive about his relationship with them; no smiling, no chitchat, rarely would they speak to him unless spoken to first, never would they seek him out after class, but once this One-ness was established—and these kids very quickly picked up on the fact that it had been—the air between himself and that boy or girl was always taut with anticipation. They were romances of a sort; at the time, Ray liked to imagine these kids thinking about him outside of school roughly as much as he thought about them; sometimes he would even envision them at home, around the dinner table, or in the kitchen, talking about him, or not being able to talk about him . . .

Narcissistic, self-aggrandizing—yeah, yes, guilty as charged; but, in his defense, he knew that he would have done anything for them: paid their college tuition, paid their family's rent, hooked up their older sibs with jobs; responded to any financial or spiritual 911 they could have possibly sent his way, although none of them had ever sought him out for anything above and beyond his continued presence in class. Nor did any of them become writers, as far as he knew—but that was OK too.

"So how'd you come to read *Spoon River Anthology*?" Ray asked Myra, as the kids gathered their books.

"Mr. Barkeley said I would like it," she answered, zipping up her backpack.

"Do you?"

"Yeah," her voice so small, "I like olden-days stuff."

"Like what else?"

"Charles Dickens?"

"What did you read of his?"

"Nothing yet. But I have his book at home. I'm going to read it next."

"Who's Mr. Barkeley?"

"He was the guidance counselor."

"Was?"

"He left."

"You know your story was excellent," Ray said, Myra looking off, fighting down a smile. True to type, she had yet to look him in the eye.

"If I'd read it in a book . . ." he faltered, then, "I'd never have guessed it was written by a teenager. How old are you?"

"Fourteen."

"Fourteen. What do you want to be in life?"

"I don't know," she said in a shrugging singsong.

"You keep it up like this, you're going to be a monster writer someday," he said, gassing her head unconscionably now. "And I'd be able to say I knew you when."

Myra swallowed another grin; he could see the physical struggle in her face; Ray begging himself to stop.

When he finally turned away from her, he saw that the entire class save for Rashaad was still in the room although the change bell had rung over a minute ago. They were lingering, eavesdropping; their expressions hungry, disturbed and alert.

.   .   .

Tromping down to the school's lobby, Ray saw that the other security guard was on duty now, the young lean unsmiling one who was under the illusion of being a corrections officer, and he faltered before getting in line to sign out, waiting his turn behind a dumpy older woman hunched over the visitors' log, a five-year-old boy at her side.

One of the main doors to the street banged open and a tall overweight girl came splay-footed into the school. Ignoring the security desk, she hung a leisurely right toward the stairs.

"Where you goin'." The guard's voice whip-cracked across the hall.

The girl, snapping gum, turned dead-eyed, sizing up this hawk-faced bitch.

"Bafroom."

"You coming from outside?"

"Yeah. I was outside."

The guard just stared her down, Ray noticing the five-year-old hypno-tized by the lean unsmiling lady behind the desk.

He took another look at the older woman holding the kid's hand, standing there openmouthed, as sucked into this showdown as the boy. She seemed faintly familiar to him; a face just out of memory's range.

"So can I go?" the big kid finally said.

"No, you cannot *go*."

Ray became entranced too, thinking, She's got to be kidding. But she wasn't.

He could tell that the big girl wanted to mouth off, register some face-saving gesture, but she was too intimidated and left the building without even a cluck of irritation.

Ray took another look at the older woman with the child, convinced he knew her but . . . More like he recognized the essence of her, the set of her mouth or something, the rest a papier-mâché swaddle, a thickening of years.

She caught him staring at her, Ray thinking, Can't be . . . But he saw that she was doing the same visual stutter-step on him.

"Ray?"

"Oh shit. Carla . . ." seeing her full on now, stripping her back down to seventeen.

"Oh my God . . ." Carla said, and they embraced in the epicenter of the school, the moment not lost on Ray who barely had the nerve to even look at her back when they were students here.

"Oh my God." Carla's voice rasped like boots on gravel, her eyes, eyebrows all that was really left.

"Yeah, wow . . ." Ray stepped back to take her in, then quickly looked away, afraid his disorientation at her physical decline was all over his face.

"You look just like you did. You look just like you," she said, her lower teeth now sepia-toned and quarter-twisted at the bottom of her mouth.

"Jesus . . ." He didn't know where to rest his eyes. The last time he had seen her, maybe thirty years ago, Carla Powell was exiting their building in Hopewell strapped into an upright gurney, drying blood on her skirt and both forearms, her wrists thick with tape. Her face, as always, even on that day, was makeup precise, brows plucked to a whip-line of black, eyes, despite their tranked-out glassiness, still somehow managing to project a fierce and angry sexuality. There had been rumors about her and her father.

"How *are* you," he said, beaming mechanically, but really wanting to know.

"I'm just . . . They got a preschool program here." She jerked on the little boy's arm. "I'm trying to get him squared away."

The boy was still fixated on the security guard, still staring at her wide-eyed.

"Your son?"

"Grandson," she said, and Ray got lost in the math.

"So how *are* you," he repeated mindlessly, and this time Carla seemed to take the question seriously, her face suddenly buckling from forehead to chin.

"Not so good," she said hoarsely, let go of her grandson's hand, fished out a cigarette and fired up.

"What's wrong."

"No smoking, Ma'am," the guard blared flatly as if they were at the far end of the lobby.

Carla blinked, said "Sorry," then absently stubbed out the freshly lit butt into the palm of her hand, Ray getting a cold whoosh off that.

"No, I'm not so good," she repeated, pocketing the broken cigarette.

"How so . . ."

"So how are you?" Carla ignored the probe. "You married? You happy?" saying it like it was an either/or proposition.

"I'm over in Little Venice for now," he said, leaving it at that.

"You know, Ray, I swear . . ." Her voice dropped to a rusty mutter. "I can't believe I'm in this goddamn building again. I hated this school."

"Then maybe you should leave," the guard said coolly.

"*Excuse* me?" Carla cocked her head in astonishment, Ray equally startled, almost thrilled, not so much by the comment itself but by the fact that he was sure the guard had said it just to see what would happen.

"You save that mouth for the *hoodies*." Carla leaned forward, flashing fire, but despite the words her voice was more distraught than pugnacious, and her hands were shaking. "I am a *grand*mother . . ."

Ray went hollow with dread, with epiphany. This whole home-from-the-hills fantasy that he had engineered for himself here was all wrong; retreating into the past like this just another way of advancing to the grave.

He quickly scribbled his name in the log and started backtracking toward the main door.

"Carla," calling out to her as he became a silhouette in the blinding afternoon sun. "Be well."

C h a p t e r   8   >

Hospital—February 13

Already in tears, Nerese pulled up in front of her sister-in-law's sway-backed clapboard house, where her nephew Eric was sitting on the steps waiting for her, a Raven .25 semi-automatic in a see-through sandwich bag resting across his knees.

She had intended to go over to New York today and interview Ray's daughter about the assault, but that was before the hysterical predawn phone call from Butchie's ex-wife that had jump-started her morning. Nerese sat there now in her gargling Chevy, thinking of her mother's favorite saying: "If you want to make God laugh, tell him your plans."

Checking the empty street both ways before rising to his feet, Eric slowly walked around to the passenger side of the car, slid in front and handed the Raven over to his aunt.

"What the fuck is *this*," Nerese said through her tears.

"What," Eric more sulky than anything else.

"I said for you to put it in a *bag*."

"It's in a bag."

"Not a *see*-through bag, Eric. Where's your brain at?"

The kid shrugged, looking away from her, his kneecaps pumping like jackhammers.

Nerese put the Raven in her purse, then shoved the whole thing deep beneath her seat.

The two of them sat there in the mid-morning silence of the ramshackle street, Nerese sniffing and periodically palming the wetness from her cheeks.

"What my sup*posed* to do," her nephew finally said, his voice an explosive whine. "He hit my brother in the back a the head with a *bat*."

"*When*," Nerese snapped.

"What?"

"*When* did he hit your brother in the back a the head with a *bat*. What *day*."

"Sunday."

"Sunday, huh? And you shot him on *Tues*day? That's premeditated murder, Eric."

"I was scared." The kid looked away again. "I had to work myself up."

"Premeditated . . ." Nerese looked at her hands, the world a blur. "I used to push your stroller."

"Yo, Aunt Neesy, you bring me in all crying like this, you gonna make me look guilty."

Nerese bounced a slap off her nephew's near-side temple so fast that it seemed as if her palm was stinging before she had even acted.

"You *are* guilty, you dumb shit!"

Eric stared straight ahead, a bright red bloom marring his profile.

Nerese gulped air, put a hand to her own forehead, regrouped.

"Where's your mother."

"She went to work."

"She *what*?" Nerese shocked, not shocked. "Jesus."

"I need to go back inside," Eric said, still staring straight ahead.

"No you don't." No way would she let him out of her sight now.

"I need to change my clothes before we go."

"Why?"

"These are like brand-new," plucking at his baggy jeans and ENYCE sweatshirt. "I got to give them up down there, I don't know what they're gonna do with them."

"My God," Nerese's voice was high and faint with marvel. "Do you have any idea how much jail time . . ." She stopped herself, not really wanting him to think about that right now.

They sat in silence again, Nerese deciding that he could change his clothes if that would make him feel better; she wouldn't even follow him into the house, but Eric, starting to look a little gut-sick, made no move to leave the car.

"OK, look. I'm going to take you in over at the South Precinct. The reason we're going there is that my old partner is in South Detectives now. He knows we're coming, and he'll make sure everything goes smooth, no bullshit, no head games, OK?"

"You get me a lawyer?" he asked, eyes on the street.

Nerese stared at him, his self-centeredness, his lack of gratitude a little breathtaking.

"All right, listen to me. I put a call in to the supervising attorney over at the public defender's office? She promised me that come the arraignment, the right PD's gonna grab your file from the basket."

"Aunt Neesy, I can't go up in there with a PD!" Eric finally looked at her, his eyes glistening with panic. "I need a *pay* lawyer!"

"Eric. A pay lawyer needs to get paid. I don't have it and I know your mother doesn't either. Now, this woman I talked to? She's always been as good as her word. I promise you, whoever you get is gonna be rock-solid, and it's gonna be on the house."

"OK." Eric abruptly turned submissive, and again they just sat there, Nerese trying to drum up the heart to put the car in motion.

"So how's Darren doing," asking after his cousin with strained formality, his voice near to breaking.

"I don't even want to hear his name on your lips, today," she said, then after a beat, grudgingly added, "Darren's fine."

The silence came back down again, Nerese able to hear the tick of her wristwatch.

"You want something to eat before we go?"

Eric shrugged, palmed his gut.

"How about McDonald's?"

"OK."

And with a nonjail destination, Nerese finally pulled away from the curb.

Two blocks from the McDonald's off Highway 440 in Jersey City, Eric turned to her. "Can we go to Burger King instead? I don't like McDonald's."

The nearest Burger King was ten minutes away on a demoralized stretch of John F. Kennedy Boulevard, Nerese driving past block after block of boarded-up storefronts, homemade shop signs and clots of Eric-aged dopeslingers lounging on every corner, a few of them still able to read her as police despite her civilian dress, sex and personal car.

The Burger King was boarded up.

"There's one on the city line in Gannon," Eric said. "Near the Armstrong Houses?"

Nerese dutifully took off, only to find herself bumper to bumper on the New Jersey Turnpike, a jackknifed sixteen-wheeler closing down every lane but one, and after twenty minutes of inching along, the absurdity of what they were doing finally became too much for her and she drove the shoulder to the next exit, whipped around a jug-handle and pulled in to a Wendy's.

They ordered via the drive-through window, Eric letting Nerese choose his last civilian meal, then parked in the lot, neither one of them making a move to open the humid greasy bags that heated up their laps.

"When did you turn eighteen, Eric." Nerese had started crying again.

"I'm nineteen," he said.

"Shit." She blew her nose. "You're still working at Caldor's, though, right?"

"I quit."

Nerese tossed her food bag out the driver's window.

"I have to go to the bathroom," he said.

"Hang on." Nerese held up a staying hand, fearful that if he left the car now he'd bolt, although a good part of her would be rooting for him to do just that. But if he took off he'd risk the dangers of an armed arrest, and even if he escaped harm, being hauled into court as a fugitive would kick his bail sky-high.

"All right, let's go."

Nerese walked him into the Wendy's, walked him into the men's room, Eric squawking, "Aunt Neesy, what the hell . . . ," but not until she could reassure herself there was no way out but through the door that they had entered did she leave him to his business, standing directly outside in the vestibule in order to escort him back to the car.

With the flat of her hand resting lightly against the small of her nephew's back, Nerese steered him into the lobby of the Southern District precinct house, the Raven, still in its sandwich bag, now stuffed into the zippered side pocket of her North Face coat.

Eric faltered only once, between the two sets of double doors that would put him directly inside the house, but Nerese kept nudging him forward.

There were three uniforms standing behind the chest-high receiving desk, not one of these cops reacting to Eric's presence despite his at-large status and the freshness of the murder.

"Ammons, how're they hangin'?" one of the cops drawled without looking at her. Nerese ignored this asshole and addressed the oldest of the three.

"Is Willy Soto back there?" She tilted her chin to the squad room around the bend.

"I'm not sure, hang on . . ." The cop disappeared into a short narrow corridor.

With her hand still lightly pressed against Eric's back she could feel him trembling right through his winter coat as he gawked at the dozens of wanted posters taped to the glazed-tile walls.

"Why the *fuck* did you wait for Tuesday," Nerese hissed in his ear, making him jump; the kid breathing through his mouth now, suddenly two heartbeats away from a full-blown panic attack.

The uniform returned to the desk followed by a bull-necked black detective whom Nerese straight-out loathed: Aaron Kirkland, an old-timer with no use for women on the Job, and with a reputation from back in his squad-car days as a sleeper-hold freak; a cop who, if given the option, always preferred bringing in his suspects unconscious.

"Soto had a family emergency," Kirkland said in a slow rich voice as he gave them a languid once-over that started with the feet and ended just short of the eyes.

Even though Eric had set up house in her from the day he was born, was as blood close to her as family could get, Nerese powerfully resented Kirkland's group X ray, as if she and her nephew were two peas in a pod.

For a blind moment she contemplated taking her nephew out of there and restrategizing the surrender, but then Kirkland deigned to make eye contact, first with Eric, then with Nerese.

"Anything I can help you with?," this twenty-six-years-on-the-Job prick knowing exactly who Eric was and what the both of them were doing here.

. . .

For the next hour and a half, Nerese lingered outside the precinct holding cell, keeping Eric company until two Dempsy County homicide detectives came to bring him back to their own squad room across town in the basement of the municipal building.

Re-cuffing her nephew, they told her, as respectfully as possible but with no mistaking the message, that it was time for her to step off on this one, promising that the kid would receive every courtesy and consideration they could give him short of not doing their jobs.

Nerese sat in her car in the small ruptured-asphalt South Precinct parking lot overlooking fogged-in marshland and an urban creek so polluted you could set it on fire. She made three attempts to reach Eric's mother at work only to be told time after time that the woman was still on her lunch break, and recalling the frantic wee-hours phone call that had set all this in motion, Nerese was left musing on the fact that after two decades of dealing with all kinds of behavioral extremity out here, there were no people in the city of Dempsy whose mind-set and logic systems left her more straight-up bewildered and exasperated than those of her own tragically erratic family.

Heart-sore, physically exhausted, she fell asleep where she sat, slept for nearly an hour, then awoke with a start to the vibrating cell phone bouncing around in her lap.

"Nikki?" Nerese trying to come alive for Eric's mother.

"Guess again," Bobby Sugar said. "OK, I got into that First Dempsy account."

"The what?" Nerese not even sure who was calling.

"First Dempsy. The checking account."

"Bobby?"

"Yes. It's Bobby."

"What are you talking about?" Nerese rooted around in her purse for breath mints, came up with Eric's now empty sandwich bag.

"Your guy Mitchell. I told you I needed to get the check disbursement on his First Dempsy account. I got it."

"Yeah, so . . ." Her eyes felt puffed and sandy.

"There's two checks he wrote that you might want to ask him about."

· · ·

After taking down the information from Sugar, Nerese peered across the creek again. Somewhere out there in the muck and mist was the Dempsy County Correctional Center, like a massive cement wagon wheel lying on its side: Eric's new home for the foreseeable future. And once he set up house in there, she could see him only with the written permission of the police commissioner, cops otherwise barred from jailhouse visits, even to family.

And with that thought in mind, Nerese, despite the courteously delivered warning to stay away, drove across town to the Homicide office, determined to see her nephew one last time before they took him to the Bureau of Criminal Identification and then to the Intake Center. But traffic was bad and she got there too late; both Eric and the detectives who had picked him up were already gone.

Standing alone in the large, windowless squad room, she could hear the buzzing of the overhead fluorescents, the place deserted right now save for the receptionist out of sight in the vestibule, who at the moment was busy transcribing a taped confession via headphones. And with no one around to bust her, Nerese impulsively slipped into the Homicide evidence room—basically, a converted storage closet filled with stapled shopping bags holding worn-at-the-time blood-stained clothing and a coat rack hung with death-tagged outerwear, and finally, finally, after six months of trying to work up the nerve, boosted a beautiful leather-and-wool FUBU jacket, the objective of a year-old robbery-homicide that had already been prosecuted, the near mint coat just hanging there, keeping no one warm in this shit-ass February weather.

Roughly an hour later, in an effort to avoid being alone with her black-dog thoughts, Nerese exited the oversized and geologically slow hospital elevator on six and headed down a building-length corridor to visit Ray in the monitored-care ward.

Halfway there she saw a cluster of kids, maybe thirteen, fourteen years old, huddled at the entrance, their collective gaze fixed on something or someone inside. Even at some distance from them, Nerese was struck by the fact that she had never seen a crew of young-side teenagers so silently fearful as this group before her.

Coming abreast of them, she saw that one by one they were tentatively entering the ward and heading for Ray's bed, where, propped upright, he received them like dazed and damaged royalty, shaking their hands while trying to avert his garish face, each kid coming off somewhere between seasick and frightened, backtracking to the safety of the hall as soon as they pressed the flesh.

Nerese stood alongside the group observing the queasy procession; the kids were overseen by a stocky female teacher who acted as jumpmaster, holding the next kid by the shoulder then giving them a slight shove into the ward as soon as the previous kid had returned from his or her mission.

As for Ray, all traces of yesterday's motormouthed agitation seemed to have vanished, replaced with a wooden self-consciousness, as if he was trying to mask the fact that he couldn't quite place these children, his manner both formal and discombobulated.

"How are you doing," Nerese said in a near whisper, touching the teacher's elbow. "I'm Nerese Ammons with the Dempsy PD?"

"Evelyn Bondo." The handshake was solid.

"Are these Ray's students?" Nerese asked, backing away from the group as she spoke.

"They're his writing class," Bondo said, following her only to the point where she could still propel them with a touch of her hand.

"Nice kids," Nerese said, just to say it, the woman waiting for more. "Do you have any idea of what happened to him?"

"Not really," Bondo said.

Nerese watched the kids for a moment; a black girl with frosted hair and oversized glasses quietly slid a red and black notebook onto Ray's night table without saying anything. Ray looked from the notebook to the girl, a momentary light coming into his eyes.

"Are these all the kids?"

"These are all the kids."

"Small class, huh?"

Bondo nodded, poking a boy. "Rashaad. Go."

"Did he have problems with any of them? Run-ins . . ."

"No . . ." Bondo taking a hair too long to say it.

"No, but . . ." Nerese pushed.

"No," she said more cleanly. Nerese reinterpreted her previous hesitation as some kind of personal disapproval of the man, more than any kind of suspicion.

"How about other kids in the school, maybe not in his class?"

"I can't say for sure, but I doubt it. He's only in there two hours a week."

"He's a good teacher, Ray? I'm asking because I know kids hate hospitals and to come here . . ."

"They like him," Bondo said, and left it at that.

"Hey, gorgeous, how you feeling today?" Nerese took her customary seat, the stolen FUBU jacket folded neatly in her lap.

"Why won't they feed me. A chip of ice. Give me a chip of ice at least."

"They don't feed head traumas until they're out of the woods," she said for the second day in a row.

Ray stared off. "I feel like I sleep all the time but I don't sleep at all. I have these dreams but I'm wide awake," speaking to her as if from under a pile of coats, his words muffled and affectless.

"Who did this to you, Ray?" Nerese jumping on his confusion, hoping to win the lottery here.

"This . . ."

"Who hit you."

Ray said nothing, Nerese unable to tell whether his silence was willful or just a by-product of today's glaze, the poor bastard having definitely gone sour over the last twenty-four hours.

She reached for the composition book left by that kid with the frosted hair and exaggerated glasses.

The pages were filled with the rotund swan-necked penmanship of an adolescent girl—poems, prose and an old runny photo Scotch-taped above a story entitled "Baby." Other titles: "Living Dead," "Our Mutual Enemy," "Living Dead II," "Blue Dempsy" and "Dempsy River Anthology—Dead Man Talking."

Nerese replaced the book on the night table and regarded her charge.

Lying motionless on his side, the right cheek of his empurpled fright mask pressed into the pillow, Ray stared right through her, stared at nothing; the blood-dipped eyes beneath the skull and skin suggesting a second hidden face more terrible still.

"Ray, can I ask you about two checks you wrote?" Nerese almost embarrassed by the absurdity of the question given his condition. "One was made out to cash, three thousand two hundred dollars endorsed by the McCloskey Brothers Funeral Home. That was for your mother?"

"My mother?"

"Yeah."

"My mother's dead."

"Yeah, I know, and I'm sorry about that. Did you bury her through McCloskey Brothers?"

Ray just lay there, unresponsive; Nerese let it go for now.

"The other's for seventy-three hundred dollars, written a few days later, also made out to cash," squinting at her own handwriting, "endorsed by, Ray Mitchell. That's you."

"I don't know," he said.

"Seventy-three hundred in cash. That's a lot of pocket money to 'I don't know' about. You have some kind of major under-the-table expense a little while back? Something you couldn't pay for by check?"

"You know, I'm lying here," he said thickly, ignoring her questions. "And, I have these memories . . . Things I didn't even know I ever knew . . ." He faded for a few seconds, then came back. "Like now, right now I can tell you about the first time I saw her, exactly what that felt like."

"Saw . . ."

"Ruby."

"OK," Nerese said tentatively, wanting to pull him back to the seventy-three hundred dollars, but also curious as to where he would go on his own.

"Room 331 NYU Medical Center, December 15, 1990, five-thirty in the morning. I'm sitting on a pink plastic chair. There's no bed in the room, they had rolled it out with Claire to the OR, it's just me in the chair, a big space where a bed should be, and some drapes . . . I was driving a cab then, no more teaching, a fucking strung-out cokehead just sitting there crashing, and the anesthesiologist, all of a sudden the anesthesiologist walks in with a baby wrapped in a blanket, hands it to me, says, 'Here you go' . . . And, all I want to do is just get back in the cab, get high and drive . . . So I'm like, 'Excuse me?' as if, as if he had just said, 'Hey you, hold this for me?' I can barely bring myself to look down at her. I'm thinking, Why did he give me this baby here? Where's he going . . .

"And when I did, you know, look? There's this little thing in my arms, red face, blue eyes, black hair, see-through fingertips . . ." Ray's voice started to quiver. "Three hours later I'm out there like the Flying Dutchman, whacked, wasted, picking up fares, supposedly to support my wife and child? But every other dime was going up my nose."

Ray went south again, Nerese on the verge of touching him when he came back on his own.

"And for the next four years, Claire stays home with Ruby, starts writing those kids' books of hers, *being* with Ruby . . . But *me* . . . For four years, coke coke coke coke . . . And, if I want to torture myself? I ask . . . I ask, Where *were* you, asshole. Do you have any idea what you missed? What you can never get back? And for what. For *what*," his voice momentarily rising to an angry quack.

Nerese restrained herself from offering any solace, letting him unreel.

"And I remember, *oh*"—he flinched—"I remember this one time— Ruby, she couldn't have been more than three, quiet little girl, always . . . She's sitting on some steps and she's got her knees together and her palms flat on her knees very prim, and on either side of her, she put her Batman and Robin dolls, they were about a foot high, she's in the middle, and she had bent their arms and legs so that they were seated exactly in the same posture as her, and she just keeps looking from Batman to Robin to Batman. And, she's talking to them, I can't really hear and there's something so sweet about her at that moment, so babyish, and I wanted to join in, jump in, but I knew it would ruin whatever fantasy she had going right then, so all I did, all I really could do, was watch from a distance, but I don't remember much else of her as a child, a toddler, a baby."

Ray subsided, Nerese watching him breathe, wide-eyed open-mouthed exhalations.

"And whenever I tried to kiss her or hug her back then, she'd say, 'I don't *like* kissing.' She'd do the same to Claire, she was very much in her own world, but it would upset me, it would upset . . . but I'd be like, 'OK, if that's the way you want it . . .' And I'd be off in the taxi, fucking idiot . . ."

"OK, but Ray, that was then," Nerese just having to say it. "She's still just a kid."

"And, when she turned five? Claire kicked me out . . . It was a long time coming. I don't even think Ruby noticed. I mean of course she did, but . . ." Another hypnotic pause, Nerese starting to acclimate herself to Ray's ebb and flow.

"The thing is . . . The minute I left? I stopped. On my own. No N.A., no A.A. Stopped on a dime."

"Good," Nerese said, angling for a way back in now. "Good for you."

"Quit drugs, quit the cab, back to school. Polygraph school. As a student. A year and a half by myself, cleaning up, to go back to them."

Nerese grunted, something not happy coming up.

"A year and a half. I was so ready . . . I call her, 'I need to talk to you,' she's, 'Great, me too.' We go, sit down, she says, 'I need a divorce. I met someone and I'm in love.'"

"No . . ."

"So I gave it to her. What else could I do."

"I hear you," she said, restlessly refolding the jacket in her lap.

"I had, I had completely forgotten about other people, new people. A year and a half, that's a long time . . ."

"For some." Nerese still looking for a way in.

"Two days later, I'm back driving a cab, driving fifty, sixty hours a week, back with the coke, back like I never left . . . And Ruby knew. She knew . . . Didn't know it as, as cocaine or even drugs, I don't think, but you can't fool a kid . . ."

"No, you can't," Nerese said, drifting off into thoughts of her nephew, her dumb-ass nephew and his incomprehensible mother, thoughts of how some people should have to pass a test before they were allowed to have children.

"So do I stop?" Ray's voice rose in a febrile lilt. "No. 'I can't make it this week, sweetheart.' And at first she's, 'Daddy, you promised.' Then after a while it's, 'OK, whatever.'"

And then Ray began to cry. Head-bashed, sleep-starved, drunk on his own remorse, he began to quietly weep, like a solitary lush at the short end of the bar.

"'OK, whatever,'" scourging himself. "I can't, I can*not* believe I wouldn't stop for her."

"But Ray, that was a long time ago. You're all squared away with her now, right?" Nerese not knowing if he was or wasn't, not even knowing if his drug problems were in the past tense but assuming they were: he never failed to make his monthly payments—mortgage, child support—and even more tellingly, he still had over three hundred thousand dollars socked away from that television gig. Nerese had learned the hard way from her son's father how cocaine could go through a bank account like fire through dry timber.

"Do you want to know how I finally stopped?"

"Actually I want you to tell me about that seventy-three hundred in cash you needed."

"I'm back driving the cab. Back on coke. And it was bad. Worse than before, because now I don't have anyone to answer to."

Nerese, in her restless anxiety flapping out the FUBU then refolding it, wasn't sure whether he was responding to her question or his own.

"I'm at La Guardia, pick up a fare, black guy in his twenties, beautiful suit, going to the Four Seasons. I'm driving, and I see, every time I look in the rearview, he's looking at me, studying me. I'm high, but not too bad, not too jagged yet, but I'm starting to get spooked—what's he looking at me like that for?

"Halfway to the city, I just can't stand it. I check in the rearview, sure enough he's looking right back at me. I say, 'Do we know each other?'

"He says, 'Mr. Mitchell?' Says it kind of cautious, but it's on my license right in front of him on the partition so I don't . . .

"He says, 'Don't you remember me, Mr. Mitchell? John Shaker.'

"And I almost died. He was an old student of mine from the Bronx."

"From that Shakespeare class you took off with?" Nerese resigned herself to hearing this out.

"No," Ray said, slipping into another mini-fugue, then coming back with a fragment of a smile. "His year? The class trip was two hours in a Times Square video arcade, my treat, after fifteen minutes in the Morgan Library checking out handwritten drafts of nineteenth-century novels."

"You know something?" Nerese said softly. "I would have fired your ass, too."

"I was a good teacher. It wasn't clicking for them. Believe me."

"Yeah, OK."

"I couldn't believe it was this kid Shaker. We talk, it turns out he had become some kind of hot-shit TV producer, writer-producer. Starts telling me how I was his favorite teacher, how I had turned him on to writing, how I'm responsible for his life path. Looks like nine million dollars in the back of my cab, and he couldn't have been sweeter. I'm feeling so torn— happy, but all fucked up, embarrassed to be driving him, he can't even call me by my first name.

"And then he asks me, 'How about you, Mr. Mitchell? How's your writing going?'

"And, I just pull off to the shoulder, stop and I just, just . . . I couldn't drive, I just . . .

"And he's great, doesn't look at his watch, isn't like, 'Hey Shaky, let's go, let's go.' He's just . . . He's great.

"Finally I suck it up, come back to myself. He asks me if I know anything about TV, writing for TV, one-hour dramatic series.

"I'm, you know, 'Not really.'

"He says, 'I have this show in development, *Brokedown High*, takes place in an inner-city New York high school. I'm looking for writers, do you want to take a crack at it? It would be an honor for me to hire you.' I tell him I never did anything like that before. He says, 'What's to know. It's based on our old school,' says, 'I know you have the heart for it. You'll learn by doing. Earn while you learn. Trust me.'

"And I'm . . . 'OK.'

"We get to the Four Seasons, I refuse to take his money. He's getting out of the cab, at the last second, he leans back in, says, 'Just one thing . . . I don't mean to be disrespectful, but I don't tolerate drugs in my shop and I believe you need to know that.'"

Ray took a breather, then: "And see, this is why I still have hope for myself leaving this world as an honorable person, Tweetie. I respond so well to shame? I haven't touched the stuff since. But I wouldn't stop for my daughter . . ."

"Stopping is stopping," Nerese said, thinking, And not stopping is not stopping; once again brooding over her son's father, wherever he may be. "Tell me about the seventy-three hundred dollars."

"I don't know," he said dejectedly.

"Sure you do." Nerese shrugged, guessing, drugs, blackmail, some kind of scam, something not good.

"Stuff . . ."

"Stuff."

Another long pause. "It's nothing. Just let it be."

"Look, it's easy enough for me to find out on my own."

"Then do," he said lifelessly, and Nerese put it on a back burner.

"I take it you haven't seen Ruby yet," she said.

"No."

"You know my next stop is to talk to her."

"Who."

"Ruby."

"Oh, don't." Ray's face suddenly melting.

"Make it so I don't have to."

"I swear to you, she doesn't know anything about it."

"Oh, you'd be amazed at how people who don't know anything know something."

And, suddenly anxious about time, Nerese once again began folding and refolding the FUBU jacket in her lap. With his eye drawn to her movements, Ray abruptly jerked back, his face stark with fear.

"What." She leaned forward.

"Oh, I thought . . ." He pointed at the jacket. "I thought . . ." Then breathing deep with relief.

"You thought what?"

"Nothing." Embarrassed now.

"It's a jacket."

"I know." Ray was big-eyed, spooked at how he had spooked himself.

"A jacket, see?" She held it open by the shoulders, black leather body and orange wool sleeves, then turned it so that he could see the big chamois FUBU stitched across the back.

"I said I *know*." Nerve-blown, exhaustion-wracked, Ray squawked like a parrot.

"How are you feeling today?" The neurologist materialized at bedside.

"Like shit," Ray said.

Nerese rose from her seat and began gathering herself up. "Hey, Ray?"

"Like I'm underwater," Ray said.

The doctor went to work, once again testing his pupil reflex.

"Ray, I know you're beat, but let me just . . . You say you buried your mother through McCloskey Brothers, right?"

The neurologist made his swamilike passes with the light.

"Your people are Jewish. Why'd you go there?"

He took one of his interminable pauses; then: "Dead is dead."

"Can you tell me where you are?" the neurologist asked in a preoccupied murmur.

"Unfortunately," Ray said, sounding more rueful than feisty.

"Can you spell the word 'world' backwards for me?"

"Not . . . not right now," he said apologetically.

"You know, Ray . . ." Nerese sweating the test, unable to leave.

"Can you tell me who's the President of the United States?"

"Reagan," Ray said.

"Reagan?"

"No. Bush. Bush."

In contrast to the day before, he was coming off as earnestly wanting to do well now. Nerese marginally wondered whether she was in some way being played here.

"You know, Ray"—she moved closer to the bed—"I'm never the fastest horse on the track. But more often than not I wind up finishing in the money."

"Which one?" the neurologist asked, moving to the crook of Ray's right elbow, the one opposite the wound site, tapping it for deep tendon reflex.

"Which one what." Ray's arm jerked emphatically in response to the contact, Nerese not knowing if that was good or bad.

"Which Bush is President?"

Ray hesitated. "I don't understand the question."

"What the hell's going on?" Nerese demanded. "This guy just took me down enough memory lanes to crisscross a continent."

"Sometimes, with a head trauma like this?" the neurologist said softly as he ran a Babinski, Ray's toes splaying a little more than yesterday, "The mind remembers what it wants, off-loads the rest."

"Really." Nerese thinking, How convenient.

"Hey, Tweetie?" Ray said her name almost meekly. "Can I see that jacket again?"

Fighting off a wave of irritation, Nerese once again held it up by the shoulders, the arched chamois FUBU in his face.

"Yeah, OK, I thought so," he said, sounding almost relieved. "It's got two holes in it," limply gesturing to the small of the back, a small ragged perforation there. "Turn it around again. See?" pointing to a corresponding hole at solar plexus height in front. "Did you buy it like that?"

"I'll have it patched," giving him her own eye exam.

"Where'd you get it?"

"Evidence room yard sale."

"Evidence room. So, what . . . Those are bullet holes?"

"I don't know," Nerese said brusquely, suddenly on the defensive. "What I *do* know is that this is something like a three-hundred-and-fifty-dollar coat."

"For your son?"

"I don't know," in that same curt sing-song. She took a deep breath.

"You'd give your son a jacket that some other kid got shot in?" he asked without reproach.

"I *said*, I don't know." Nerese began to plummet.

"Jesus, Tweetie," Ray murmured in that new flattened-out way of his. "You're almost as bad as me."

< Chapter 9

Ruby and Ray—January 10

Ray sat in his living room pretending to watch the tape of *Buffy the Vampire Slayer* that he had made the night before, but really just studying his daughter, cat-curled in front of the TV, the girl a graceful swirl from her folded-under legs to the long sweep of her spine to the swan arc of her neck to the slope of her profile and the smallish features there, her eyes both mournful and attentive.

He sat there pretending to experience Buffy with her but in reality churning with frustration, unable to engage her, desperate to engage her.

"Is Angel still a bad vampire?"

"He's back to good," she said.

"A good vampire . . ."

For the first years of her life, before the divorce, his sense memory of her was an affectionate blur: hey there hi there and out the door to score, cash or cocaine, Ruby always quiet and around when he finally made it back home, but now that they only saw each other one night a week, minutes were like diamonds and the sensation of loss was unshakable.

"You know, I met David Boreanaz two years before the show even started," he said.

"I know, you told me."

"You hungry, sweetie?"

"No thank you," delicately scratching her nose, her eyes never leaving the screen, even now, during the commercials.

When he took over this place from his parents he hadn't set up a bedroom for her; he was afraid that when she was back with her mother, that room would feel like a shrine, so instead she slept on the living room couch, and as a result, the entire apartment felt like a shrine.

"I got another letter from that old student of mine who's in jail. Do you want to see it?"

"Mom said it was really dangerous to write to him." She finally looked at him, face puckering. "What if he gets out of jail?"

"Well you tell your mother . . ."

"Will he come here when he gets out of jail?"

"I don't know," happy for her concern. "He's not a bad kid."

"Then why's he in jail?"

"He messed up," Ray said mildly, unwilling to go into the fine points separating manslaughter from homicide. He had about as many ex-students in jail as he did in four-year colleges.

"Will he come here?"

"He has a home. Don't worry about it, sweetie."

Buffy returned and he lost her to the screen again.

"You know if I sat with my legs curled under me like that they'd probably snap off at the knee."

"Sorry . . ." she said, straightening them out.

"No no, I didn't mean . . ." Ray's skull ready to pop with exasperation. "Do you ever use that camera I got for you?"

"What?"

"Do you ever . . ."

"A little."

A little; Ray's eyes roaming the room for a love weapon, some kind of fireworks.

It drove him wild with despair that he felt incapable, when alone with her, of treating his daughter like anything other than an awkward first date; this self-consciousness only seeming to worsen as she got older.

He sat through the last ten minutes of the show, some more commercials—Ray belatedly remembering that this was a tape and he could have just fast-forwarded through all the goddamn commercials—sat through next week's teaser, then pulled a large book from the bottom shelf of the case.

"Honey, can I show you my favorite photographer?"

"Sure."

And he opened her eyes to *Weegee's World.*

"See, I love news photography, photojournalism, because every picture is like a story," he said, his voice taking on a Mister Rogers–like inflection in keeping with the depth of his commentary.

She sat there, the book balanced on her thighs, and began leafing through image after image of catastrophe-stunned women, eyes big as dishes; drunken diapered dwarfs; and death: sidewalk death, facedown, fedoras floating in blood, neighbors looking on death; ankles crossed, one pants leg up, one-shoe-in-the-gutter death; Ruby taking it all in slowly, solemnly, giving away nothing.

"What's that white stuff," pointing to a floret of brain matter sprouting from the back of a dead bookie's head, the body lying in the tiled vestibule of a Hell's Kitchen walk-up.

"I have no idea," Ray said lightly, and casually closed the book on her.

But inappropriate or not, he loved Weegee, those photos: give her something, show her something.

"So how's school?" he asked, vaguely remembering someone saying never ask "How's school, how's your day."

"Good," a clipped nibble.

"You getting on with your friends?"

"You mean Hell's Bitches?" There was a faint ring of tears in her voice.

"Anybody in particular?"

"It changes. Today this one's nice, that one's a bitch. Tomorrow that one's nice, *this* one's a bitch . . ."

"Well look, honey, we're talking eighth grade. They're pretty immature . . ."

"No," she began in an angry singsong. "They're *mean.*"

"Jesus, Ruby. I wish I could help you," not sorry he asked, but knowing all he could do now by pushing on this was to make her more unhappy.

"Hey, you know this new class I'm teaching in Dempsy? The kids are like from the worst neighborhoods in the city. I think you'd enjoy it."

And what the hell did *that* mean? Give her something, show her something, the need in him chugging like a train, his daughter sitting there now quietly giving him her full attention as if waiting for him to come up with the requisite ace.

"Dad, how did you meet David Boreanaz again?" Feeling sorry for him, helping him out.

"It was no big deal," he mumbled.

The phone rang like a round-ending bell.

"Yeah . . ."

"Ray?" The voice was rough yet tentative. "This is Carla . . ."

"Carla . . ."

"Carla Powell?" The woman gave it up almost wincingly.

"Hey!"

"I hope you're not upset I'm calling you at home . . ."

"Please."

"You said Little Venice, so I got your number from information. Ray, you asked me how I was doing earlier today, remember?"

"Sure." Ray wide open, something coming.

"My son died."

"No . . ."

"Yeah, last week."

"No . . ."

"The thing is, I'm . . . They're holding his body."

"The police?" he said unthinkingly.

"The funeral home," she said after a wounded pause, then quickened the pace. "We can't bury him. We don't have any money, and I *know* I just saw you for the first time since like forever, but . . ."

"Please . . ."

Ruby reopened the Weegee book.

"Ray, please don't be offended, we're calling everybody we know. If you can lend us fifty, a hundred dollars, if you can see your way to help us out for whatever you can spare, I'll give you a signed IOU, anything you want and you will definitely get paid back. We're calling everybody we know, whatever you can afford . . ."

"Carla, please . . ." he said huskily. "How much are you needing to raise?"

"Thirty-two hundred dollars," she said, then, "Ray, I'm so embarrassed to call you like this. Anything you could spare . . ."

"Hang on . . ." He put the receiver to his chest, regarded his daughter poring through *Weegee's World* on her own steam, asked himself, Isn't that enough for now? answered himself: No.

"Carla, give me your number. I'll call you back in a minute."

He sat there, receiver dead in his hand, as he studied his daughter, wary of the impending elation that was welling in him, trying very hard to police his own impulses, but it was hopeless. He rang her back.

"Carla?"

"Yeah, Ray," something defeated yet quick in her voice.

"Where do you live now?"

"In Hopewell."

"Still?" Ray belatedly flinched at yet another unthinking jab.

"Still."

"Your mom's apartment?"

"It's mine now."

"Can I come by?" Something proprietary in the question, something in the nature of not-quite-rightness.

"Sure," she said after a hesitation. "You remember our windows? Where we are?"

"Yeah, of course."

"How long will you be."

"Half hour?"

"Look for me in the window."

Ray hung up, thrown by the window business, and once again eyed his quiet daughter.

"Honey? How'd you like to see where I grew up?"

The commercial strip under the PATH tracks that ran past the Hopewell Houses wasn't as desolate as he had anticipated; more beat-down, for sure, but if anything livelier, the Italian and Jewish stores replaced by the ubiquitous red-and-yellow awnings of bodegas and Caribbean vegetable marts, of Jamaican jerk chicken and patty shacks. The corner candy store was now a dispatch office for a dial-a-cab outfit, the movies an Iglesia Pentecostal, the florists a Church of Cherubim and Seraphim. Food Land was now the Cinderella House of Beauty, a formerly vacant lot the site of an abandoned prefab IRS annex. The German homemade-ice-cream parlor was a fire-blackened ruin, probably standing like that for God knew how long, and the bowling alley a discount carpet outlet that had gone out of business and had, Ray assumed, been preceded by half a dozen other enterprises each in its turn having gone belly-up too.

He drove wall-eyed under the latticed shadows of the tracks, taking it all in, absorbing memory hits right and left, too full to pump a line of chatter at his daughter, who was nose-down in her homework in any event.

The towers of Hopewell were draped over a hill, his old apartment two stories below Carla's in one of the bottom-end corner buildings facing the elevated PATH tracks, 1949 Rocker Drive, aka Six Building.

Rising from the car, Ray was struck by how the relatively new aluminum window frames that monotonously bordered every window of every building along Rocker picked up the color of the grit-flecked snow, the soupy driven-through slush and the dull bituminous cast of the sky. It was the monochrome of his childhood.

Carla was leaning out of the fifth floor as promised.

"Stay there," she called down, yet made no move away from the window.

The PATH train barreled overhead, the slow calliope groan of steel on steel as it veered past the windows as musically primal to him as a nursery rhyme.

"This is my daughter," he offered up to Carla.

"Hi . . ." Ruby whispered, making a faint window-wiping gesture.

"Hi, sweetheart . . ." Carla smiled, dropped a cigarette butt into the bushes below and turned back to someone in the apartment. "They're down there now. Just *go*."

"That's the lady that just lost her son," he said softly.

"OK." Ruby readjusted her backpack.

"We're gonna see if we can help her out."

There was no one on the snowcapped bench in front of the building, no one anywhere.

A gypsy cab glided past, disappearing into the shadows under the PATH tracks.

Ruby readjusted her backpack.

"Carla, are we coming up, or what."

"Hang on." And as if on cue a younger sweater-clad woman exited the building, hugging herself against the cold, then carefully tiptoed her way over to them through the beaten-down snow. She was light-skinned like Carla, heavyset, but softly so, something satisfyingly complete in the fullness of her face, green eyes didn't exactly hurt, her hair the same cinnamon tint as her skin.

"I'm Danielle." She smiled at him. "Carla's my mom."

Ray had never known whether Carla was black, half-black, Hispanic or Italian, but her daughter's features were definitely black. Maybe.

"Oh my God, you're so beautiful," Danielle abruptly cooed at Ruby, touching her cheek, and then Ruby did something that Ray had never seen her do before, even with her mother—she reflexively leaned into this new woman as if expecting to be hugged, Danielle doing just that, and Ray, as usual hanging by a thread, choked back a sob.

"That's *my* daughter," Carla said proudly from five floors up.

The lobby of his old building, as he'd expected, seemed smaller to him now but the smell caught him off guard: a claustrophobic stankiness— urine, old bacon grease. Half the mailboxes were dented and crowned with scorch marks.

"You didn't have to come down to get us," he said to Danielle.

"Yeah, well, this building, you never know."

"I'm sorry about your brother . . ."

Danielle shrugged, her face closing up. She had a broad bold Chinese character tattooed on the right side of her neck.

"Can you believe I lived here for eighteen years?" he asked Ruby, then froze, in no way intending a put-down of the place, but Danielle was lost in some private anger, absently and repeatedly slapping the elevator button, and Ruby seemed transfixed by a poster taped to one of the greasy lobby walls: a close-up head shot of a starkly tense black woman staring out as if having just gone blind. OUR CHILDREN ARE PRECIOUS. IF YOU CAN'T TAKE IT CALL US, and in smaller type beneath this entreaty the number of a parent hotline.

As the three of them squeezed into the elevator, Ray was hit with another jolt of miniaturization compounded by a half-shift in odors, the ever-present alkaloid reek of urine now mingling with a moist ghost waft of Chinese takeout.

The ascent to the fifth floor was excruciatingly slow, the car gravely clanking every ten feet up the cables.

"Eighteen years I took this elevator," he announced, starting to bore even himself. Ruby bugged her eyes as she stared at her shoes; Ruby-mime for Shut Up.

"Parents . . ." Danielle smiled at her. "We're like the worst, right?"

"You go to school?" he asked her, his eyes helplessly straying to that tattoo again.

"*Me?* I'm thirty years old."

"No . . ." Ray laying it on a bit, but truly surprised.

"Thirty going on seventy," she added. "But yeah, in fact, I do." Then to Ruby, "How old are you, sweetheart?"

"Twel— no, thirteen." Ruby grinned at the mistake, eyes closed in pleasurable embarrassment. "Thirteen."

Carla was waiting for them in her doorway at the end of the hall. She had a cigarette in one hand, a beanbag ashtray in the other. She shifted the cigarette to her lips and affectionately palmed Ruby's face, Ruby reflexively saying, "Thank you."

As they stepped into the small L-shaped living room–dining alcove, Carla's five-ish grandson was jumping on the plastic sheathed couch, but at first sight of Ruby he stiffened mid-leap, landing spread-legged on the crackling fabric protector, and gawked at her with savage fascination.

The layout of the apartment was a cookie cutter of Ray's own childhood digs and in his excitement he did it again: "Ruby, could you believe—"

"*Please* . . ." she murmured almost desperately, and he stopped.

Besides the couch there were two plastic-covered easy chairs, a low Formica coffee table and a television. The dingy walls were the color of smoke and covered with framed graduation photos.

"Are you hungry?" Carla gestured to the dining alcove, where the table was laid with a plug-in coffeepot, a half-gallon bottle of Coke and a deboxed supermarket cake. "That's all I had time—"

"Please . . ." Ray cut her off. She looked like she was having a hard time breathing, like she knew what was coming.

"Honey?" Carla addressed Ruby, gesturing to the food, Ruby whispering her standard "No thank you."

"She's just going to do homework, OK?"

"Absolutely," Carla said overemphatically, her chest rising and falling with each breath, Ray thinking, This is not even about her; thinking, This is fucked.

"Let me make you some room, sweetheart." Danielle stepped over to the table and cleared a space, Ruby quickly burying herself in her books, her hyper-alertness to her surroundings betrayed by the instantaneous ferocity of her concentration.

The boy jumped off the couch and stood at Ruby's elbow, staring up at her.

"Do you want some food?" she asked him in a soft, high, self-conscious murmur.

"David, leave her alone," Danielle snapped and the boy assaulted the couch again.

Another PATH train roared past, fifty yards from the building and at eye level with Carla's windows.

A toilet flushed in the apartment above.

"So, Ray . . ." Carla wheezed, sitting on the couch squat as a pasha, her grandson once again bouncing next to her. She attempted to light a cigarette, the trembling match jerking in synch with the kid's gymnastics.

Ray perched tensely on the arm of a chair.

"Make yourself comfortable." Danielle gestured to the seat, then sat facing him flanking the bouncing boy on the couch.

"I'm good. I'm good," Ray catching Carla's breathing disorder. "Carla . . ." He swallowed, then proceeded as if reading from a semilegible script. "Carla, I don't think for something of this nature, you should have to call people for dribs and drabs of money, you know, for something like this. So please . . ." And, as he had envisioned himself doing over and over in the last hour, he extracted the check for thirty-two hundred dollars from his shirt pocket, and after a fleeting, almost unconscious glance at Ruby to see if she was bearing witness, launched himself off the arm of the chair, extending it to Carla in a crouched lunge.

But he saw that Carla had caught that reflexive look to the kid in the dining alcove, and it threw her off, turned her off, just enough to miss the exchange, the check flipping and fluttering between their outstretched hands before finally swooping to rest under the coffee table.

Shaken, glaring dumbly at Ruby, Carla made no move to retrieve it, so Ray, already torn between denying and acknowledging how quickly, how artlessly, how helplessly he had just given himself away, dropped on all fours and delivered it to her on his knees.

Carla and Danielle, temple to temple, read the amount together, Danielle softly grunting as if a padded weight had been dropped on her chest.

Carla, however, sat stiffly reading and rereading the amount. "You don't—"

"Carla, please . . ." Flush-faced, Ray cut her off.

The grandson started jumping on the couch again, sideswiping Carla on the upstroke, the downstroke.

"All I asked you for . . ."

"Please, Carla . . ."

"Mom . . ." Danielle started to argue, the grandson bouncing bouncing, until Carla abruptly reared back and swatted him hard on the arm, hissing, "*Stop* it!"

The boy looked at her in astonishment, looked at her in a way that told Ray that she had never laid a chastising hand on him before, his stunned silence momentarily sucking the air out of the room, until at last he started to cry, flinging himself at Danielle's breast.

But she needed the money, he told himself; she has a son to bury.

"Thank you so much," Danielle said. "You have no idea . . ."

Ray stole a quick glance at his daughter, his audience, his all, Ruby fiercely focused on her work, Ray telling himself again, But she has a son to bury . . .

"How do you want us to pay it back?" Carla asked almost angrily.

"Look, just get through it. Worry about it later. I don't really care . . ."

"You have no idea," Danielle said again.

"Have some cake," Carla said flatly, then, turning to her daughter, "Give them some cake."

"No, really . . ." he began, his eyes fixed swimmingly on the framed graduation portraits, each sober head cocked at the identical angle.

"Sweetie?" Danielle called out to Ruby at the dining table. "Sweetie, are you OK?"

Ray turned to see Ruby blindly staring at her binder, her eyes shining like wet steel, chin trembling with the effort not to cry.

"Ohh . . ." Danielle sighed in sympathy, her voice soft and pillowy.

Ray knew enough not to ask Ruby what was wrong in front of strangers, but that was about all he knew, all he was good for.

The check lay face up on the coffee table.

"You know, we should really go." He rose to his feet.

"Go down with them," Carla said quickly to Danielle, "walk them to the car."

"Carla, that's OK."

"You don't know this place," she said, once again almost angrily.

"Come on, I lived here eighteen years."

"Well, you don't live here now."

At the door he was about to ask as tactfully as he could what her son had died of, or at least what was his name; but he shut himself down, knowing that there was absolutely no question he could ask of her that wouldn't make her feel more profoundly humiliated and used.

. . .

"I hope your mom's OK with this," Ray said to Danielle, once they were back out on the street.

"She's a little thunderstruck, I guess." Danielle shrugged it off.

"I just wanted to help," he said, seized with the need to revise what happened up there. "I just wanted it to be OK."

"To be OK?" Her teeth glistened in the encroaching twilight. "You're a *god*send, how's that?"

Ray felt his face glow.

"Can I ask what your brother—"

"Died of?" she offered with perky vehemence. "Reggie, Reggie died of not wanting to deal with himself."

Ray didn't know if that implied an overdose or a suicide.

"Speaking for myself?" She touched her own chest. "I buried him years ago. My mother, she's shook up but she knew it was coming."

An overdose.

A car shot up the hill. Danielle turned her head briefly to track its progress, and Ray's eye was drawn once again to the thick blue lines of her tattoo.

"Ruby, check it out," he said easily, extending his hand to Danielle's throat and something in the way she stared at him without shying away from his almost-touch had him patting his pockets and looking about as if he had just lost his keys.

"Cool," Ruby murmured lightly.

"Soon as my back's turned, Ruby's gonna do herself up like a comic book," he said, a little too burbly.

"Shut up," Ruby murmured again, this time fighting down a smile.

"You know what this means, sweetheart?" Danielle pulled down the neck of her sweater so Ruby could get a good look. "This means 'The Hunter.' See, most people when they get Chinese symbols, they go for 'Love,' 'Eternity,' 'Hope.' But me, I got the Hunter, because once you got a child? You got someone who's counting on you, someone who didn't ask to be here, and you need to be a hunter. You need to be on top of it. Food, shelter, education, spirit, you know, spirituality? Ask your daddy . . ."

Ray wanted to ask about the father, the husband, but didn't.

Looking up to the fifth-floor windows he saw Carla's restless silhouette.

"OK then," he said.

"Where do you live, Ray, in New York?"

"No, I live right here in Dempsy, over in Little Venice. Ruby's mostly in New York with her mom."

Danielle cut loose with another soft "Ohh . . ."

"It's OK, we got it covered," he said meaninglessly.

"Come here, you." Danielle embraced Ruby.

"Thank you," Ruby said.

Danielle then embraced Ray. She was sporting some kind of vanilla-musk body spray, the scent so dense that it made him dizzy.

"I've never been to Little Venice," she said, looking right at him, then waved good-bye to Ruby and walked back into her mother's building, Ray watching her until she was out of sight.

For a long moment after Danielle had gone, the two of them remained standing there in the rapid winter twilight; Ray eyeing the thick mounds of snow that lay atop the chained-off bushes planted snug against the building, roughly half of them garnished with air-dropped cigarette butts.

"Ruby, what was bugging you up there?"

"I don't know," her voice rising and falling minutely.

"C'mon, give me a break."

"I was just worried that everybody would think you're conceited," the words coming out of her in a tumble.

"That I'm what?" Ray getting it, not getting it. "Ruby, I just saved that lady a hundred phone calls," determined now to sell it both to himself and his daughter.

"I know." She shrugged.

"Do *you* think I'm conceited?"

"No."

"Do you love me?" he asked shamelessly.

Ruby recoiled from the question. "Of course."

Something else.

"What." Ray braced himself.

She gave him another shrug.

"Ruby, I'm freezing my ass off. *What.*"

"I don't know." She began to get teary again. "I never knew about this part of your life before and it scares me because it makes me feel like I don't know you." For Ruby, a major speech.

"Whoa honey," Ray scrambling for the right words, his old building seemingly bearing down on them, hunkering forward with its twitching TV-light eyes. "Honey, I haven't been around here since before you were born. It's just fun to see it again. Actually, what *makes* it fun is to see it with you."

"Do you wish you still lived here?" Her voice was freighted with worry.

"What are you, nuts? I wouldn't live here now if you put a gun to my head. Don't be an idiot."

Ruby's mouth twitched; Ray seeing an opening.

"Don't be a dipshit."

The twitch became a smirk; profanity, for some reason always did the trick with her, at least temporarily.

Another train racketed by overhead, the noise making Ray blink.

"That train? Every day, every night, that train went right past my window. When I went away to college the first year? I couldn't sleep."

"Because it was too quiet?"

Her providing the punch line like that made him ridiculously happy.

"Let me tell you something. When I was a kid, there was a guy in the building, Eddie Paris, a black guy, he was a motorman on that train, you know, a conductor? His family lived on the top floor, and every time his train passed our building he would toot the whistle twice, like, saying Hi to his wife and kids."

"So cool." Ruby was listening now, open-faced.

"Yeah." Ray nodded. "Ruby, you know what? I don't feel like . . . Do you want to walk around a little?"

He took her backpack and they began trudging up the hill, the grounds still so eerily deserted; came to the crest and cut into the heart of the projects, Ray steering her to a small playground buried in untrampled snow; Little Playground they had called it back then, monkey bars, crawl-through barrels and cement seals peeping up through the pristine crust like soldiers in a trench.

There were four black teenaged boys huddled at one end of the single long bench, Ray hesitating for a tick before settling down with Ruby at the opposite corner.

"You want to hear something else about Eddie Paris and his family?"

"Sure."

"Eddie had two sons, Winston and Terrance. Terrance was called Prince, and Winston was called Dub, don't ask me why."

"Dub?"

"Dub. Anyways, Prince was really smart and he had this great voice— you know, singing voice—but Dub was a handful. He wasn't dumb or a bad kid, but he was tough and he got into a lot of fights. His father did, too. In fact, Eddie Paris was like the only parent I knew back then that got into fistfights. Handsome guy, had kind of like, Old School straightened hair, mustache . . . Anyways Eddie, he was a really strict parent, brooked no bullshit from his kids, so Dub, he was kind of in and out of trouble with his dad on a steady basis."

"But his dad got in fights, too," she said.

"You're absolutely right. Jesus, you should—" He cut himself off from saying "be a psychologist," for once in his life not wanting to blow everything up past the moment.

"Anyways, this one day after school, Dub goes upstairs, comes into the house, he's got ten, twelve new comic books on him. Now, Eddie's home and he knows something's off. Dub can't buy, hasn't got the *money* to buy that many . . . He takes one look at Dub's face, Dub's like"—Ray went all pop-eyed—"Eddie's like, 'Where'd you steal them.' And he starts chasing Dub around the apartment."

Ray paused, sensing the kids at the far end were possibly listening in, acknowledged to himself that he had been consciously talking louder than necessary, going all Danny Kaye on them. Fuck it, he liked kids. This workshop thing was the best, most honorable idea he'd had since quitting the show.

"Anyways, next thing, Eddie's coming out of the building with the comics in one hand, Dub's ear in the other, like . . ."

Ray got up wincing, head tilted sharply, and took a few mincing steps.

"Dad . . ." Ruby furtively eyed those other kids.

"OK." Ray sat down. "So Dub's being dragged out by his ear and, he's crying. From the humiliation, I guess. And, me and my friends, we're sitting on the bench in front of the building, and it's like, we *know* if anyone makes eye contact with Dub right now he'll come back and kill us.

"Anyways, what happened was, Dub stole the comics off a spin-rack at this little grocery store about two blocks from here called Food Land. OK, so Eddie marches his kid all the way back to Food Land and makes Dub go in there, go up to the owner, guy's name was Fat Sally, big Italian guy with a white mustache, makes him go up to Fat Sally, *hand* him back the comics, *tell* him that he stole them and apologize. And Dub is crying, remember?"

"How old was he?"

"I don't know, fourteen? Fifteen?" aging him past his daughter.

"Dad, do you know who steals stuff in my class?"

"Ruby, I'm on a roll here . . ."

"Go on." Ruby easy about it, smiling.

The four teenagers got up off the bench and filed out of the playground, Ray having to deal with a quick wave of disappointment.

"OK, so Eddie plants himself in the doorway of Food Land, Dub walks in, still crying a little, pissed off, embarrassed, but he manages to mumble out what his dad told him to say, gives back the comics and leaves."

"What did Fat Sally do?"

"Fat Sal? Nothing. He didn't say anything, yell, nothing. And Dub leaves, him and his father go back home. And *here*, right here, is where Eddie, in my mind, does an amazing, excellent thing. They go back upstairs, him and Dub. Eddie takes out a dollar, says, 'I want some Hostess cupcakes, go back down to Food Land and get me some.'"

"*Why?*"

"*Exactly.* And Dub is like, '*What!*' Eddie's like, 'Just do it. And don't get them at the supermarket. If you do I'll know, and then me and you are really gonna dance.'"

"Dance?"

"It's an expression. So Dub goes back down, me and my friends on the bench are staring at our shoes, OK? Dub goes back to Food Land. He walks in, Fat Sally's all alone, just him and Dub. Dub says Mumble Mumble cupcakes, Fat Sally rings up the sale, Dub's walking out the door, Fat Sally says, 'Hey, kid . . .' Dub turns, Fat Sally goes, 'I'm looking for somebody to make food deliveries for me. You feel like making some money after school?'"

Ruby smiled; Ray's throat tightened on him.

"And Ruby, dig this . . . from the next day on? Dub works five afternoons a week and eight hours every Saturday. Does that all through high school. Four years. He's working the cash register, buying groceries from the wholesaler, he becomes like Fat Sally's right-hand man."

"Oh my God that's so cool . . ." Ruby's voice floating high.

"But dig *this* . . . Dub graduates high school, Fat Sally wants to retire to Florida? Guess who he sells Food Land to."

"Dub." Ruby saying it like he was an old friend of hers.

"You got it. And guess where Dub got the money to buy the store from . . ."

Ruby just stared, not knowing.

"From his father." Ray swallowed hard.

"That's so cool," Ruby cooed.

"From his . . ." Ray had to look away. "From his . . . From Eddie. As a graduation present."

"Dad, are you crying?" Ruby wide, wide open now, all his.

"Absolutely not."

They sat in silence for a moment, Ray not oblivious to his surroundings, not a fool, but just knowing that for tonight this place was safe for them, knowing it in his bones.

"Dad?" Ruby said. "How did you know what happened with Dub and his dad upstairs and with Fat Sally in Food Land if you were out on the bench in front of your building?"

"How do I know? I know because I know." Ray indestructible, the night a joy. It was a good thing he had done earlier for Carla and her family; a great good thing; Ray fleetingly beatific, experiencing himself somehow as both the benefactor and the recipient.

Carla would come around; Ray thinking of her trapped, stricken expression, the sudden violence of swatting her grandson; then thinking of Danielle, her Chinese hunter tattoo, her soft pillowy "Oh."

"Dad, what was Dub's brother's name?"

"Terrance. But everybody called him Prince."

"Did everybody have a nickname?"

"Pretty much."

"What was yours?"

"Mine? 'Ray.'"

"Tell me the others."

"There was like a thousand kids, Ruby," Ray said happily, as if they were still here, packing the playground. "How many do you want?"

Ruby threw him a look, guarded and greedy.

"All," she said.

Chapter 10 >

Ruby—February 14

Ray's ex-wife and their daughter lived in a loft on Bond and Broadway, three floors over a skateboard megastore, in a souklike neighborhood lined with vaguely hippyish street vendors, dump-and-fly three-card monte games and too many sneaker stores; the foot traffic, at least on this mild Saturday, a nonstop salmon run of mostly high school–aged kids from the outer boroughs, Long Island, Westchester and New Jersey.

Nerese loved downtown New York but invariably lost her head in the face of its abundance. By the time she was buzzed into the Bond Street building, she was carrying two shopping bags, one filled with bootleg videos and homemade earrings for herself, the other containing two probably counterfeit Triple 5 Soul sweatshirts for her son.

Ray's ex, an indifferently dressed, thin, pale, clear-eyed woman whose long hair was in mid-transit from red to gray, met her at the door.

"Hi, I'm Claire," offering her hand.

"Hey there, Claire. I'm Nerese." She had to put down her stuff in order to shake, and the other woman's nonreactive glance at the goodies peeking out of the bags made her feel as if she had come through the Holland Tunnel on the back of a mule.

Claire led her through a narrow dark hallway that abruptly opened up into a vast window-lined space; opened up into an explosion of sunlight so exalted and airy that Nerese just dropped her shopping bags again like overweight luggage and involuntarily drifted off into a dream of new beginnings.

"Can I get you something to drink?" Claire moved to the far end of the room, the kitchen end.

"Water's good."

If she had a place like this, a space like this, Florida wouldn't even be a thought. But then, almost gratefully, she noticed the water-buckled ceiling above the kitchen area, the damp flaking chevrons of plaster running down the walls between a few of the windows; heard the street life three floors below coming through way too loud and clear. Not that she didn't have six kinds of water damage in her own home; and not that it wasn't Bonehead Central 24/7 right outside her own living room window. However . . .

Drawn by the low drone of a television, Nerese spied, through a door barely ajar, Ray's daughter sitting on a bed, surrounded by schoolwork.

But as if intuitively reacting to danger, Claire, carrying the requested glass of water, swiftly came between Nerese and her daughter's bedroom and pointedly closed the door.

Then, still carrying Nerese's glass, she led her to a long pinewood table in the main room.

Protective, controlling, probably a little pissed off and/or frightened: Nerese knew the type, knew that if she wanted to get anywhere near the kid, she was not to ruffle or challenge this woman in any way.

"You know, Claire, I have to say"—Nerese stroked the rough planks of pine—"this is like my dream home."

"Yeah, well, beware what you wish for."

"No, I hear you, I hear you."

The table was centered by a tall cylindrical glass vase, which held a half-dozen austere sprigs of bittersweet. Nerese had never really thought about that before, branches instead of flowers, and it struck her, like everything else in this loft, as both exciting and right.

"Can I ask what you do?"

"I write children's books," Claire said.

"Any I might have heard of?"

"I don't know. Do you read children's books?" Claire asked, a little too innocuously, her face bright-eyed and tight.

"Used to," Nerese responded in kind. "My son's eighteen now."

"They grow fast, don't they."

"Way too fast," Nerese said, thinking, Not fast enough.

"Anyways, they're on the wall." Claire pointed to a framed poster, Nerese rising, then reading out loud:

"*It Makes Me Laugh When* . . . by Claire Draw, author of *It Makes Me Mad When* . . . , *It Makes Me Sad When* . . . , *It Makes Me Feel Cozy When* . . . , wow," Nerese said, retaking her seat. "I used to write a little poetry in college; now mainly I just write checks."

Claire sat there, waiting.

"OK, here's the deal. I don't want to be invasive, but the fact is whoever did this to Ruby's dad, he's still out there." Nerese paused, trying to pick up how Claire felt about her ex, but the woman was still waiting for the meat of it.

"So let me just ask you straight up, is there anybody or anything you can think of . . ."

"No, not really," answering a little too quickly for Nerese's taste, so she just let Claire's words hang for a while, see how she would fill the void.

Half a minute passed in silence, Nerese trying to look pleasant while maintaining eye contact.

"You're kidding me," Claire finally said.

"About . . ."

"Look, you can spend a few days running down whatever you need to run down about me or you can take me at my word, it'll come down to the same thing. I had nothing to do with it."

Her smile, in fact, was a dazzler, filling her face with light and adding ten pounds to her frame.

"Whoa, hey, no, I didn't mean to imply . . ." Nerese put out a placating hand, thinking, A woman did it? That could explain his noncooperation, too.

"Jesus." Claire shook her head as if clearing cobwebs, this never-was accusation somehow serving to break the ice.

"So you guys are OK with each other?" Nerese asked.

"Me and Ray?" Claire shrugged. "We're co-parents."

"Separated?"

"Divorced."

"You know who's in his life these days?"

"Other than Ruby? I have no idea."

"Ruby and her dad, they have a good relationship?"

"I guess."

"What."

"It's nothing."

Once again, Nerese resorted to silence, got to Four Mississippi . . .

"Maybe it's just me, but Ray, he overparents. Overthinks, overreacts, overagonizes. You know the type I'm talking about?"

"To be honest?" Nerese said. "I personally have never met the male 'over' type. The ones I know range from 'under' to nonexistent."

The woman didn't laugh, but her face remained open.

"Claire, why won't he talk to me about what happened?"

"No idea."

"Look, this is an unpleasant question, but sometimes when the victim won't cooperate . . ."

"He's not a drug dealer, drug addict or a gambler. And he's not into sexual, you know, anything, what's it, problematical."

"OK—well, thank God for all that." Nerese smiled.

"I don't know." Claire shrugged. "In terms of things to be thankful for? Those are all kind of grounders."

"Claire, did you know that Ray and I kind of semi grew up together?"

"You mean over in that housing project in Dempsy?"

"Yeah," Nerese said, thinking, That housing project . . .

"Why 'semi,' because of the white-black thing?"

"White-black?" Nerese thought about it. "Yeah, I guess, among other things. Claire, listen." She hunkered in, touched the other woman's knee, went eye to eye again. "Because she's got her own relationship with her dad, independent of you, I'm gonna need to speak to Ruby. Now, I'll be as brief as possible, and as sensitive as possible, but if you could see your way to going along with this, it would be much better if I could talk to her alone."

"Not on your life," Claire said almost cheerfully.

Nerese stood in Ruby's small bedroom, the girl just thirteen but already having three lanky inches on her, showing her around while Claire stood in the open doorway, arms folded across her chest like a cop.

The room contained a narrow bed, a work station and a wall-mounted TV. There were six bookshelves, the bottom three covered with more than a hundred miniature plaster or wood or pewter gods, goddesses and the like, the top three holding an equal number of souvenir shot glasses.

The closet doors were covered with taped-up magazine photos of cast members from *Buffy the Vampire Slayer* and *Angel*, interspersed with a few dewy-eyed head shots of some androgynous blond actors that Nerese couldn't identify and an equal number of shirtless black hip-hop stars, all cobblestone abdomens and jailhouse eyes.

"Would you look at this," she marveled, zeroing in on the god shelves. "Now, I know that's Buddha, that's a Viking, this one here's a mermaid, but who are all these other guys?"

"Dhurga, Lakshmi, Rama, Krishna, Hanuman, Ganesh, that's just a dragon, and that's the Weeping Monk."

"The Weeping Monk . . . Man, you like to cover your bets, huh?"

"What?" Ruby didn't get it. She was trying very hard not to stare at Nerese's scarred eyebrow.

"And what's this trophy for?"

"Basketball." Ruby shrugged. She had an abundance of foamy light brown hair that fell in lazy ringlets down past her shoulders. "Everyone in the league got one. It doesn't mean we won."

"Well how'd your team do?"

"Second place."

"Out of . . ."

"Eight."

Nerese snorted. "Good enough for me." Then: "Ruby. You ever hear of Ruby Dee?"

"Ruby Dee, Ruby Tuesday, Ruby Baby," listing off tiredly.

"Who's Ruby Baby?"

"It was a song my dad liked when he was a teenager."

"Your dad, huh?"

Ruby's eyes strayed helplessly to Nerese's scar again.

"You looking at this?" Nerese put a smile in her voice.

"No no no." Ruby looked mortified. "I'm sorry."

"That's OK, honey," Nerese loving this sweet kid, but then floored by what she said next.

"Dub did that, right?"

"Come here." She put her arms out and Ruby obediently stepped inside her embrace, her chin touching the stocky detective's forehead, wisps of her bounteous hair lying like a veil over Nerese's face.

"So you know me and your dad go back a long way, right?"

She was holding Ruby at arm's length now, and saw the girl's face crumple. "What's the matter, sweetheart?"

"I don't *know* anything," Ruby's voice a teary whisper.

"Anything about . . ." Nerese starting the head games but then heard the mother rustling in the doorway behind her.

"Well honey, can I just ask you a few questions? Because maybe you know more than you think."

"OK," Ruby whispered brokenly, palming her blotched eyes.

Normally Nerese didn't like to go at kids this directly, but she sensed the mother was already on her toes for anything she perceived as trickery.

"You see your dad how often?"

"I stay with him one night a week."

"Yeah? What do you guys do together?"

"Watch TV, homework, have a catch . . ."

"Yeah? You ever do stuff with other people?"

Ruby hesitated, flicking a worried glance in the direction of her mother. Nerese read New Girlfriend in that look and wished that Mom over there would take a small hike.

"It's OK, Ruby," Claire said evenly.

"Danielle?" Ruby said tentatively.

"Danielle." Nerese turned to the mother, Claire shrugging: news to her. "Danielle." Nerese nodded. "Do you know her last name?"

Ruby shook her head no.

"You met her?"

Ruby nodded yes.

"On a scale of one to ten . . . You like her?"

"Eight." Her eyes then going to her mother. "Four."

"Six." Nerese shrugged. "Tell me about her."

"She's got a tattoo."

"A tattoo," Claire muttered.

"Yeah? What kind of tattoo?"

"A Chinese symbol, right here." Ruby touched the left side of her throat. "She says it means the Hunter."

"The Hunter, huh? OK, Ruby. What I'm gonna ask you right now is very, very important . . . Do *you* have a tattoo?"

Ruby tried to smile.

"You want to know who else had a tattoo?" Nerese asked. "My grandmother. On my father's side. She was a nightclub dancer over in New

York," Nerese forgetting that she was in New York at the moment. "Up in Harlem. She was a part of an act called the Blackbird Follies and she had a bird tattooed up inside her leg. Can you believe that?"

"Huh . . ."

"She had long long legs, my grandma. As you can probably tell, I take after the other side of the family . . . So this Danielle, she and your dad get along?"

"I guess so. He gave her mom money for a funeral."

"Danielle's mom? He gave money to Danielle's mom for a funeral?" Hence the McCloskey Brothers; Nerese finally able to scratch that itch. "Yeah."

"Oh for Christ's sake," Claire said wearily.

"How do you know this, honey?" Nerese asked, wishing now that the mom would fucking vanish.

"I was there. My dad took me."

"Took you to . . ."

"To her apartment."

"Danielle's mom's apartment?"

"Uh-huh. Yeah."

"Jesus." Claire again. Ruby looked worried, burdened.

"Do you remember Danielle's mom's name?"

"I'm sorry . . ."

"No problem. Do you know where Danielle's mom's apartment was? What kind of building?"

"Yeah, it was where my dad grew up."

"In Hopewell? The Hopewell Houses?"

"I don't know the name."

"But it was a housing project?"

"Yeah. Right by the trains."

"By the trains. Was the building itself right by the trains?" Nerese envisioned four possible addresses.

"It was my dad's old building. The trains went right by the windows. He told me Dub's dad used to toot the whistle when his train went by."

"My God, I haven't thought about that for going on thirty years," Nerese said softly, thinking, 1949 Rocker Drive. Danielle. Chinese tattoo. "Yeah, Dub's dad was something else."

"He took you to the hospital with my dad, right?" Eyeing her scar again. "My dad was holding his T-shirt to your face to stop the bleeding," Ruby spoke in a slightly reverential tone as if reciting a cherished tale.

"Yes, he did." Nerese was touched that the girl knew of this, that Ray had told her of this. "He did, indeed. Why'd your dad give Danielle's mom money for a funeral?"

"Because she was poor."

"Do you know who was being buried?"

"Her son."

"Danielle's son?"

"No, Carla's . . . Carla! Danielle's mom is Carla!"

"See? Didn't I say you knew more than you thought?" Nerese beamed, thinking, Carla. Carla Powell? She could still be there, generations tending to stack up in the projects these days. And Carla, Nerese vaguely recalled, had had a child when she was a teenager, possibly this Danielle. And Carla Powell was black, Nerese thought, so Danielle could definitely be the lady friend that Ray's neighbor gabbed about.

"Ruby? Can you tell me what race Danielle is?"

"Race?"

"Black, white, Latino, you know, Hispanic . . ."

"I didn't . . . I'm not sure. She's kind of tan."

Black or Latino, there being no more whites of a sexable age in Hopewell, just a few stranded seniors. And "Carla," "Danielle"—the names could be of either group.

"Did you meet anybody else in Danielle's family?"

Ruby shrugged, turned sullen.

"Uh-oh," Nerese mugged, hoping against hope. "Who."

"Nobody," Ruby looked away.

"Nobody?"

"Just some kids, little kids."

"Little kids. That's it? No other grown-ups?"

"No."

"No?" Nerese was almost positive that Ruby was holding something, someone, back. "Honey . . ." taking hold of her hands. "I have to get real serious with you here," hating to do this to her, but knowing there was nothing like fear to focus a child's mind. "Whoever did this to your dad, I'm gonna get 'em. And when I do? I'm gonna nail their behind to a tree and sell postcards. But the thing is? They're still out there and I don't want them coming back to hurt your dad again." Nerese could sense the mother steaming up behind her; saw tears pop in the corners of Ruby's eyes like glass beads. "So I just need to ask you straight out . . . was anybody mad at your father?"

"Yeah," she answered after a long moment, then added, "Me."

"*You?*"

Ruby shrugged, took back her hand.

"Why?"

"I don't know," her voice that teary climbing whisper again.

"Enough," Claire said, finally stepping inside the room. "Interview's over."

Nerese took Ruby by the elbows, sought out her eyes, but the kid wouldn't look at her. "You're a sweetheart, you know that?"

"Thank you," she whispered, nodding quickly, pressing the heels of her palms to her eyes.

Nerese stood in the third-floor hallway, her two embarrassing shopping bags at her feet.

"So I take it this Danielle is news to you."

Claire shrugged.

"It's understandable. You know, loyalty to her mom and all."

"It's fine."

Claire seemed impatient for the elevator to come; jamming her hands in her jeans pockets and restlessly dancing in place as if they were standing inside a meat locker.

Actually, Nerese hadn't quite rung for it yet, just palmed the button to forestall the bum's rush.

"You had kind of a reaction when Ruby said he gave money to the mother."

"Ray. He always says 'I just want to make a dent.' But what he really wants to do is make a splash. There's a big difference. Paying for a funeral . . ."

"I would say that was pretty decent of him," Nerese said, offended by the woman's above-it-all tone.

The elevator began its clanking ascent from the lobby on its own.

"Ray likes to save people, you know, sweep them off their feet with his generosity. It's a cheap high if you've got the money, but basically it's all about him."

"Yeah well, that character flaw most likely eluded the family he helped."

Claire folded her arms across her chest, gave Nerese that minutely upticked smile from her photo.

"You sure you don't have any problem around him knocking boots with this Danielle?" Nerese just saying it to get under her skin.

The elevator groaned open, a tall slope-shouldered fiftyish man rearing back in surprise from Nerese, then smiling at Claire, a set of house keys in his hand.

"I'm sorry." Claire blinked at Nerese. "What was the question?"

Chapter 11 >

Hospital—February 15

Nerese walked into the monitored-care ward with a headful of calculated banter, but one look at her audience and the script just blew off the page. Ray was sitting upright as if lashed to the headboard, his smudge-pot eyes haunted and blank, the encircling purple mask breaking down now into the marbled ambers and browns of overripe tropical fruit. But the skin show was both typical and not as bad as it looked; what caught her up short was the impression she had that his immobility was both purposeful and absolute, as if there were a coral snake asleep in his hair, as if one sudden or imprudent move would reduce his pain-packed skull to shards.

"The fuck, Ray." Nerese stood gawking at him from the foot of the bed.

Taking a moment to find her, he slowly raised his left hand in greeting like a feeble pope.

"It's global," he murmured.

"Global. What's global?"

He continued to raise that same hand until it was above his head then traced an encircling halo.

"Tell him it's global."

Nerese walked out to the nurses' station. "Can you tell me what's going on with him?" chucking a thumb back toward Ray's bed.

"The neurologist is on his way."

"But what's his status, what's the deal today?"

"The neurologist is on his way."

Reentering Ray's glass-lined stall, Nerese went right into his multicolored face. "Ray, what's going on."

His eyes slid past her hunkering presence and tracked the progress of something moving along the baseboards: dustballs, elves, mice or maybe, just maybe, she thought once again, he was putting her on, ducking her.

"*Ray*," Nerese near shouted, "Ray, I saw Ruby. I talked to Ruby."

"No," he murmured. "Why."

"She's scared for you. She's terrified of this bastard coming back to finish what he started."

Ray almost imperceptibly shook his head from side to side. "He won't. Tell her."

"How can I tell her that?" Nerese came kissing close, then pulled back, Ray's breath suffused with his deterioration. "I can't guarantee that."

"When's your son coming to see me," he slurred dreamily.

"What?"

"I'll get him in college." Then: "Oh . . ." raising a time-lapsed hand to the side of his head, saliva sizzling through clenched teeth.

Nerese was struck by the oddly detached thought that if Ray were to die before she could make an arrest, the case would automatically be taken from her, kicked across town to County Homicide; the investigators over there, she knew from past experience, probably not even interested in reading her notes, let alone keeping her as part of the team.

"You know, Ray, I don't even need to come back here anymore to do what I have to do on this," Nerese was back to shouting. "But I just keep hoping you're either going to grow a pair of balls or come to your senses and just tell me who the fuck did this to you."

"Senseless," he muttered, then looked away.

"Excuse me?" Nerese waited, then plowed on. "For example, I can just go to see Carla Powell over in Hopewell and from there over to see her daughter Danielle. I mean, I guess I could go to see Danielle first since she's the one you're banging, or *were* banging, stop me if I'm wrong."

Ray closed his eyes.

"But I need to work from the outer circles in towards the center. That's the way I've been taught to do it, and that's the way I *like* to do it because with every face-off I just get stronger and stronger so that by the time I get behind a closed door with my bull's-eye? I just know too much, and it's over."

Ray appeared to lose himself in the pain, delicately bringing his fingertips to his temples, eyes moving laterally under lightly fluttering lids as if he were about to receive a message from the beyond.

"See, right now I'm liking the idea of some pissed-off boyfriend or husband didn't appreciate your taking his honey over to Little Venice like that. Or if this was some kind of setup, you know, some kind of half-assed extortion, somebody seeing how easy that thirty-two hundred came, squeezing you a few days later for another seventy-three in cash, we're still talking the immediate family and now you're too embarrassed to come forward on it because you let your dick get you into this mess."

Nerese waited, Ray still taking dictation from the dead.

"Now, I don't really know this Powell family per se, just vaguely from back when we were kids, but I *do* know that this Reggie? The son you buried? He was an overdose, so that doesn't bode well in terms of casting aspersions on the lot, but in any event, I hope one way or the other I'm looking for someone connected to that house because otherwise the list of potential doers is like the phone book."

Ray stared off, unresponsive.

"Did you *really* give Carla Powell thirty-two hundred dollars to bury her son?"

He grunted, gave up a small smile.

"Shit, you do that for a stranger, where'd you bury your mother, the Pyramids?"

"Money," Ray grunted through his teeth.

"What about it."

"Weighs you down."

"How we doing?" A doctor Nerese had never seen before breezed into the stall and, like the other one, went directly for Ray's eyes.

"The President is George W. Bush," Ray said, the slurring in his speech giving Nerese knots.

"Good. How about the first President?"

"Of the United States?"

"Of wherever you want." The doctor stepped back to size up the package.

"Washington," Ray said. "Booker T. Washington. Booker T. and the MGs."

"'Green Onions.'" The doctor smiled, flipping up the bottom of the blanket and running a Babinski, Ray's toes now spastically arching and splaying.

"What's going on?" Nerese asked.

"Little of this, little of that. He's scheduled for a CT later today." Then, to Ray, "How are the headaches?"

"Bad."

"Global or banded?"

"Global," Nerese and Ray said together.

"Are you the catching detective here?"

"Yes I am."

"Can you hold your hands straight up over your head?"

Nerese was momentarily thrown by the request until she saw Ray lethargically comply, both hands wavering at high noon.

"Close your eyes please?" the doctor stepping back watching Ray's arms shift slightly, as if buffeted by wind.

"Well, I'll tell you." He addressed Nerese in a lowered voice without taking his eyes off his patient. Ray's right arm, the extremity directly affected by his left-side injury, began to drift, floating down to twenty past the hour, Ray seemingly oblivious to the movement. "If this was my case and I was still needing information from the vic?" The neurologist finally turned to face her. "I'd shake a leg."

Back down in the hospital lobby, Nerese ran into Ruby and her mother as they headed for the elevators.

"Hey!" She gave the kid a real smile, took hold of her long-fingered hand. "You here to see your dad?"

Ruby nodded, her face trembling like a raindrop on a leaf.

"You know, I have to tell you," Nerese threw a wince into her voice as she spoke to the mother through the daughter. "I just came from trying to see him myself? The thing is, he's kind of sleeping right now, which the doctors told me is very important. And, it's not my place, I realize, but maybe today's not such a good time to visit," flicking a glance Claire's way, Spare your daughter a freak-out; Ray's ex breathing deep but otherwise keeping it together.

"Well, that's probably good advice, then," Claire said in a tone of strained breeziness.

Ruby took back her hand, made a quick swipe at her eyes.

"You know your dad's gonna be OK, right?" Nerese, despite being shorter than Ruby, needed to duck her head in order to get into the girl's eyes. "You *know* that, right?"

Ruby nodded, but remained mute, as if to speak was to lose it.

"We'll come back, see him tomorrow," Claire said lightly. "Hey, Ruby? Maybe you want to leave that with Nerese, she can put it on your dad's night table for when he wakes up, what do you think?"

Without making eye contact, Ruby handed over the nearly spherical Weeping Monk from her gods and goddesses collection.

"I'll go right back up there now," Nerese said, rotating the softball-sized sculpted wood and discovering that the kid had minutely inked ST. SIMON'S HAWKS onto the monk's bowed back, converting his prayer robe into a varsity jacket.

"We'll come by tomorrow," Claire repeated. Then, moving closer to Nerese, her voice became hoarse and shaky. "He's a good guy, you know? Take care of him, OK?"

Nerese watched mother and daughter navigate the lobby traffic until they dissolved into sunlight; then she headed back up to six.

Ray's eyes were open as Nerese reentered his stall, but they appeared glazed and sightless.

Carefully setting the monk on the corner of his night table she turned to leave.

"You know what I just remembered?" addressing her in a low slurry monotone as if she had never left the room.

"What." Nerese stood by the edge of the bed.

"That day you were caught spray-painting by the housing cops and all the kids from Big Playground started following you and ranking you out?" He paused for breath. "Your brother Antoine was with them. He walked in the pack like the two of you weren't even related. He wasn't shouting out any shit like the rest of them, but he wasn't telling anybody to shut up either . . . And then about halfway to the management office he lost interest and went back to the basketball courts."

"What else do you remember," Nerese said, easing herself down on the side of the bed, Ray staring off.

"I remember you were wearing mustard-colored shorts, kind of linty . . . And sky-blue plastic sandals."

"Linty," Nerese said.

"How would I remember that . . . Is that from this?" He languidly gestured upward.

"So I guess you were a part of that crowd too," she said without heat.

"Yeah, I was. But I didn't call you out, tease you or anything. You were just in such deep shit and I wanted to see what would happen to you," taking another rest, then: "It was more like I was riveted by it."

"What else do you remember?"

"I remember," his chapped lips working, "I remember one of the two cops? He kept turning around and trying to shoo us away, saying how we should all be ashamed of ourselves for making fun of you like that, but when he turned on us, all we did was scatter a little, then when he turned forward again we just regrouped and kept following. He couldn't really do anything about it."

"Which cop was it?"

"What?"

"Which cop was the one who tried to shoo everybody away. The white cop or the black cop?" Nerese telepathically egging him on: The white one, the white one, the white one . . .

"The white cop," he said. "The white one."

"No kidding," Nerese growing hot-eyed, thinking, Of course; grateful for this confirmation, this gift.

"Do you remember his name?" She was holding her breath now, Ray taking forever on it, then, "No."

"No problem . . ." Nerese unthinkingly stroked his hair, regarded him with a welling tenderness. "Ray, please let me get some payback for you on this."

But he responded by instantly shutting himself down again; she could feel it through her fingertips.

"My gut says it was a boyfriend or a husband pissed off about you bringing his squeeze back to Little Venice for some sex, wasn't it . . ."

A waste of breath, but no matter. She felt doubly indebted to him now, sticking to him like glue.

Chapter 12

Danielle — January 15

Danielle entered the apartment in Little Venice trailing two boys: Nelson, twelve, and Dante, an eight-year-old who just took off, flying around the place like his ass was on fire.

Wearing dry-cleaned jeans and a white T-shirt under a red bolero jacket, she gingerly wandered about, lightly touching things, her perfume, that vanilla musk, laying down a heavy sweetish track wherever she went.

Unlike Dante, the older boy, Nelson, pretty much hung at her side from the door on in.

He had a big head, this Nelson kid, accentuated by smudgy rings around cautious intelligent eyes and a monkish high-walled bowl-cut that left him with a stranded bird's nest of wavy hair at the crown.

"Oh Ray, this place," Danielle said, her voice husky with want.

When he first picked them up at the Hopewell Houses he was eager to show off where he lived, but now, embarrassed by that eagerness, the cheap-shot easiness of impressing them, he was eager for them to go.

Besides, even as he tried to reenvision his digs through Danielle's eyes, he couldn't shake how much he hated it here, his parents' apartment always feeling dead to him — militantly color-coordinated as it was, in plum and gray; more like a first-class airline lounge than any kind of home.

"Nelson," Danielle said, "could you imagine . . ." She let her fantasy hang.

The boy shrugged and did an about-face, clearly embarrassed by her saying his name out loud like that.

Nelson had three cut-glass studs in his left ear, wore an oversized Jets jersey and clown-sized baggy jeans, but Ray could tell the kid's heart wasn't in it.

He wasn't drawn to Dante, the eight-year-old too hyper, too much like an unknotted balloon, but Nelson had that hungry-hearted watchful aura that Ray always responded to, that made him keen to connect, to let the kid know he wasn't out there on his own.

And the boy also made him ache for Ruby. Often when he was around children not his own he experienced sharp pangs of sentiment cut with a panic about "losing her," whatever that might mean, which tended to make him much more focused on the kids in the room than on whatever adults were around.

"Ray." Danielle gave him that unnerving straight-on stare. "I would die for this place."

Her hair was drawn up into a topknot so taut that it lifted the outside corners of her eyes.

On the other hand, maybe all his misty-eyed kid focus this evening was nothing but self-generated smoke to cover the fact that he hadn't been alone with a woman, not just sexually but socially, for a little more than a year.

Danielle slid back the glass door and stepped out onto the cement terrace which faced the Statue of Liberty and the moon-bleached water.

"Check it out," both Danielle and Ray said simultaneously to Nelson, Danielle indicating the view, Ray pointing to the full-length funhouse mirror that he had brought back with him from Los Angeles.

"Or whatever," he quickly demurred, but Nelson gestured for his mother to hang on as he made his way in front of the silver-chipped undulating surface, instantly turning himself into a dwarf with a five-foot forehead. Fighting off a grin, the kid looked like his mouth was stuffed with grapes.

"You remind me of my daughter," Ray said easily.

Nelson looked stricken.

"You know, I mean in a masculine universal way," Ray scrambled. "I can tell, you got that watchful thing going on, kind of guy likes to lay back in the cut, check out all your options before you finally make your play." Shit-talking in a way that would make Ruby cringe. Then more soberly, "It's a compliment, Nelson."

"It's a compliment, Nelson." Dante mimicked him in a deep dull voice, the kid just materializing, a wooden veal mallet from the kitchen in his left hand.

"Whoa!" Dante jerked back from his image in the funhouse mirror, then promptly took out his dick, the glass giving him back a foot-long loop of Turkish taffy.

Nelson ran out of the living room with a hand over his mouth. Hearing him howl a moment later from the far end of the apartment, Ray became faintly repulsed by the kid's need to flee.

Sidling up to Danielle on the terrace, Ray rested his forearms atop the guard rail.

"Is that the Trade Center?" she asked, pointing to the hemispheric glow of floodlights across the river.

"Yeah. Not much to see," he said quietly.

They stood in silence for a moment, watching the silhouette of a titanic crane move jerkily behind the waterfront skyline like a prehistoric forager.

"You know," she finally said, delicately scratching a corner of her lipsticked mouth with a long red pinky nail, "if I had this place? I would be out here around the clock. I would set up a desk and do all my homework right where we're standing."

"Homework?" The breeze brought scented wisps of her hair across his face.

"Yeah. I go to Dempsy Community College. They got a two-year program in Public Policy. Housing said that if I get the degree they'd throw me a desk at Hopewell, make me the tenant liaison officer."

"That's great," Ray said, half-listening, mostly just soaking up being next to her.

"Yeah, see Hopewell, they're so sick of the tenants bitching about this, that, the other, they decided to make some of us management. See how we like it."

"You want to neutralize a threat? Give it a job."

"Didn't work on my husband."

"Oh yeah?" Ray was all ears.

"The thing is, I never graduated high school and, they'll let you into the college, but I can't get my degree until I get my GED, so I'm kind of doing both at the same time."

"Straddling two horses," Ray said, still stuck on Husband.

"Try three. I work a forty-hour job, too."

"Damn, that tattoo's no lie," wanting to touch it, her. "So where's your other son tonight, with Carla?"

"What other son?"

"That little boy jumping on the couch at your mother's."

"David? That's my brother's boy. So's Dante, thank God. My mom keeps picking up the ones that fall off the back of the truck."

"Really." Ray thinking, I can help.

"Really."

"But Nelson's yours?"

"All mine."

"Does his . . ." He faltered; how to put this . . . "Does his dad live with him too?"

"Yeah, OK." Danielle smirked. "What you're really asking . . ." She cut herself off, briefly leaned her arm into his, just a playful bump but it made his head spin.

"He's out of the picture," she said.

"Out, like . . ." Ray pushing, losing control a little.

"Like three strikes you're out," she said, enjoying this game.

"In English?"

Danielle sighed. "There's two institutions in this city start with the words 'Dempsy County.' I attend one, he lives in the other."

"What's he in for?"

"Guess."

"What kind of sentence he get?" Ray assumed she meant drugs.

"Year and a day. Like always."

Ray repeated it to himself, Like always; then let it be.

Back in the living room, Dante, for some reason shirtless now, came up to Ray with a baseball-sized rock that belonged in the bedroom.

"What's this?" The kid offered it up to him on twinned palms.

"That's coprolite."

"What?"

"Petrified dinosaur shit."

Dante let it drop to the floor. "What's *wrong* with you, man!" A chip shot off the hardwood in a powdery spray.

"Dante!" Danielle snapped.

Nelson quickly, anxiously, looked to Ray, then, clucking in irritation at his cousin, stooped to pick it up.

As they left the apartment, heading for a restaurant, Ray became aware that Danielle's perfume would still be in the air a few hours from now when he returned, just hanging there like an unmitigated longing, and there would be nothing he could do about it.

Oriente was a big red Cuban-Chinese restaurant in Hoboken, gaudy and loud.

Ray picked it not for the food, which was OK, but for the fifteen-foot papier-mâché hand suspended from the ceiling: a life-sized Chinaman complete with lampshade hat and pigtail, struggling to free himself from two chopsticks held by gigantic green-nailed fingers.

"So Nelson, what are you into these days," Ray asked over a plate of plantains and mu shu pork.

"So Nelson, what are you into these days," Dante aped him, once again nailing his self-conscious attempt at breeziness.

"He's into books," Danielle answered for her son. "His father was a college graduate, not that you'd ever know it."

"Oh yeah?" Ray made himself smile. "What do you want to be?"

"He told me Vice President of the United States."

Nelson glared at his mother.

"Vice?" Ray asked.

"He says being the President's too much pressure," Danielle answered for him again.

It dawned on Ray that Nelson hadn't said word one since being picked up at Hopewell over two hours ago.

"So what kind of work you do?" he asked Danielle.

"Me? Bullshit work. I'm a receptionist over in New York. You know this movie guy, Harold Krauss? The producer?"

"Does TV movies?"

"Him. I'm a receptionist at his company."

"Really."

"Really." Dante again.

"You know I worked in TV for three years myself," Ray said cautiously.

"On *Brokedown High*, right?"

"How'd you know that?"

"I watched it once with my mother. She saw your name in the opening credits and got all excited. 'I know him! I know him! He lived in the building! He lived in the building!'" Danielle quoted her mother in a high hissy whisper.

Back when he was working on the show, Ray had often fantasized about people who had known him from childhood turning on their TVs and reacting to the sight of his name; but in the few instances where that pipe-dream scenario had actually become an in-the-flesh encounter, it invariably left him feeling more embarrassed and shallow than vindicated.

"You don't want to get deeper into TV work yourself?"

"As what, a seasoned receptionist?" Danielle said with a twist of the lips. "Well, actually what I do is more interesting than it sounds. Like, three days after I got hired, OK? My boss Krauss, he buzzes me, says to come into his office, bring a notepad. I go in, he's auditioning this actor for some movie, like a disease movie, a virus movie, or some such. I go in, he points to a chair in back, says, 'Take notes.' And I'm thinking, 'On what?'

"So, the guy reads his lines with an actress, the audition lasts maybe ten minutes, Krauss gets up, says, 'That was wonderful. We'll call,' the guy leaves, the actress leaves, it's me, Krauss and this other producer, Krauss looks to me, says, 'So what you think?' I'm like, 'About *what* . . . ?' Krauss says, 'Would you fuck him?'" lowering her voice on the f-word. "And I'm, in my mind, I'm, 'How *dare* you.' I mean I was shaking I was so insulted, but scared too, because I needed that job. But all I say is, 'I don't know. Would you?'

"And at first he's like, his face is, 'Who the hell are you to . . .' But the other guy starts laughing like, 'Hey, good one, Hal,' and I guess that broke the tension. He never actually apologized to me but he's been kind of, I don't know, tasteful about things ever since."

"Tasteful."

"I mean he still calls me in every time he's auditioning actors, you know, 'Take notes,' but after they leave, all he says to me is, 'So what do you think?' and all I give him is thumbs up, thumbs down. But I'll tell you one thing I learned about movies? It all boils down to 'Would you fuck him, would you fuck her.' Everything flows out of that."

"Understanding what you just said?" Ray aching for her. "That's a six-figure salary right there."

"Jesus, Krauss has this wife? Two weeks into the job she comes in, slips me a hundred-dollar bill and her cell phone number, says to me, 'Any woman goes in that office, the door's closed more than fifteen minutes, you call me.'

"I'll take the money, but screw you, bitch, I'm not playing pussy police for her and I *know* he's layin' carpet with two of the office staff plus about every third or fourth actress goes in for a part, but she's not getting shit out of me. I mean, the presumptuousness of asking me to do that."

"He ever put the moves on you?"

"Me? I don't know, kind of. I mean, right from the jump I can tell he's sizing me up, sees the tattoo, figures anything goes, right? Like, day two he comes out of his office, sits on my desk, says, 'Hey, good news. I just bought the film rights to five of the Ten Commandments, got a two-year option on the others.' You know, it was a joke, but I believed him, and I think that turned him off."

He heard regret in her voice, like she would have been up for it if things had broken another way.

"Nah nah nah," Danielle said, reading his eyes. "Mainly I just felt stupid about not getting the joke."

And with that gentle correction, Ray decided he was in love.

"So, Nelson." He beamed at the kid, who had been listlessly stabbing the same shrimp with a single chopstick for the last ten minutes. "What's your favorite subject?"

"He's good at everything but gym," Danielle said.

"That's exactly like I was, except I wasn't even good at gym."

"You hear that?" Danielle asked him, Ray fending off irritation, the boy not needing a translator.

"How much money you got?" Dante asked him.

"On me?" Ray was sick of this kid.

"Can you buy me something?"

"I'll buy you a beer."

"I'll drink it."

"Dante, shut up," Danielle snapped.

"Was I talking to you?" he shot back in a high railing voice.

"He's like the demon seed, this one." Danielle palmed her forehead.

"Oh yeah? You're like the *water*melon seed, you big booty bitch."

Nelson covered his mouth again, swallowing another howl as Danielle snatched Dante clean off his seat and had him dragged halfway to the rest-rooms before Ray could react.

Now that he was alone with Nelson, some of the kid's wallflower vibrations made it across the table, had Ray tongue-tied for a long moment.

"Nelson, I tell you, when I was in school? The only good thing about seventh grade was that I was finally done with sixth. And the only good thing about eighth grade? I was finally done with seventh. What grade are you in?" trying to get him to verbalize at least one word.

Nelson held up seven fingers, Ray wondering if the kid had a speech defect.

"When I was in seventh grade, a lot of our classes, we were set up in squares of four, you know, four desks in a block, the students all facing each other. They still do that?"

The kid nodded yes.

"Anyways, in seventh-grade math? I was such a pain in the ass, I was so disruptive, the teacher took my desk out of the square and put me alone right under the blackboard, you know, facing the whole class, so she could keep an eye on me, keep me from contaminating anybody with my behavior. Can you believe that?"

"That's like . . ." Nelson began, then quickly shut himself down, Ray surprised by the thrill he felt just getting the kid to say those two words.

They sat in silence for another moment, Nelson studying his untouched food and Ray wondering why he always resorted to sad-sack stories of his own childhood to get on the inside with kids.

Danielle and Dante returned to the table, Dante flinging himself sullenly in his chair, his downturned lips tight as a drum, a residual sparkle of tears in his lashes.

"I swear," Danielle said, "I told my sister-in-law when she was pregnant with this one, 'Do the cops a favor, swallow a pair of handcuffs now.'"

The waiter dropped a check on the table but left before Ray could give it back to him with a credit card.

He pulled the gold AmEx from his wallet and left it face up on the tab.

Nelson glanced at the card, then did a double take, abruptly leaning forward and gaping at it fish-mouthed.

"Ma!" More a gasp than a word.

Snatching the card off the bill tray, he buried his mouth in his mother's hair, a cupped hand shielding his whispered words from the table.

Danielle nodded, took the card from Nelson and carefully placed it back on top of the check.

"You know what he just said to me?" she asked softly, tapping the oval-framed profile of the AmEx centurion. "He just said, 'Ma. That's one of the guys who killed Jesus.'"

Near ten o'clock, he pulled the car in front of Carla's building, Danielle in the passenger seat, Nelson and Dante in back.

Directly overhead, the PATH train tore apart the night. Ray sat there thick-witted, adolescent, wanting to kiss her at least—but the presence of the kids made it unthinkable.

Even so, there was a swollen moment of inaction, of expectation, of avoiding each other's eyes . . .

Dante opened his door and hopped out, followed by his cousin, neither one of them saying a word to him or even looking his way.

But Danielle remained in the car, frowning at her nails, working something out. Ray began to lean across the stick shift.

"You don't want to come upstairs." It was a statement, not a question, and it checked his timid progress.

"No, I guess not."

He ducked down and twisted his head up in order to see if Carla was on fifth-floor window patrol up there, but he couldn't get low enough.

With nothing to lose, he tried to kiss her again, get his nose up in that vanilla-scented hair.

"Wait here." She opened her door. "I'll be down in five."

She disappeared into the building without a backward glance.

Wait here: Ray sitting there now, stupid with shock, trying to do the math; Carla's daughter, but thirty years old, a mother. Down in five. He tended to get up two, three times a night, walk around, take a leak, write down the odd dream. He couldn't, just couldn't fall asleep without reading. Wait here. The car smelled of her, smelled like panic. She had been frowning at her nails, something else was going on with her; something having nothing to do with him. He'd come way too fast; how could he not? It would be over before it started; Ray already working on what to say after, how to make it up to her.

He was halfway across the stick shift again, lost in her scent, when she abruptly opened the passenger door, making him jerk back in surprise.

"Hey," she said, then exhaled heavily, free of the kids, of Carla too, maybe.

"I like your terrace," she announced, staring straight ahead.

"Yeah, no," Ray said. "Me too."

She had put on fresh lipstick, her mouth glistening with it.

They drove back to Little Venice in taut silence, as if the trunk were packed with nitroglycerin, both of them staring straight ahead, Ray not knowing fuck-all about what was going on in her head, and not intending to ask until it was too late.

The first time all evening Ray became truly aware of Danielle's blackness, or her nonwhiteness, or her whateverness, was in the long moment before he could find his keys—his old-bat next-door neighbor, Mrs. Kuben, with her usual uncanny timing, opened her own door a crack as if some phantom had rung her bell, then, apparently shocked by the sight of Danielle, she just stood there flatfooted, lost in her own surprise, before finally reclosing her door without even acknowledging Ray's presence.

There was no dirty look, no blatant hostility or disapproval, just naked disorientation; Danielle saying nothing about it, just pursing her lips and briefly closing her eyes as if exhausted.

Reentering his apartment, Danielle instantly turned it inside out with her child-free presence—her touch, her glance, suffusing everyday objects with both life and menace.

Standing with her back to him in the middle of the living room, she slipped out of her red bolero jacket and, with the languid purposefulness of a toreador, extended her arm to drop it on a chair, Ray understanding right then that whatever was about to go down would be all her play.

"Do you want a drink?" he said, just to say something.

"No thank you."

She pulled back the sliding glass door and stepped onto the terrace as if stepping into a shower, Ray easing on out after her.

For the second time this evening they stood alongside each other, leaning forward against the guard rail and staring out this time at the Statue of Liberty, glowing frog-belly white and encircled by foam-flecked waves.

Upriver in the opposite direction, the floodlights behind the financial district skyline had been turned off for the night.

It was cold, the city-borne breeze damp and acrid, still dense with dread after all this time, but the swollen silence between them was interesting enough to keep him out here like this until the sun came up.

He inched his arm along the rail until there was contact. She didn't pull away.

He became aware of a faint tremor in his jaw.

She exhaled heavily through her nose.

"Do you think if we stared hard enough at that statue we could get it to levitate?" He had said it four times to himself before saying it out loud.

"What?" She finally looked at him, a faint smile of incomprehension playing across her face.

"Do you think . . ." he ran out of breath. "I'm no good at this."

"Good at what . . ." Teasing him.

"The, the international playboy routine."

"International, huh?" she said, then turned so that her back was to the rail.

She took his left hand and placed it on her belly, which was full and round and solid. She then unsnapped the top button of her jeans for him while slipping her other hand between his legs, seeking the heated outline within the folds and creases of denim.

In a daze of sensation Ray imagined he could feel the tint of her skin through his fingertips. He dropped his hand into her curls and she thrust herself outward to meet his touch; hard bone sheathed in a padding of flesh.

She roughly rubbed the flat of her hand over the thickness between his legs and there they stood, hip to hip, but facing in opposite directions, like tango dancers awaiting the music, working on each other in fiercely minute circles.

The lack of eye contact combined with the furtive urgency of their touches shrank the enormous night into a stolen pocket of dark.

She kept grinding against his fingers, until, faintly growling, she suddenly lurched forward like a drunk, bringing her free hand to his shoulder for balance.

Ray, knees trembling like jackhammers, didn't know whether to concentrate on her hand or on his own.

Once again, he was afraid to fuck—he'd go off in a heartbeat—and, thinking You first, he dropped to his knees, mouth pressed to her belly, both of his hands now trying to gently ease her tight jeans down below her hips.

At first she was still swoony, not sure where he went, what was going on, but she figured it out fast enough, said, "No," brought him back to his feet, tugged on his belt as if to cut him in half and, before he could start any negotiations, had him in her mouth, Danielle down there balanced on her haunches, the crook of one arm between his legs as if holding him up, the flat of her hand splayed against the small of his back pushing him forward into her rhythm.

He felt that to touch her hair or her shoulders as she worked on him would be a violation. He let his head drop back and gawked at the stars until the hand on his spine slid back down to between his legs, cupped his balls, one finger grazing behind and he went off; holding onto the terrace rail to take the pressure off his bubbling legs.

Still perched on her haunches, Danielle wiped her mouth with a flick of her thumb and said as if to a third party, "We know he can dish it out, let's see if he can take it."

"Me?" Relaxed now, Ray was happy to oblige.

"What?"

"Me?"

"No," she said.

"Then who . . ."

A half-hour later he drove her home, then came back to the terrace, the over-rich scent of her still hanging in the air, as palpable as breath.

Chapter 13 >

Nerese — In the Field — February 16

Nerese sat in the outer lobby of the Hopewell Houses management office on the same heavily varnished municipally issued oak bench that she had sat on twenty-nine years ago on the day of her arrest as she waited and waited for her mother to come pick her up. Sat there on that same damn bench and in her discomfort and boredom rediscovered the room, taking in the long familiar, now half-century-old framed architect's drawing of the about-to-be-built housing project, the hypothetical landscape peopled with white Bob and Betty tenants and never-to-be-planted trees—then studied the wall hangings that spoke of Hopewell in the moment: the Gunbusters Anonymous poster, the No Pit Bulls notification, the buoyant group photo of Hispanic kids clustered around some monkey bars, the legend beneath declaring YO TENGO ASMA PERO ASMA NO ME TIENE A MI; and the stunned-looking teenaged football player—a dead ringer for her son—cradling a baby above the warning: AN EXTRA EIGHT POUNDS CAN KEEP YOU OFF THE TEAM.

A PATH train roared by overhead. Nerese watched it through the heavily paint-glopped iron window grilles. Flushing toilets and running water could be heard from various apartments above the office. She hated this place, always had.

Mr. Rodriguez, the projects' current manager, came out of his office to meet her; a small stocky man sporting a parted mustache, wire-rimmed glasses, a button-down dress shirt—the outline of his undershirt visible through the fabric—and a tie patterned with the logo of the Dempsy County Housing Authority.

Nerese's greatest asset as a detective was her ability to make anyone feel like she was so damn glad to finally meet them—victim, perp, witness; it came across in her eyes, her laugh, her body language and especially her smile, but this guy Rodriguez had his own smile—that of a career stonewaller, tight as a crab's ass. Nerese knew to save her wattage; the only thing she'd be walking away with here today was a tension headache.

"Powell . . ." Rodriguez frowned as he punched the name into his computer, acting as if he'd never heard of these fifty-year Hopewell tenants.

"Anything you could tell me . . ."

"Apartment again?"

"Five C, Six Building," she said evenly.

The office itself had cinder-block walls painted a glossy sky blue; four desks and a large blackboard that served as a work-order chart. Besides Rodriguez and Nerese the only person present was a heavyset black woman wearing a rust-colored pantsuit and a bright African head wrap, this individual standing over a rear desk and filing time cards. Nerese read her as a tenant exchanging labor for rent credit.

"You know I grew up here," she said to the manager.

"Oh yeah?" Rodriguez murmured, like he could give a shit. "Powell, Carla," he announced, studying the screen. "Pays rent on time. No complaints, no . . . What are you looking for?"

The tenant-worker at the corner desk caught Nerese's eye, shook her head, Nerese not sure how to read the gesture.

"Can you tell me exactly who's living there?"

"Powell, Carla . . . Powell, Reginald."

Nerese knew Reginald was the son that had just died.

The other woman rolled her eyes, Nerese reading her now as dying to blab.

"Two minors: Powell, David, and Powell, Dante."

"She have a daughter living there?"

Rodriguez was a long time studying the screen, said, "Nope . . ." just as the woman behind him nodded yes. Nerese winked at her, then thanked the manager for his time.

Standing outside the management office, Nerese idly watched the kids on the netless basketball courts at the far end of the block-square Big Playground, a lot of these boys her son's age, although Darren was more into soccer, a sport that put her straight into a coma.

Scanning the buildings around her, she caught sight of a floral crucifix suspended over the entrance of Eight Building, the browning of the petals telling her someone had been killed there maybe three, four days ago, Nerese trying to remember the name from the report sheets—Aretha, no, Aurora Howard; five days ago, stabbed by the ex-boyfriend, once again demonstrating that an Order of Protection was about as effective as a string of garlic.

Nerese spotted the tenant-worker from the management office exit the building and slowly make her way over, the woman firing up a cigarette, not looking at her until she was in conversation range. "She in trouble, Carla?"

Nerese shrugged. "Not with me, she isn't."

"This about Reggie?"

"Who?"

"Her son, died last month."

"First I'm hearing of it."

"Because that was drugs." The woman removed a fleck of tobacco from the tip of her tongue.

"Yeah, huh?"

"That boy's been breaking his mother's heart since he was a child, and now it's broken in half, although anyone around here not deaf dumb and blind could of seen that one coming clear as a bell."

"How about the other kid?" Nerese asked.

"Which other . . ."

"I just know one. There's more?"

"Well, she's got the other boy, he owns a drugstore down in Maryland. She did real well with him, although I believe he married a white woman."

"And the daughter, right?"

"Yeah, Danielle."

"Danielle." Nerese nodded.

"Danielle's doing good too. Got a job, goes to college. Only has the one child herself, a boy Nelson, because the doctors messed up the delivery, had three-four operations after that, wound up with a hysterectomy at nineteen years of age, God have mercy, finally won a one hundred and twenty-five thousand dollar settlement about six years ago? Not that any of it's left."

"Unh," Nerese grunted, thinking, The shit people know.

"But Carla, she's two for three with her kids, that's more than most these days except for me. I'm three for three, two boys in the Air Force and a girl at Dempsy Community, transferring to Rutgers-Newark in September on full scholarship, and I mean *full*," taking a satisfied drag on her cigarette, Nerese saying, "All right," throwing her an admiring smile, thinking, Darren would be lucky to get accepted to the University of Pizza Hut—then thinking, Air Force . . .

"So, Danielle, she does or doesn't live with her mom. I couldn't tell in there."

"Yeah, well, you couldn't tell in there because Rodriguez don't want to know about it. Man makes a ostrich look curious. Yeah, she'd been living with Carla for about six months, just left maybe ten, twelve days ago, but she'll be back."

"Left for . . ."

"For to go back with her husband now that he's out."

Out.

"What's his name again?" Nerese squinted helplessly.

"Freddy."

"Yeah, Freddy. Freddy . . ." Snapping her fingers.

"Martinez. Just say, 'What's the name of the guy Danielle's married to, because I don't know it.'"

Nerese laughed, always appreciating dryness in people.

"What was he in for?"

"Same thing he's always in for. He's a college graduate, too, can you believe that? I mean, he's a nice guy and all, you know, a gentleman. Lets the ladies out the elevator first, holds the door for you, always says hello, good evening, good night. You know what his problem is? He's educated but he doesn't have the drive. And then he sulks because the world don't beat down his door with job offers. Then he goes and puts his business on the street. Then he sulks about how much money he's making *that* way, him with his college degree, how ironic and whatnot."

The woman rolled her eyes again; Nerese feeling so close to it now, the situation laying itself out like a highway.

"Anyways," she yawned into the side of her fist. "Freddy, he got out about two weeks ago, so Danielle moved back in with him a day or two after that. They live over his mother; she owns a two-family brick on Taylor Street, although she's mostly in Atlantic City these days with her sister, rents out the top floor to her son and his family, but I have to tell you I'm kind of surprised at how quick she got back with him this time, because normally when Freddy gets out of County? On the average it takes her three, four days just to even start talking to him again, OK? He usually has to go and leave all kinds of phone messages for her on Carla's machine, make all kinds of promises, put on a suit, circle some job ads in the paper, show up at her work over in New York or at Carla's apartment; let her yell at him until she goes hoarse, takes it, you know, 'You're right, you're absolutely right, give me one last shot,' et cetera et cetera, but you know, living with Carla is no picnic either, they're always on each other's case those two, so this that and the other, once he's out she can usually hold him off for a week, ten days, if she's really pissed, two weeks one time, but then she always gives in and goes home, you know, goes right back to square one squared, see you back in Hopewell in about nine months."

Nerese made a grateful enlightened noise. She had nailed it, Ray taking up with a jailbird's wife a few weeks before his release. If love was war, then Ray was shaping up as one of those hapless recruits accidentally shot and killed with his own gun while still in basic training.

"So what's this all about?" the woman finally asked.

"I'm sorry." Nerese shook her head as if addled. "What's your name?"

"Brenda. Brenda Walker."

"Hey Brenda, it's nice to meet you. I'm Nerese Ammons." She handed her a detective's card.

The woman took a moment to study it, then asked again, "So what's this all about?"

"Nothing, really. There was an incident awhile back. Someone in the family might've witnessed it."

"Witnessed, huh?" Brenda Walker drawled, then, despite the stonewall, got right back into it. "See, Danielle, you know what her problem is? She's no dummy, but she's been running with Freddy since she was fifteen years old. That's half her life, had a child together . . . She just don't know any other way than but to be with him."

Nerese nodded, thinking, Not exactly.

"Well, Brenda, let me ask you, what's he like, Freddy? Other than sulky."

"What do you mean?"

"I don't know. He got a temper?"

"Actually, *she's* the one with the temper. I think he's a little afraid of her, if you ask me."

"Does he ever get physical?"

"With who, *her*?" She laughed. "Yeah, I'd like to see that."

"How about with anyone else?"

"Freddy? I assume push comes to shove he can take care of himself, he's been in County enough times, in fact there was that incident in there, but if he's got a fuse, it's a long one as far as I can tell."

"What incident in there?"

"Oh. You never heard? OK, about two years ago? This other inmate had come at him in the showers with a knife or a shank or whatever they call it but Freddy was the one walking away breathing on two feet."

"No kidding. What happened to the other guy?"

"Dead," Brenda Walker said without drama, removing another shred of tobacco from the tip of her tongue.

"No kidding," Nerese repeated lightly, walking around herself in a tight circle.

She decided not to push for details; there were other people for that. "And their son, what's his name again?" Then she added quickly, "And this time I really did forget."

"Nelson. Twelve, thirteen, kind of smart, quiet, does what he's told."

"Let me ask you, you say it usually takes about a week, two weeks, for Danielle to move back in with him, right?"

The woman nodded.

"You have any idea why this time around she moved back in so fast?"

"I couldn't really say." Brenda Walker flicked her cigarette into the bushes. "Fact is, I don't really know the family all that well."

Instead of heading back to her car, Nerese decided to take a walk around the outside perimeter of Big Playground until she came upon Eleven Building, where she found herself reflexively scrutinizing the approximate section of brick face upon which she had done the deed, spray-painted "White Bitch," so many years ago, searching now for any faint trace of the crime, but the surface was so weathered and defaced that it was impossible to tell what she was looking at here.

The White Bitch referred to had been Miss MacGowan, her seventh-grade homeroom teacher. The class, a low-expectations vocational-track group, was composed almost exclusively of black and Hispanic kids, a rowdy already defeated bunch, but Nerese, placed there primarily because of her legendary brothers, was the teacher's pet; fastidious, dependable and attentive, everything the others, and the other members of her family, were not—and Miss MacGowan had on more than one occasion nearly gotten her killed by using the example of her deportment as a cudgel to pound the other kids into feeling worse about themselves than they already did.

Endlessly picked on, provoked and ridiculed in the schoolyard and cafeteria, Nerese steadfastly refused to rise to the bait until the one time she simply lost it, bloodying a boy's nose for him and nearly tearing his shirt in half.

Returning to her homeroom after an hour's wait in the administration office followed by a terrifyingly choleric fifteen-minute chewing out by one of the assistant principals, Nerese had instinctively moved to Miss MacGowan's desk at the front of the room for some vague token of support or sympathy. The acidic bitch, however, knocked her on her ass with a sour smirk and a jerk of the head to the rest of her zoo, saying, "And I thought I had one that was different."

Five days later, six blocks from school and three towns over from Miss MacGowan's home, came the impulsive vandalism, Nerese back then barely aware not only of why she had done it, but even of White Bitch's identity.

Turning her back on Eleven Building now, she faced the twenty-foot-high chain-link fence that bordered the north end of Big Playground, draped that day, as she recalled, with a mute pop-eyed brace of Hopewell kids; Nerese trying to recapture, as Ray had courtesy of his brain damage, how quickly they had transformed themselves into a gleeful crew of young shitheels, streaming out of the basketball and handball courts to jeer and dog her every step of the way once it became apparent that she was in police custody.

And before she was fully aware of what she was doing, Nerese began retracing her mortified march from Eleven Building to the management office, walking along the bush-trimmed footpath lined with low chain-looped stanchions, walking past Nine Building, Seven, Five, Three, but rather than reexperiencing the shame, she became instead filled with a sneaky low-key sense of pride in herself—she was a police officer, a detective who in the course of nearly two decades had saved lives, restored and/or maintained order, locked up every conceivable kind of transgressor from bus-riding ass grabber to multiple murderer, and had been responsible at least in part for delivering to innumerable people over the years varying degrees of justice, solace, comfort and revenge. She was also a solo parent, the master builder of a reasonably intact son on the cusp of his majority. She was a mortgage-free homeowner and, for better or worse, the sole source of financial support for half a dozen people. Truly, as she had announced to Ray the first time she visited him in the hospital, she was blessed; truly truly blessed.

And along with the plummy glow of pride that came over her as she continued along the path of her childhood calvary came an exhilarating epiphany—above and beyond her avowed creed of reciprocation—and purely on a more selfish note: If she could successfully work Ray's assault, bring in a Closed by Arrest—Freddy Martinez the obvious doer here—it would grant her the perfect coda for the last twenty years of her life. Ray, the Powell family, Hopewell Houses—Tweetie: if she could wrap this one up, it would bring her not-easy career full circle, yield her an exit suffused with a degree of symmetry and grace that she had never thought possible.

"Yes," Nerese saying it out loud, so jacked by the rightness of this. Where it had all begun for her was where it would all come to an end.

As the management office, the finish line of her walkabout, once again came into view, Nerese saw that the tenant-worker who had given her the lowdown on the Powell family was still standing there as if waiting for her return, the woman taking slow thoughtful drags off a cigarette and staring into the middle distance.

"Can I ask you something?" Brenda Walker cocked her head as Nerese drew close, then gestured with the detective's card between her fingers to the rotting floral cross hanging over the entrance to Eight Building. "You have anything to do with that up there?"

"Not, no, this isn't my district."

"Well, I'll tell you, just so you know," she said. "That lady that was killed? She had just moved in about three months ago and I believe she had brought her trouble in with her. Because all things being equal? This project's still a pretty good place to call home."

Nerese headed over to the Bureau of Criminal Identification, situated in the basement of one of the smaller courtroom buildings in Dempsy. It was a greenish place consisting of two rooms: one, a vast and dusty warehouse lined with ancient oak filing cabinets which held thousands of criminal records still awaiting conversion to a county-wide database; the other, much smaller, almost claustrophobically so, set up for processing the catch of the day. It included a fingerprinting station, a fixed camera and backdrop for mug shots, an ancient scale and a small steel table for last-minute negotiations. There was also a tiny holding cell in here, no bigger than an elevator car but which in the course of the last century had temporarily housed two German saboteurs working the Dempsy waterfront in World War I; Longy Zwillman, the behind-the-scenes founder of syndicated crime; Dutch Schultz; Carmine Galante; Henry Hill; and Abbie Hoffman.

Sitting on the edge of the small steel desk, Nerese studied the rap sheet of Freddy Martinez. Yes, there was a murder charge that had brought him before a grand jury midway during his second stretch in County, but they had failed to indict, which invariably meant that he had acted in self-defense, as Brenda Walker had claimed; and in front of witnesses, the guards themselves most likely, as required for a No Bill judgment. So for now, Nerese put this incident aside in order to get a clearer picture of the whole; on the face of it, a fairly run-of-the-mill history of mid- to low-level drug transgressions, but for those who could read between the charges and dispositions, the trajectory was a little trickier. There were four arrests over a period of twelve years; for the earliest, on a County-based charge of possession with intent, he was sentenced to three to five years but only served nine months—not that unusual for a first offense. But of the three subsequent arrests, all initially for PWI, two were downgraded to simple possession and one to a disorderly persons, each in turn kicked back to municipal court, where the longest possible sentence was a year and a day. He served nowhere near that: two months on the first municipal complaint, during which he had killed the other inmate; a desk appearance on the second; and, for this most recent one, six weeks.

If all things were on the up-and-up, each arrest should have led to more time than the last, and the fact that after the initial bust County kept downgrading the charges, then booting them into city court, told Nerese that after Freddy's first arrest County Narcotics had turned him into an informant and pretty much kept him out of jail save for just enough time to keep his street credentials intact. In addition, as these relationships primarily worked on a don't ask, don't tell basis, his handlers most likely turned a blind eye to his continuing career as some kind of dopeslinger. The scale of his dealings was difficult for Nerese to tell from the paper in her hands, except that there always seemed to be a bigger fish out there that justified County's perpetual catch-and-release policy toward whomever they happened to have on their hook at any given moment.

Nerese sat across the desk from Kenny Howell, a lieutenant in the Dempsy County Narcotics Squad ten years her junior.

It was common knowledge that Kenny owed his quick rise up the ranks to his foresight in casting his lot with a dark-horse mayoral candidate who pulled off an upset victory in the last election; the lieutenant's shield a reward for volunteering thirty hours a week during the campaign and dropping $3,000 into the war chest from his own pocket. On the actual lieutenant's examination, Howell had finished fourteenth out of one hundred and forty candidates, usually well beneath the cutoff for new appointments, but the mayor got around this by simply declaring that the Dempsy PD needed fifteen new lieutenants, the guy beneath Howell lucking out in order to make the reward a touch less obvious. Not that anybody would complain. This was how things were done in Dempsy; Nerese knew it, the newspapers knew it, the governor of the state knew it—it was just how things were done.

For a cop like Nerese, though, the downside of all this realpolitik was that although she knew exactly what to do in order to get ahead, she basically lacked the moxie, the hustle, the desire to gamble, had no interest in advancing herself by playing the political ponies—attending the right dinners, joining the right organizations or investing a couple of paychecks into this one or that one's campaign fund. And it had nothing to do with race—there were as many black and Hispanic ponies to bet on as there were white ones—but she just didn't have the appetite for it. And as a result, whenever she found herself around high-stakes careerists like Lieutenant Howell here, she always wound up feeling like an outsider in her own department, a borderline nonentity, and if she gave the slightest bit of a damn it would probably have pissed her off.

"Freddy Martinez." Kenny tore off a mouthful of sandwich, held up a finger for Nerese to wait as he chewed and swallowed. "Interesting guy." He put the sandwich back on his desk, passed a hand across his mouth. "He brings the shit in from Washington Heights, sells it to guys who sell it to guys who sell it on the street. No Pablo Escobar but not exactly Bonehead Jones, either. And he's smart. We can never catch him with weight. Usually it's him being in the wrong place at the wrong time."

"OK." Nerese nodded.

"On the other hand, I have to be honest, we kind of like the guy. Never gives us shit, always comes along without a fuss, throws us a useful nibble now and then, you know the type."

"Sure." Nerese was almost choking on the horseshit.

"Yeah, he's an interesting hombre, Freddy. Did you know he and I both went to Montclair State? The thing is, me? I dropped out after two years, but Freddy, he hung in for the full ride and got his degree."

"Degree in what." Nerese just asking.

"You're an aspiring drug dealer, what are you going to major in?"

"How the hell do I know. Chemistry?"

"C'mon, chemistry's for your underlings. Marketing, baby, marketing."

"OK." Nerese thinking, Whatever.

"The thing is, we must have nailed him what, four, five times over the years? When my son was born last July, Freddy came by the office and dropped off a miniature Yankees uniform for him. When I told my wife who it was from and how I knew the guy, she gave it to Goodwill, but it was a nice gesture."

"Well, I'm kind of liking him for an assault."

"Who, Freddy?" Howell clasped his hands across his gut, made a face. "I don't see it."

"What do you mean, you don't see it? He was charged with murder."

"That was no-billed." Howell held up that finger again.

"But he did it, right?"

"Whoa, hang on hang on, you want to know how that went down? Because I can tell you."

"Sure." Nerese shrugged, suppressing her dislike for cops who so eagerly rushed to protect the good names of their street connections.

"OK." Kenny briskly rubbed his hands. "Each residential pod in County's got its own mini-gym, right? Like a twenty-by-twenty workout cage? Freddy's in there, working the speed bags, some three-hundred-pound tattooed numb-nuts comes in has it in his head that Freddy did him some dirt, on the inside, out in the world, who knows, comes at him with a sharpened toothbrush, OK? Now, like I said, the room's a twenty-by-twenty cage. There's a guard posted on the outside, but he's forbidden to enter that space without backup. So, Slobbo goes after Freddy, Freddy's dancing away best he can, screaming for the guard, who finally removes the thumb from his ass and hits the panic button, which, once again is all he *can* do. Meanwhile, the guy finally corners Freddy, takes a swipe and opens his forehead like a tin can, at which point, Freddy just straight-out wigs, and by the time the response team shows up, which was maybe all of ninety seconds later? That big tub of shit is laying there with his toothbrush in his heart, and Freddy's back to working the speed bag again like nothing happened except you can't see his face for the blood coming down plus he's hyperventilating. And when they go to grab him? He starts freaking again and blind as a bat, runs face first into the edge of a barbell, breaks his own nose, knocks himself unconscious and spends the next three days in the psych unit. Overall, not what you'd call a cold-blooded killer, you know what I'm saying?"

"Well, I didn't ask anything about him being cold-blooded," Nerese said, trying to fend off the image of Freddy as a buck-wild berserker. "I'm just liking him for this assault and I wanted to know if you thought . . ."

"If it was in his general nature?" Kenny shrugged disparagingly. "I believe that thing in jail was a one-time-only situation. I mean, hey, who can say for sure, but . . ." He threw her another uninspired look, then inched forward across his desk. "I mean, it's up to you, but do you want to throw me the specifics of the situation? Maybe I can . . ."

"Nah, that's okay." Nerese sensed that not only wouldn't Howell give her anything to work with here if it meant putting one of his primo informants in some kind of jackpot, but he might even go so far as to give Freddy a heads-up.

"I'm just curious," Nerese said, slipping this in as she made a show of gathering up her things. "Do you know anything about his domestic situation?"

"His home life?" Another shrug. "All I know is what I need to know to do my job, you know?"

"OK, then." Nerese was about to rise, get some fresh air, but was distracted by another narcotics lieutenant—Billy Herman, steroid-puffed chest, salt-and-pepper ponytail and a face like a frying pan—marching into the office with some sorry-ass-looking street kid in cuffs, Billy steering him with a hand at the back of his neck, planting him in a chair facing Nerese and Howell.

"Kenny, check this out," ignoring Nerese as he turned to his grab. "Tell him your name."

"Aw, c'mon, man." The kid winced, looked away.

"*Hey.*" Billy towered over him, hands on hips.

"Michael Jackson," the kid muttered.

"Michael Jackson," Billy marveled.

Howell made a token noise of amusement; not really—much to his credit, Nerese thought—into the usual niggers-as-God's-clowns school of cop humor.

"Say it again."

"Michael Jackson." The kid looked away, then added, "They din't ast me when I was born, they just gave it to me."

"Michael Jackson," Billy said. "Live and in cuffs."

Nerese had a history with this prick Herman. She began to leave again.

"Hey, Nerese." Billy smiled. "I didn't even see you there. You meet Michael Jackson?"

"She's asking about Freddy Martinez," Howell said so blandly that to Nerese's ears it was insulting in its blatant effort to talk around and through her.

"Oh yeah?" Billy gave her a long look. "How's your brother Butchie doing? I heard he came down with the Package."

"Well, you heard wrong," Nerese controlling her temper, not wanting to put on a show in front of this kid in cuffs.

"Then I must've heard it about Antoine. Is it Antoine?"

Nerese just glared at him, unable to lie. A mug of hot coffee sat on the edge of Howell's desk, steam rising in lazy intertwining swirls.

"So how's he holding up?" Billy pushing it.

"Not so good," Nerese answered flatly.

"I'm sorry to hear that. He wasn't a bad guy."

"He's still alive," Nerese said, trying to lock eyes with him; Billy Herman was having a good day, though, immune to any *malocchio.*

"Well you tell him he's in my thoughts, OK?" he said, then gave her his back.

Livid, Nerese rose to her feet. She wasn't even aware that Kenny Howell's coffee mug was in her hand until she felt the heat coming through.

She carefully, casually returned the mug to its ring of condensation on the edge of the desk.

"Thank you for your time, fellas," she said dryly, then headed for the door.

"Hey, Nerese?" Howell turned her around. "You know, like I said, Freddy, he's smart," taking another bite of his sandwich. "Maybe you got something for us?"

White Tom Potenza stood waiting for Nerese on the stoop of his building, a five-story walk-up wedged between the Dodi-Diana Smoke Shop and the Ship of Zion daycare center on Tonawanda Avenue.

He stood there rickety-legged, leaning into his cane, face hidden behind large impenetrable shades and a push-broom mustache.

Having been born on the same day and in the same housing project as each other, Nerese had known White Tom all her life; had known him when, before the Great White Exodus from Hopewell, his name had simply been Tom.

As she stepped to the curb, White Tom said what he always said when greeting her—"Officer Nerese, keepin' the peace"—then ceremoniously opened his arms, his cane held aloft like a baton.

Embracing him always gave her the creeps, his torso feeling somehow both bloated and insubstantial; she likened it to hugging a large trash bag filled with dry leaves.

"Come up."

He pulled a rickety about-face and entered the tiled vestibule, Nerese following behind as he began briskly one-stepping his way up three flights of cracked marble stairs.

Although part of her was dying to take a run at Freddy—today, right now, this minute—she willed herself to do it right, which meant slowly, patiently continuing to work from the outer rings on in. And no one and nothing in Dempsy—no human, no filing system, no data bank—had the between-the-lines lowdown on so many shady-side individuals as White Tom Potenza.

Sober now for over a decade, he had become over the years something of a local phenomenon, a great and driven fisher of men who, despite multiple health problems, ran his own N.A. and A.A. meetings; and working for a cop who owned a chain of federally funded methadone clinics, tirelessly prowled his old haunts, cajoling and conning his surviving running buddies and the younger generation of lost souls to come in for HIV tests, free counseling and a three-week methadone maintenance program.

He was HIV-negative himself, had been tested twice a year for the last ten years with that result, but pulling a perverse reverse denial on himself, steadfastly refused to believe that his days weren't numbered.

"So who's on the menu today," he asked, shouldering open his apartment door, then, once Nerese was inside, pushing it shut with his cane.

"Don't you lock that?"

"Why? Anybody breaking in here's got to face Arletta." Then, "Honey, I'm home," calling out to a faint rustling at the back of the railroad flat.

The apartment was tilted, the rake not quite as high as a pitcher's mound, but a round object placed motionless on the north side of a room would definitely roll across the linoleum until it hit the south wall.

Tom steered her into the small, flaking front parlor and gestured toward the plastic-sheathed couch directly beneath a roughly concentric set of tobacco-tinted water stains on the ceiling. Despite his necrotic hip, White Tom remained on his feet, the man so chronically antsy and tense he couldn't even take a seat in his own home.

The wall hangings in here consisted of a laminated meditation on Christ's bleeding hands, an ornately framed eight-by-ten wedding picture of White Tom and his black wife, Arletta, two smaller studio-shot portraits of their three-year-old twins, Eric Sosa and Maceo McGwire Potenza, and a simple reed crucifix pushpinned into the wall over the TV, the frayed unadorned thatch giving it a crude power that moved Nerese every time she saw it.

"Who we talking about today, kid?"

"Freddy Martinez."

"Freddy Martinez. He's in County, right?"

"Just got out," Nerese said.

"Just got out."

White Tom took off his shades to briefly rub his eyes, which were pale, piggy and dazed: a blind man's eyes, set back in sockets as deep as teacups.

This wreck, this gimp, had been the only kid tough enough, athletic enough, to ever kick her brother Antoine's ass in all the years that her family had lived in Hopewell; kicked his ass good, then gestured to the encircling Brothers that day on the handball courts of Big Playground, a little beckoning waver of his fingers—Who's next—no one taking him up on it, either.

Nerese looked away until the shades were back on.

"What about Freddy Martinez," Tom asked.

"What's his story . . ."

"Freddy? Mid-level dealer. Sells to guys who sell to guys. Probably ratting out some Colombian or other to County in order to avoid any kind of serious time. Just like every other jibone out there."

"What else . . ."

"What else?"

She waited.

"What else like what, criminal activity or just human interest?"

"Whatever."

"Personally, I like him," White Tom said. "Intelligent, well-spoke, never touches the stuff himself. Says, 'It's not like I'm selling Marlboros or malt liquor. Those are the *real* killers.' You know the type, right?"

"Yup."

"But I'll tell you, when the twins were born? He came by and dropped off two baby-sized Minnesota Twins uniforms, had their names already sewn in back—a very thoughtful gesture. Required some imagination, too. You know, the twins and the Twins."

"Kenny Howell over at Narcotics? When *his* kid was born, he got the Yankees." Nerese fucking with him a little.

"Up your ass with the Yankees." White Tom waved her off. "I live in *Dempsy* yo, home of the underdog."

"Well then, go Freddy."

"No, well look, all I'm saying is . . . Well, fuck it." Tom shrugged. "Bottom line is, at the end of the day? He's still one of the bad guys. You know, the 'good German.' Still wears the death's head, right?"

"Uh-huh," Nerese said, staring at the stark, undeniable crucifix.

"You want something to drink?" Tom shifted from side to side. "I want something to drink."

Nerese got up and followed him into the kitchen.

He opened the refrigerator to reveal a synthetic bouquet of knockoff-brand sodas: orange, grape, lemon-lime, root beer.

Despite the last ten years of sobriety, White Tom retained many of his junk-head proclivities: the sweet tooth for candy bars, glazed doughnuts, sodas, sugar-laden coffee and more coffee—vats of it. He couldn't pass a pay phone without flicking the coin return, still stopped dead in his tracks at the sight of salvageable debris—rubber, copper, iron, aluminum—all of it cash on the hoof at a scrap yard. He assembled the day's paper out of cast-off sections in diners and coffee shops, and he still walked around with a set of works, although these days they were for shooting insulin, not scag.

Preceded by the dry-whisk shuffle of flip-flops on linoleum, Arletta entered the kitchen wearing a poncholike housedress, a heavy gold crucifix nesting in the bony hollow at the base of her throat.

"Lettie, you remember Nerese, right?"

Arletta nodded without changing her expression, took one of the sodas and retreated back down the hallway.

Nerese had never cottoned to that woman. An ex-junkie like her husband, these days she worked at the Armstrong Houses Homework Club, aka the youth center. She was a well-respected figure in the life of the projects, known for a program she had started there designed to combat juvenile nihilism with manners. She believed in salvation through the practice of common courtesy, through ritualized consideration of others. Nerese was all for anything of a positive nature, but the woman was a humorless pill; had the grim-lipped visage and burning eye of the A.A./ N.A. proselytizer. Plus, it was hard to forget Arletta from the brief time when Nerese had worked vice and Tom's future wife had been out there all night in front of the abandoned section of the Dempsy Medical Center wearing nothing but shorty pajamas, platform shoes and a copper wig, the part in which slowly revolved like a nocturnal sundial hour after hour as she made her way in and out of the backseats of cars.

In those days, Arletta had weighed maybe a hundred pounds, but she was easily double that now, more in danger of a heart attack than any kind of sexually transmitted disease.

Nerese knew that she was being hard on a soul who had basically clawed her way up from degradation and oblivion to some kind of purposeful life, but she just didn't like the bitch and that was that.

White Tom and Arletta: ebony and ivory; dope, in Nerese's experience, the Great Equalizer, the only thing that truly brought people together across the color divide. And she was far from alone in her thinking on this.

She knew, for example, that Port Authority cops set up on the Jersey side of the Lincoln Tunnel, if desperate or bored enough, would always stop a car coming through from New York if the occupants were males of different races—reasoning that the only motive a white man and a black man would have to cross a state line together was to score. It would always be a two-bit bust, users not dealers, but the cops would be on the money just enough times to justify the perpetuation of this policy.

Ebony and ivory; even White Tom and her brother Antoine got thick as thieves around dope about six months after the big fight.

"So what's up with Freddy that you're asking?" Tom said, then, before she could formulate a deflecting answer: "Oh. You know his brother-in-law Reggie? Reggie Powell? He OD'd a few weeks back, or so they say. I personally think he was given a hot shot, but I heard his people were having trouble coming up with the scratch to bury him and this Hopewell guy from the heyday threw his mother a check for thirty-five hundred zorts to get him in the ground. What was the guy's name?" Tom rapped his cane on the floor. "Roy. Roy. *Ray.* No, yeah. Ray. Ray."

"Ray Mitchell," Nerese said, then instantly regretted it.

"Ray Mitchell? Yeah, I don't remember him."

"He was a few years older than us."

"That was a good deed, though, right? But now wait. I heard that that guy took a real beating. He's in a coma or something?"

"Not quite that bad."

Tom looked at her; click, click, click. "Oh."

"I'm just exploring things."

"But why would Freddy . . ."

"I'm just exploring."

"Unless he was banging Freddy's wife or something."

Caught off guard, Nerese hesitated half a beat.

"No," Tom said. "Get the fuck out of here. Are you shitting me?"

At first Nerese balked, but then thinking, In for a penny . . .

"Do you know her?"

"Freddy's wife?" He shrugged. "She's got to be a straight shooter because I don't even know her name. Sorry."

"You think he's the type who'd go after somebody like that?"

"Freddy?" White Tom humped his shoulders. "Who's to say."

"How about that guy he stabbed in County?"

"That was kill or be killed."

"Guy just came at him out of the blue?"

"Out of the blue, huh?" His face narrowed with knowledge. "Where'd you hear that?"

"Kenny Howell." Nerese already feeling like a sap. "You know something I should know too?"

"Let's just leave it at 'kill or be killed.' That part's true."

"C'mon, what . . ."

White Tom looked away, Nerese knowing from past experience that once he had made the decision to shut down a line of inquiry it was a waste of time to push him.

"Who'd you hear about the money from?" she asked, working the other angle.

"Who'd I *hear* it from? Around here, are you kidding me? He might as well have given it to her live on pay-per-view. Forget about it."

"But if you're looking hard at Freddy for this, he's not a thief per se," Tom said, back to propping himself up against the living room wall.

"I'm just exploring things."

"It could be that this guy Ray stepped in and paid for the funeral before Freddy could get a chance to do the same. You know, it not even being his family, like a pride thing for Freddy, but no. I don't . . . Scratch that, scratch that. I like the fucking-his-wife approach."

Nerese nodded noncommittally, White Tom not really having anything for her on this.

"OK then." She began to rise from the couch.

"But that was amazing of him to do something like that, right?" he said softly, speaking more to himself than to Nerese. "That's a good guy. Ray Mitchell . . . *Wait.*" He snapped out of his musings. "He lived in Six Building. Played handball all the time. Good-looking mother. I remember his mother, too. Yeah, OK. A handball player. Ray. He's older than us, yeah?"

"That's what I said." Nerese not sure whether to unpack or not.

"Now he's an actor, right? Something?"

"A writer."

"A writer. *I* should be a writer, the fucking story and a half I got to tell. So you know him, huh?"

"A bit."

"Well, I'll tell you. I got something in the works now, I can't go into details, but . . ." White Tom shifted his weight to take the pressure off his dead hip. "I would very much like it if you could arrange some kind of sit down for me to talk to this guy."

Nerese just stared.

"Neesy, people like him, it makes them feel good to help people like me." Then: "Just think about it, OK?"

Chapter 14 >

Hospital — February 17

Armed with the Freddy Martinez mug shot, Nerese entered the monitored-care ward and once again felt the fist clutch the back of her blouse and yank. Ray was lying there today as if awaiting his embalmers, his head wrapped in pristine cotton, eyes shut, mouth agape, spaghetti-thin nasogastric tubing running into one taped-down nostril.

"We had to drill," the neurologist said, sidling up to Nerese, arms crossed over his chest. "The bleed was starting to fill the cranial cavity, put pressure on the brain, so we needed to open her up, clip the site and evacuate the buildup. But when we got in? There was nothing to do . . . The site had closed on its own and the bleed had drained itself off into the vault. I mean, better safe than sorry, but as it turned out he needed the procedure like a hole in the head."

"When's he going to be good to talk?"

"To *talk*? To actually talk, I'm not sure. To come around, I'd say tonight? Tomorrow?"

"And he's going to get good?"

"Should. I don't know what kind of residual damage we're talking about here."

"Damage . . ."

"Physical, verbal, memory. It's the brain. It's like the futures market, up, down, you're busted, you're flush, you're busted all over again and it's not even time for lunch." He cocked his head and squinted at Freddy Martinez. "That the guy?"

"Maybe. You know if anybody's been in to visit him the last day or two?"

"Like the actor coming back to admire his handiwork?"

"Just anybody."

"You have to ask the nurses. I'm like the Road Runner around here, you know, *Meep-meep.*"

"OK."

Nerese stood at the foot of the bed and watched Ray breathe, his lips parched and peeled, his chest almost imperceptibly rising and falling beneath the smock.

There was a very good chance that they had left his skull open to allow for easier access in case there was another buildup in fluid. Nerese momentarily wondered where they would keep the disc of removed bone until the time they saw fit to permanently plug the hole.

Her business was done here for the day, her next stop in the tour a sit-down with Carla Powell—Danielle's mother, Freddy's mother-in-law; then, after Carla, Danielle; after Danielle, the birthday boy himself, Freddy Martinez, that sit-down resulting in payback, vindication and a one-way trip to the Sunshine State. But the sight of Ray in his present state kept her rooted to the spot, leached her of all confidence, all purpose. Abruptly seized by a notion that if she were to let him out of her sight right now, if she were to leave his bedside, he would never regain consciousness, never live to see her bring it home for him, she wound up taking a seat. After a few interminable minutes of stilted silence, of simply sitting there watching Ray suspended in his own ether, she began to talk to him.

"You know," Nerese murmured self-consciously, leaning in close, "I've been thinking about how pissed off I am at everybody these days, bitching about this that and the other, and I kind of concluded that that's pretty much symptomatic of pre-retirement around here in general. Because, if I think about it? If I think back, I can't ever remember *one* cop, no matter how much they loved the Job, who didn't leave bitter, leave pissed off at the department, you know, just like me."

Like the last man on earth still reflexively obeying traffic lights, Nerese found herself pausing, waiting for a response.

"But the thing is? I *love* being a cop. Even with all the bullshit, the politics, the pettiness, the racial shit—I mean, hey, after twenty years I got enough chips on my shoulder to build a fucking tree house—I love it, and, I don't want to retire. I mean what can I *possibly* get into out there that's got half the juice of what I'm doing now, you know what I'm saying?

"Greatest show on earth. You said it yourself. Run *to* trouble instead of away from it. Nothing like it in the world."

A nurse came in to check Ray's IV. Nerese leaned back, her face half-turned, until the woman was finished. She then leaned forward again, elbows on knees, her voice now directed to the space between her feet.

"That being said, I *did* run into this one fucking asshole yesterday over at County Narcotics?" Nerese's teeth locked at a slant. "I mean what kind of hypocrisy is it that a guy taking anabolic steroids by the fistful can bust some bonehead street kid's got thirty dollars' worth of weed in his sock. Where's the justice in that? I mean, we all have our demons, we all do shit that's fucked up or abusive or bad judgment or whatever, but this guy, Billy Herman? I had a run-in with him about three years ago, or actually the problem is, I *didn't* have a run-in, *should* have had a run-in with him about three years ago . . . I mean, shit, man, seeing him again?"

Nerese leaned back, covered her mouth with an arched hand—what the hell was she doing?—then shrugged. Fuck it. She had never been able to get this one out.

"See, three years ago I got put on loan to County Narcotics, the city and county tend to move us around like checkers. So, you know, first they check to see if Butchie and Antoine are locked up, which they were at the time, and I temporarily go over to County for a series of summertime raids.

"And, OK, it's going, it's going, until finally this one night? It's August, hot night, we hit this apartment in Armstrong, supposed to be a full-blown crack factory in there."

Nerese tilted forward, her voice once again furtively directed to the floor.

"OK, so, everybody, we're all vested up, hearts pumping, guns out, we go through the door, like boom . . .

"What's in there? Six scagged-out junkies, pipes, needles, triple-beam scales, all kinds of paraphernalia but *no* dope. A handful of bullets but *no* gun. It's like ninety-nine degrees, we're all wearing those heavy Kevlar vests but there's *no* air-conditioning, *no* fan. And because it's a ground-floor apartment we have to keep the windows shut and locked, not that anybody there was even physically capable of trying to escape . . . OK, so, we spend the better part of an hour tearing up this hot, greasy, stinky four-room roach palace, got these six skeletons sitting on the sofa all cuffed together, gonna be back on the street before we finish the fucking paper-work . . .

"And the thing is, given that the apartment is on the ground floor? Over the course of that hour, this crowd of tenants starts to collect right outside the windows. We pull down the shades, but you can hear them laughing at us . . . I mean, hey, it happens. You win some, you lose some. I mean, we're all pissed off, fed-up, embarrassed. It goes with the territory.

"Anyways, we can't stay in there forever and when we leave, we know we're going to have to walk through that crowd to the van.

"So we do. And what happens is what usually happens. The seas part, the assholes in the back rows start woofing you out, you bite the bullet and you split.

"Except, except this Billy, Billy Herman . . . I'm walking next to him as we come out of the building and, as we start walking the gauntlet? I see Billy, you know, pissed off like the rest of us, I see Billy look at this black kid maybe all of sixteen, seventeen years old, pregnant out to here . . . Billy, as he goes by her, he looks her in the eye, then looks at her big belly, and all he does, is shake his head and hiss a little, you know, like when you're disgusted with something? Looked at her unborn child and shook his motherfucking head like, 'Great. Here comes another one.'

"Now, he didn't *say* anything to her, barely made *eye* contact, but when he shook his head and made that hissing sound? That young girl reacted like he had just kicked her in the belly, like he had just punched her in the face. I mean she actually staggered back like he had *hit* her. Can you picture what I'm saying?

"He just condemned that unborn child. He just judged and juried it in a split second but you know, I mean really, he didn't do, you know, technically speaking, he didn't do or even say a thing.

"And what can that girl say—'That cop just gave my stomach a dirty look'?

"But I tell you, Ray, in a world full of shit? It was one of the worst things I ever saw, the look on that pregnant child's face . . .

"And to this *day* I'm mad at myself for not calling him out, but the same with me. What could I have said, 'Why'd you give that kid's belly a dirty look?' He would've looked at me like I was crazy. I doubt he even knew that he did it, you know what I'm saying? I mean really, what could I have said?"

To cover her self-consciousness, Nerese began rooting around in her purse but after a moment of this mindless activity, when Ray abruptly breached the void by croaking "More," she shot to her feet, tissues and tubes flying off her lap.

But the word had come from deep within the black pool, Ray following it up with a dream-gabble of language, a flock of nonsense, before once again subsiding into silence.

Numb, embarrassed, Nerese suddenly saw herself as if from across the room, ladling out her grief to an insensate presence with a hole in its head the size of a silver dollar, and she just fell through the earth.

As self-congratulatory as she had been the day before, during her walkabout in Hopewell, regarding the state of her life—her achievements, her responsibilities, her career; as euphoric as she had been, envisioning the beauty of going out on a last solve rooted in personal history, in the repayment of a childhood debt; sitting now at Ray's bedside, her own ludicrously furtive monologue still resonating in her ears, she began to see everything through a violently opposite lens. The people she was so proud to support were, in fact, a grim assortment of the diseased, the deranged, the addicted and the criminal; the mortgage-free house a soggy rat-trap that she couldn't wait to flee; her son as mewling and unformed as a newborn; and her career—twenty wounding years of little or no respect from her peers, of being regarded as a cosmetic statistic, an outsider, a nonplayer and a malcontent—forgotten but not gone.

Twenty wounding years . . .

But rather than provoking her to walk out in despair on Ray and his stonewalling ways, as she studied his assault-marbled face, his gapemouthed exhalations, she now felt desperate to work this last case successfully, desperate for the potential of grace offered by this last clearance.

In fact, as she sat there, fighting down the impulse to shake him awake, rattle whatever brains he had left into a state of pliable alertness, she came to recognize that if for any reason she should be denied this last professional satisfaction now that she had come to fully appreciate its soulsoothing promise, it would elevate the pain of her impending retirement from run-of-the-mill bitter to near-unbearable.

Eager to roll, Nerese took Freddy Martinez's mug shot and wedged it under the base of Ruby's Weeping Monk on the corner of Ray's night table.

Then, wheeling for the exit, she nearly collided with a slender young black man who had materialized at the foot of the bed. The kid's instinctual reaction to her was to immediately backstep the hell out.

"Yo, sorry . . ." He made it to the nurses' station.

"Whoa! Whoa!" Nerese automatically reverted to cop tone, pointing a finger at him—Do not move—the kid, apparently with equal experience and instinct, showing his hands but otherwise doing as he was told. "In here," beckoning him back to the bedside.

"How you doin' today." He smiled easily although he continued to play statue from the waist up.

" 'What's Mine Is Mine,' " she said without thinking.

"What?" The kid blinked, then: "Yeah," his smile broadening. "How'd you know that. Did Ray show you my stuff?"

He tentatively eased out of the freeze, face still unclouded. "I'm Salim." Offering his hand, fine-boned, like the wing of a bird. "How you doin'," he repeated, that smile of his staying put.

"Had days better," she said cautiously, still sizing him up.

He was tall but rail-thin, the suggestion of physical frailness underscored by high cheekbones, pronounced orbital sockets and a carefully groomed pencil-line mustache.

And he was natty, too: spotless Mets jersey, baggy jeans and near-mint powder-blue Timberland boots.

"Can I see Ray?"

"He's out," she said, blocking his access to the bedside.

"*Out*. Out where?"

"Unconscious," Nerese looking straight into his face. "They had to drill a burr-hole in his skull to drain the excess blood that was pushing in on his brain," watching the eyes.

"Oh, shit." Salim reared back, wincing in honest disgust.

"How do you know him again?"

"He's my teacher," he said, this grown man stating it in the present tense, then finished with her, slipping around to the head of the bed. Nerese flared at the dismissal.

"Oh *shit*," he hissed, hovering over Ray's gauze-wrapped dome. "You can see right *in* there."

"Come away now," Nerese commanded, thinking, Finished with *me*?

< Chapter 15

Salim — January 18

"I wasn't even *doing* nothing, just hanging with my boys when the shots went off.

"Somebody said 'you bleedin', I didn't even feel it and now I'm down here, don't have no one to talk to, no TV, no phone, no Z100, and this is like for*ever* . . . I didn't deserve this."

"Good." Ray nodded at Jamaal. "Any comments?"

The challenge had been to create voices for the Dempsy River Anthology—the dead of the city looking back from the solitude of the grave on lives spent/misspent.

The idea had come from Myra's having mentioned that she was reading *Spoon River Anthology* a few classes back, although he was very careful not to point that out when he announced the assignment—not that she wouldn't know where he was coming from with this.

"Comments?"

"Z100?" Rashaad reared back. "That's *white*-boy music."

As one, the class turned to check out Ray's reaction. Bondo was out sick.

"I do believe my daughter listens to Hot 97, blazin' hip-hop and R'n'B," he said, the kids grinning with surprise that he even knew of that station's existence.

"Yeah," Rashaad said. "See, that's what *I'd* listen to down there."

Altagracia started waving as if she were trying to flag down a lifeguard.

"Go," Ray said.

"Yeah, OK." Clearing her throat. "And nobody say nothing till I'm finished."

"Just go."

"OK." Then,

> "Man, I *knew* I shouldn't have gone in on that business. The thing looked shaky from the door but the money was large.
>
> "My mother always tried to set me straight but I never listened to nobody, not even her, and so now I'm down here with nothing to do for forever except think about how stupid I was.

"And that's it," she said looking up.

All four of the stories read so far, if stories were what you could call these bite-sized epitaphs, had equated being dead with being bored—being buried with being sent to your room with the added hitch of an eternal power outage, no TV, phones, boom box, just you and the four walls until the cows came home.

"Comments?"

"And not stupid ones," Altagracia said.

He had pretty much given up on the idea of the class getting any kind of real criticism; it was enough that they were writing.

"No comments?"

"I liked it," Felicia said, the girl as usual trying to turtle down below her starched collar.

"OK," he began, then faltered as the door to the teacher's lounge opened and a young black man of indeterminate age quietly slipped into the room. Gliding along one of the walls, he sat himself down behind the big scuffed desk that stood catercorner beneath the windows.

Ray didn't know who he was, a student most likely, but maybe a little older. He decided to let him be.

"Efram."

"Yeah, OK." The chubby Latin kid did an Art Carney, extending his arms, twirling his wrists, official class wisenheimer; the other kids already half-grinning, bracing for his latest stylings.

> "Even as a corpse I look good. Just a little hole where the
> bullet went in.
> "There's a real cute girl in Row 6, Plot 9."

And the howling began. Efram looking up. "Man, how come nobody ever lets me finish?" pleased with himself.

"All right, all right, calm down."

"Yeah, please." Efram shot his cuffs. "Control yourselves."

The newcomer took out a small notebook and started sketching, his eyes flicking rhythmically between his handiwork and the seminar table.

"OK." Efram cleared his throat. "As I was saying,

> "There's a real cute girl in Row 6, Plot 9. She's already
> sent me like a dozen dead-o-grams, but I'm still considering
> my options because I heard there's an even cuter girl gonna
> be buried tomorrow in Row 8, Plot 4, and since two-timing
> my women is how I got laid out down here to begin with, I
> better stick to one corpse at a time.

"The—the—that's all, folks!"

Ray let the kids cut loose. After only three classes, he had already worked out a natural batting order; the four other kids first, then Efram for comic relief and then, for the grand finale, Myra.

The class was working in ways that had nothing to do with school as school—it was more like a goodwill free-for-all, the readings themselves like short toasts at the end of a banquet.

"OK. OK," Ray said, intending to gesture for Myra to bring out the big guns, but instead found himself turning in his chair to check out the visitor again; the kid still quietly sketching.

He met Ray's eye with an amused, oddly intimate smirk.

"Myra?" Ray called out distractedly, still turned to the kid; something . . . "Myra, go ahead . . ."

"Uh-oh, here we go," Rashaad clowned, getting shooshed by everyone.

Modest in her power, Myra kept her eyes downcast, fussing with her notebook, then for the third week in a row began to read in a near inaudible murmur.

"Start again," Ray said gently.

"This is called 'Dead Man Talking,'" Myra said, then coughed into the side of her fist.

"As a famous actor I created desire and excitement everywhere I went. However, no one knew how miserable and alone I really was. Everybody around me wanted something but had little or nothing to offer in return.

"Then one day I was walking in the neighborhood of my youth, and I was reminded of how happy I used to be living here before I became a celebrity.

"I decided right then and there to escape my present life for a little while, go up to my old apartment where my mother still lived and move back in until I felt better. My mother was overjoyed, and I returned to my old bedroom.

"There was only one problem. When I looked out the window I saw not the world of today but of twenty years ago. All my childhood friends were downstairs again, hanging out on our old bench, even though I knew in reality that most of them had gone on to die of drugs or gang-related violence. They were looking up at me smilingly and silently waving for me to come down and join them just like when we were all kids.

"The next thing I knew, I was on the floor of my bedroom, unconscious.

"My mother called a doctor who said I had a bad heart.

"For seven days I lived in my old bedroom hiding from the cold uncaring world, and each day I looked out the window and saw only my childhood friends on the bench, beckoning for me to join them. And each time I woke up on the floor of my bedroom unconscious.

"On the eighth day, when I looked out the window to see their beckoning waves I decided enough was enough and I called out that I'd be right down.

"They said I died of a heart attack that day and buried me

with much fanfare. But it's only my shell that you will find here six feet under. For the rest of me, look out that window and if you're lucky, me and the boys will gladly ask you to join us on the old bench of our carefree youth. The end."

Myra closed her book and coughed into her fist again.

"That's a for-real story," Efram said soberly.

"How do you come *up* with that." Altagracia winced.

Myra shrugged, fought down a smile, spoke in her tiny voice. "It's just in my mind."

"The mind of Minolta," Rashaad announced.

Ray sat there moved by the sentiment and impressed with the kid's ability to bring the story to completion the way she did, but except for a terse "Very good," as if he were commenting on a single-malt Scotch, he held himself in check.

The class-ending *boop* came over the PA, everyone rising except for Ray, intent on not gassing up Myra's head anymore—not even a low-five at the door.

Instead, he turned to watch the quiet visitor uncurl himself from behind the big desk, the sketch that he had been working on now tucked between elbow and ribs. Even from across the room Ray could see it was something extraordinary; something deeply detailed, and despite the use of a ballpoint pen, subtly shaded.

As the visitor made his way around the desk and over to the long seminar table, Ray quickly got to his feet to maintain a sense of psychic balance.

The kid was tall but bird-boned, the delicacy of his frame underscored by a carefully tended razor-thin mustache.

Face-to-face now, he fixed Ray with that same teasing gleam and waited.

"Can I help you?" Ray said awkwardly. "Are you in, you're not in the class, are you?"

"Not really," he drawled, shiny-eyed, holding something back; something delicious.

Ray got a closer look at the artwork—a drawing of a stubby, guttering candle, a moth with a minute human face hovering precariously close to the flame.

Something about it spoke to Ray of jail, and off-balance, the words were out of his mouth before he could check himself. "Were you in the joint or something?"

"The 'joint'?" the kid said with gentle mockery, ducking his head to make better eye contact.

"No offense. I just meant . . ."

"Mr. Mitchell, you don't remember me?"

Ray looked at him for the first time, really looked. "Coley?"

"There you go," his eyes dancing.

"Jesus, Coley . . ." He couldn't remember the kid's last name, Coley a member of that notorious English class of his that had ducked out on Shakespeare in the Park nearly a decade ago.

"Except now it's Salim."

"Salim."

The kid had to be close to thirty years old.

"And yeah, I was incarcerated," he said soberly. "This is my hundredth day back out."

"OK." Ray nodded, not knowing what to say. "So how's it going?"

"You know, I'm trying to maintain. Get out from under all the negativity, you know? So how *you* doing, Mr. Mitchell?"

The question, sweetly put, nonetheless made Ray uncomfortable. He always preferred to be the asker.

"I have a daughter," he answered reflexively, Ruby his ace in the hole these days.

"Oh yeah?" Salim/Coley said, reaching for his wallet and pulling out a photo of a toddler, ash-gray eyes and niblet teeth. "That's my son. That's Omar. He's two and a half now."

Ray felt himself go puttylike with goodwill.

"I don't have any pictures of my daughter."

"That's OK." Salim beamed. "I see her in your eyes."

"Really." Ray winced, then noticed that the kid had a paperback in his hand, something entitled *Where Is God, When* . . .; and automatically began compiling a reading list for him. "So you just came by?"

"Yeah—well, no. Felicia Stevenson, in your class? She's my stepfather's niece and she was talking you up in the house last night, you know, how you were all positive with her writing and that made me remember how you . . . You know, you remember the day you took me to that art school over in New York?"

"School of Visual Arts. Sure," Ray said carefully.

"Yeah. You had hope in me back then, and that was important so I just, you know, I just wanted to come by and say hello."

In his last year of teaching, when Coley was technically still on the books but pretty much a full-blown dropout, showing up in class once a week if that, Ray had taken it upon himself to reach out to a college friend of his who was an art director at Young & Rubicam to arrange for the kid to get a tour of the agency, see artists getting paid.

This friend of Ray's took one look at Coley's untutored portfolio, gave him a long speech about how talent without training gets you nowhere, dropped a few hundred dollars' worth of pens and markers and manuals in a shopping bag for him, scribbled out a letter of introduction to one of the deans at the School of Visual Arts twenty blocks south and set up an admissions interview on the phone before Coley and Ray had even hit the elevator banks.

Out on the street they had parted ways, Ray heading uptown, Coley, his letter and his goodie bag allegedly heading downtown to a new life. But he never quite got there; he claimed later that night on the phone that the shopping bag was too heavy, so he hopped a subway at Grand Central and went back home to the Bronx.

Ray had been furious with him for the rest of the term; in fact, it wasn't until years later, when he was coked up driving a cab and had occasion one day to drop off a few SVA students in front of the school, that he realized with belated clarity that the problem wasn't Coley being an ungrateful shortsighted jerk that day—it was just that it had all been too much for him; too much, too soon, and the kid, most likely unbeknownst to himself, had simply freaked.

"You still live in the Bronx?"

"Nah. Not for a while. Like, right after I had gotten finished with high school? My mother married this guy from around here, so we moved."

"You still drawing?" Ray nodded to the candle and the moth.

"Yeah. Like this, though." Salim shrugged.

"You working?"

"Yeah, well no, not like an employee per se. However, I'm working *on* something. I got this idea for a nonprofit organization to help inmates return to so-called society? I call it LIFE—Living in Fear of Extinction. I want to set up a whole reentry program, you know, literacy, computer literacy, how to fill out résumés, how to communicate, how to be prompt, how to be inspirational, how to make eye contact. See right now, I'm at the research stage, I need to learn how to file an application for tax-exempt status, how to find sponsors, how to—"

"Anything else?" Ray unable to hear this shit.

"Other? Well, yeah, I had this T-shirt thing goin' on, you know, bought shirts in bulk, designed my own logo, hooked up with this printer did the silk-screening on a delayed payment schedule but that's all on financial hold for the time being, and I was also working on a comic book I wanted to publish, called *Dawgs of War,* about the future, when America wages war on the Republic of Nubia and it was gonna focus on one platoon of guys from the hood, how they get educated over there, you know, come to understand that they're fighting . . . you know, that they're on the wrong side, you know what I'm—"

"Do you want to grab something to eat?" Ray cut him off again, offering the meal half out of curiosity, and half just to shut him up.

The school was surrounded by fast-food outlets, diners and burger taverns but Ray drove Salim over to Jersey City, to a small café reclaimed from the shell of an old Chinese laundry on a regentrified street of brownstones.

"Yeah, this is nice," Salim said, his gaze slick with pleasure.

The room was small and dark with a pressed-tin ceiling painted chocolate brown, a framed movie poster for Cocteau's *La Belle et la Bête* on one wall, and Ingrid Bergman's *Joan of Arc* on another. A refrigerated display case featured three small cakes and an array of petite tarts. They were the only customers.

When the sole waitress came to the table, Salim threw her a terrific smile. "How you doing?" he said. "You having a good day?"

"So far."

"Yeah? Me too," Salim said. "I'll have the, what's . . . Is there any meat in the Asian salad?"

"Chicken."

"Yeah, no, I don't eat meat. Can I have it without the chicken?"

"How about I just bring you a garden salad."

"OK. Yeah. And is there any caffeine in the raspberry tea?"

"Nope."

"Yeah, OK, good. I'll have that too."

Ray studied Salim. He looked thin but healthy, almost untouched by the years.

"I'll have the same," Ray said, too keyed on the kid to put any thought into food.

When the waitress turned away with the orders, Salim fired up a New-port, and she pulled a reluctant about-face. "I'm sorry . . ." she began.

Ray watched, waiting for some kind of blowup.

"No, *I'm* sorry," Salim said, jumping up and flicking his cigarette out of the front door and into the gutter.

"You ever see anybody from the class these days?" Ray asked.

"Not, not really. I'm kind of running in different circles right now. How 'bout you, Mr. Mitchell, you been keepin' tabs?"

"Not . . . well yeah, but just . . . Do you remember a kid, John Shaker? Maybe a year younger than you? Had rimless glasses, shaved head?"

"Yeah, Shaker. I used to hang with his brother Doobie."

"Well, he's a TV producer now, and I actually kind of wound up work-ing for him out in Los Angeles for a few years, you know, writing this show."

"No. Yeah. No. John. I remember him. He was always a pa-positive individual." Salim foundered. "Never got into the street thing, just avoided that whole crab-cage mentality. That's good, that he's doing good."

Ray had only brought up his ex-boss, ex-student's name in order to keep the conversation moving, but he felt like an unthinking jerk for it now.

When the salads came, Salim performed what Ray assumed was a small prayer to Allah: eyes lightly shut as he whispered his grace, hands open before him, palms up in supplication, then gliding across each other as if washing, then sliding down over his face like a veil; the whole of it exquisitely delicate.

"What's that?" Ray said.

"I was giving thanks to the animals who sacrificed their lives, the labor-ers who prepared this meal and to Allah, the life force, the causeless cause behind all beings."

"For real," Ray said, as always, genuinely moved by anyone's unflinch-ing commitment to anything.

"Oh no doubt," Salim said. "But see, yeah, OK. For me? Islam? I'm not in it for the militancy, or the separatism or whatnot. Especially after, you know . . ." He tilted his chin toward what Ray assumed was New York. "I'm just . . . It keeps me from giving in to the darkness, you know what

I'm saying? Like in jail, right? They can and do anything they can think of to break you, not just the so-called correction officers, but the, your fellow inmates. It's like a sea of negativity and contempt in there and you just got to keep your eye on your aspirations or you can go down so fast and so deep you're never gonna see the light again."

"So that's how you made it through?" Ray said with restrained awe.

"Yeah. Uh-huh. That and who I chose to spend my time with. Most often I was either by myself or with the old-heads. You know, read, played chess. The old guys, they even said to me, 'Salim, you ain't like the others. You got a mind on you.'"

"What were you in jail for initially?"

"Me? For nothing. For violating parole. OK. I was in this cab, right? I had my laptop and everything because I was heading over to have a meeting with this accountant my cousin knew? He was gonna help me get my tax ID number for the nonprofit organization I was gonna set up.

"The driver of the cab, he was from Pakistan or somewheres, can't drive to save his life, sideswipes a car chock-full of niggers. Four jump out, everybody's got a gun. The police roll up, alls they see is *five* niggers and a bunch of guns, you know, so it's . . . We're holding up the cabdriver, it's a holdup. I say, 'I ain't with them,' wavin' around the laptop like, 'Who'm I gonna rob with this?' But they ran me through the computer, comes up that I'm on parole. So I got violated."

"Jesus Christ," Ray said, half-believing it. "What were you on parole for to begin with?"

"You mean what did I go to jail for *before* that?"

"Yeah . . ."

"Same thing. Violation of parole. OK see, I was selling T-shirts in this club? The owner liked my drawings, right? Gave me a concession. I had silk-screened up about two hundred tees with my design. Sold about seventy-five at twenty dollars each less the owner's cut is a lot of cheese to be holding in that kind of environment, you know what I'm saying? I get outside to go home about five in the morning? Nigger steps up, puts a gun in my mug, I take it away from him, you know, just so he wouldn't kill me, I wouldn't kill him? It's called Temporary Innocence of Possession but the thing went off by accident. Nobody got hurt, but everybody starts runnin', police come around, and when I saw them? I got scared, you know, and just out of reflex I started runnin' too, and you should never do that, run from the cops, unless you can get away, but I got caught, cuffed, thrown in the back of the police car. Then, like, at a light? I slipped the cuffs over my legs, ran off from the police car. Got caught again. Didn't look too good, but I didn't even get indicted 'cause the witnesses bore me out. All they had on me was violation of parole. Not supposed to be out that late without permission, not supposed to be near any scene like that club, so I had to go back in. My parole officer even said, 'Salim, I can't believe this is you, you were doing so good . . .'"

"OK, but *before* that arrest, there was . . ." Ray stopped, too tired, and shifted gears. "Tell me about your kid."

"Yeah OK, my son." Salim's face lightened. "See, that's the other thing keeps me maintaining, because he didn't ask to be born, you know what I'm saying? So I'm beholden on his behalf to do the right thing with myself."

"He lives with you?" Ray asked gingerly.

"He lives with me and my fiancée."

"His mother?"

"Yeah, uh-huh." Salim swallowed a burp, even though he hadn't touched his food. "It's not . . . Now *that's* a relationship that tries men's souls."

Ray was half finished eating, Salim's untouched plate starting to make him anxious.

"See, I'm, I am *trying* to get something going here, and, you know, as an individual I feel strong in and of myself but as of yet I can't contribute to my son's upbringing on a financial basis. I'm like a hundred days out of incarceration and like I have all these ideas, but I need capital, I need time, and she's all up in my face about not coming up with my end, gives me twenty dollars a week for myself like I was a child, but she is not supportive of me. She's all negativity and it's like, hey, out in the street? I can *go* that way, bring home in a night what she makes in a *month*, but I'm trying to maintain, I'm trying . . ." Salim burped again, as if trying to swallow a bubble. "Excuse me," a hand resting on his unfed plank of a stomach.

Eyeing Salim's untouched salad, his now-cold tea, Ray sensed the potential explosion ready to blast through his carefully constructed sentences, his delicate prayers, his inability to eat. A precise dot of white spittle marked the corner of his mouth.

He reached for another cigarette.

The waitress, sitting alone at a far table and reading *The Dempsy Dispatch*, caught sight of it and began to rise in order to play reluctant health cop again.

Ray quickly moved to stay Salim's lighter, but the kid reined it in on his own.

"Something wrong with the salad?" the waitress asked with genuine concern.

"No, no, thank you. I'm sure it's delicious." Salim threw her another smile.

"Do you want me to bring you something else?"

"I'm OK, thank you."

"You sure? Because . . ."

"Yeah, no, but thank you for your consideration, though."

The waitress returned to her paper.

"I like this place," Salim said, leaning across the table. "People treat you with respect. That's a object in short supply in my neighborhood."

Ray felt it lurch to life in him, the slightly suspect craving to give, to do, and attempted to police it, convert it into mere words of advice.

"To be honest, Coley . . . Salim, sorry."

"That's OK."

"To be honest, right now I think you'd be getting quicker results just getting a job with somebody. You know, take home a paycheck every week."

"No doubt," Salim said, not really hearing him.

"This entrepreneur stuff, the nonprofit . . . That's a little dicey in terms of getting paid off it, you know? You have to start kicking in on the diapers, otherwise you're going to blow a gasket."

"I hear *that*," Salim said automatically, touched the edge of his salad plate as if it were hot.

Ray studied the remains of his own meal, a thrum racing through him, building, irresistible.

"Let me ask you. Would a thousand dollars tide you over for a few weeks? You know, make peace in the house with you and your fiancée?"

Coley/Salim became motionless, his facial expression stiffening into a gawk as he furiously attempted to process Ray's offer.

"I'm just trying to buy you a little grace period on the home front here. I think you need it."

"Just a loan, right?" Salim fighting with himself, all ten fingertips touching the edge of the table.

"A whatever. Just to take the weight off. We can work it out down the line."

"I mean I *would* pay you back." His face became more fluid. "Because what I believe is, that if you *give* a man a fish he'll eat for a day, but if you *teach* a man *to* fish, he'll eat *every* day."

"Hey, this is just to buy the fishing pole and a bucket of bait."

"I will most *definitely* pay you back," Salim all the way happy now, Ray having to fight off a worm of queasiness, of embarrassment before returning the kid's smile.

Joy-locked, shiny-eyed, Salim took in the vintage movie posters, the vivid palette of tarts under the ice-cold case light.

"Yeah, I love this place."

"Good," Ray murmured, stroking his gut like a cat. "Glad to hear it."

Chapter 16 >

Carla — February 18

Once again perched on a corner of that small steel desk in the processing room of Dempsy's BCI, Nerese pored over another rap sheet, this one belonging to Salim El-Amin, formerly known as Coley Rodgers. She was just being thorough here; Ray, before the craniotomy, had given up the kid's name easily enough, and the kid himself hadn't really put out any kind of stress vibe when he ran into Nerese at bedside. And although Salim did have a record to be pored over, it was more sad-sack than sinister — first arrest for Possession With Intent eight years earlier, the kid considered salvageable enough at the time to receive as an alternative to jail a two-year stint at New Dawn Village, a nonresidential rehab center over in Hudson County. Hard time there, Nerese knew, was equally divided between being yelled at in group therapy sessions for four hours a day and attending classes in English and math geared toward passing the state exam for a high school equivalency diploma.

But a year after leaving New Dawn, he was busted again, same charge — no more school for you, my man — and wound up serving two years in the Dempsy County Correctional Center. And then, only six months after his release, he was back in the slammer, this time for violation of parole — a charge of resisting arrest downgraded to disorderly persons, which usually meant it was the cops that were in the wrong. He'd been remanded nonetheless at the discretion of his parole officer; another two years. And then, four months after he finished that, the same shit—a charge of assaulting an officer, downgraded to disorderly persons, the PO once again swinging the hammer. All of which told Nerese that basically the kid had one real problem: no matter what the cost to him personally, in the heat of the moment he chronically refused to go along with what-ever the cops wanted him to do in order to pass muster, which in most sit-uations usually meant submitting to a pat-down, then cooling your jets as they ran your name through a dashboard-mounted computer. Coley/Salim's history was more that of a thin-skinned knucklehead than a hard-core criminal; the idiot managing to get himself locked up time after time basically over nothing, as if jail were the place to be.

Unfortunately, Nerese knew this type well. Her nephew Eric was like that—*had* been like that, that was, until the week before, when he went and killed someone. But even that homicide was pretty much the deed of a career nitwit, the kid waiting a good forty-eight hours after the provoking incident before busting a move, as if conscientiously holding off for the requisite time to pass in order to deny himself any heat-of-the-moment defense. But the bottom line for Nerese as she sat and pondered the self-defeating résumé in her lap was still Ray and Salim's tone when speaking about each other, open and anxiety-free.

Sliding off the edge of the desk, Nerese returned Salim El-Amin's jacket to the BCI clerk and began the three-story climb back up to the street.

She still liked Freddy Martinez for this.

Nerese sat at the small dinette table in Carla Powell's Hopewell Houses apartment, Carla sitting across from her and scowling out the window as if the sun were in her eyes. All she had offered Nerese was the glass of cloudy tap water that sat before her.

"I don't imagine you would remember me. Tweetie Ammons? The Ammons family from Four Building?"

"No, I don't," Carla said too quickly, pushing her glasses up the bridge of her nose.

"You probably remember my brothers from the benches, though. Antoine? Butchie?"

"Nope." Another bitten-off response.

Carla tapped the ash of her cigarette into her palm, Nerese eyeing the unused ashtray sitting before her.

This whole thing was a charade from the door on in, both women knowing exactly where Nerese was headed with all the small talk. She took a sip of the furry metallic water.

"C'mon, you don't remember Antoine?" Nerese challenged playfully, her sex cartoon of a brother back in the mid-sixties, early seventies, having been borderline unforgettable.

Carla shrugged with feigned indifference.

"Well, I have to say, I certainly remember *you*, though," throwing Carla one of her world-class smiles. "I would see you leave for school in the morning? Man, you'd come out of this building in those tight skirts, mascara, *hair* all teased up. You looked like Miss Rheingold or Miss Subways or something. I would've done anything—"

"I have a doctor's appointment," Carla said, cutting her off.

"Well then, let's see if I can make this quick," Nerese said, giving up on memory lane. "Like I said, I'm sorry for your loss."

Carla nodded, tapped another ash barrel into her palm.

"I assume you heard what happened to Ray Mitchell?"

"Yeah, I heard." Carla studied the world outside the window.

Nerese had grown up in a building situated barely a hundred feet from this one, yet the slight change in angle of vision was enough to make her dizzy.

"I understand Ray helped you out with your son's burial arrangements. Is that true?"

"You don't need to ask me something you know the answer to already."

A train racketed past at eye level, a cyclone of steel, Nerese waiting it out.

"Well, can I ask you for how much?"

"You just did," Carla said. Then, "Thirty-two hundred dollars, three thousand two hundred dollars, and I know he doesn't expect to get paid back, but he will, every cent."

Nerese nodded noncommittally; she had lost count of the number of homicides she worked on that had at their source the pride of poor people.

"Can I just . . . Ray, did he offer you or give you any other money besides for the funeral? You know to maybe help out with some emergency . . ."

"He didn't give, he didn't offer, and I most certainly didn't ask."

"OK, the, for the burial . . . Did anybody else know about that money?"

"I'm not a talker, but who's to say."

"How about family members?"

"How about family members *what.*"

"Any of them know about it?"

"Hey." Carla leaned forward, getting in Nerese's eyes. "My surviving children *work* for their living. The boy in Maryland is a licensed pharmacist, owns *two* drugstores, my girl holds down a nine-to-five in New York and attends *college,* so I don't appreciate your insinuations. Not every family in this shithole projects is as fucked up as yours was."

Carla immediately reared back from her own words, a small tremor blooming in her cigarette hand.

"So I guess you do remember us," Nerese said evenly, experiencing an odd, not unpleasant sensation somewhere between confirmation and vindication.

"I'm sorry," Carla said shakily, staring out the window again, the PATH tracks a brutal band bisecting this family's view of the outside world.

"How did you feel about Danielle going out with Ray?" Nerese asked mildly, jumping on Carla's momentary disorientation.

"She's a grown woman," not giving an inch.

"But how did you feel about it?"

"I didn't like it," she said, still staring out the window, Nerese intuiting that, angry, embarrassed, Carla would probably not make eye contact again.

"You didn't like it. Why not?"

A preadolescent boy, twelve, thirteen, shambled into the living room in his underwear, eyes sleep-gummed, hair a bird's nest.

"Hey, honey." Nerese smiled.

"You don't want to be having this conversation in front of him," Carla murmured, then, "Nelson, put your pants on."

The kid vanished.

"Grandson?"

"Yeah."

"Danielle's?"

Carla nodded.

"And you didn't like her seeing Ray."

"That's right."

"Why not?"

Carla shrugged.

Nerese counted to twenty; no dice. "Because he's white?"

"No, I don't care about that. I'm one-quarter white myself." Carla eyed another dull red train approaching her window at an aggressive slant.

"Because she's married?"

Carla's gaze tracked the lead car until it shot past the kitchen window.

"Look, Carla." Nerese reached across the table and laid a light hand on her arm, feeling the agitation still bubbling beneath the skin. "The poor guy almost died. And whether you have some kind of bone to pick with him or not, he did you a major kindness. And I just don't understand why you won't return the favor here."

"Because I don't *know* anything," she moved her arm out from under Nerese's touch.

"Hey, I'm not here looking to hurt you or your family, but I *am* going to find out who did this."

"I hope you do," another shrug.

"Does Danielle usually see other men when Freddy's in jail?"

Carla exposed her lower teeth, dark and twisted at the bottom of her mouth. "Now, I just told you I don't know who did this to the man. But if you feel the need to, you can come at me fifty different ways to hear me say it fifty different times, or you can hear me say it just this once, it'll come out to the same thing. I, don't, *know.*"

"No, I hear you, I hear you," Nerese said amiably. She took great pride in the thickness of her skin, the job oftentimes boiling down to sitting there calmly until the interviewees exhausted themselves blind throwing every kind of insult and self-righteous hugger-mugger at you imaginable. "What's Freddy like with your daughter?"

"He's her *husband*," Carla said, as if Nerese were too thick to live.

"Is he the emotional type? Physical?"

Not liking this question either, Carla sank down into herself like a big-breasted bird on a wire.

"Well, I'll tell you." Nerese took another sip of water. "What I don't understand is, like you yourself said, Danielle, she's holding down a job, taking classes over at DCC, raising a son, and this Freddy, he's been locked up, I believe this last was his fourth trip to County? So my question is, why is she still with him?"

"Are *you* married?" Carla surprised Nerese by looking right at her on this.

"Not anymore," she said warily.

"Me neither." Carla flicked her cigarette out the window. "How many of your girlfriends still live under the same roof with the father of their children."

It was more of a challenge than a question and Nerese didn't think it was necessary to respond.

"Yeah, I thought so," Carla said. "Same with my friends. How old are you."

"Forty-one."

"Forty-one." Carla lit another cigarette. "You like being alone?"

"I have family," Nerese grudgingly answered.

Carla waved that away with a sweep of her hand. "Do you *like* being alone?"

"Tell me Freddy didn't do this," Nerese said with more heat than she'd have liked.

"If he did, you can throw his ass right back in jail, I wouldn't shed a single tear. But as I told you before, I just don't know, so instead of wasting *my* time with this, why the hell don't you just ask him?"

Chapter 17 >

Hospital — February 19

After exiting the hospital elevator on the sixth floor, Nerese halted directly outside the monitored-care ward, overcome by a premonition that she was about to discover that her time had run out, that in her absence Ray had departed for the far shore. But when she finally crossed the threshold and approached his stall, to her great relief she saw that he was still in town, marginally at least, the poor bastard lying there today head-wrapped, immobile, but open-eyed, tracking her expressionlessly from the prison of his own body.

"How you feeling, gorgeous?" Nerese muscling the bounce into her voice but worried, sensing that she'd need to be right on top of him today to have any kind of meaningful communication.

Ray swallowed, a slow and painful exercise, his face contorting with the effort.

Nerese's gaze strayed to the night table where she saw Freddy Martinez still wedged under the Weeping Monk, untouched since she had placed him there the day before.

She slipped the photo free and held it before Ray's face. "Hey, look who's here," making it dance.

He stared at it impassively, Nerese wondering if Martinez still had the goatee from two years ago, but then Ray must have made the connection, goatee or no, because he closed his eyes again and attempted to turn his head to the side.

"What . . . "

Ray opened his eyes, stared at the night table.

Nerese blocked his view with Freddy again. "This is him, right?"

Ray closed his eyes.

"Oh yeah," Nerese crowed falsely.

Eyes still shut, Ray shook his head infinitesimally, either in denial or in woe.

"No, huh?" Nerese almost in his ear. "Your face tells me different."

Breathing deep, Ray stared at the Weeping Monk.

"Look at it again." Nerese propped it upright against the wooden carving. "All I need for you to do is nod, and it's a done deal."

"No." A hoarse shadow of a whisper.

"'No.'" Nerese flushed. "No *what* . . . No, I won't help myself? No, I'm too scared? No, the guy fucked me up so bad I can't remember? No *what*."

Ray swallowed another razor, his face contorting with the effort.

"The man put a *hole* in your head, Ray. Just *nod*, for God's sake."

"No." Another lip reader's special.

Nerese eased herself down onto the edge of the bed, fighting off a depression-induced wave of fatigue.

"I don't know, Ray, this whole thing, I understand, I appreciate that you wanted to do a good deed or whatever, but that entailed going in there and laying a fat-ass check on a woman living in a place eighty percent of which is on some kind of public assistance, in a place that's got *no* walls, your business is out on the street before *you* are, that isn't bad enough, the money-flush white boy starts boning the woman's daughter, *that's* out on the street, gets to her husband in County faster than a speeding bullet, and so for me, sitting here right now the amazing thing isn't that you got beat for your troubles but that you only got beat once. Now, I like this guy for what put you here, and unless you give me another name, I'm going straight to his parole officer and getting him violated."

"You can't," Ray whispered.

"I can't?" Nerese reared back in mock surprise.

"Not without a complaint." Ray stared off, red-faced with the effort.

"Then *complain*," leaning into him.

"No."

"No. OK. You know what, then? *Fuck* you. I will *let* his murderous ass come back down on you and finish off what he started, you brain-whacked son of a bitch." Nerese hissed in his ear. "And believe me, I have seen it happen, some strong-arm psycho go down and down on the same vic time after time like they're a goddamn soda machine. And won't your daughter have fun, feeding her dad like a baby, pushing him through the park or whatever the fuck shape he'll leave you in what is *wrong* with you." Nerese fighting off a powerful urge to straight-out beg, the victim himself the true mystery here, intractably blocking her way home.

"Tweetie," Ray said hoarsely, then faded, his lower face dropping away from his teeth like the hinged jaw of a marionette. "Tweetie," seeking out her eyes as he hauled himself back up to the surface. "What if I had it coming," the question an atonal balloon.

Nerese studied the beseeching fright mask before her, tried to connect it to the hack license photo in his apartment, couldn't.

"Nobody has this coming," she said.

Two orderlies and a nurse came into the stall and began detaching Ray from his IV and fingertip vital-signs monitor, moving swiftly and efficiently, one of the orderlies squatting to release the catch that would make the bed mobile.

"Where's he going?" Nerese asked.

"It's time to put Humpty Dumpty back together again," the nurse said, standing behind the head of the bed as if it were a dogsled, gesturing for the two orderlies standing in front to move on out.

"What were you doing messing around with her to begin with," Nerese asked hopelessly as Ray, like a prince on his royal barge, glided past her into the hallway. "It's just ass," she called out after him. "You're not supposed to *die* for it."

‹ Chapter 18

Danielle — January 20

"I don't know how else to ask this," Ray said staring at Danielle's gleaming compact torso, "but what are you?"

The scent of vanilla was everywhere: the nape of her neck, in her brass-tinted hair, her mouth, between her legs, on his own fingers and belly, rising from the sheets like a mist.

"What do you mean, what *am* I . . ." She lay on her side, her head propped on a cupped palm. Since the sex ended she hadn't looked at his body once.

"I mean, you know, ethnically." He wanted to say "racially," but thought "ethnically" a softer word.

"Well, that's an interesting question." Her legs brushed against each other with a dry slishing sound. "I have one grandfather, he was Dominican, a grandmother who's black, still alive, and another grandmother who was, I'm pretty sure, a Russian Jew."

"How about the other grandfather?"

"The other grandfather? He was a sailor."

"Really," Ray said, witless with desire. He wanted to touch the crest of her hip where her body began to swoop in then roller-coaster back out again at the base of her rib cage, but the fucking was over for now and he wasn't sure where he stood.

Her body was on the heavy side but solid; thick-waisted, blunt-toed, with small high breasts that were almost lost in the expanse of her chest and wide swimmer's shoulders. And she was strong—stronger than him; he'd never been in bed with a woman so physically powerful before—and she used that strength to make him come, leisurely almost absently riding him with a controlled density of muscle that made him despair of dragging things out.

But in fact, the sex, at least in spirit, had been over and done with well before she had ever thrown a leg over him and began the too-short ride.

When he had brought her over to the apartment a few hours earlier, for what he had hoped would turn out to be some slow-boat-to-China fuckery, he was jarred to discover that the initial aura of pillowy gratitude with which she had driven him wild on so many levels in their first two encounters had completely evaporated.

And once in bed, Ray, recognizing a lost cause when he saw one, knew it as such for sure soon after he had worked his way south from her tattooed throat to between her legs. Glancing back up at her after a few languid minutes beneath the rise of her belly, he saw that she had pretty much vacated the premises; her expression was composed, absent, her eyes open and gazing off as if trying to remember something, the remnants of a to-do list, perhaps.

There was nothing cruel or willful in her sexual distance; just a wall of preoccupation that he instantly and accurately knew to be unbreachable, but which also turned him atomic with want. And the hell of it was that, even though she was lying in bed now as detached as if she were waiting for a bus, he was pretty sure she'd go at it again if he wanted to; now, later today, tomorrow, probably anytime up to a few days before her husband was released—Ray at his deluded worst didn't belive her "three strikes, you're out" speech—but it would be in the spirit of holding up her end of a deal, and her continued unreachableness would make him insane; make him feel as isolated as if he had lived in one of those talking tombs he had his students imitate from *Spoon River Anthology*.

"Do you know in eight years of marriage I never fucked around once?" he semi-announced in an ass-backwards effort to get her to talk about her husband, about the big picture here. "And it wasn't like we had this great sex life, you know, never-ending passion. You sleep with someone long enough you know every square inch of their body. After a while, it's like getting turned on by staring at yourself in the mirror."

"I don't know about that," Danielle said mildly, rattling him.

"No, I mean, the sex was fine, I'm not saying . . . It's just, for me, you start screwing around, you can either lie or you get all candid about it. You choose candid, next thing you know you're both doing it, you have this, understanding, quote unquote, it's worse than being best friends, so I decided right out of the gate, in for a penny, in for a pound."

"In for a pound," she lightly aped him, once again bumping him off balance. "Let me ask you something," blocking her body with a pillow. "Why'd you do that for my family."

"Do what . . ."

Danielle waited.

"Because I could."

"Bullshit. *Why.*"

Ray wondered how honest he could be, decided that saying he had paid for her brother's funeral at least in part to impress his daughter was too much.

"Because money's only money and it was a good way for me to come home."

"Home. You still think of Hopewell as your home?" Squinting with skepticism.

"It's like, you can live under many roofs in this life? But you're always only from one place," he decreed, half believing it.

"She's going to pay you back, you know." Danielle still sizing him up as she said it.

"If it'll make her feel better about taking it, fine. But I don't really care. I mean, I'd never lend money to someone, if they wound up stiffing me it would make me crazy. For me, it's like Hi-Yo Silver, and go. See you when I see you. I'm not in it for the static."

"Not for nothing, but do you really think you can do things for people, help them out then just walk away like nothing sticks to you? No offense, but I think that's incredibly naive on your part."

"Nonetheless." Ray attempted to shrug it off, everything out of her mouth like a broomstick tossed in the path of a runner. "Do me a favor, make sure she knows that, OK?"

"Yeah, OK," she said, still not buying it; not buying him.

Her foot grazed his leg, an accident, and he just came out with it. "I need for you to tell me about your husband."

"You want to know about Freddy?"

The quiet way she said it, with the smallest pause beforehand, told him that she was utterly alive to the drama, that what was going down here was probably a time-honored routine, a ritual between husband and wife involving crime, punishment, purge and forgiveness, and that he was merely a player, a disposable second banana — that in fact, his disposal was most likely critical to the climax.

But it had been so long for him . . .

"Just tell me what's going on," he said cleanly. "And don't tell me it's over, OK?"

A pager went off in the heaped rumple of her clothes on the floor and she stretched across his belly to pluck it from her jeans, the impersonal pressure of flesh on flesh turning his thoughts into white noise.

She scowled at the number coming up on her beeper. "Pass me the phone please?"

Sitting up cross-legged now, she frowned at her nails as she waited for her call to ring through.

"*Nurse's* office?" She reared back in surprise at the greeting. "Yeah, hi, this is Danielle Martinez, Nelson Martinez's mother? Did you just page— Is he there? Can I talk to him?" running a long-nailed hand through her short hennaed mane. "What's wrong, Nelson . . . You got a 58. A 58 *what* . . . You're in the nurse's office because you failed a *test*? . . . No. No. You had the flu *last* month. Did you study for . . . Nelson, if you didn't understand what you were studying, why didn't you say some-thing? . . . To me, to your teacher. Which teacher is it . . . *Who*? That woman should be teaching like I should be in the circus. I'll talk to her. I'll . . . Well, if you don't want me to step up for you then why are you call-ing me? . . . What do you mean 'just to tell me'? Couldn't you just tell me when you got home?"

Ray flinched at that, Nelson's misery coming through loud and clear.

"Are you missing a class right now? OK. I want you to hang up the phone, tell the nurse you feel better and get your ass back in class . . . No. Right *now*, Nelson. Right *now* . . . I love you too. Go."

Danielle hung up and stretched across Ray again to replace the phone on the night table. "He's such a mama's boy. 'I got a 58, I got a 58,'" mim-ing her son in a whispery bass. "What's he got to call me for?"

"I don't know. He probably feels like crap and you're his mom." Ray said it as lightly as he could, afraid the obviousness of it all would in some way backfire on him.

"No, I'm sorry, I will fight to the death for my son when it's called for, but he's getting a little too old to not start sucking it up when shit doesn't break his way. See, that's why I'm so pissed at his father . . ."

"Freddy?" Ray said quickly, all thoughts of Nelson gone like smoke into a vacuum.

"Yeah," Danielle responded, looking at him, Nelson fading a little for her, too. "About Freddy, what did you want to know?"

"Be me," Ray said. "What do I want to know."

"You have to be more specific," she said, loving this.

"C'mon, give me a break."

"Shit, I'll tell you all of it." She shrugged. "I don't owe that bastard anything . . . I mean, you talk about marriage and faithfulness and sex and all that? Do you know I have been with my husband for exactly half my life? Since tenth, *grade.* I mean, it's not like I haven't been out in the world. We must've gone off, gotten back a dozen times in the last fifteen years. Mostly it's his fault. He disappears now and then, finds some short-term shortie for himself, or says he needs to get his head together, otherwise known as sulk, or he gets locked up again, and for me, that's the bad one, that's right on the line with unforgivable, although I always do, and once or twice, it's me. I got to get away, can't breathe with all the bullshit in the air. But the thing is, we've made up so many times? It doesn't even feel like making up anymore. It's more like we've just come back from separate vacations at the exact same time. 'Hey, how you doing.' We don't even make promises to each other, you know, 'I'll never do that again,' or, 'This the last time, baby, I really learned my lesson' or whatever. It's just time to get back to each other until the next time."

Gone Off: Ray thinking, That's what I am here, Danielle's latest Gone Off.

"But I tell you, the worst time when he left? Was right after I had Nelson. He disappeared for four months, said he had to be alone to prepare himself for fatherhood, can you believe that shit? And to this day I don't know what he did or where he went for that time, but when he came back he was most definitely still unprepared for fatherhood. Still is.

"See, he's not like you with Ruby. You love her, it's so obvious, your face gets all, *alert* when she's around. You're alive to her. Even with Nelson, I see it in you with my son, like just now, on the phone, telling me how bad he felt. I mean, he's not even yours, but there's no doubt in my mind you'd be a better father to him than his own. You're not afraid of children, you're not afraid to, to re*ceive* them. Freddy, for all the shit he deals with? Jail, cops, the business he's in? He's not like you. He's an emotional coward."

There were no words he could think of to describe how deeply moved and flattered he felt by the dry-eyed sureness of her observations.

"No, I tell you," Danielle said. "You know who's Nelson's real second parent? My mother. And it's sad because now, these days, people look at her, my mom, and what they see is this broke-down woman, all gone to fat, no sex in her, she's what, three, four years older than you? It looks more like twenty. But she's had a life; you don't know what she's had to overcome in her time.

"Like, I'm sure you remember her back in the sixties, all hot and made-up, looked like Rita Moreno, everybody says that, and she hates it when they do, but upstairs in that apartment? You cannot believe what she had to deal with back then. She was abused . . ."

"Sexually?" remembering rumors.

"No. Violently. My grandfather used to beat on her, my uncles and my grandmother. I don't really remember him but I was told he drove a truck for Pepsi, drove from five in the morning till three in the afternoon, came home the same time as the kids from school, came home drunk, never said a word to anybody, just emptied his wallet on the dining room table for the, you know, for whatever was needed, then collapsed in his TV chair without ever turning the TV on. Used to sit there with his eyes open, maybe he's asleep, maybe not. And my mother told me if anybody in that house made any kind of noise for the next hour or so? Or even if the phone should ring, he'd go off like a rocket, start whaling on people. My mother was in and out of Dempsy Medical Center she can't even remember how many times, bruises, shiners, stitches, even for trying to kill herself, and my grandfather never got arrested for it because my grandmother was too afraid to press charges."

"Jesus," Ray breathed.

"Jesus didn't have fuck-all to do with it," Danielle said. "And so how does she get out of that house? How else . . . She marries the first idiot who asks her. Seventeen years old, drops out of school with like six months to graduation, married, pregnant, and guess what? The son of a bitch was just like her father, surprise surprise, except in addition to the beatings? She got one bonus extra—he didn't drive a truck for Pepsi, my father, he sold drugs."

Just like your husband, Ray thought—surprise, surprise.

"We lived in Jersey City, and our house used to get raided like clockwork, so they tell me, but he was pretty slick, my father, they never found anything until the one time they did. Then he got locked up, and me and my brothers, when I was very little, we were all placed in a foster home. I mean, I have no memory of this, I was three, four . . . But my mother, she didn't deserve that kind of punishment because she didn't do anything except put all her time and energy and wits into protecting us, you know, trying to keep us whole."

"Why didn't she just take the kids and leave?" Ray regretting the question the moment it came out of his mouth.

"To *where*," Danielle rightfully snapped. "She had no money. Three kids and no money. Where was she supposed to move to, back to her prick father's house? Life's not about 'Why didn't she just do this, just do that.' People don't 'just *do*' things. There's no 'just *do*' out there. It's all about complications and bad habits and being afraid and wanting to be loved. I mean I read these, these *text*books, you know, Urban Studies, Sociology, Public Policy . . . I get ten pages into the author's shit and I want, I want to strangle the bastard. And don't get me wrong, half the time I want to strangle my mother too. Just because she had a hard life doesn't qualify her for sainthood. She laid a *dump* truck of grief at my feet. But still, she's my mother and she's come through for me more than you'd have any right to expect."

Danielle took a breath; Ray seized by what she was telling him and almost physically aching for more. It wasn't only the secret history of Carla Powell that she was revealing here, or even the secret history of the Powell clan; it was the secret history of 1949 Rocker Drive, its hallways, elevators, apartments and smells; it was the secret history of his childhood world, the mouths, eyes, bodies and scents of others, of those he had brushed up against every day of his younger life, and therefore the secret history, marginally at least, of himself.

And the fact that Danielle was not only the gatekeeper of this intimate knowledge but its living offspring; not only the teller of the tale, but the tale itself made flesh—to Ray, an individual who saw personal history and anecdote and his ability to communicate through them as his lifeline to the rest of the world—his lifeline to love, expressing his love—for someone like Ray to be in the physical presence of memory incarnate, sentiment incarnate like this—intensified and complicated his hunger for her way beyond lust, which was painful enough, into something excruciatingly sublime.

"The thing is," Danielle started up again, gazing past Ray, oblivious to the chaos she was unleashing in him, "the thing is, I *know*, right now, my mother blames herself for my brother's death, for his life. She raised him in a dope house, then lost him to foster care for two years. Like I said, I have no memory of it, and Reggie was even younger than me, so, if any one of us was old enough to be scarred by it, it's my older brother Harmon, who's a pharmacist, owns two drugstores in Prince William County, Maryland, and me, I'm pretty much good to go, so Reggie . . . It doesn't make any sense. But it's like, whenever I try to say something to her about how she can't blame herself? She just won't hear it."

Ray was tempted to say that the tattoo on her throat was there for life whether she remembered the visit to the tattoo parlor or not, but he had just enough self-control to keep his mouth shut.

"Anyways, when my father got locked up, in the two years it took for my mother to get us back from foster care? She got her GED and took a semester at Dempsy Community College—although nothing came of it, because the minute we were returned to her she had to go on public assistance. She couldn't continue with her education or go find a job because she couldn't afford a baby-sitter, and wouldn't drop us off at our grandparents' apartment because of her father.

"I mean, a few years later, two seconds after the bastard died, we moved right back in with my grandmother so my mom could finally look for a job, but it turned out she couldn't really hack it, work, went through something like three gigs in six months, wound up on medication for depression, been battling that ever since, no wonder given her life, fighting diabetes too, a parting gift from my grandfather.

"The thing is, when we moved back into Hopewell to live with my grandmother? Nana was like my second parent. And after Nana died and my mother took over the apartment, and me and Reggie had kids? My mother's Nelson's second parent. Dante, David from Reggie—for them, she's the sole parent. She embraces all the kids, never complains, never gets overwhelmed. Says it's her second chance to get things right.

"And I say to her, 'Mom, you did the best you could with us given the circumstances,' but she just won't hear it. Always says, 'I fucked up with you.' Gets all teary. 'I fucked up.' Won't buy anything else in the store.

"And I'll tell you one other thing she did for me, which is let me witness her life so I can say to myself, I will not have a life like that. I will be my own person, my own way, no apologies to anybody."

"Huh," Ray grunted; married to a dope dealer, in and out of living in that same apartment: he just could not understand how she didn't see it, but was afraid to point it out to her, afraid of losing this woman lying in bed with him, even if she was here only for an interlude, even at the price of some kind of future beatdown or worse. Made diplomatic by desire, all he could say to relieve the pressure of his perceptions was "So your husband, he doesn't, he never laid a hand on you, right?"

"If he had, it would be me in County right now, not him. And I'll tell you something else. My mother, when she was a teenager, before she left and got married? She was wild, did everything there was to do. But once she got pregnant and learned what it's like to live with a dealer? To see junkies around the clock? To have their addictions, their, their self-destructiveness to thank for putting the food on your table? She stopped cold. To this day, she doesn't drug, she doesn't, hasn't had so much as a can of beer. However, she smokes like a bonfire, takes medication for depression, for diabetes, high blood pressure, insomnia, asthma . . . She's a walking drugstore. Can't go to sleep or get out of bed without a fistful of pills and, once again, unfortunately by negative example, I see her and say to myself, Unh-uh. No way. I don't drink, smoke or take so much as an aspirin. Same for Nelson. I don't know that much about Christian Science, I mean, if Nelson needed an operation or lifesaving antibiotics, yeah, of course, but otherwise our bodies are our temples and we keep them pure."

Ray nodded approvingly, thinking, You live, with a drug dealer.

The light coming through the bedroom window abruptly changed, a flotilla of clouds drifting across the afternoon, and impulsively, using the flattening gloom as cover, he reached for the clean swoop above her hip, but oblivious to his too little, too late move, she simultaneously slid to the foot of the bed, got up and walked to the window, Ray craving and mourning, mourning and craving every inch of her; the flexed tendons at the backs of her knees, the soft inverted triangle of flesh at the base of her spine, her earlobe, throat, mouth, and when she stepped back into her jeans he experienced a sense of loss that just tore him apart.

It wasn't love as love—he didn't want to have a child or grow old with her—but as the combination of lust and sentiment hunkered down in him, the afternoon finally evoked a sensation that he could recognize: a long-lost misery-hunger from the time in his life when girls still got to him, when they had the power to put him in bed in the middle of the afternoon with the shades drawn so that he could be alone with his punch-drunk heart. Basically, she made him feel like he was back in Hopewell—sixteen, suffering and home.

"The thing about Freddy?" She turned to him as she pulled on her T-shirt. "Well, let me . . . My father and my grandfather? They just did what they did because that's what they did. They didn't, they weren't what you would call reflective individuals. They were more like . . . See, there's no animal on earth that ponders or analyzes their own actions. And that's what they were, animals. But Freddy . . . Whenever Freddy pulls any kind of Freddy shit? He feels bad after, he feels remorse, he'll talk about it, for whatever that's worth, which as I hear myself right now, is not much . . . But the fact is, he's thirty-three, and he's getting to the point of no return. He's got to start doing some serious soul searching or he's going to wind up being who he is for the rest of his life."

Half-listening, nodding like a bobble-head doll in response to whatever, Ray slowly sat up and began to look around the room for his pants.

The thing to do here, he knew, was to end it. To be running with this woman right now was the equivalent of willfully standing on train tracks, the train out of sight so far, but the rails beneath his feet beginning to vibrate like mad.

On the other hand, Ray thought—for boys at least, nobody went through life without getting a little bloody now and then; he'd been unnaturally lucky on that score so far. But given that as more or less an inescapable, maybe the best he could hope for was to at least choose the time and circumstance.

"What's wrong," she asked, cocking her head.

"What?" Ray said, startled and vaguely embarrassed. "Nothing."

"You look like you just lost your best friend in the entire world," she said with benign amusement, reading him like a billboard as she unsnapped the top button of her jeans again.

Part II

BLUE DEMPSY

Chapter 19 >

Home — February 23

Four days after his last surgical procedure, Ray, wearing a Dempsy PD Crime Scene Unit baseball cap supplied by Nerese to cover his shaved and resutured scalp, shakily emerged from the passenger side of her sedan, and with thick tentative fingers began fishing in his pockets for his keys.

He had escaped any serious residual damage from the assault but sustained some minor, short-term impairment — his right hand tended to curl up until his fingertips were touching the inside of his wrist, his right-foot to land inward, the heel not quite touching the ground — and she had pulled up directly in front of his apartment to minimize the distance he had to cover.

Nerese had to believe the doctors wouldn't have released him if they felt he was still in any kind of medical jeopardy. But she knew that head injuries like Ray's tended to revisit — if he started experiencing headaches or became faint, it might signal a new bleed, a buildup of fluid. If his right-side extremities became any floppier, it meant that rebleed was compressing nerve tissue; if he passed out, if he developed a fever, if this, if that . . . All of which had to be interpreted through the usual shakiness, soreness and knock-knee characteristic of any ambulatory post-op reacquainting himself with the outside world.

Once he was free of the car—Nerese had to lean across again and reshut the passenger door after his weak shove—she drove the hundred yards or so to the nearest Little Venice parking lot, then walked back, not all that surprised to see Ray still outside the building waiting for her, the key in the lock unturned. Not many assault victims were too keen on revisiting the scene of the crime for the first time without some company.

Following him into his apartment, she wound up stepping on his heels when he froze at the sight of the EMS debris that littered the floor tiles closest to the door.

"Shit," he whispered.

She sidled past him into the living room, Ray stuck in the doorway, glaring at the discarded rubber gloves, torn gauze wrappers and needle-sharp shards of vase.

"That's the one thing I hate about paramedics," she said, gazing out at the river. "When they come and save your life? They never tidy up after themselves."

She had left the bloody scatter as she'd found it two weeks ago, wanting him to see it first thing over the threshold.

Without a word, Ray moved off toward the rear of the apartment, came shuffling back with a small trash basket, a plastic bristle brush, a roll of paper towels and a spray bottle of Tilex.

She made no move to help, just stood there leaning against the windowsill as he eased himself down and went to work.

He looked furious, tight-lipped. Nerese intuited that for Ray, the act of getting on his knees and cleaning up his own browned blood was a symbolic gesture to mark his resolve to be done with it, for now and evermore. But she had been an observer of moments like this too many times to count, and as she watched him attempt to obliterate the evidence of his own mortality, she began to speculate when the terror of being back here would truly start to kick in.

With his impatience and anxiety allowing him to do at best a half-assed job on the floor, Ray struggled to his feet, his right hand hugging his side, and began working on the black fingerprint powder that stippled his front door.

"Don't forget those," Nerese said, breaking the implosive silence as she gestured to the set of greasy handprints flush against the wall about ten feet down from where the forensic team had called it a day.

"Those what." Ray swiveled, squinting, searching, then finally picking up on them, oily and luminous in the sunlight.

"What's—" he began, then, "Oh . . . ," turning ashen with some kind of memory hit and, forgetting about his smudged door, he set to work on the hands, going at them with a haunted determination.

Nerese imagined Ray right now reexperiencing standing there up against that wall in frisk mode, alert yet helpless, waiting for it . . .

"Seconds seemed like hours, huh?"

"What?" Ray leaned into his work, half-listening.

"That guy must've had you up there like the St. Valentine's Day massacre . . . Did he give you a little speech first about fucking with OPP? Or did he just go all home-run derby on you without a word."

Ray turned to her. "You have no idea what you're talking about."

"No?"

"No," he said, then, "No."

Nerese pushed off from the radiator she had been perched on, walked over to the wall and, locating the remains of the prints, assumed the position, twisting her head to look at Ray over her shoulder. "Man, this had to be one of the worst moments of your life."

At first, he seemed paralyzed, gawking at the re-creation with slack-jawed distress, but then he simply walked away. Soon after Nerese heard the sound of running water from behind the bathroom door, and envisioned him in there gripping the sides of the sink, too unmanned to even splash water on his face.

And when he finally returned to the living room a few minutes later, she was set up for him on the couch facing the TV: the mug shot of Freddy Martinez, and the framed photo of Ruby playing basketball that had a place of honor on one of the bookshelves, laid out side by side on the glass coffee table.

Ray staggered back on his heels. "Oh, for Christ's sake."

"Nah nah, I'm never going away on this one. Don't you get that by now?" tapping a long artificial nail on the glass table.

"Tweetie." Ray stood there—"Tweetie . . ."—then simply gave up, dropping onto the couch next to her, pinching the flesh at the inside corners of his eyes.

"You know he killed somebody, right?" nudging Freddy's portrait.

"What?" Ray straightened up a little. "When?"

"Two years ago. In County. Stabbed some inmate in the heart with a shank made out of a sharpened toothbrush. Grand jury no-billed, said it was self-defense, but I heard rumors that it was business-related. Three-hundred-pound man, too."

"Fuck," Ray hissed, his left hand starfished over his chest.

"Do you know how physically hard it is to puncture a big man's heart with a weapon like that? How determined you have to be?"

"*Stop.*"

"What," Nerese said blandly.

"Just . . ." Ray fanned the air between them as if erasing words on a blackboard.

"In the hospital you said to me, 'What if I had it coming.'"

"I don't remember saying that."

"Trust me, I was right there."

"Hey, I had a hole in my head." Ray shrugged, but Nerese could tell he was good and freaked by what she had told him.

"Did you talk to him yet?" he asked with strained casualness.

"Who, Freddy? Unh-uh. I just got through with Carla. Next stop's Danielle."

"Danielle," he repeated.

"She's been ducking my calls for four days now, but I have my ways."

Ray opened his mouth, thought better of it, looked away.

Nerese picked up the photo of Ruby and the black girl simultaneously levitating off the hardwood during tip-off.

"You see her yet?"

"I called her last night from the hospital. I told her to give me a week. I'll be in better shape in a week. The poor kid feels things deep as a river. I don't want to shake her up unduly."

"She's scared for you, you know."

"Yeah, well, thanks to you."

They sat in silence for a moment, Nerese thinking, Let him stew over Freddy, then just start to leave, abandon him to his secrets, see what that pulls out of him.

She got up and walked to the window. "I would think you could see the World Trade Center from here."

"Not really," his voice more fluid now with the change of subject. "It's too far north. At night you can see the floodlights for the cranes; sometimes you get that dense wet-ash smell if the wind is right, but that's it."

She watched out of the corner of her eye as Ray furtively tried to wrestle his right hand free of its shrimp-head curl.

"So what was it like being a cop around here at that time?" he asked, his face a little wooden with the strain of his efforts.

"I'll make a deal with you," Nerese said, walking back and retaking her seat next to him on the sofa. "You tell me why you needed to pull seventy-three hundred dollars in cash out of the bank a few weeks back and I'll tell you what it was like around here when all hell broke loose."

"I'm not bullshitting you, Tweetie, there's nothing there for you. Just drop it."

"If it's nothing, why don't you just tell me what it was for, get me off your back?"

"Why? Because it's my life."

"All right." She shrugged, letting the marlin run.

"You know, growing up, there was this kid a year or two older than me, Franklyn Brown," Ray said, giving up on straightening out his hand. "Had cerebral palsy, a mild case I guess, it only affected one side of his body, but he used to walk around with his hand curled up. Left hand, I think, and, being the sweethearts that we were back then, me and all my friends, we used to call him Captain Hook." Ray looked down at himself. "It's almost enough to make you believe in karma."

"So what are you going to do now, Ray?" Nerese asked, angling for another way in.

"Me?" palming his chest. "Eventually I'll probably go back to LA and start over, but not now, not yet. No more cutting and running."

"What do you mean, 'cutting and running'?"

"I need to see things through. You can't not see things through," talking to himself now more than to her.

"What things."

"I don't know. Certain relationships. That class at the Hook. I want to pick up where I left off with those kids. That was a good thing for me to do."

"What relationships."

"Ruby. Others." He scooped up Nerese's two-card gambit and turned it facedown on the table.

"Others like who—Danielle?" Could he *be* that stupid?

"No. No way."

"Then who. Salim? That kid Salim?"

Ray shrugged. "Mostly I'm thinking of that class."

"That was two hours a week."

"So I'll do more. I just want to make a dent while I can. And I can as long as I have enough dough not to do anything for money. When the money runs out?" He gestured with his left hand to the framed Emmy nomination on the wall. "I can always go back to that. Some dopey show or other. TV writers, we're like baseball managers, two minutes after you get canned by one team you get picked up by another, because there's only so many of you floating around."

Nerese was still hung up on "certain relationships," but she sensed that to push further right now would shut him down.

"So you won the Emmy, huh?"

"Just nominated. You ever watch the show?"

"Not all the way."

"More power to you," he said, reaching into his shirt pocket, uncapping a vial and popping two pills without water.

"What was that?"

"Vicodin."

"For a headache?"

"Yeah."

"You have a headache?"

"Yeah."

"You're not supposed to have headaches."

"Well, I do."

"Then you need to go back to the hospital."

"It's not a headache. They put a hole in my head. It *hurts*."

"And why are they giving you painkillers for it? That could mask symptoms."

"She's a doctor, too."

"And it's addictive."

"And a counselor."

"Popping Vicodin," she said out loud to herself. "Ray, don't you see what's happening to—" she cut herself off; enough with the ragging.

She weighed getting up to leave, decided it was neither the time nor the right note.

"So tell me about the show," she said.

"About *Brokedown*?"

"It's about this inner-city high school," making a circular unfurling gesture to get him going.

"Hang on." He struggled to his feet, walked halfway to the window, then turned to face her, drawing himself up as if he were about to deliver a recitation. "OK. Right. Inner-city high school, the trials and tribulations, like, 'Rashaad, you have every chance of getting that scholarship, why are you wearing gang colors?'

"'Chlorine, you're fifteen years old. You're too *young* to have that baby.'

"'I don't *know* how that gun got in my locker, Mr. Johnson! It ain't mine, I swear!'

"'Chamique, you did *not* get that black eye from walking into a door, and I *will* be coming to your house tonight and find out what's going on.' 'Please, please, Miss Rosenberg, don't do that! I'm clumsy! That's all, I'm clumsy!'

"You know, one from column A, one from column B. It's on a teen-based network, eight p.m. drama following four half-hour black comedies, and you know, every episode has its pat little lesson about tolerance or the hard-knock life or whatever. And I'm at best a run-of-the-mill writer but writing for TV is more like learning how to dance a particular dance. You can have a little variety here and there, a little quirky move now and then, but basically it's one, two, cha-cha-cha over and over, so hey, I can do that." He shrugged. "I mean, there's probably a few well-trained dolphins out there that can do that."

He closed his eyes and expelled a lungful of air, Nerese sensing a deflecting performance coming up, designed to both keep her here and keep her away.

"Anyways, like . . ." His eyes popped open. "OK, for example, the show that I worked on that got the nomination? The plot, the thing, centers around this basketball hotshot, the kid is first-team all-ghetto, has like fifty college scouts at his house, cock of the walk, banging all the cheerleaders, all the Urkels are lining up to do his homework for him, everything's all good and well, except, five days before graduation? His English teacher realizes that the kid never handed in his paper on *The Great Gatsby*.

"Now this teacher, Mr. Montone, he's supposed to be this old-time hard-nose dinosaur from back in the day when the school was predominantly white—and even though a lot of teachers have looked the other way as far as this kid and class requirements went, this crusty old sports-hating sonofabitch refuses to give him any kind of grade for the year unless he coughs up a paper. Not only that, but he calculates that in order for it to be a passing grade? This paper has to be worth at least a B."

"You know, I think maybe I did see that one," Nerese said, thinking maybe she actually had.

"Believe me, even if you didn't, you did. Anyways, the actor who plays Mr. Montone, he had gone AWOL, you know?" Ray mimed upending a bottle. "Nowhere to be found. This ex-student of mine, the producer? He looks at me, says, 'Fuck it, the character's only been on twice, nobody'll remember. You're Mr. Montone. Go get fitted for a bow tie.' And I'm like, *Me?* Shaker says the same thing he said about the writing, you'll learn by doing. Next thing I know someone slaps a SAG card in my hand and I'm wearing makeup."

"Are you kidding me?" Nerese encouraging him, letting out a little more line.

"The episode centered around two big scenes. One, I confront this kid about the paper. He's all full of himself, 'Yo man, I was touring colleges, playing in the McDonald's All-Star tournament. I din't have time to write no paper.' You know, and then I say, 'Well, you better *make* time, Mr. Jefferson'—I'm always calling my students Mr. and Miss—'because if you don't, you won't graduate.'

"He's like, 'Aw man, that Gatsby book, it ain't got nothing to do with around here. Why you stressing me? Why you standing in the way of my education?'

"And I'm, these aren't the exact words, but, I'm like . . ." Ray drew himself up again and went all stern for her, tap-dancing for his life. "'Mr. Jefferson? I don't give a damn about basketball, I am not impressed by athletes, I am not impressed by celebrity. I *am* impressed by accountability, by personal integrity and by personal initiative, none of which you are exhibiting to me at this moment. And as far as getting in the *way* of your education? Unlike many a faculty member in this school, I absolutely refuse to turn a blind eye when it comes to your obligations in my classroom.'

"'And let me tell you, those colleges that are so, so ardently wooing you? For the most part, they could care less about your education. You're simply an athlete to them, a source of income and prestige, and mark my words, Mr. Jefferson'—I think I actually used that expression, 'mark my words.' Anyways, 'Mark my words, Mr. Jefferson, once you leave this building for the last time, I seriously doubt that anyone will ever make an academic or intellectual demand on you again beyond memorizing a playbook, which at your age, as far as I'm concerned, at your tender and unformed age, is both borderline criminal and a crying shame. And believe me, if you allow this, this, *pampering* to continue, you will suffer for it. So hand in that paper, Mr. Jefferson, and then, if you choose to cruise through the next four years, there'll be no one and nothing to stop you. Certainly not me.'"

"Damn, Ray, you're good." Nerese, despite her awareness of the underpinning here, was starting to enjoy the show for its own sake.

"Why thank you," he said. "Anyways, the kid Jefferson, he's storming out and I call to him, 'Mr. Jefferson, four years from now when your athletic career most likely comes to an end, what do you envision doing with the rest of your life? What will you be prepared for?'

"And he hesitates just a tick, like I had laid some serious food for thought on him, then he storms out.

"I mean, the reality of it is, is the kid could do a million things after four years of college ball—go into coaching, go into construction, be a cop, I mean what is *any* college idiot prepared for after four years? At least this kid would have some glamour, some prestige to his name, right? Give him a job in the alumni office, whatever . . .

"Anyways, so word goes out that Mr. Montone is flunking Hammurabi Jefferson—big-ass hue and cry. Everyone's calling for his head, he's a racist, he's this, he's that.

"So the second big scene is this huge meeting two days before graduation, demanded by the PTA and half the faculty. What's this dinosaur still doing teaching in this school. He doesn't like it here, he's contemptuous of our children, he doesn't understand the day-to-day reality of life around here, he doesn't know what it means for one of our kids to get a four-year scholarship. Off with his head, off with his head . . .

"And I'm standing up there on the auditorium stage in front of this mob, I'm not saying shit. Just taking it in, got a face like a rock, I shall not be moved, racial politics be damned. You want my resignation? You got it, but this kid is not passing English. I mean, this is all said without, you know, just by my expression, thank God, because I'm an actor like you're a ballerina," Ray immediately flinching after he said that, but Nerese just shrugged it off: Tell me something I don't know.

"So anyways, everyone's going all bughouse on me and just as everything is reaching like this crescendo of outrage? I look up over the heads of all my detractors, my eyes, the camera goes to the back of the auditorium and like slowly everybody turns to see what I see and there's the kid, Hammurabi Jefferson, just standing there and when it's all silent? He starts walking down the center aisle to the podium and, oh shit . . . He's got some paper in his hand and he comes right up to me, says, 'Here,' and hands me his report on *The Great Gatsby*. I'm all like thunderstruck, the crowd is wobba-wobba, you know, milling and murmuring, this kid says to me, and this actor, Tariq Howard, was a lot better than he had to be, he says, 'Yo, I been thinking about what you *said*, Mr. Montone, and I realized that you was demanding stuff of me that I should have been demanding of myself all along, man. You were demanding that I be responsible, that I have respect for myself and that I have standards for myself. Man, I been skating through this school since day one, but that's gonna stop. Next year at college? Wherever I go, I don't care *how* much slack they're ready to cut me, man, I'm gonna get me the best education I can. I'm telling you, the next four years? I'm gonna make you proud of me.' Then he turns and faces the PTA, his parents, the other faculty. 'I'm gonna make you *all* proud of me, and I ain't talking about basketball.'

"And then, right back at me, he says, 'I tell you, Mr. Montone, whatever you think of that paper I wrote? Far's I'm concerned, you're the best damned teacher in this school.'

"At which point I'm just supposed to give this terse nod of, I don't know, communion, vindication, but what I do instead is, I just burst into tears on the set. I couldn't help it. I was so, this actor kid, the scene, it just *got* to me, and I started to fucking sob and everybody's like, stunned, all the extras, the PTA people, the director, the cameraman, the script supervisor's flipping pages like crazy, but they keep shooting because I guess my crying is so, so gut-wrenching. I even heard somebody say, 'Fucking *great.*' I guess it looked like here's this die-hard teacher Montone who's been bucking the social winds for years refusing to give in, he's on the verge of annihilation and he finally gets validation at his darkest loneliest hour or who the fuck knows, I just can't stop crying. Finally the kid, the actor playing the kid, he wings it, takes it on himself to come on up to where I am and hug me, and the show fades on that image.

"And Tweetie, it freaked me out like you can't believe. I was so scared at how I lost control. I . . . And the reason I'm *telling* all this to you instead of showing it to you on video is that I never watched it. I never wanted to watch it. I don't own it, I never saw it when it ran, nothing. And I had offers to act after that. No way. I'd just as soon be a rodeo clown.

"And, oh! You want to know about actors? After we wrapped, I was still so shaken and I wanted to connect with the kid who played Hammurabi Jefferson, somehow keep the communion going but like in real life? You know, find out what *he* thought happened between us? So I go to him and I say, 'Jeez, Tariq, I'm sorry I lost control like that. It was so powerful. What do you think . . .'

"And he looks at me, big grin, says to me, 'Yeah, thanks, I *thought* I nailed it,' turns and goes off with one of his honeys. And to this day I don't know what happened to me, I swear to God."

But Nerese got it, was starting to get it. The guy fell apart because the moment was about gratitude; he had manufactured a situation that was to the heart of him and then personally, physically played it out like it was the real thing.

Video arcades and football instead of libraries and Shakespeare, coming out of the blue to pay for Reggie Powell's funeral, volunteer teaching in that shithole of a school, playing some kind of mentor-muse-patron of the arts with Salim El-Amin . . . And taking up with the jailbird's wife. The constant white-black casting made her uncomfortable—no, made her angry; but that anger was tempered by the intuition that this compulsion in him wasn't really about race; that the element of race, the chronic hard times and neediness of poor blacks and Latinos was primarily a convenience here, the schools and housing projects of Dempsy and other places like a stocked pond in which he could act out his selfish selflessness over and over whenever and wherever the opportunity presented itself, and that he was so driven by this need, so swept away by it, that he would heedlessly, helplessly risk his life to see it played out each and every time until he finally drew the ace of spades, or swords, and got the obituary that would vindicate him, bring tears to his eyes; key word, "beloved," if only he could figure out some way to come back from the dead long enough to read it.

Agitated both by his own dramatic reenactment and fighting off the mounting terror of being back here, Ray paced the room blindly. From her seat on the couch, Nerese took in his small yearning gestures, the language of fluttering fingers, of tightening mouth and twitching eye, and she had to remind herself why she was here, why she was voluntarily putting out for this man; but for the first time in her life, the childhood memory of Ray coming to her aid with that blood- and sweat-sopped T-shirt made her feel hollow and enraged. Had that been all about this? Had he been working his shit out on her too?

But then and with great relief, she brought back—she made herself bring back—the frightened, disoriented expression on Ray's face as they sat rib to rib on that filthy curb, the great exhalation of deliverance that came out of him when Dub's father, Eddie Paris, showed up and took over the show.

And that was the problem she had with passing judgment on Ray: at heart he was a decent individual, an "honorable person," to use his own words, or at least he consciously tried to be . . .

She had no doubt that it honestly thrilled him, for whatever reason, to truly come through for people even if only in the short run—which was fine, unless in the euphoria of the moment he was in the habit of making long-term promises he had no intention of keeping, or unless he chronically confused, as his ex-wife had said, making a dent with making a splash.

But on the other hand, what the hell: a cash crisis was a cash crisis, poor people needed to bury their dead too, Paulus Hook kids were desperate for passionate teachers, no matter where their true motivations lay. And who in this life wasn't carrying around a suitcase of hidden agendas?

The mug shot of Freddy Martinez was still lying face up on the coffee table. Nerese mused on the fact that even though twenty years as a cop told her that this was the guy who had laid open Ray's head for him, she was sure that if this murderous sonofabitch were to call up Ray tonight and ask for—well, maybe not a loan, but a job reference, or some advice on how to be a better husband to Danielle, Ray, his heart swelling like a balloon, would instantly and unhesitatingly come through for the guy. And feel like a million bucks for doing so.

"So, Tweetie." Knitting a ladder of fingertips, Ray tilted tremulously into the windowsill. "How'd you become police. You were going to tell me."

"No, I got to go," she said tersely, finally jerking the line.

"Aw c'mon, don't be like that . . ."

"Next time." She began gathering herself up, wondering if in addition to springing the trap she wasn't also throwing a little payback his way for the discomfort of some of her perceptions.

"C'mon, hang in a bit," Ray forcing some cheer through the panic in his throat. "It's kind of freaky around here."

"See, what you're scrambling to do right now," Nerese said with one hand on the doorknob, "is to figure out how to make me stay without giving me what I want. The thing is? You can't."

"I'll tell you why I left the show," Ray blurted.

"Some other time."

"You don't want to hear about my, *racial* incident?" Dangling it like a bracelet.

. . .

"OK . . . By the way, I have no idea why that episode was nominated for writing. We used just about every cliché in the manual, but I guess . . . I just don't know . . . I just don't." Ray stood before her again as if onstage, Nerese back down on the couch, grudgingly giving him her eyes, telling herself a few more minutes to finally scratch an itch wouldn't make any difference here one way or the other.

"Anyways, about two weeks after I go all blubbery in front of the cameras, there's a birthday party for one of the actors. Guy plays the gay black art teacher, so you can imagine the tolerance punch lines whenever *he's* center stage, right?

"And the actor who plays this character, Tony Raymond? He got his start in the blaxploitation flicks, *Cleopatra Jones and the Casino of Gold, Blacula, The Mack,* and everybody loved this guy, great guy, one of those feast-or-famine actors, nothing doing for fifteen years, and now he's working again and just, in general, happy to be alive practicing his craft, joy to the world. And for his birthday, it was going to be a surprise costume party with a seventies theme, you know, everybody dressing like popcorn pimps, disco ducks, dashikis, bell-bottoms, Afro wigs, medallions, marshmallow heels, muttonchops, miniskirts.

"But me, I don't want to do the matching vest and pants *Saturday Night Fever* thing. Me, I have to have a fucking brainstorm. Me, I'm going as Curtis Mayfield, you know, 'Superfly,' 'Pusherman,' 'Freddy's Dead' . . . Me, White Ray Mitchell, as Curtis Mayfield, OK? Not offensive enough? How about this. Mayfield's died since then, but at that time he was a quadriplegic. So how about in addition to wearing an Afro-trimmed bald wig, jawline beard and big pink tinted shades, I go in a fucking, *wheel*chair.

"We were in New York shooting exteriors at the time, so we have the party at B. Smith's, food, music, costumes, it was a blast. They even hired Pop Staples from the Staple Singers, guy was in his eighties, had everybody going crazy on the dance floor. Except me, of course, because you know, I'm in character.

"Anyways, pretty quickly into the party, one of the actors, the guy who plays the black principal of the school, comes up, says, 'Ray, what's with the wheelchair? You OK?' I say, 'I'm Curtis.' 'Curtis? Curtis who?' 'Mayfield.' He's like, 'You're . . . I don't get it.' So I explain. I say, 'He got hit by a light pole onstage at some concert a few years back . . . He's, he's a quad . . . he's paralyzed, I think.' Guy says, 'He's in a wheelchair?' At which point I'm, I say, 'Well, yeah, he is.'

"And it's not like I was oblivious to the possible downside reaction to what I was doing, Tweetie, it's just, you get caught up in the excitement, the, the *hit* you could make if you pull this off. I did, at any rate. And the guy says to me, 'You're coming in here, to this party, and you're Curtis Mayfield in his wheelchair . . .' And I look, and I can see in his eyes, him processing the information. I can see the mental violence that I had just perpetrated on him, and I'm . . . I want to die, you know, finally. So, I can't even look at him, I'm so horrified by myself. I just mumble, 'No, man, I *love* Curtis Mayfield. He's like my hero,' or some such shit, but the guy's not even there anymore, he's stormed off into the crowd, and as I'm sitting there, I know the word is going around the party like the Ebola virus, and I'm ashamed, I'm heartsick, and I'm frightened. And I know I have to get out of that goddamn wheelchair instantly, but I *can't*. I'm so fucking mortified that I can't, get, *up*. And so I sit. Every, every atom in me is bubbling with horror. No one goes near me. No one says hi, all these people I've worked with for over two years, and I can't get up. Finally I just roll myself into a corner of the room, rip off the Afro beard, the wig, toss the glasses, try to rearrange my hair into some kind of half-assed pompadour and I'm ready to tell people I'm George Wallace, which I'm not sure was a hell of a lot better, but of course, nobody asks, because everybody knows I'm Curtis fucking Mayfield."

Ray paced in front of Nerese like a manic sentry, addressing first one wall then the other, the words rattling out of him as if he had delivered this tale verbatim every day of his life, although she was fairly sure that if he had, he'd delivered it mainly to himself.

She had no gut reaction to the story yet, no inclination to pass judgment one way or the other; Ray's self-castigating rhythms neutralizing any real sense of outrage in her.

"So, OK, I'm sitting there in a corner, maybe fifteen, twenty minutes, I don't know whether to sneak out, try to apologize, what . . . Finally, just as I'm about to make a break for the door? The actor that I, exposed myself to comes tearing out of the crowd, corners me in my wheelchair, and at first I thought he was going to slug me, but instead he says, 'How would *you* have liked it if I had come in here tonight wearing striped pajamas and had numbers tattooed inside my arm, huh?' And the die-hard wiseass in me wanted to say, 'But it's a seventies party.' But of course I don't.

"And I could tell he had put some time and effort into the wording of what he'd just said, which made me feel worse but it also made it easier for me because it gave me the chance to say I'm sorry, which I do, and then I leave.

"Except that night I kind of lose track of what was freaking me out and I go from writing this guy an apology note to thinking where the hell does he get off comparing the Holocaust to a singer having an accident at a concert, you know, tearing up the note, getting all Zionic, coming off it, redrafting the note . . .

"Anyways the bottom line is, I just walk into the producer's trailer the next day, you know, my ex-student Shaker, and the minute he sees me he says, 'Oh my God, it's Curtis Mayfield! And not only is he walking again, folks, but he's turned white! Great glory to God!'

"The next day I fly back to LA with everybody else, but a week after that I was off the show."

"You got fired?"

"I quit."

"Your boss, he was black?"

"Yeah."

"And he didn't fire you?"

"He thought what I did was in bad taste but people would get over it."

"But you quit."

"Yeah."

"Because of that."

"Yeah. What would you have done?"

"If I were you?"

"If you were him. My boss."

"I don't know shit about TV except how to watch it."

"C'mon, Tweetie, you know what I mean."

"Like I said," she muttered, not particularly interested in being his race priest, "I don't know shit save for how to watch it." Then, to change the subject, anything to change the subject, "So that was it for you and TV?"

"Yeah, pretty much. Save for one last trip, one last stab." He stepped over to the sliding glass doors and gazed out at the river, waiting for the go-ahead.

Nerese glanced at the sun going down, wondering if by staying for more of the show she'd be allowing him to sate himself with anecdote and achieve a state of repose that would undo the fear. But as she watched him minutely jig and jerk before her even now, in this fleeting moment of

calm, she decided that for people like Ray, the state of repose was a lifelong mirage, perpetually just ahead but never experienced.

"Go on," she said with a blatant heaviness.

"Yeah, so after I quit?" Ray wheeled back to her as if someone had
flicked his switch. "Pretty soon after that I came back East, and after all
the insanity around here somewhat settled down I kind of develop this
three-point game plan. One, I was going to get my own place in New
York. Two, I was going to maybe try and take a shot at some serious
writing. And three, I had this fantasy of really connecting with Ruby, for
the first time, like, *connecting*." He paused to draw a tone-shifting breath.
"But I have to tell you, after a few weeks? It was like, one, I wound up here
on the geriatric Riviera, two, all I wrote of consequence was checks,
and three, with Ruby? It was 'Hello, Ruby! Here's your unemployed dad,
coming back to New York, expressly to *be* with you!' The pressure's enormous. What do you say, what do you do. Anyways'—waving himself off—
"everything's boomeranging on me, I feel like the man without a country,
so what I did was, I didn't want to go back to *Brokedown*, but I reached out
to John Shaker with this idea I had for a new show. It was going to be
about cabbies—not like *Taxi*—but a drama that— See, in New York you
can always tell the newest influx of immigrants, which nations were coming over in force because they all become cabbies, it's the easiest job to get
right off the boat. And, if you really want to know which group is the most
recent to have arrived? All you have to do is check the registration number
on the hack license posted on the partition. If it starts with a zero, it's some
old Jew with hair coming out of his ears, been driving since DiMaggio's
hitting streak. But if the numbers start with a five or a six? You got the
newest wave. So, for example, last winter it was all Fukien Chinese,
spring it's Sikhs from Punjab, summer it's Hindus from Gujarat, fall it's
Albanian Muslims or whatever. And I wanted to do a show that would
have different main characters, follow their newborn lives in the city, you
know, living in cramped basements, sending their money back home, the
loneliness, the culture shock . . . I'm making it sound way more of a bum-
mer than it was, although my first idea for a title was *Wretched Refuse*."

"Meaning . . ."

He stared at her for a beat without answering, then forged on.

"Anyways, I catch Shaker coming through town, and he loves the idea.
Well, I mean everybody loves everything in that business, at least to your
face. The thing is, Shaker tells me his own contract is up at the teen network and he's probably not going to renew, he's been talking to various

networks looking for the best deal for himself and he's sort of leaning towards this one particular network at the moment, let's sit down with some of their guys, run it by them, see how they react.

"Now this is in New York, right? We go in, I do my thing, the pitch, everybody's like, 'Wow, I love it I love it I love it.'

"Me and Shaker, we're all V for Victory, it's in the bag, the only thing left is to get together with the Head Guy in Burbank, get his OK, and we're off to the races.

"And I can't wait. I'm so excited, especially because if we pull this off? What we're talking about is a New York–based production, which means I can have my cake and eat it too, you know, in regards to not bailing on Ruby. Plus, it'll be much more relaxed between us because I won't have all this free time to moon around in . . . In any event, the next step is flying me out to LA to sit with Shaker and the head of programming, get the final OK.

"And I ask Ruby to come with me. She'd never been to California and it just sounded like the best idea in the world, you know, watch Daddy score.

"So off we go, the network puts us up in a beachfront hotel in Santa Monica, she takes one look at all the movies we can order on the TV? She doesn't even glance out the window. And I'm not one of those 'It's a beautiful day, go outside and play' type parents so . . . And in all fairness to her, she *did* take a peek at the Pacific Ocean on her way to check out the minifridge, but whatever.

"OK. This sit-down, it's for the next morning, right? About nine o'clock that night, Shaker calls the room, tells me he won't be attending the meeting—he's not sure, he's developed some doubts about the premise, doesn't think he can go in there and say for sure he wants to do it.

"And I'm like, 'Shit, man, we just flew out.' He says, 'It's still a great idea, Ray, maybe just not for me.' Which means he's definitely not going to do it. 'But hey, man, you've been around the block. Take the meeting yourself, it's your baby, you don't need me, the networks have producers coming out of their ass, don't sweat it, get what's yours, brother!' I get off the phone, I know him well enough not to take it personally, and I start thinking, You know? He's right. Let me see what I can do on my own. It's my idea, I don't really need him godfathering me wherever I go.

"So come the morning, the studio has sent a car and driver for us. It was a town car, not a limo, which I was hoping for, you know, for Ruby's sake, but the driver's wearing a suit at least and off we go out to Burbank.

"I'm so jazzed. I feel like I'm both showing Ruby off, and showing off to Ruby. We go up there, the corridors are lined with huge blowups of the network stars, the kid's all big-eyed, I go in for the meeting, there's the guy, there's the bottled water, he says how he's such a big fan of *Broke-down High*—which in my mind makes him either a moron or a liar—and I start laying out the taxi thing and I do it very well. I'd much rather talk than write, and he's listening, nodding, making appreciative noises, takes me about fifteen minutes, and I'm done. He says, 'I just love it. This is exactly what I've been looking for. It's gritty, it's real, it's got heart.' Says, 'Screw all this other crap we do. I'm an old Brooklyn boy, Midwood High class of '66, and this is getting me right where I live. Great. Just great.'

"So I say, 'Great.'

"He says, 'Great, OK. Let me just talk to John Shaker, get him on board, and we'll put you guys to work.' And I'm, 'Uh, Shaker's not, he's not coming on board, I don't think . . . Didn't you . . . I assumed every-body . . . Uh, duh, uh.'

"And the guy doesn't miss a beat. He never stops smiling, doesn't come out and say to me, 'Well, if John Shaker, who we desperately want to be in business with, is *not* involved on this, why the fuck are you wasting my time?' He just says, 'Well, OK, look, give me a few days to live with it, let it sift down . . .' You know, like his head was some kind of colander, and I knew the thing was dead in the water and it hurt. I felt like two cents and, shit, I have Ruby out there, what am I . . .

"So we shake hands, I go out to the reception area, try to be cool, happy, Ruby takes one look at me and says, 'Dad, did you get fired?' Whis-pers it, and I'm like, 'No honey, not at all,' which is technically true since you need a job in order to get fired from it but like any sensitive kid, she can *smell* it on me.

"So we go down to the car and I tell the driver that I'll pay him to stay with us until the evening. I'm gonna show Ruby a great time. In fact, after that meeting, in my mind, it's life and death that I show Ruby a great time. So I have him take us to the Beverly Center, which is this six-story indoor mall. I mean, we just came from Gray York and, so far, Ruby's take on California is that it's all indoors. But I know my kid. I know what's fun for her so, screw the Pacific Ocean once again and off we go. Unfortunately my kid also knows me, and she's looking very troubled.

"We get in the mall and I say, 'Ruby, the hell with it. Let's just buy shit. Whatever you want, who cares . . .' She says, 'That's OK, I'll just look.' I'm like, 'Ruby, c'mon, I just swung a big deal, a dollar's like a penny today.' And I sort of bully her into buying some studs for her ears, can't get her to buy clothes, can't get her to buy any skin stuff, she grudgingly lets me buy her some teen magazine and it got really tense, the both of us like in this battle in the mall. And at one point she stops at a kiosk where they're selling belly-button rings, she just got hers pierced a few weeks before and I see her eyeing this one ring, sort of a curved silver rod with dice at either end and, I'm instantly breathing down her neck, 'You want that? You want that?' Which of course makes her want to run away. She says, 'Just looking,' and wanders off. I'm so panic-stricken, the minute her back is turned, I buy it plus two others, then I sort of mosey up behind her, say, 'Miss, did you drop these?' and show her the three belly-button rings in my hand and she, goes, berserk. She starts sobbing and screaming at me, 'Stop buying me stuff! Stop buying me stuff! Please! Daddy! Please! I don't *want* anything!'" Ray had to pause.

"And she's so freaked, and everybody around us just freezes and the tears are just running and she's just about doubled over. 'Daddy! *Please!*' And she *flings* away the ear studs I made her buy, and *throws* away the teen magazine and people just won't stop staring and her eyes are like . . . she can barely open them and I just . . . I just grab her. I didn't know what else to do. I've never been so miserable. I'm just holding onto her until she stops crying, and the people are like, 'What's he doing to her, get security, get a cop,' and I'm like, 'Ssh ssh ssh,' rocking her, *I'm* crying, *she's* crying, holding her, holding her until she starts calming down and I'm, 'Ruby, I'm so sorry,' she's, 'I don't *want* anything, Daddy, please, please.' And finally she gets a grip, steps away a little, embarrassed in front of all the people, and I'm, 'Sweetie, screw it, let's just leave the shit where you threw it,' and then I make a big show of tossing away the belly-button rings and I'm, 'Hey, you want to go see a movie? They have a whole multiplex on the top floor. How about it.' And she says, 'Yeah, sure.' Her eyes were almost swollen shut from crying and from jet lag—I never even factored that in—although, well, fuck the jet lag. In any event, we start heading to the escalators and now that she's kind of blown it out, aired her misery, my first instinct, in order to cheer her up is, of course, to *buy* her something . . . Which I don't, but as we pass one of the belly-button rings on the floor, I see her kind of checking it out from the corner of her eye, so I took a chance, just picked it up, put it in my pocket, and we went to the movies.

"And for the rest of the day we had a good time. Saw the movie, went back to the hotel, ordered room service, watched TV, and when it got dark we walked down to the Santa Monica Pier where they have this half-assed amusement park set up.

"We check that out for a bit, then we walk back to the hotel along the beach, the only time she likes the beach is at night, go upstairs, watch another video selection, halfway through which she just conks out. I mean it was one hell of a day, but I'm thinking in its own way it turned out OK. Ruby got to blow some stuff out, I might or might not have gotten some insight into myself but we both hung in, went to bed reasonably happy. I mean I couldn't even remember the pitch session I had had that morning that, you know, set everything in motion. I mean that Burbank sit-down seemed like a year ago, the day was so intense. And right before I rack out myself, I slip the new belly-button ring in the secret stash compartment of her overnight bag and then I'm out like a light, day is done, OK? Three o'clock in the morning I get woken up, Ruby's having a nightmare and she's screaming her head off, sitting up in bed, half in, half out of it, just shrieking. I wake her up, 'Ruby Ruby Ruby,' she comes to . . . You know what her nightmare was? She dreamt that we were walking around Hopewell, me and her, and I was showing her all the secret places where jewels were hidden, except that every time I opened my mouth to speak to her, blood spurted out. No words, just blood, and she was desperately trying to shut me up so that no more blood would come out and I wouldn't bleed to death, but I just kept flapping my lips, walking and spurting blood. Nice, huh?

"So we come back to New York. The TV thing never happens, of course, and I just stop writing. But, because I'm kind of at square one again? Man, I start thinking about cocaine, having incredibly realistic cocaine dreams. I never actually *do* the cocaine in the dreams, it's more about scoring it, figuring where I can hole up with it. But I never get around to doing it. And I know I never will in real life, either. I just won't.

"And since then I'm trying real hard with Ruby, you know, just to be a little more relaxed. I'd like to think I'm better with her these days but probably not. And, like I told you, I volunteered to teach that class at Paulus Hook because I have to do something, everybody's got to do something so it might as well be the *right* thing. You know, as in fight the good fight . . .

"I mean, half the time I'm teaching there I don't know what the hell I'm doing, or *why* I'm doing it, but I get some good hits off it, click with some of the kids, you know, see them open up a little, reach for things that they normally wouldn't have any inclination to reach for, and that kind of feeds me for now. I mean, like I said, anytime I want I can go to LA, get back in the saddle on some dopey show or other, but . . ." Ray went off somewhere, came back. "I'll tell you Tweetie, do you know what I'm really doing these days? I'm waiting . . .

"Some days, I feel this, this *thing*, this great, thing inside me, I can't . . . It's like a welling sensation. How can I . . .

"OK. For example. Back in that mall in LA? After me and Ruby go to the multiplex we go down to the food court, get a table. Ruby had this homework assignment for English. She had to write, just sit somewheres and write about the life around her, mankind or whatever.

"So, we're sitting there, she's pretty much OK by now, still had that splotch-mask a little from crying, but she's settling into it and I'm watching her, her posture, her repose. She's got these long arms and she's got her chin in her hand, elbow on the table, very, she's elegant, everything's so, *long* on her, you know, arms, fingers, neck, and I just watch her settle into this rhythm of jotting stuff in her journal, stops, looks around, focuses on this or that person, kind of holds them in her gaze then drops her eyes to the page, jots a little, looks up, observes . . . It's like I'm watching her mind work—writing, looking, writing, and all of a sudden I get hit with this feeling, and I can never nail it, what it is, but it's regarding something I'm about to *become* or *do*, I don't know which, but it feels gigantic, and at the same time it feels very very fragile, and when it comes down on me I always wind up getting teary because, because there's a *goodness* in it, this thing, like, a passing on to others, from me to them, so like I'm both the source and the receiver of something. But I can't, I can't really describe or articulate . . ." Ray's voice finally trailed off.

"Maybe it's just feeling good about being with your daughter," Nerese said, carefully. "You know, a nice quiet moment together. Maybe it's just that."

"Yeah, well, no, there's that, of course . . ." Ray laughed it off but she could sense his embarrassment. "So what's your deal. Come on. How the hell did you become police . . ."

Now that he had come to the end of his string of stories, she could sense the fear coming back on him, hear it in his voice.

"I don't think so, Ray." The world outside had fallen into the tail end of twilight, and Nerese, getting back with the program, finally struggled to her feet.

"Jesus." He started pacing again. "So you're just going to leave?"

"Hey, give me what I want and I'll camp out on your couch all night," Nerese offering that rather than an exchange of autobiographies; something indefinable in the texture of his history—the racial stuff wasn't it—made her want to safeguard the details of her own transformation from disaffected kid to police officer for at least another conversation or two. Or possibly indefinitely.

"Going once," she said, gathering her things. "Going twice . . ."

"No. OK. You just don't . . ." Then, "Fine." And once again she lost him, the fear of coming forward on this and finally giving up Freddy's name apparently still greater than the fear of being left alone with the hovering smell of his own blood.

If fear, in fact, was the operative emotion here.

"Take care now," she said.

"Hey, before you go. How's your guy doing?" Ray grabbing at straws.

"My guy?" Nerese was thrown. "I don't *have* a guy."

"I meant your son."

"Darren? Darren's good," she said quickly, to be done with it.

"I thought he was going to come see me or call me about colleges."

"He didn't call you yet?" She froze in a posture of astonishment. "Man, I have been on his case to reach out to you for a solid week now." A straight-out lie.

In addition to her usual ban on bringing Darren into work conversations, she discovered that the same elusive instinct that made her balk at telling Ray her own life story inclined her to keep her son out of his orbit too, ban or no ban, and that this protective wariness about Ray would probably hold sway even if the circumstances were purely social.

"All right, let me go home and have a conversation with his ass," Nerese said, once again turning for the door.

"Tweetie." Ray stood there in the middle of the room, his right hand curled into itself, a deer hoof. "No. OK. No. If you have to go, you have to go."

Nerese made it to the door and, despite everything, faltered, not having the heart to just walk out on him like this without giving him something.

"Do you remember a Hopewell guy, Tommy Potenza?"

"Potenza?" Ray shrugged. "Not . . . No."

"Well, he remembers you and he wanted me to ask you if you were game for hooking up with him. I took the liberty of saying you were."

Ray shrugged, then said almost shyly, "Whatever. Sure."

"Good. I'll set it up," reaching for the door again but then still feeling guilty. "Actually, you know what? Give me your phone. I'll call him right now."

Ray stepped to the portable sitting on the end table among the surviving vases, but found only the base there. He spent a moment scanning the room for the receiver, then pressed the locator button. The high-pitched beeps came from under the dining table nearly twenty feet away, and he had to get down on all fours to retrieve it.

"Battery's dead," he said from his knees.

"What's it doing under the table?"

"I don't know." He said, looking off.

"Battery's dead. So it must've been laying there since . . ."

"I don't know," he repeated, cutting her off, suddenly as eager to see her leave as he had been for her to stay, and by the time Nerese had made it to the street, she had already contracted Bobby Sugar to lift Ray's phone records, incoming and outgoing, for the last month, up to and including the day of the assault.

Although it was only seven in the evening, as she walked to the parking lot Nerese was enveloped by the stillness of the place, the sound of her own footsteps seemingly louder than they should be, until a solitary figure stepped into a cone of streetlight from out of the darkness, heading toward her, Nerese's right hand instinctively dropping to thumb-graze her sidearm.

"Hey, how you doin'." Salim El-Amin, smoking a cigarette and sporting a backpack, casually raised a hand in greeting, then just kept trucking past her toward Ray's building.

"Hang on," Nerese called after him, Salim wheeling to face her. "You going to see Ray?"

"Yeah, uh-huh." He stepped on his cigarette butt.

"Where you coming from?"

"Out there," pointing to the unbroken darkness, the lights of downtown Dempsy and the Gothic spires of the hospital center.

"Out there *where*." Nerese squinted at him. "How'd you get here?"

"I took the bus to the front gate then I walked," Salim said, looking antsy now.

"The guard just let you in?"

"I din't see no guard." He pulled a loose Newport from his jacket and fired up as if settling in for a long interrogation.

"Is Ray expecting you?" Nerese asked.

"Me?" He touched his own chest. "Not like, *expecting* expecting. I tried to call, but nobody answered so I thought I'd just, you know . . ."

"What." Nerese cocked her head.

"See how he's doing."

"Nobody answers the phone, so that's a sign to you he's home?"

"I don't know." Salim briskly rubbed his temples. "I thought maybe the phone's broke."

"What time did you try to call?"

"A hour ago?" Looking away.

"I was up there an hour ago. The phone never rang."

"Yeah well, see? That's what I'm saying." He shuffled in place. "Maybe it's broke."

Maybe it was, maybe it wasn't; Nerese not knowing if the other extensions in the apartment were affected by the dead portable under the dining table, but she said nothing, letting a silence come down between them, an awkward half-grin on Salim's face the only sign of resistance to her overwhelming authority in this and in all future encounters.

"Well, Ray's sleeping now," she finally said.

"OK." Salim still not looking at her.

"Anything *I* can help you with?"

"Not, not really." He stepped on the second cigarette, Nerese for a fleeting beat thinking the kid was actually going to take her up on her offer.

"Where do you live?"

"On Tonawanda? I don't live there per se, it's my mother's apartment but I'm staying there at the moment, allegedly with my fiancée, until I can get myself fully composed."

"I'll give you a ride home," she said.

"Nah, that's OK. I'll take the bus." Salim was finally on the move, backstepping in the direction of the gate, half a mile down the road.

"I'll drive you to the bus." Nerese was on the move too, now.

"Nah. I like walking around here. It's peaceful, you know what I'm saying?" Salim called back to her as, slim as a blade, he passed through the solitary cone of streetlight again. "But thank you for your consideration."

< Chapter 20

Salim — January 26

In the midst of a pallidly sunny winter afternoon, Salim entered Ray's apartment lugging a yard-square portfolio with one hand and gently pushing his son ahead of him with the other. The boy, maybe three years old, had luminous gray eyes and wore his hair in tightly braided furrows that were pinned straight back on his scalp like ram horns.

"How you doin', Ray!" Salim sounded downright joyous. "This is my son, Omar."

"He's so . . . *Look* at this guy," Ray said with a forced cheeriness, feeling awkward, watching the kid as if he were being watched himself.

Omar was dressed head to toe in denim: jeans, jacket, flop hat and tiny backpack.

"Can you say hello, Boo Boo?" Salim spoke loudly and slowly as if the boy were in shock.

"Hel-lo," Omar said in a surprisingly deep singsong, then made a bee-line for the television, gluing his body spread-eagle to the bottom of the wide screen like a press-on Garfield.

"No TV, Boo Boo."

"Hel-lo," the kid said again, shrugged, tossing his head from shoulder to shoulder as if working out neck kinks, and marched out of the room.

"He's a pisser," Ray said.

"Yeah, uh-huh. His name is Omar but I call him Boo Boo."

Being able to present his son like this, to display his boy in all his effort-less three-year-old glory, seemed to put Salim in a state of near euphoria; and Ray loved him for that.

"Boo Boo!" Salim called after him. "Come here, Boo Boo!"

The kid marched back into the room.

"Count to fifteen, Boo Boo."

Omar just stared at his father with those cat's eyes.

"C'mon, Boo Boo, *one* . . ."

"One . . ." the kid said.

"Two . . ." Salim said.

"Two . . ." Staring at his father.

"Three . . ."

"Three . . ." Staring, waiting.

"See, he usually just does this on his own. He might be shy today."

"No, he's great."

Salim, despite his hyper-pride, didn't seem overly anxious about his son's performance; this impressed Ray no end.

"Can I get him something?"

"Boo Boo, you want some juice?" Salim near shouting again.

The kid made a blur of his hand, rejecting the offer.

"Do you want anything?" Ray asked.

"Nah, I'm good." Salim touched his gut. "Here." He untied the black carrying case, revealing maybe a dozen drawings in there, then finger-walked the edges until he found the one he was looking for.

"Yeah, here." He handed it over to Ray. "This is for your daughter."

It was a seventies stylized odalisque, a long, curvy black woman lying on her side in a leopardskin string bikini. She had a high Kathleen Cleaver Afro and heavy-lidded, almost Asian eyes, like a calendar girl for a malt liquor distributor.

Ray knew he was being buttered up for something but he was touched nonetheless.

"Beautiful," he murmured, striving for a tone of awe.

"Yeah," Salim said. "That money you gave me? I gave five hundred to my fiancée, you know, for future house contributions? Took three fifty and opened a checking account, took the rest and went and bought art supplies over in New York. Like here . . ." He squatted alongside his portfolio and started laying out his sketches on the black-and-white tiled floor. Half of them were studies of Bambi-eyed ragamuffins brandishing automatic weapons—a marriage of Japanese animé and Keane orphan; the others were portraits of Deco-style black men, street people angularized almost to pure geometry, every one of them either on his knees and in chains, or with arms outspread crucifixion style.

"Beautiful," Ray said again.

"Yeah," Salim purred. "You really got me going again with my art. You saved my life the other day."

"Why are all these kids packin'?" Ray asked, to deflect the flattery.

"Yeah, OK. The reason they all got guns? It ain't to rob nobody or hurt nobody. It's for protection, you know, protecting what's theirs because that's the way it is."

Omar stepped on one of his father's drawings. "Take care, Boo Boo," Salim said gently, pushing his son backward off the matting. "OK, but now here's the one I really want you to see."

Salim singled out another ghetto waif with a Glock-19. The kid, sporting comically oversize hand-me-downs and a sideways baseball cap, was pointing his hand-cannon at the viewer, squinting one-eyed to draw a bead, the tip of his tongue peeking out in concentration.

"What's Mine Is Mine" ran in bold letters beneath his sneakered feet.

"It's strong," Ray said.

"Yeah. That's what I think, too. It's gonna be my new logo."

"Logo for what?"

"Yeah, OK. This is what I want to talk to you about."

"OK," Ray said, thinking, Shit . . .

"I got a business proposition for you. See, the other day, like I said, you really got me going about my future, and look . . ." Salim produced the slim catalogue of a sportswear wholesaler; page after page of item codes and order forms, Ray's eyes getting heavier than lead.

"OK, this here?" Salim touched his new logo. "It's gonna cost me seventy-five dollars to make a silk screen, OK? Now I can handle that off my savings. But here . . ." He ran a finger down one of the stock lists. "I can get me a dozen T-shirts white or black for like twenty-five dollars, OK? I order say, fifty dozen? That's fifty times twenty-five is like twelve hundred and fifty dollars, or a hundred dozen, that's . . ."

Salim extracted a slip from his jeans pocket; Ray saying, "Twenty-five hundred."

"Yeah, uh-huh. Now. Those hundred dozen I just bought? I take them to this printer with my silk-screen? That's like four dollars a shirt for the 'What's Mine Is Mine' logo to go on, OK? So that's like four times twelve hundred shirts is forty-eight hundred dollars plus the twenty-five hundred dollars for the shirts themselves is like a seventy-three-hundred-dollar investment, breaks down to a little over six dollars per shirt except for I am *selling* these shirts for fifteen dollars each, which is like a nine-dollar profit or a ten-thousand-seven-hundred-dollar profit on the whole thing minus five hundred for a vendor's license which is still over ten Bigs free and clear, no overhead, no store rent, no nothing, just me and a folding table right on the street, or hey, I don't even *need* a folding table, I'll sell 'em on the hoof straight out the backpack 'cause I love to walk and I ain't *never* been afraid to meet the people. I'm telling you, Ray, Mr. Mitchell, I'll be paying you back in like three weeks, reinvest the rest in more shirts and I'm off to the races."

"Seventy-three hundred . . . Jesus, Salim."

"OK, OK . . ." Salim grinned, prepared for this. "See, you talk about John Shaker, how he's a prominent television personality now and that's great because he never took his eye off the prize and he got what's his . . . But like, that's just inspiration for *me* because I *know* what it took to be a focused individual in that school, how hard that was back then. See, W.E.B. Du Bois in *The Souls of Black Folk*, he called it the crab-cage effect, how if one crab starts trying to climb out of the bucket the others by reflex pull him down, but Shaker got out irregardless and more power to him but see, I'm in that same crab bucket still and you know, back then I didn't even know enough to try to climb out. I mean, back then I was all about the street, being a kingpin on the street, and we all know where *that* leads, right? And that day you took me to the advertising agency? And then I was supposed to go right away to the art school and I didn't? You was trying to hoist me out of the bucket but I was too naive to know that, my vision was too limited to see that, and I blew it. I disappointed you, I disappointed myself . . . But whatever has been done to me since then . . . I got shot," showing Ray a starred scar on his shoulder, "stabbed," raising his shirt to reveal a whitish keloid on his rib cage, "got incarcerated three times, *two* times for being in the wrong place at the wrong time, nothing more, been in the joint like, six years altogether but here I am, you know what I'm saying? I'm still here, I don't eat meat, I don't drink, I don't use profanity, I read everything I can get my hands on, I'm observing the, the *tenets* of my religion, get up five o'clock every morning to perform my prayers. I got my son, my health, and now, *right* now I'm finally about crawling up and out of that crab bucket and yeah, seventy-three hundred dollars is a lot of cheese, and there may be a few other people I can try and touch for it like my mother, who frankly has been in contempt for me since the day I was born or one or two others that in terms of my legal and spiritual well-being I don't even want to associate with no more let alone be in *debt* to, but I'm coming to *you* for it, because ever since I blew off the art school thing? I need for you to be proud of me. I need for you to see your faith in me was not unabated."

Salim delivered all this while balanced on his hams, surrounded by his artwork in the middle of the floor, Ray uncomfortably standing over him, remembering one of his mother's favorite sayings: On your back can be a very effective fighting position.

"Are we talking fifty dozen or a hundred," Ray dropping to one knee in order to achieve psychic balance. "Because you started out talking fifty."

"I'll leave that up to you."

"Because fifty dozen is half that amount."

"No, I hear you."

Omar had found a pen and squatting splay-footed started scribbling lines across one of his father's drawings, long flattened interconnected Z's, like the polygraph readout of a liar.

"Watch it, honey," Ray said, then repeated to himself, Honey.

But Salim simply turned the drawing over, tapped the blank back and said in that overloud voice, "Draw a picture for Ray, Boo Boo. Draw."

"Jaw," the kid said, once again delicately squatting, and continued his back-and-forth lines.

"Make a face, Boo Boo."

As Ray crouched there, squirming over Salim's pitch, Omar drew two wobbly circles inside a larger circle, like two eggs in a frying pan.

"See, all this I'm talking about with you?" Salim bounced to take the burn out of his knees. "I mean it's for me, yeah sure, but mainly it's for my son, you know what I'm saying? I mean, I'm not gonna be one of these no-show fathers. I'm determined on that."

"No, I hear you," Ray said faintly.

"OK, then," Salim said, then, gingerly duck-walking toward Ray, embraced him in a light hug, Ray staring at Omar over his father's shoulder, the boy untroubled, one eye shut in a luxuriously feline yawn; Ray thinking, Fifty dozen and be done with it.

Both men rose to their feet, Ray self-consciously brushing the knees of his jeans.

"Hey, Mr. Mitchell?" Salim began, his voice suddenly awkward. "Can I ask your advice on something?"

And with that simple vague pre-request, something in the tone of it, the genuine tentativeness of it, Ray completely melted, suddenly found himself more at Salim's disposal than he had been at any other point in this visit.

"I have got to tell you, I'm like almost thirty years old, right? And you won't find many African-American men admitting to this, but I don't understand jack about women, I really don't."

"I'm divorced myself," Ray said easily, this flip self-effacement masking an eagerness to successfully field whatever was coming his way.

"See, my fiancée, Michelle, right? She works in Jersey City, is like the receptionist for this stockbrokerage company on Exchange Place? Started out as a office temp after Omar was born, they liked her so much they gave her the job full-time, OK? And she brings home three hundred and ninety-two dollars at the end of the week and I told you how she had me on this allowance, was breaking my back about me not being able to contribute to Omar's upbringing, the house maintenance and everything else, right? OK. So. The other day I come in with the five hundred of the money you gave me to finally pitch in, there you go, right?"

Ray knew exactly what was coming now, and almost physically flexed for it.

"So I give her the cash, right? She's like, 'Why'd that guy give you this money. What's he want you to do for it. What are you into,' all bitching me out. And I'm, 'What the hell, 'Chelle, you always complaining about me not holding up my end around here, coming through around here, the man's my old teacher, has been trying to get me to believe in myself since the dinosaur days, what is your *problem?*' And Ray"—Salim reached out, touched the back of his hand—"when I was in jail? She'd come every week to visit. Always had a smile on her face, always brought the baby, food, cigarettes, books. Whatever I asked for, and she never missed a visiting day. And you know, just because I wasn't bringing in money, that didn't mean I wasn't partaking in the house, you know what I'm saying? When I first met her, she had a alcohol problem. Nineteen years old with a alcohol problem. Pint bottles of Hennessey in the hamper, under the bed, behind the couch, and I helped her clean up. I was like a bombardment of positivism. I went to meetings with her and everything. I couldn't bring her into my religion, she's still Christian, but she ain't had a drink for five years. *I* did that. *Me.* But now here's the thing . . . I'm *free.* I'm on the brink of making it all happen for myself, for *us,* I ain't *never* been in better shape physically, mentally, spiritually, I walk in the door for the first time in *years* with money for the table?" He reached out and touched Ray again. "Mr. Mitchell. She won't *talk* to me, be in *bed* with me, look me in the eye . . . What's it *about.*"

"Look, Salim," Ray began, almost incandescent with goodwill. "Now that you're finally out, she's probably having a delayed reaction to your going in to begin with. That being said, and I'm just speculating here, so don't . . . But there are some people, they piss and moan about having to carry you, about how everything's always on them, blah blah blah. But what they get in exchange for that is total control over you. And, I don't know your fiancée, but for a lot of people, being on top like that is well worth the carrying charge, do you understand what I'm saying?"

"Yeah, uh-huh. I hear you, I hear you," Salim said. "Domination through financial takeover. But see, I'm not like most men, you know, be they African-American, white, Jew. I don't have a need to, to *dominate* in return. I just want to be equal with her. I just want to hold up my end, you know?" Salim's voice started to get away from him, become feathery and hoarse. "And I will. No doubt about it. I survived six years of penitentiary life, and there is nothing out here, and I mean *nothing*, that can compare to that. End of the day?" Salim stopped, tried to remaster his delivery. "End of the day? My son . . ." He quickly swiped at his cheekbones with the heels of his palms, a graceful fanning motion outward toward the ears. "End of the day . . ." he repeated, the words then coming out of him in a burst as if racing the tears. "My son will look backwards and have great pride for his father."

Salim turned his face away. "I'm sorry."

"No problem," Ray said, desperately trying to hold onto the notion that this kid was maybe still working him, but then losing all self-control himself.

"Oh, what the hell, Coley. Let's go for the hundred dozen."

Chapter 21 >

Danielle — February 24

Nerese waited for Danielle Martinez in the encroaching twilight under the marquee of the RKO Rajah in downtown Dempsy.

The first time she had ever come to this place was as a kid to see *Enter the Dragon* with her grandmother in the early seventies; the last time was as a uniformed cop, helping to oust the more than two hundred homeless who had taken up semipermanent residence inside the long-dark theater in the early nineties.

In its seventy-seven years of existence, the Rajah had gone from splendiferous vaudeville house to movie palace to multiplex to crack squat, to in its most recent incarnation, school building; the city, a few years back, had finally unloaded this white elephant by leasing it for a dollar a year to Dempsy Community College which, with minimal modifications, had converted the eight smallish theaters into lecture halls.

A moment after hearing a prolonged rasping bell from inside the building, Nerese was enveloped by exiting students—working adults, for the most part—separating then closing around her like streaming water around a rock. Everyone and his cousin was seemingly making a break for the street through those doors—everyone, that is, except Danielle Martinez.

She was in there, though, most likely trying to wait Nerese out, but

Nerese loved pissing contests and patiently stood her ground in the gray flannel gloom, as the rush-hour rage began to build: an endless stop-start caravan of SUVs, black-and-orange gypsy cabs and red-and-yellow buses, all plowing through the near-black slush and hammering their horns as if they had never encountered traffic lights before.

And in the midst of her determined idleness, Nerese found herself recalling that last visit to this place nearly twenty years earlier, specifically the half carrying out of one old geezer, a milk-eyed, scabby guy who, despite the fact that Nerese was literally in the act of eighty-sixing him into the street, nonetheless in his fear and disorientation began to speed-rap to her in a disturbingly cheerful voice about the Rajah in its glory days during World War II, when on consecutive Saturday evenings he and his wife had seen Charles Laughton, Ray Milland and Walter Brennan deliver patriotic speeches from the stage before the lights went down; Nerese politely ooing and ahing until the poor bastard was out in the cold with everything he owned—one of those days when she was less than proud about doing her job.

After having kept Nerese on ice for thirty minutes past the agreed-on meeting time, Danielle finally, reluctantly exited the theater, Nerese easily ID-ing her by the turgid anger in those cat-light eyes.

She came out swinging. "You think my life's a game or something?"

"Excuse me?" Nerese blinked, thinking, We can play it that way.

"Two thousand messages. I got my boss, the school, everybody going 'What's with you and the police, what's with you and the police.'"

"Well, as far as I knew you didn't *get* any of my messages"—Nerese shrugged, eyeing the traffic—"being that not a one was returned."

"Yeah, I got 'em. I just didn't want to talk to you. You're a detective, couldn't you figure that out?"

Nerese just stared at her for a good fifteen seconds before responding, Danielle still hot but having to look away.

"You don't return my calls, not only does it piss me off, but worse for you, it makes me think I'm on to something."

Danielle flashed fire, leaning into whatever she was about to say but . . .

"*Think* before you talk," Nerese leaning into it herself. "*Think* who you're about to mouth off to," locking into her eyes.

Outgunned, Danielle grudgingly toed the line, looking off again, down the darkening boulevard.

"Let's just do this nice and easy," Nerese said placatingly now that she had won the initial face-off. "C'mon, I'll buy you dinner."

. . .

Nerese steered Danielle to a corner booth in the Red Robin Diner—no window views—then nudged her to a seat that put her back to the room, so that she had to look either directly at Nerese or at the clown painting for sale above her head.

Danielle carelessly, wearily hauled her schoolbag up on the table, some textbooks spilling out across the damp-wiped Formica.

Nerese eyed the titles: *Case Problems in Organizational Behavior; Regulating the Poor; The Vertical Cage; Elementary Statistics.*

"What's your major?" she asked, signaling for two coffees.

"Public policy." Danielle began snapping toothpicks, her left leg jiggling restlessly.

"Public policy." Nerese tried it out. "Can I see one of your notebooks? I'm just curious."

"Which one?"

"Any."

She slid a spiral notebook out of the bag and inched it toward Nerese.

The pages were a pale mint green; the class notes written small in some kind of bronze-toned ink, exquisitely neat.

Danielle leaned forward, trying to read upside down whatever was being scrutinized.

"You have a nice hand," Nerese said softly, turning a few pages. "Beautiful . . ." It appeared to her that Danielle took down every word out of her teacher's mouth. "Look at this," brushing her fingers across the back of one page, feeling the minute raised impressions. "My notebooks in college? They looked like someone upended a numbers runner, glued on a page whatever paper scraps fell out of his pockets."

"You sound like what's it . . . *Columbo*," Danielle said, reaching for more toothpicks.

"Me? Nah. I like *Law & Order*. But damn . . ." She gave Danielle's calligraphy one last caress. "That's it. I'm going back to college."

The waitress bellied up to the table. "How you doing, baby," she said to Nerese. "Turkey cheeseburger?"

"Yeah, and throw me some cottage fries with that?"

The waitress turned to Danielle.

"Just coffee," she said, exhaling adrenaline.

Nerese watched the waitress shuffle across the room, then returned to Danielle.

"Six months from now, I'm moving to Florida? There's three different colleges within twenty miles of my house, and I'm just twenty-four credits shy a bachelor's," Nerese said.

"A bachelor's in what," Danielle asked, without interest.

"In what? Hell, I don't know, addiction counseling, rehab management, youth services, family services, social services . . . You know, whatever retired cops tend to major in. What's public policy?"

"Two years of horseshit followed by a job in city housing if you know the right people."

Nerese gestured at the book bag, the copious notes. "That doesn't look like horseshit to me."

Danielle didn't answer, started chewing on her thumbnail, waiting.

Over by the counter Nerese spotted two men whom she'd personally arrested in the last year and a half and three others whom she knew to have been locked up in that same time span; the Red Robin Diner was in walking distance of the County Correctional Center and was often the first stop for just-released inmates or those lucky enough to make bail.

"You know I'm from Hopewell, too," Nerese said as the turkey cheeseburger came to the table with suspicious speed and the coffee cups were refilled.

"Ammons in Four Building," Danielle said. "My mother told me."

"You'd be too young to remember us."

"You had a brother Antoine, he was gay, right?" Danielle asked carefully.

"Yeah, uh-huh," Nerese said. "Although I do believe the correct term back then in Hopewell was faggot."

"My mother said he beat up my brother Harmon once in Big Playground."

"Hey, Toni beat up everybody. Just because you're a faggot doesn't mean you're a fairy."

"What kind of counseling did you want to study again?" Danielle drained her second cup of coffee.

Nerese shrugged. "It's just us Hopewell girls talking here."

"Right." Danielle turned her head away, biting down on a smirk.

"So, Danielle, talk to me." Nerese leaned forward on her elbows.

"About . . ."

"Guess."

"Hey, you called me."

Nerese sighed heavily, then, "So how did Freddy take to you sleeping with Ray while he was stuck in County?"

"Whoa." Danielle reared back, the blood coming to her face.

"I'm sorry. Am I going too fast?" Nerese kept up the eye contact.

"No," Danielle said, after a moment of pulling herself together. "No. He had it coming."

"Ray did?"

"Freddy did." She seemed to relax for the first time all evening.

"Did he ever react to any of your other boyfriends while he was away?"

"Step Two," Danielle said. "When interviewing a suspect or witness, always try to come off like you know more than you actually know."

"That's good." Nerese laughed, fending off a third cup of coffee.

"Look, I'm really sorry about what happened to Ray, he was a very sweet guy." Danielle was almost chatty with relief now that the bottom line had been broached. "But you're wasting your time studying Freddy for this."

"Well," Nerese shrugged, "maybe you're right. I mean, I ran his sheet and there's no real pattern of violence on it. But there *is* that one body, indicted or not. And we *do* have a situation here, you know, the three of you . . ."

"Hey." Danielle leaned forward. "Ray broke up with *me*."

"Yeah, so . . ." Nerese shrugged. "Did Freddy know about you and Ray?"

"Probably."

"Probably?"

"Hey, he gets locked up like that, he knows the drill."

"The drill."

"Look. I know my husband inside out, and I'd never put another human being in harm's way like that."

Nerese just stared at her; the intermittent clatter of dirty dishes tossed into a gray rubberized busing bin punctuated the silence.

"You got to do better than that," Nerese finally said. "Make me a believer."

Danielle frowned at her cup for a moment, then came up bright-eyed. "Tell me when it happened, then ask me where Freddy was."

"OK. Two weeks ago Tuesday, where was Freddy . . ."

"Two Tuesdays ago? He was home with me."

"Yeah, OK." Nerese laughed. "That takes care of that."

"Ask me if anybody saw us."

"OK," gesturing for Danielle to proceed.

"My son. He was sick. Came home sick from school."

"How old is he?"

"Twelve. Almost thirteen. Nelson."

Nerese remembered the boy from Carla's apartment, the name from her chat with Brenda Walker. "If I need to, can I speak to him?"

"Not without me there."

"You'd have to be there. It's the law."

"Then hell yeah, no problem."

"Do me a favor. Just, lay out that Tuesday for me. What did you do, where'd you go. Get me off your back."

Danielle studied her for a wary moment. "Well, I didn't see my family till about seven o'clock because I had classes until six-thirty."

"So you came home at seven?" Nerese eased a reporter's pad onto the table, began jotting things down.

"Yeah, at seven." Danielle frowned at the notepad.

"This is just"—Nerese dismissed the pad with a flicking gesture—"I have a head like a sieve."

"Whatever you say, Columbo." Danielle sipped her coffee.

"So you came home at seven. Was Freddy there?"

"Yeah."

"What was he like that night, you know, mood-wise."

"You don't want to know."

"Why's that?" Nerese asked, ostentatiously dropping her pen as if they were off the record.

"Nothing illegal," Danielle said. "Just in a bad mood."

"About . . ."

"He doesn't need an about."

"Still . . ."

"He's trying to learn day trading now, sits at his laptop from can to can't . . . I mean, I will give him this. He is trying."

"OK, so you come home, Freddy's there in a bad mood."

"Like Darth Vader with his helmet ripped off. I say, 'Where's Nelson.' He says, 'In bed.' I say, 'Why.' He says, 'He's sick.'"

"He's sick." Nerese casually took up her pen again.

"I go into Nelson's room; he's sleeping, so I wake him up because I don't want him disrupting his biological clock with any naps. You know, all of a sudden it's two a.m. and he can't sleep or something."

"Right." Nerese scribbled.

"I feel his head and he's hot a little but I say, 'Come into the living room, lay on the couch. You can watch some TV.' See, normally he's not allowed but a half-hour of television a night but I'd rather him just keep his eyes open until his bedtime. I mean, if he's sick, I'll write him a note for his teachers about not doing his homework but . . ."

"Do you remember what he was watching?"

"What else. MTV."

"Same by me," Nerese said. "Drives me up a wall. So you sit down for dinner . . ."

"Me and Freddy. I give Nelson a TV tray on the couch. We eat, Freddy goes back online and I do my homework, put Nelson in bed about eleven, go to bed myself about twelve-thirty, one."

"Where's Freddy?"

"In bed. Still with the laptop. That's his new girlfriend."

"Did you talk about anything during dinner?"

"I guess. I don't know. Oh wait. Yeah. You know what he says to me? He says, 'I'm sorry.' Not during dinner but later when I'm getting ready for bed. He says, 'I'm sorry.'"

"For what?" Nerese said lightly.

"That's what I said. He says, 'For everything.'"

"OK," Nerese waiting.

"I say, 'Gee, where'd I hear *that* before.'"

"I hear you," Nerese going all sister-sister. "But you don't think he was referring to anything specific."

"Like being sorry for putting Ray in the hospital?"

"Or whatever."

"Or whatever, huh?" Danielle said dryly. "I'm just trying to give you a flavor for Freddy. He keeps wanting to be something better than he is. He keeps trying. And that's why I'm still with him. The minute I feel like he's given up, I'm gone. But I'm not going to walk out on someone who's fighting for his own soul, no matter how bad that fight's going most of the time. That's all I meant by telling you that."

"OK then." Nerese smiled, arched her back and signaled for the check.

"That's *it*?" Danielle reared back.

"For now."

"That was worth turning my life upside-down with two million phone calls?"

"Yup." Nerese now having a foot in the door, an interview with the kid plus an orally documented record of events which would invariably be contradicted by both Nelson and Freddy—these things rarely matched up in the retelling—and each contradiction to come was an excuse to open the door wider and wider.

Nerese weighed asking Danielle if she could speak to Nelson tonight, right now, before she changed her mind about offering up her son like that.

"So how's Ray doing?" Danielle asked, rearranging the contents of her book bag.

"You go see him in the hospital?"

"Not really."

"Did you call him?"

"What are you, my mother?" Danielle snapped, but Nerese could tell she was embarrassed.

"Why not?"

"Why not?" Danielle stopped moving. "You got to be kidding, right?"

"Do you think I could talk to your son tonight?"

"Nelson?" sizing Nerese up. "Tonight's not good."

"Why's that?"

"He's sick again."

"Really. With what?"

"Not walking pneumonia. Walking something though. It's been dragging on like forever."

The waitress placed the check and two foil-wrapped mint balls on the table.

"Well, you know, the sooner I can speak to him, the sooner . . ."

"Give him a day or two to get back on his feet. You have a card or something?" Danielle put out her hand, Nerese trying to read a stonewall in any of this, didn't think so. Besides, at this point if she sensed any further ducking on the part of Freddy or his family, she'd just have his PO threaten him with a revocation of parole, the POs often able to swing a heavier hammer than any cop.

"I'd very much like to talk to your son by tomorrow night," she said, handing over her card.

"I'm in school to around eight tomorrow."

"You want to make it nine, then?"

Danielle hesitated. "Sure."

"Good." Nerese laid out $8.50 on a $7.75 tab, then reluctantly added another fifty cents.

"So how's Ray doing?" Danielle asked again, hauling the strap of her book bag over her shoulder but waiting for a response before rising to her feet.

"You know. Shaky. Better," Nerese opting to downplay what he'd been through, not wanting to spook her with the direness of his injuries, the direness of the criminal charges.

"He was one of the nicest guys I've ever been around," Danielle said. "Very unselfish. I'd go over to his place with my son and a lot of the time I'd have to study and, he's got a terrace there, it's like heaven for me, and he'd never complain, just hang with Nelson, have a catch, tell him stories, sometimes I'd even bring my nephew. Ray never said Boo."

"You'd bring your *son* with you?" There was no revelation here; Nerese had known of this almost from the beginning; nonetheless, hearing about it directly from the mother made it difficult to keep her voice judgment-free.

"We weren't *doing* anything." Danielle darkened. "Shit, what do you take me for?"

< Chapter 22

Nelson — January 27

The day had the kind of unseasonable warmth that made people fret about the greenhouse effect, sixty-one degrees in the shade; and Ray had been waiting on his terrace for the better part of an hour before Danielle finally pulled up in her Bondo-daubed Vega. The weight of her schoolbag made her stagger as she swung the strap up onto her shoulder.

Her son, Nelson, cautiously emerged from the passenger side with the self-consciously physical jerkiness of a kid crossing an empty gym floor to ask a girl to dance.

She had said that she would be bringing him; Ray thought he was pre-pared for that, and he was, in terms of no sex, but he was surprised to find himself oddly excited by the kid's presence, too, in a way that was unclear but left him feeling vaguely embarrassed.

At the door Danielle and Ray avoided any physical greeting; Ray wasn't sure if it would have been any different if the kid wasn't present, but that was OK, he told himself, really . . .

"Check it out." He steered her across the living room to the cement terrace, where he had set up a work station: scratch pads, pens, pencils and a spool of roll-on correction tape.

"Oh my God, this is so nice of you," she said in that high furry tone of gratitude that had first drawn him to her at Carla's house.

"Knock yourself out," he said, then turned to Nelson. "You have homework, too?"

"No," Danielle said sharply, as if to a puppy, not in response to Ray's question but to her son's getting to know Ray's TV. "You read your book."

"I left it in the car," he murmured.

"Oh for Christ's sake," she squawked, pulling a slim tangerine PC from her backpack, all the little stationery touches he had laid out for her now charmingly archaic.

"What are you reading?" he asked the kid.

Nelson murmured something indistinct.

"What?"

"*Roll of Thunder, Hear My Cry,*" mother and son said simultaneously.

"About the black family down south? Ruby just read that."

"Well, I'm not going back downstairs to get it," she said.

"I'll go," Ray offered.

"No. Let him go." She lugged out a huge academic-press paperback, *Collective Violence: A Roundtable.* "Everything is half-cocked with this kid."

Ray had had a faint impression of this before, and Danielle seemed to be confirming it now; she was one of those people who equate a chronic tone of low-key reproach, of constant verbal sternness, with being a responsible parent. On the other hand, she knew what her son was reading, which, by Ray's lights, was no small thing.

"You go down and get your book, Nelson."

"Actually, you know what?" Ray said. "I think I have Ruby's copy in the bedroom. Come on." He signaled for Nelson to follow.

Danielle returned to the balcony.

Ray closed the bedroom door behind them.

He had no intention of giving Nelson Ruby's copy of *Roll of Thunder, Hear My Cry*: with Danielle doing homework and this kid with his nose in a book, what the hell was *he* supposed to do? Ray scanned the room for show-and-tell, something to delight and entertain. The cards. He never got a chance to show anybody the damn cards.

"Nelson, you like baseball?"

The kid shrugged.

"Me neither," he said, opening the bottom drawer of his dresser and pulling out a couple of three-ring binders. "But this isn't baseball. It's baseball *cards.*"

Sitting at the foot of his bed with the binders in his lap, he patted the mattress in invitation and opened one of the fatter books to reveal his collection of '55 and '56 Topps, eight clear horizontal pockets to the page.

"Beautiful, right?" He passed a hand lightly across a sheet of '55 Tigers, the head shots all set against a reddish background, the tint building gently from a dusty rose at the bottom of the card to a bloody sunset at the top, the Detroit players all gazing skyward, whatever they were looking at up there making their lips part in wonder.

"This guy here, Ferris Fain? You know what they called him? Burr-head."

Ray had amassed these cards, Topps from 1952 to 1958, in the months immediately after he kicked cocaine. Newly flush with TV money and desperate for a relatively harmless surrogate obsession, he had settled on retrieving material fragments of his childhood—actually, pop artifacts from the years that preceded his childhood, for some reason—first the cards, then a few years' worth of vintage *Mad* magazines and *Playboys*, then spin-off products from early sixties TV shows: lunch boxes, board games and figurines; then mambo and cha-cha LPs, the risqué comedy albums of Belle Barth and Rusty Warren, two hundred first-edition *Classics Illustrated* comic books and a thousand paper cocktail napkins embossed with a variety of semi-dirty jokes.

He found all of this fairly embarrassing, kept most of it hidden away and eventually sold it all off—all of it, that is, except the cards.

He had never been a baseball fan, but the cards were another story. As a kid he had been a helplessly compulsive collector, and the mere sight of them thirty-five years later, even those that were manufactured before he was born, still tugged at him: Warren Spahn's goofy grin, Wally Moon's massive beetle brow, Hoyt Wilhelm's pear-shaped head, the Karloffian rings around Don Mossi's eyes, the nicknames, the flattops, the jug-handle ears, the way Bobby Richardson stared off and Junior Gilliam up—at what? And all of it set against those vivid background colors: Halloween orange, emergency yellow, hot pink, royal blue, kelly green, arterial red, all of it, even now, right now, sitting here next to a twelve-year-old stranger, the albums open on his lap, each card was as immediately and viscerally tantalizing to him as a dissolving dream.

"You have to be a four-star moron to collect this stuff at my age, don't you think?"

Nelson shrugged, his hands twisted in a figure eight between his knees.

"Thanks for saving my feelings. You wouldn't believe the names some of these guys had." Ray began flipping pages, juggling albums. "Cot Deal, Coot Veal, Hank Bauer, Hank Sauer, Memo Luna, Hobie, Smoky, Pumpsie, Choo Choo, Yatcha, Schoolboy, Noodles or these . . ." His fingers flying. "Alpha Brazle, Sibby Sisti, Dee Fondy, Whammy Douglas, Suitcase Harry Simpson, Vinegar Bend Mizell and this guy here, my favorite"—opening his slim book of '53s, again to the Detroit Tigers—"Dizzy Trout. Man among fish."

"Huh," Nelson managed, arching his elbows inside out, his hands still entwined between his knees.

"How old are you again?"

"Twelve."

"See this guy?" Ray flipped to Joe Nuxhall of the 1952 series Reds, his face a little out of focus against a brilliant butter-yellow background. "He pitched his first Major League game at the age of fifteen. Lasted two-thirds of one inning, gave up two hits and five walks, didn't throw pro again for eight years, so stay in school, OK? I don't care *how* many millions they want to give you. Promise me you'll do that?"

"OK," Nelson murmured, fighting down a grin.

"Then you're even dopier than I thought."

A shaft of sunlight came through the bedroom window, whiting out the furniture and flashing off the plastic sheets like cold fire. Nelson's arms were entangled between his legs up to the biceps, blue veins bulging in the inverted crooks of his elbows.

"Enough with the prelims," Ray said, rising to his feet and lightly whacking the kid on the side of his leg. "It's showtime, baby."

Nelson was using Ruby's glove, a lefty, so at first Ray thought the reason his tosses were more like shot-put heaves than throws, his attempts at catching so ineffectual and spastic, was that the kid was all inside out, but after he switched gloves, giving Nelson a righty's mitt, his hand-eye coordination became even worse, and Ray was surprised to find himself in the company of a twelve-year-old boy who had no idea how to catch or throw a ball.

They were standing on the dead wheat-colored grass beneath his terrace, the Hudson River slapping its banks fifty feet away.

The air smelled of sea funk and overturned earth; the only thing Ray loved about living in Little Venice, the raw and heady scent made him think of new beginnings, of second and third chances to get things right.

Tossing around a softball had always been a lifesaver for him, a mode of nonverbal communication between himself and his daughter that they both had come to count on in times of awkwardness, and so he felt a little like a philanderer bringing this boy out here. But Nelson made his own laconic kid come off like a babbling brook, and he had no other idea of how to connect.

"Get over here," Ray said briskly, the kid stepping forward. "Give me the ball.

"OK . . . Hang on, hold on . . ." Ray faltered in his demonstration; throwing a ball so second nature to him that he had to go through the motions himself just to see how it was done. "Hold on . . . OK. You're a righty or a lefty?"

"Right."

"Good. OK. Good."

Ray planted his feet, discovered that you had to stand slightly sideways, the foot opposite the throwing hand a little forward. "Do this."

Nelson took up the stance, then cut a glance at his mother up on the terrace, but Danielle was nose-down in her homework. Ray looked up there, too, then found himself fighting off a wave of frustration; she could at least *fake* an interest . . .

"OK, let's . . . OK," planting the ball in Nelson's right hand. "Put your hand behind your ear, the ball behind your ear."

Nelson held it there like a transistor radio.

"No . . . OK. Cock your . . . Bend your elbow. Get it up, elbow up, ball behind your ear, OK?"

Ray stutter-skipped backward about fifty feet, gave Nelson a target.

"OK . . . When I say? I want you to snap it. Snap your wrist and just *whip* that bad boy to me, OK? Like this . . ." miming the act, Nelson watching him with his arm frozen into the position Ray had sculpted for him. "OK? Ready? Go ahead. Take my head off. Go."

Once again Nelson let loose with more of a heave than a throw, but less of a heave than before.

Ray tossed back the ball. "Again."

And they worked that snap-and-release for the better part of an hour, Nelson steadily improving, not ready for the majors but less of a potential embarrassment to himself in a schoolyard.

And over the course of that time, each of them periodically looked to the terrace with the same desire for Danielle's attention, the physical ache in Ray diminished by what he had going on with her son right now, Ray telling himself that if he couldn't command her passion, he'd settle for her admiration.

"Nelson, you want to hear a sad story?"

Ray tucked the glove under his arm, took a seat on the ghost grass, inviting the kid to do the same.

"Seventh grade, right? My class, the boys were in an intramural soft-ball league, each homeroom had its own team. And I had a glove," he splayed his fingers, "it looked like an elephant fell off a skyscraper and landed on it, right? But the night before the first game? My grandmother, of all people, takes me to a sporting goods store and spends thirty bucks on a new one. And thirty bucks was some serious cheddar back then.

"But this new glove, Nelson, it was state-of-the-art. I'm talking a *dead* man could catch with that thing. You with me so far?"

Nelson bobbed his head, swallowed.

"OK . . . The next morning, I'm so excited, I get on the train to go to school, go the two stops with a million other kids, get off on the platform, train pulls out and . . . I left the goddamn glove on the train."

Nelson just sat there, studying his sneaker.

"I wanted to die. I never left anything on a train before. I wasn't that type of kid. Plus, I spent the whole ride showing it off to my friends and— I assume twelve-year-old boys are still like this—these guys? Nothing made them happier than one of us having some kind of disaster. So when I started freaking on the platform they were howling like hyenas. Just loved it.

"Are the boys in your class still like that? Someone rips their new jacket, everybody starts high-fiving each other?"

Nelson shrugged.

"I'll take that as a yes. Anyways, the game was after school, indoors in the gym. And I was the first baseman, that was always my position. And I had to borrow a glove from the other team. I get one just like my old glove, looked more like leprosy than leather. Anyways, we're playing, and this glove sucks but I'm doing OK . . . So, ninth inning. We're ahead four to three. The other team's up, last licks. It's two out, bases loaded. Kid hits a dribbler right to the pitcher. Now, our pitcher, Eric Abruzzi, was a very fat kid, but very, very cool. And Eric, as a rule, would never stoop for a ball, would never commit himself to any physical act that would make him look, ungainly, or foolish. But this was the ball game right here, right? So he goes down for it, tosses it underhand to me, the toss was so soft and per-fect it could've been a newborn baby he was throwing. And, I got this kid out by a mile. But, as this grapefruit, this *beach*ball, is coming to me, I say to myself, I'm gonna drop it. I, Raymond, Randolph Mitchell, will *not* catch this ball, and guess what . . ."

"What," Nelson finally said.

"I dropped it. I fucking dropped it, two runs scored, and we lost, five four. How do you like them bananas . . ."

The kid looked buzzed by Ray's profanity, half smiling, half dis-oriented.

"And after the game, going home? All I heard from my friends, my, my *team* mates, was '*Fuck* you, Mitchell, Fuck you Fuck you Fuck you."

Nelson developed frog's eyes, fought back a smile, fought back anar-chy like a balloon rising in his gullet, Ray leaning into him, whispering, "Fuck you, Nelson. Fuck you Fuck you Fuck you."

"*Stop* it!" Danielle barked from above, both Ray and Nelson raising their eyes to the terrace.

"You have *no* say in this!" She was fighting with someone on the phone. "You have no . . . You have . . . You respect my wishes . . . No . . . No . . . It's *my* life. It's . . . *Fine.* I'll come home and pack. I'll come home *right* now and pack."

Ray assumed the fight was with Carla, the topic Freddy Martinez, himself, trouble.

Nelson resumed scowling at his sneakers.

"You did good today." Ray forced some air into his tone. "We have to work on your catching, but you did good." Then, "You ever do stuff like this with anyone else?" The question, he knew, was a sleazy one, his artful avoidance of any direct reference to Freddy making it feel sleazier still.

Nelson didn't respond.

"Anybody ever teach you anything off the charts? You know, ventril-oquism, carpentry, celestial navigation, midwifing . . ."

"My dad once," Nelson muttered, shrugged.

"Your dad once what," Ray pushed, unable to help himself.

Nelson shrugged, looked away.

"Talk to me, baby."

"He tried to teach me to box."

"Oh yeah?" Ray said lightly, it coming to him like the Annunciation: Just end it. "How'd that go?"

"He got mad."

"What do you mean he got mad."

Another shrug.

"How'd he get mad?"

"He walked away."

They resumed their catch in the near-dark, Nelson having to chase after every ball tossed to him; flinching and turning his head each time as if Ray were flipping him a series of grenades.

The game finally came to an end when he uncorked a moonshot over Ray's head, the ball rolling down the lawn's embankment, plopping into the river and bobbling away on the current.

Nelson's face turned gray with apprehension. Ray, pained to see fear rise up so quickly in a kid like that, briefly wondered where it came from, then quickly shut down that line of thought.

"Hey, it's just a ball, Nelson," he said easily. "That's why God gave us two."

Up in the apartment, Ray regarded Danielle with dispassionate eyes. "You were on the phone?"

"Yeah," she said, packing her book bag. "I'll pay you for the call."

"Don't be ridiculous," her offer just one more turn-off. Nonetheless, he couldn't help but ask, "Everything OK?"

"My mother." Danielle straightened up, arched her back. "She drives me nuts."

"What. About us?"

"Among other things." She resumed packing.

"What other things."

"Don't sweat it."

"OK," Ray thinking, I won't, seeing her for the last time now; Nelson, too.

But then, at the door, with her son already halfway to the elevator, Danielle abruptly turned and almost violently threw her free arm around his neck, yanking him close and hissing in his ear. "I'll be back in an hour."

Chapter 23 >

White Tom — February 25

This time around, the hospital smelled like terror; a pervasively astringent reek that set up house between Ray's eyes and made the two-month-old *Entertainment Weekly* spread-eagled between his fists flutter as if caught in a gentle breeze, Ray reading and rereading the same paragraph about Ben Affleck and his new eighty-five-pound girlfriend as if his life depended on it.

On this, his first visit back to the medical center since his release, he found himself molting in the waiting room of the outpatient physical therapy wing, surrounded by the palsied and the frozen, the stuporous and the forlorn, in-curled wrists, stroke-locked mouths, walkers, canes, wheelchairs, the only other sign of fluid life Nerese, his stick-like-glue escort these days, sitting next to him on the bench and speaking softly into her cell phone to some childhood friend of his that he had no memory of, neither face nor name.

"He's right here, right here. Here," she semi-whispered both to Ray and to whoever was on the line, putting the phone in Ray's hand.

"Hello?"

"It was a fucking mitzvah and a half, what you did for Carla, you cock-sucker."

"Thanks, thank you," Ray staring at Nerese, who nodded in encouragement, then commandeered his magazine.

"I'll be there in ten minutes. Do not fucking move."

Ray gave the phone back.

"Tommy Potenza. White Tom. How can you not remember him?" she said.

"Because, like I told you before, I never *knew* him."

"Well, he knows you."

"This is bullshit," Ray hissed, rocking now, his stomach sprouting wings. "I have to sit here half a day to go in there for thirty minutes so they can watch me squeeze a rubber ball and do some leg lifts? No. I don't think so."

"Did I tell you I spoke to Danielle Martinez last night?" Nerese asked, her eyes on the magazine.

"Yeah, so," Ray feeling one of his post-op head-stabs coming on; pawing himself for a Vicodin.

"She didn't even say to say hello," Nerese said, then, "My God," her voice going high and faint with astonishment. "Look how much weight Leonardo DiCaprio put on."

White Tom Potenza came striding into the waiting room twenty minutes later as fast as his cane-assisted gait would allow. He was roughly Ray's age, wore a beret, shades, a charcoal turtleneck, black leather car coat, sunglasses and a broad black Pancho-style mustache.

"I'll talk to *you* later," he said to Nerese with mock menace, then took a seat next to Ray, embracing him at a right angle, Ray's shoulder pressed into his chest, kissed him on the cheek and whispered, "You're a good, good man."

Then, holding Ray by the biceps, he leaned across him to address Nerese.

"You would not believe this dream I had. This fucking dream and a half . . ."

His face was misted with perspiration and the grip he had on Ray's arm was tremulous.

Ray still had no idea who this was, but that "good, good man" lingered in his ear like a butterfly kiss.

"I'm sitting in a movie with my son, he's three years old, right?" White

Tom's voice a heightened whisper. "And next to him is this big fuckin' shvug, no offense, with an Afro out to here and I see on the elbow rest he's pushed my son's arm off, like, *pushed* it, and my son's a sweetheart, he never complains but this push was so fuckin', fuckin' *rude*, and violent that he made Maceo spill his soda. So I say, 'Mace, change seats with Daddy,' and so now *I'm* next to Afro-boy and I say to him, 'You want to try that with me?' And then I shove *his* fuckin' arm right off the elbow rest.

"And this big mamaluke, he pulls out this fuckin' *hand* cannon, puts it right in my face, I say, 'What are you gonna do, throw shots in here in front of a child? What kind of animal are you?'

"And because, and *only* because it's a dream, Neesy, the guy actually, mentally, *absorbs* what I'm saying and reholsters his piece.

"I say to him, 'Forgive me. I'm an overprotective parent. I was upset.'

"So the guy goes back to watching the movie, I'm sitting between him and my son, staring at the screen but now that this guy's relaxed, all's I can think is how I can nail this nigger . . . Like this?" Bisecting Ray's Adam's apple with the flat of his hand, Ray feeling like an asshole.

"Like this?" Resting a thumb against the corner of Ray's eye.

"I'm like murder on a stick. And then I wake up . . ." White Tom seized his head. "And I am so ashamed of myself. I'm still with the violence. My little boy's right there and I can't even . . . I'm still with the violence. I even used my son to set the guy up, soften him up."

"Oh for Christ's sake." Nerese waved him off. "It was a dream, Tommy."

"It's an ongoing issue, so fuck you," he said without heat. "I don't want to be that way. *Ever.* Like today, right?" He addressed Ray now. "Guy cuts me off on JFK. We pull up at the light? I didn't even make eye contact. Now, *that* is a big first for me, but do you know why? Because I refuse to surrender to the darkness anymore. I mean what good can come of it. What possible good, can you *feel* me on this, you sonofabitch? Look at you, you still look like a kid."

"Oh yeah?" Ray, creaming to get away, tried to catch Nerese's eye, but she seemed to be enjoying the show.

"No, I remember you back then, chugging along . . ."

"I never chugged anywhere in my life," Ray said awkwardly, trying to get in the spirit of whatever this was.

"Oh yeah? Well fuck you then." Tommy kissed him on the cheek again, Ray at least distracted from the amorphous dread and interminable wait.

White Tom pulled a square of brown paper towel, public restroom towel, from inside his car coat, then turned his head away as he removed his glasses and mopped his face, Ray thinking, speed, crank, coke, looking to Nerese for an explanation but she just smiled.

"No, listen to me." White Tom got back into it, the hand on Ray's arm damp and shaky. "I have buried way too many friends. I have seen so many friends go down over the years I have fucking survivor's guilt. Remember Hector Santos? Big Hector? Six-foot-five, built like Man o' War. Fucking Hector, could crush a raw potato in his fist, make basketballs explode with his bare hands. Hector, my soul brother, dead at thirty-two, a needle in his arm, sitting in a wooden chair, no other furniture in the room except a stack of books on the floor and a picture of his nephews hanging on the wall. His *nephews,* you hear what I'm saying? So fuck the darkness, OK? God has given me so many second chances in this life, but I *know* at some point, some point sooner than later, He's gonna lose patience with me and then the sheets go up over the mirrors and my mother's sitting barefoot on a wooden crate. So, no. I'm not marching in that parade no more."

"So Carla's son. He OD'd, right?" Ray just saying it to say something.

"Who, Reggie?" White Tom wiped his forehead again. "No, he was murdered." He then leaned across Ray's chest to go in Nerese's face. "He. Was. Murdered."

Nerese just waved him off. "Coroner said OD."

"Bullshit. That kid's been robbing Peter to pay Paul since he was in diapers. Somebody gave him a hot shot."

Nerese plugged a yawn with the back of her hand. "Coroner said OD."

"You know how you get that one off her ass? Put the doughnut at the far end of the table."

"Doughnut jokes," Nerese muttered.

"So what are you doing when you're not playing guardian angel." Tom's eyes wagged like dog tails behind his shades.

"Well, until a few weeks ago I was teaching," Ray said stiffly.

"Teaching where . . ."

"Paulus Hook?" Then, just having to add it, "Pro bono."

"Pro Bono, who's that, Sonny's brother?" the guy too jumpy to smile at his own joke.

"On the house. Volunteer."

"You were teaching for free?" He suddenly seemed to slow down, gather focus.

"Yeah," Ray said, encouraged. "I'm going to try to go back to it next week."

"For free. Motherfucker. You're the real deal, aren't you?"

"I don't know." Ray fought off a smile.

"You married? Kids? What . . ."

"Divorced."

"Fuck her, right?"

"Got a daughter, just turned thirteen." Ray usually began to glow when Ruby came up in a conversation but for some reason this time her name pulled him down like a plumb line.

"What . . ." White Tom on it instantly.

"Nothing."

"What's wrong, the kid?"

"No."

"It's the kid. Tell me."

Nerese was quietly listening in, her chin in her hand, a watchful tentative smile on her face. Unannounced, the Vicodin kicked in, and bookended by the two of them, by their expectant eyes, he found himself unable to keep the huskiness from his voice.

"I don't know, she's going through a patch right now, and, or, you know, maybe it's just me, I'm the one, but it's like, I don't know how to *be* with her, you know, how to be her friend."

"Her *friend*?" White Tom said in a way that made Ray flinch, made him want to take the word back.

"Excuse me, Ray, for stepping over the line here, but let me just remind you that you're not her friend. You're her father."

"No no, I know, I know. What I meant . . ."

"Listen to me." He gripped Ray's wrist. "When they're adults there'll be plenty of time to become friends, but not now. Right now she needs guidelines. She needs yes and no. Your displeasure has to be *worth* something to her, or all is lost."

The only thing keeping Ray from shutting out the lecture was his sense of the extraordinary effort this Tommy guy was making to slow down his racing metabolism and carefully pick his words.

A nurse came out into the waiting room and finally called his name. Ray looked to Nerese and shook his head—forget it—Nerese opened her mouth, then closed it.

"I just want to keep her talking to me," Ray said.

"Well . . ." Wincing, White Tom slowly straightened out one leg until the outline of his kneecap disappeared. "The reality of it is, at her age she's gonna do what she's gonna do, they're all like that, but she needs to know that this shit is *not* OK with you. She needs to know that just because everybody else is doing it, it still doesn't float under your roof, and you have to make that very clear. No waffling, no politicking, no worrying about your popularity rating. I don't tolerate it, I don't accept it and I don't approve of it. It is *not* OK, so don't do it."

"Do what," Ray said, coming back to himself a little.

"Drugs sex alcohol whatever. Once again, forgive me for stepping over the line with you, but if you really want to be a friend to her? Then don't be her friend. Be her father."

Ray nodded as if in deep thought, restraining himself from reiterating that all he meant was what he had already said, that he increasingly did not know how to be with Ruby these days, and that he feared that this self-defeating self-consciousness was also self-perpetuating, driving an ever-widening wedge between him and Ruby that he felt helpless to arrest.

In their first encounter after his release from the hospital, he had been so worried about her being freaked out by his appearance, he had projected so much intense anxiety toward her, that the first words out of the kid's mouth after taking in the damage to his face had been *"Dad. You're the one who got hurt. Stop looking at me like that."*

He restrained himself from reiterating all this now because he sensed that, given White Tom's physical distress, the issue, the only issue in his eyes, his life, was self-destruction; and Ray just didn't want to make the guy, or himself for that matter, feel like a fool.

Using his cane, White Tom struggled to his feet like a man trying to hoist himself out of a pool, his forehead beading with the effort; then, turning, he dropped a hand on Ray's shoulder. "I got to book, but very soon, you and I, we're going to sit down and break bread like human beings, because I have a business proposition for you that's really gonna ring your bell."

"OK," Ray said neutrally.

White Tom continued to stand there, smiling down at him from behind his shades; Ray waited.

"Listen to me," he said. "I want to give you something. You gave to Carla, now I'm going to give to you. I'm going to teach you a trick to defeat the darkness."

Ray heard Nerese cough into her fist and figured she knew what was coming word for word.

"Think of it, the darkness, as a ball, small, a golfball, a Ping-Pong ball that's like hovering in the air right in front of your face. You defeat that fucking ball by keeping your eye on it, your mind's eye. As long as you do that? You contain it. But the minute you take your eye off it, turn your back, *indulge* in a little something? You look back, that ball just got bigger. Now it's a baseball, a tennis ball. Take your eye off it again? Indulge in another little, somethin'-somethin'? Ho-ly shit, now it's a softball. Next time a basketball. Drop your guard enough times it becomes one of those ten-foot-high nudist colony beach balls with the happy broads hanging on it, mow you down like a bowling pin. You don't *ever* take your eye off the darkness, Ray. You heard of one day at a time? I'm talking one *minute* at a time. You understand me?"

Ray nodded, touched and inarticulate.

"I'm out of here." White Tom stooped to embrace him, then straightened up. "You're gonna be OK, brother. I know it. You're gonna be A-OK."

And then he was gone.

Ray sat in silence with Nerese for a long moment, wondering how to word what he wanted to say.

"So, what's he on?"

"What do you mean?"

"You're kidding me, right?"

"Tommy? Tommy's clean as a whistle."

"He's always like this?" Ray raised his hand, made it tremble.

"Nah," Nerese said softly. "That was just about him being in here."

"Here. The hospital?"

"He's got a history, so it's kind of hell on him, places like this."

"So what did he come in for?"

"Because this is where you were and he wanted to see you."

"Why?"

"Because he loves you, Ray," Nerese laying it on a little. "Didn't you get that?"

< Chapter 24

Salim — February 25

As twilight hit the Hudson, Ray's intercom went off, pulling him in from the terrace where he had been playing around with assignment themes for his first return class.

"Yeah?"

"How you doin', Mr. Mitchell. This Salim." The kid's voice came through the crackle like an ancient radio signal. "I need to come up and see you."

"When?" Ray asked stupidly, instinctively balking at this unannounced house call.

"Now."

"Now's not . . ."

"I got something for you," he said. "Take like a heartbeat."

A moment later, Salim, his backpack hanging off one shoulder, came striding into the apartment as if there had been no one at the door to greet him.

"Mr. Mitchell, how you doing, how you doing . . ." Smoking, pacing, eyes bouncing off surfaces, something goal-oriented in his distraction, in his reverting to Ray's teacher name right now. "I came here the other night but your phone wasn't working."

"Oh yeah?"

"Yeah. I visited you in the hospital, too, but you were unconscious. How you feeling now, OK?" The words flying out of him with the impersonal pitch of an auctioneer.

"I'm good," Ray said at a remove, studying this new Salim. "What's goin' on?"

"Oh shit . . ." The kid abruptly came to a dead stop in the middle of the room, eyes lightly shut, hands up in surrender. "I can't . . . OK, it's like, OK last week? Michelle, has lost her job. They had like a budget cut? And she was a temp, so . . ."

"I thought you said they changed her over to full-time," he said cautiously.

"No, no. That's not . . . No, she's out, she's out. And she started drinking again."

"Oh no," Ray said. He didn't know whether to sit or stand in his own home, settled for perching on the radiator.

"Like, OK . . . The first morning after she had got let go? Ten o'clock, she's still layin' in bed, she ain't even tryin' to hide the pint, I say, ' 'Chelle, you got to bounce back from this. You got to get up on your feet.' She tells me to mind my own fuckin' business, excuse my language . . ."

"She sounds depressed."

"Naw, man, *I'm* depressed," he said. "She's *drunk*."

"She can't get another job?"

"Like *that*?" Salim cupped a hand under his cigarette, then brought the ashes to an open window. "Naw man, she won't even try. Yeah, I guess she's depressed, like you said. That job was important to her, you know, to her self-esteem."

Ray flinched, the buzzword putting him on even higher alert.

"But it's all coming right at *me*. And like . . . OK, the night before last? The night before last I had to go to the police. I had to have the police come over to the house."

"Because . . ." Ray waiting for the money touch now like waiting for a bus.

"Because the last few days she started having her cousins come over. I don't . . . These guys, man, For Real and Busy? I don't . . . They're stickup niggers, and I *told* her, she *knows* I don't ever want to see them over my doorstep, you know, under my roof with my son there. She *knows* that and I think she was just doing it to get back at me, but I didn't *do* nothing. All's I'm trying to do all week is get her back on her feet, but when they left the other night? Me and her, we got into it, arguing, but just verbal, and I told her what you said to me last time, how she's into controlling me through money, right?"

"Whoa . . ." Ray came upright off the radiator. "Salim, that was just a conjecture. I don't even *know* her."

"But it's true." He shrugged, fired up another butt. "Without her job, she ain't got nothing over me. And now I'm back to being the breadwinner out there with the T-shirts."

"But you told her *I* said that?" Ray unconsciously palmed his injured crown.

"Hey. True is true," Salim missing the point here. "Next thing I know she's coming at me with a steak knife. Look . . ."

He raised then dropped the hem of his sweatshirt, revealing a flash of flat gut and an oblong pinkish something under the left-side ribs; Ray unable to make out what he was supposed to have seen.

"And I don't even hit her back. I'm like, ''Chelle, why you doin' this?' All's I did was disarm her, you know, with a chair. She starts sayin', 'I'm gonna go to the cops, say you beat me, say you sellin' drugs. I'm gonna get you violated. I'm gonna put you back in the *joint*.' And she can do that. I already gone back twice on violations. It's a sword of Damian over my head."

"Was Omar there?" Ray wanting to bring the boy in, make this PG.

"*Yes.*" Salim jumping on that. "He was right there! Cryin', scared. I said, ''Chelle! Omar's right there!'" Offering back to Ray his own words.

"She says, 'This ain't got nothing to do with him. He's irre*lev*ant. I'm gonna have you violated.' So I got out of the house, go right over to the police station, file a, a domestic violence report myself. You know, to cover myself? Here . . ."

He pulled a pale blue carbon of the report from his rear pocket and flapped it open for Ray's perusal, Ray wondering why he felt it necessary to show it to him.

"So then I go back to the house with two police? I show them how everything's all thrown around, I show them the liquor bottles, my injuries . . ."

"Was Michelle there?" Ray reached inside his shirt pocket for a Vicodin, then changed his mind.

"Naw, she had left. She took Omar and left. Then the next morning, I go to the parole office like an hour before they opened to catch my PO coming in, tell *her* what happened. Then I'm supposed to see this psychologist from the state? They say even though I never used drugs, sell-ing's an addiction too, so I have to see this guy who doesn't do a damn thing for me but I go see *him,* tell *him* what happened . . . It's like, I'm making first strikes everywhere, covering my behind on all the bases against false accusations, OK?

"But while I was out there talking to all my, my handlers? I come back to the apartment about eleven that morning, Michelle had got back in when I was gone and destroyed all my stuff. She poured soda inside the VCR, the TV, tore up the bed, the, the mattress. Stuffed up the kitchen sink with my books and drawings, turned the faucet on, water's all, every-thing's all flooded, my neighbors from downstairs start banging on the door 'cause the water's all running down into their place, and Ray, my apartment? It ain't even mine, it's my mother's, she's in the hospital right now, but she could kick me to the curb anytime she wants, you know what I'm saying? So I'm like up to my ankles in water, fighting with my neigh-bors, the phone rings, it's Michelle. She says, 'You ain't never gonna see Omar again. I'm gonna get For Real and Busy to come by and *cap* your ass and you ain't *never* gonna see your son again.'"

Salim took a breath, still leaning against the wall, smoking and staring out at the river.

Ray had balked on taking the Vicodin in order to maintain his edge against the bullshit, but now he reluctantly decided, if not to believe Salim, to at least surrender to the emotion driving his story.

"Then I go call my mother, you know, to tell her what happened? Michelle had already been to the hospital, told her some shit about me? My mother didn't even want to hear *my* side. She's all 'You're just like your father, all y'all niggers, you're all the same, you're this, you're that.' But I'm her *son,* you know what I'm saying?"

Ray un-surrendered; there had to be more to it, more to all this vicious anger coming at Salim. "Tell me again. Why's Michelle doing all this?"

"*Why?* Because she's drinking. She lost her job, started drinking, and this is what happens." His eyes went to the river again. "But, Ray, you know what? It's like, I lost my fiancée, my, my worldly possessions, I can lose the apartment, my *son* . . ." He swiped at a dry cheekbone, the tears more in his voice. "But now I have to think about myself. I have to take care of myself. I have to survive and continue because I just . . . It's some kind of test. And I don't even know if I'm ever gonna see my son again. I don't . . ." His gaze shifted to Ray—"She can't just . . ."—then back to the river. "I have to stay strong, because if I can't stay on top of things, if I can't maintain then I can't do nothing for Omar. I can't . . ." Salim dropped into a glassy silence, slowly shaking his head in awestruck disbelief at his own saga, Ray now somewhere between bored and hyperalert.

"You want to hear something?" Salim asked more calmly. "She changed her name."

"You weren't married."

"Her first name."

"Michelle?"

"Now she's Fire. Wants everybody to call her Fire."

"Fire . . ." Ray repeated, softening, thinking, He can't be making this shit up. "You worried about For Real and Busy?"

Salim waved off the cousins. "The only thing I'm worried about is staying positive."

"But the T-shirts are going well, right?"

"Yeah OK, here's the thing," Salim said, and Ray had nobody to blame but himself.

"OK, this week? Last week?" Salim counted off on his fingers, "I was out there eight, nine hours a day. I usually started out set up on the sidewalk in Journal Square over in Jersey City by the PATH trains till the police come and move me because as of yet I don't have a vendor's license. Rest of the day I just hit the bricks, here, there, you name it. Sold 'em right out of the backpack.

"But the other morning? When she destroyed the apartment? You know what else she did? She filled up the bathtub with water, took all my shirts, all my inventory, dumped everything in the tub, took a gallon of bleach . . ."

Salim mimed the pouring, his curled-down wrist traveling in a slow determined arc, over and over.

"Get the fuck," Ray sputtered, in a near panic as he desperately took stock of himself, wondering if he had it in him, for once in his life, to simply say no, to endure the disappointed reaction, the possible counter-rejection. "How many shirts . . ."

"Nine hundred. Ruined. Now I got to start over."

"Start over," Ray numbly repeated. "That was seventy-three hundred dollars I gave you."

"I know!" Salim sounded outraged; at Michelle, at Fire.

"If you had nine hundred left, that means you sold what, three hundred?"

"Yeah, well, maybe not that much."

"At a profit of what, nine bucks a shirt, right? I'm trying to remember."

Salim exhaled as if he were trying to launch a sailboat.

"Because that should be about twenty-seven hundred dollars you've cleared by now."

"Yeah, well, you know, like I said, I don't think I sold quite that many."

"Well, how many *did* you sell?"

"More like ninety."

"*Ninety?*"

"Yeah, see, I was unable to run off twelve hundred shirts, like I had originally intended, because when you gave me that money? I deposited it in my mother's checking account for safekeeping because I didn't have an account, myself, but as soon as I did? She withdrew fifteen hundred dollars for herself, said I owed it to her."

"For *what*," Ray suddenly so tired, his right hand helplessly curling into itself.

"For . . . I don't know. Back rent, food. She just said I owed it to her."

"Owed it to her," Ray repeated as if lost in thought, knowing at that moment, knowing with absolute certainty, that the remainder of Salim's life, regardless of whatever school of spirituality or industrious free enterprise game plan he embraced, would be one long unbroken cavalcade of elaborate excuses and self-defeating con jobs, and that any continued bankrolling of this kid on his part would be the equivalent of flushing money down a toilet.

Sighing, Salim lit another cigarette, stared out at the river again. "See, I should've *knew* better that my mother would've done something like that because she has always had a survival-of-the-fittest mentality, you know what I'm saying? Like a cougar eating its own young, but I keep wanting to believe that blood is thicker than water, so . . ."

"So what did you do with the money you made from the shirts you did sell?"

"What didn't go from hand to mouth is in here."

Salim lurched off the wall and pulled an ATM card from the same rear pocket that held the blue carbon of the domestic violence report.

He handed the card to Ray. SALIM EL-AMIN was embossed in the lower left corner.

"I look at this ten times a day," coming around behind Ray and leaning over his shoulder as if they were looking at baby pictures. "I can't believe I finally have one of these. I never thought . . ."

"I'm not going to refinance you for nine hundred T-shirts, Salim." Ray instantly regretted stating the quantity, as if a lesser number could be acceptable.

"Hey, I didn't even come here for that. I just needed to talk to somebody and I didn't know where else to go."

"In fact, I think the sooner money's not a part of the deal between us, the more clearheaded we can be with each other, you know, relate to each other."

"Michelle, can she just . . . She can't just take my son away, can she?" Ignoring Ray's last statement.

"I don't know," Ray said dejectedly. "Maybe she just needs to calm down, sober up or something."

"Because I already have one child I don't see, but that was for the good of that child," Salim said.

"OK . . ." Ray refusing to follow up on that one. "You know where she is right now?" keeping it to Q and A.

"She's probably at her mother's house, but I hear she's going to Atlanta next week, moving down there back in with her first boyfriend or her aunt or somebody. And, you know, with parole I can't leave the state. I can't even go through the tunnel to New York, so if she takes Omar . . ."

Again Salim sighed, his chest rising and falling once, a momentary silence coming down like snow.

"And Ray, half the time she don't even *like* Omar; he's like a obstacle for her. The only thing she likes with him is fixing his hair, that's about it. And I don't know how to do that."

"What if she left him with you?"

"Yeah see, I'd jump on that in a minute, but she *knows* that and she'd never, she'd . . . Ray, I swear, you never seen someone change so fast. Never . . ." His tears finally ran the rims then spilled. "So how's your daughter doing?" he managed to get out, running the backs of his hands under his eyes. "How's Ruby?"

"I'm not doing nine hundred shirts."

"No, I know. Excuse me," wiping his face.

"At six bucks a shirt that's fifty-four hundred dollars, Salim. I'm not doing it."

"All I want . . ." Salim locked his jaw in an effort to stem the flow. "All I want from you is to not lose your belief in me."

"All right, all right, all right," Ray said softly to shut him up, then rose once again from the radiator. "C'mon now."

"Because my mother, Michelle . . ." His lips began to tremble, his jawbone bulging aslant.

"Hey, c'mon, you stood up to worse. You told me that yourself," Ray said, wishing he could leave this apartment, leave it with Salim in it.

Salim extended his right hand palm down, back of the wrist domed up like the body of a jellyfish, the fingers dangling like tentacles, his left arm cocked wide for a wrap-around hug which Ray fell into awkwardly, patting his back, some sweet-scented oil rising from the kid's jersey.

"I will survive," Salim said brokenly. "I will *not* sub-cumb."

"So on the intercom you said you had something for me?" Ray attempted to shift gears, to delay or possibly finesse having to come forth with the final no.

"Oh yeah. Yeah." Salim stooped to unzip his backpack, a waft of moldy dampness rising up, and from a thick folded-over pile peeled off the top two T-shirts, black and bizarrely oversize, quadruple large, like slipcovers for a chandelier.

Unfurling them, Ray saw the "What's Mine Is Mine" legend emblazoned across the chest, the caricature of the pint-size thug brandishing his hand cannon silk-screened onto the belly.

Each moistly redolent shirt was spattered with a pinkish spray of bleach, one along the arm and collar, the other across the back, the visual impact both ugly and violent.

"Obviously I was hoping to make a more attractive presentation to you," Salim said with what to Ray's ear sounded like rehearsed regret. "Anyways, that's one for you and one for your daughter."

"Hang on, just . . ." And in a fit of suspicion Ray reached into the backpack himself and plucked out another T-shirt at random; this one was, if anything, more grotesquely marred than the two Salim had offered him. He then plucked a second shirt from the pile; same story; then a third; Salim stepping back almost respectfully now, as if Ray were a customs inspector.

"The running around I had to do to get these made?" he said. "It makes me sick just to look at them."

Ray yanked out another, then another; it quickly became apparent that Salim, rather than attempting to scam him with the offered T's, had in fact, selected the two least disfigured ones as gifts.

"I'll still try and sell 'em," Salim said. "I got no choice, but . . ."

"OK, look, I'll go for half," Ray said down low.

"I don't think I can get fifteen each anymore."

"I'll go for another four hundred and fifty." Ray looked away.

"Say what?" Salim blinked.

"What I said," Ray still looking away; chiding himself, You asked for this . . .

"Oh, man, Ray," Salim, exhaling gratitude, stepped forward.

But, smiling tightly, Ray danced back from a possible further embrace.

"But that's *got* to be it," he said. It was as much a plea as an edict.

Chapter 25 >

Interviews — February 25

The enforced idleness of having two hours to kill before her nine o'clock meeting with Danielle and Nelson heightened Nerese's eagerness to have at Freddy so intensely, that she nearly had to recite to herself out loud the lessons of a lifetime: Close in slow. Interview by interview. Don't, do *not*, skip. In an effort to eat the clock, she decided to check in on Ray again — their daily chess matches having taken on a not unpleasant life of their own for her — but as she rolled into his parking lot in the early-to-bed stillness of a Little Venice evening, she saw Salim and his ever-present backpack passing through that solitary cone of streetlight again, same as she had two nights before when she first brought Ray home from the hospital. The kid was heading for the gates at a brisk clip, his face creased with agitation, the burning tip of his cigarette restlessly tracing zips of light against the night.

"Hey," she said, rolling up alongside him.

Salim reared back at the sight of her, his hands briefly rising and falling with exasperation before he could rein in the body language.

"How you doin'," he said lifelessly, taking a step back from the car.

"You just coming from Ray's apartment?"

"Yeah, uh-huh."

Nerese reached across the front seat and pushed open her passenger door. "Get in."

He took another step back, quickly scanned the darkness—no help there—then did as he was told.

After a few minutes of driving in silence, Nerese nodded to the backpack, which now sat in his lap. "You have anything in there you don't want me to find?"

"Nope." Salim stared straight ahead, his mouth in a constricted pucker.

Nonetheless she pulled over next to a streetcorner trash basket. "You sure?"

"You can look for yourself," he said flatly, still not turning to her.

She pulled away from the curb, the silence once again beginning to build as she drove into the heart of Dempsy.

Salim, most likely conditioned to accept these things, hadn't even asked her where she was taking him, just went with it, his face locked into a mask of forbearance; only once, at an interminable red light, did he turn to her, halfheartedly asking, "So how's your evening, you having a good evening?" before returning his eyes to the road, not expecting and not receiving an answer.

Nerese walked him into the Northern District precinct house, one hand at his elbow, the other holding his backpack away from her body as if it were filled with bees.

The interview room, not much bigger than a walk-in closet, contained a card table and two chairs, the one on casters for her, the folding chair for him.

"Salim." Nerese leaned across the table. "You and I, we're going to have a conversation right now, and, the deal is? If you *lie* to me at any point in this conversation? If you hold *out* on me, withhold information from me at any point in this conversation, and I find out about it?—which I no doubt will, and quicker than you think—I personally guarantee that you will be elderly the next time you breathe free air."

Salim nodded, gape-mouthed now, either screwed or bewildered, she couldn't tell which yet.

"However, if you come clean with me? As easily as I can fuck you to death I can also make this a semi-skate, do you understand what I'm saying to you?"

"Can I ask you something?," tentatively raising his hand as if he were in a classroom. "How come police, every time before they interrogate you they have to start out with this big speech about how they're gonna mess you up if you lie."

"Let me hear you say you understand," Nerese said, not in the mood.

"I do," as solemn as a marriage vow.

"What's with you and Ray. What's with all the visits."

"He's my friend."

"Friend . . ." Nerese took a shot. "He gives you money, though, right?"

Salim hesitated, then, "Yeah, but not like a handout. He invests in my business."

"In your business." She let the phrase hang.

Salim hauled his backpack up onto the table, the abrupt weight making it wobble and shudder on its matchstick legs. A river-bottom rankness filled the air of the small windowless room as he unzipped the largest pouch, and pulled out two fistfuls of damp T-shirts, black randomly riddled with pink—Nerese thinking, Tie-dyed?—each one silk-screened with his Bad-boy logo. "Six to make, fifteen to buy. *Business.*"

"For seven thousand three hundred dollars I hope to hell you have a lot more to sell than just those."

The kid's startled expression confirmed the number.

Fucking Ray; Nerese suddenly had to fight down an impulse to laugh.

She gestured for Salim to reload his goods, not wanting anything between them on the table.

"So what's been going on with you the last two nights."

"Like what," his face was pinched with incomprehension.

"I saw you coming and going from Ray's apartment twice now, each time looking like you were ready to blow a gasket."

Salim blinked at her, then abruptly snapped into focus. "Aw, man, you don't want to know."

"I don't?"

"No, I'm just saying"—taking a deep breath—"I have a domestic situation in my home." He straightened up, fished a blue duplicate of a domestic violence report from his back pocket. "Ray was helping me with advice."

Nerese skimmed the sheet: Woman on a warpath. "What kind of advice." She held on to the document.

"I don't know, like . . . don't let her get the upper hand, she likes it when you're down and out, and other stuff. I don't really remember off-the-cuff per se, because I have pressures on me right now? It's like . . ." The kid worked his mouth wordlessly. "It's like, these days? I swear to God, everything's a blur."

"A blur," Nerese repeated as if chewing it over. "Let me ask you . . . You have any idea who might've assaulted Ray a few weeks back?"

Salim slowly shook his head. "Not really."

"*You* didn't do it, did you?" Nerese said it as lightly as she could.

"*Excuse* me?" Salim went motionless, his head cocked in disbelief.

Nerese said nothing, just met his eye with that placid unwavering gaze.

Salim leaned back and took in his surroundings as if for the first time: the barren room, the pitiless light. "Oh. Whoa. Unh-uh. No *way*. This is like a *frame*-up. Ray's my *boss*. He's my *teacher*. He's my *friend*. I brought my *son* into his home. You barking up the wrong tree for *sure*."

Nerese stared at him. Then stared some more.

"Hey, I'm not saying there are those who wouldn't, but no *way* can you lay that on *my* doorstep."

"Those who wouldn't, like, who?"

"How the hell do *I* know!" His face abruptly coloring. "I'm just saying in general. People. You're police, I need to *school* you about this?"

"Did you—" Nerese cut herself off, rephrased. "Who did you talk to about him?"

"Ray? Lots of people."

"Like who. Give me names. Give me *the* name."

"I don't know! I just said my old teacher's helping me get on my feet, I didn't say, 'Here's where he lives, go take him off.' Why would I do that, huh?" Salim near-shouting now, the corners of his mouth dotted with spittle. "What's in it for *me*," hitting himself in the chest.

"Well I'll tell you," she said calmly. "If the actor on this turns out to be someone you *talked* to, or *bragged* to, or anything of that nature and it's a name you could've given me right now, but didn't? There's no accessory status in this state, and I'm gonna make sure you go down for attempted homicide, aggravated assault and conspiracy to commit both just like the scumbag who did it. So I'm gonna ask you one last time . . ."

The kid cut her off with a gagging sound, Nerese at first thinking he was choking on something before realizing he was attempting a laugh.

"The po-police, man. It's like, no matter how hard I try, ha-how much I strive and suffer and persevere . . ." He leaned back and covered his mouth, his face roiling with blood. "Man, I don't even know why I fight it. You-you all don't *want* me to be any other way. It's like I got a *brand* on me or something. I brought my *son* . . ." Banging the table, then covering his mouth again.

Nerese glanced at her watch: 8:15.

"You know what? Fuck it. Why don't you all just save your ass some waiting time and lock me up for future reference. I mean, I'm here already, you know what I'm saying? So just go and get it over with." His eyes became slick and shiny; Nerese thinking, Crybaby. "'Cause I'll tell you, I'm starting to give less and less of a fuck each day, these days, so . . ."

Salim cut himself off, waved her away, then sat with his face averted, his jaw taut and bulging with outrage.

Nerese nodded as if sympathetic to his plight, understanding at that moment that she was sitting across the table from a killer.

Although she was fully aware that her dry threats and galling implacableness were at the root of his sputtering fury right now, something about how that fury expressed itself—not so much his choice of words but how quickly he had come to the edge of tears, the way his face and body and gestures had gone through what seemed to be nearly uncontrollable changes—told her this kid was both weak and dangerous. His mastery of day-to-day tribulations, which were close to innumerable in his world— this interview right here, for example—yielded far too readily to an explosive despair. And given that in Salim's neck of the woods there were so many kindred spirits for him to bump into, there was no doubt in her mind that the kid was a loaded gun and given enough time he'd inevitably go off.

"So what happens now," he demanded, his arms folded across his chest.

There was nothing to hold him on, nothing he'd done as far as she knew. He might or might not consider Ray as his friend, his mentor; he might even revere the guy—and Ray, in his desire to do the right thing, most likely saw this relationship as some kind of Give a Damn love match—but the fact of the matter was that every future encounter between them would increasingly play itself out like a game of Spin the Bottle with death.

"Can I go?"

"Let me ask you something," Nerese tilted her chin at him. "You say Ray's been backing your play?" nodding at his rolling stock, all zippered up at his feet.

"Yeah, I just told you that."

"So how much of a return has he been getting on his investment?"

"Nothing with me sitting here so why don't you all cut my ass loose so I can go back to work and then we'll see."

• • •

Nerese sat double-parked in front of Salim's apartment house on Tonawanda Avenue. She watched as the kid walked from her car to the building entrance, then did an about-face at the last minute to hook up with three young men coming out from the vestibule into the street. Salim had three too many friends right now, as far as she was concerned, but before she could brood on it any further, her cell phone rang.

"Make it good," she said.

"I'm always good."

"Bobby?"

"Your guy's phone records read like a thriller."

"How so," losing sight of Salim as he went around the corner with his homies.

"OK. The last outgoing call made on the day of the assault was to Garden State Taxi at four-thirty in the afternoon."

"Four-thirty. That's pretty much in the ballpark of when it happened. Garden State Taxi?" She reached for a notepad.

"To call a cab, I guess," Sugar said.

"He's got a car."

"Maybe it was for someone else. Maybe someone else made the call, you know, needing a ride out of there."

"The actor?" Nerese didn't think Freddy was that stupid.

"I don't know. I called them to get the dispatch log for that day? No extra charge, by the way. They don't have any record of sending a car to 44 Othello, so it's . . . Maybe the guy realized like at the last second what a bonehead play that would be, calling for a cab out of there, and hung up or something, I don't know."

"I don't know either," Nerese said, seeing that dead phone receiver skittered across the room from its base. "How about the outgoing call before that?"

"Before that? To a Frederick Martinez, 3355 Taylor Street. Went out roughly fifteen minutes earlier."

"Fifteen?" Nerese closed her eyes and saw Freddy standing over Ray's body and calling home to tell Danielle where he was, what he'd just done—Nerese then thinking, At least he didn't leave him lying there with a toothbrush in his heart. "What else you got," she asked.

"What else?" Sugar enjoying himself. "How about eighteen outgoing phone calls to the same number in a three-hour period four days before the assault."

"What was the number?"

"To a Carla Powell, 1949 Rocker Drive."

"Eighteen?"

"That's what I said. But the first seventeen were under ten seconds long, the last one for over a minute, so it sounds like a bunch of no-one-home-but-the-answering-machines, and then maybe on the eighteenth, he finally got someone to pick up or he finally decided to leave a message . . ."

Nerese thought it through, imagined Ray desperate to reach Danielle about something a day or two before her husband's release from jail.

"What else, anything else?"

"Well, I'll tell you there, Neesy." Sugar cleared his throat. "I have to say, it's some of these *in*coming calls that are truly gonna ring your bell."

Twenty minutes later, Nerese pulled into the narrow driveway of Freddy and Danielle's house, a brick two-family set in the midst of a cookie-cutter row of the same, the street monotonous but well maintained, part of a larger encircling neighborhood of Dominican, Puerto Rican and Filipino homeowners, house proud to the bone.

Although she was there ostensibly to interview the kid, Nerese was also hoping to get a first look at Freddy, see what she would be up against when it was time to go at him hard.

The trick here tonight would be to get Nelson to contradict at least a few details in his mother's account of the evening in question and to do so in her presence without her pulling the plug on the interview. The other needle to thread was to pull this off without letting the boy get wind of what this was all about: his mother's infidelity, his father's violence, the possible—no, most definite—return of said father to jail. Nerese could handle rage, bluster and deceit; innocence was tricky.

As she climbed the exterior stairs to the upper apartment, she saw that the living room windows were dark save for the shifting light show of the television playing inside. She took that for a bad sign, intuiting that she was about to be stood up.

It was the boy who came to the door on the third ring, barefoot and open-faced, still more of a child than an adolescent. He stared at Nerese without the presence of mind to either say hello or ask her her business.

"Hey, you must be Nelson." She smiled. With a nod, the kid silently acknowledged the ID, still not sure what to do or say.

Behind him, at the far end of the living room, the TV light bounced restlessly off vinyl fabric protectors, making the furniture wink and gleam in the semidarkness.

"I'm Nerese. Are your parents home?"

"Unh-uh."

"No?" Grinning through her irritation. "Do you know where they are?"

"My mother's . . . I don't know *where* she is." Nelson's voice was muffled and small, as if he weren't used to speaking.

"And your dad, do you know where your dad is right now?"

He shrugged, turned his head to briefly eyeball the TV, see what he was missing.

Nerese took out her ID and shield.

"Nelson?" Turning him back around. "I'm with the police department?"

The kid's mouth dropped open as if on a hinge, Nerese having to put some extra incandescence in her smile to keep him from freaking.

"I was supposed to meet your mom here now. Did she say anything about me coming by? Nerese Ammons? Detective Ammons?"

"No." The word like a fishbone in his throat.

Nerese's anger grew along with the wattage of her smile—the kid right here, so easy to work on, but she couldn't say a thing without Danielle present, anything he said . . .

"You OK, honey?"

The boy was leaning into the frame of the open screen door now, his hand clutching the inside knob.

"Nelson?"

"What."

She gave him her card. "You tell your mom to call me as soon as she gets in, OK? Tell her . . ." Nerese faltered. Tell her what? What kind of veiled threat or ultimatum could she deliver via Danielle's son?

On the other hand, the hell with it. Armed with the incoming calls on Ray's phone, she finally felt confident enough, prepared enough to just call Freddy's PO and compel him to have a sit-down, with or without Danielle or this kid here as a prelim.

"Nelson, does your mom have a cell phone?"

"I don't know," he said. "I don't think so."

Nerese shrugged amiably. "OK. Well you tell her to call me as soon as she gets in tonight, OK?"

The boy just stared at her.

"All right, then." Nerese touched his hand, then turned to leave.

"Why do you want to talk to her?" he asked when Nerese was halfway down the stairs, his voice barely audible.

Nerese turned and climbed back up, in order to look him in the face.

"She's helping me with some work I have to do." Then, unable to resist, "So it must be nice having your dad home again, huh?"

The question seemed to distract the kid from his own anxiety. Nelson shrugged sullenly and looked at his own shoes, guileless in his resentment.

"Have you guys been doing stuff together?" Nerese on thin ice now.

Shrugging again, the boy looked away, and in the gleam of the streetlight, Nerese found herself studying his face, something off in it . . . Not in his expression but in the face itself. Finally she zeroed in on his lips; they were riddled with the whitish pin dots of recently removed stitches, and the lips themselves were somewhat lumpy and swollen, as if someone had bashed him in the mouth a few weeks earlier.

"You have an accident?"

"What?"

"What happened to your mouth?"

"I don't know," he said, unconsciously covering his lower face with his hand.

"Someone hit you?"

"No." Nelson jerking his chin into his chest in disdain at the absurdity of her conjecture.

The phone rang from inside the apartment. The boy went to get it. Nerese held the screen door open, but remained on the porch.

The TV was on a straight sight line with the front door, Nerese watching some white hip-hopper lunge around a stage like a lewd hunchback, one hand squeezing his own balls.

Nelson came back to the door. "I have to finish my homework."

"Was that your mom just called?"

"Yeah."

"Did you tell her I was here for our meeting?"

"I forgot."

< Chapter 26

Ruby and Nelson — February 1

Ray thought it might have been a big mistake to bring Ruby into his apartment with Danielle and Nelson already there, but upon entering, Ruby looked right past Nelson, who was curled up in a corner of a couch watching MTV with the sound off, to Danielle set up on the terrace; Ray relieved to see the unguarded smile on his daughter's face.

Danielle was sitting with her back to them, apparently embroiled in another fifteen-rounder with her mother.

"Just respect my wishes. Respect . . . That's not your problem. That's not . . . *Thank* you . . . *Thank* you." Muttering, she killed the call, then half turned to finally see them standing in the living room.

She was smoking; Ray knocked off balance by that, recalling her "The body is the temple" speech from earlier in the week.

As Danielle stepped inside, Ruby once again reflexively tilted toward her, wanting to be embraced, but this time the hug she received was perfunctory, as if Danielle were a hostess greeting late arrivals at an already packed party. "How you doing, sweetheart, you doing good? Good. You're so pretty," then began to puff and pace, both Ray and Ruby disappointed that she hadn't made more of a happy fuss.

"I'm just smoking out on the terrace, is that OK?" asking for the house policy, pushing him ever further away.

"Inside, outside, whatever."

"Oh, Ruby!" Danielle wheeled to her. "Did you meet Nelson?"

At the sight of this other kid, Ruby took a step back and cocked her head like a bright-eyed bird.

Nelson jumped up, spun on his heel and, facing away, made some odd improvised karatelike moves.

"You all right?" Ray asked Danielle.

"These teachers, it's like no one has a life outside the classroom. No one has any other responsibilities."

Without another word, she went back out on the terrace.

Nelson sank back into the couch, returning to soundless MTV while Ruby pointedly gathered up all her *Buffy* and *Angel* tapes from around the television and removed them to the back bedroom.

And so, within a minute or two of introductions, everyone had dispersed into their own furious cover activities, Ray left standing there as solitary as the statue out in the bay.

He followed his daughter into the rear of the apartment, where she was now ordering and reordering her tapes around the TV at the foot of the bed. Before opening his mouth, he scanned the room for any evidence of his thing with Danielle, saw nothing but a bottle of baby oil on the nightstand; innocuous enough.

"You want to have a catch?"

Ruby shrugged, not looking at him.

"Yeah?"

"I said I don't *care.*"

Ray went to his closet, pulled out the two gloves and a softball.

"C'mon." He marched out of the room, determined to reclaim her.

At the front door he saw Nelson half-buried in throw pillows and, despite his intention to reaffirm to Ruby that she was his be-all and end-all first last and always, Ray just didn't have the heart to exclude the poor guy.

Both kids followed him out onto the lawn as if under court order to do so.

Danielle, seated almost directly above them on the third-floor terrace, threw a short wave, then dropped back into her work, Ray's portable phone propped upright on a stack of books.

Taking Nelson by the wrist, Ray walked him backward to a spot facing the building—no more river balls—and tucked his own glove under the kid's arm.

"Ruby, just back up." Not daring to touch her right now, he waved her off until she was about fifty feet from Nelson, tossed her the other glove, then backpedaled himself to create an equilateral triangle.

"Ruby, I'll throw to you, you to Admiral Nelson over there, Nelson to me." Ray choosing that arrangement because without a glove he couldn't handle his daughter's whip-crack delivery. Ruby was an unthinking natural, all her graceful lankiness effortlessly clacking into place with each rocketlike release.

Nelson on the other hand, was still pushing the ball rather than throwing it.

"OK, let's go, nice and easy, OK?"

His phone rang on the terrace. Danielle snapped it up as Ray waited for her to yell down to him, but instead she took it indoors, the call apparently for her.

"Nice and easy," he said somewhat distractedly, tossing the ball horseshoe-style to his daughter who lackadaisically snatched it out of the air, turned to Nelson and offered up her own baby-speed lob; but the boy, as if undecided between dodgeball and catch, simultaneously stuck out his glove and curled his body as far away from the throw as possible, the ball sailing past him untouched.

As he turned tail and began chasing after it, Ray saw that his daughter was studying him again with that same beaky bird-stare she had given him up in the apartment.

Danielle came back to the terrace without the phone, talking to herself so loudly that Ray could almost make out the words, and when he returned his attention to the kids, he saw that the ball was now at his feet; Nelson's throw not quite making it.

The phone rang again from inside the living room, Danielle saying, "Mother*fucker!*" clear as a bell, slapping closed her book and reentering the apartment.

"Nice and easy," Ray said, flipping the ball to his daughter, who then once again lobbed it to Nelson, who then once again did his flinchy dance and ball-chase. Ray's gaze went from Ruby's clinical squint up to the empty terrace; Danielle's voice raised in anger now came from inside the living room.

Nelson's second toss made it to Ray on the fly this time, the boy going up on his toes with suppressed excitement.

"Gettin' there, Nelson. Just keep your body turned like I showed you."

Ruby impatiently gestured for the ball, snapping her empty glove like a lobster claw. Ray threw it to her sidearm, then looked up to the empty terrace again—just for a second—but when his attention returned to his daughter, it was already too late.

Ruby's long right arm hung motionless straight over her head, the hand clutching the ball tightly curled at the wrist. And before Ray could shout out her name to stop her, she whipped that arm back and out like a bolo, a slingshot, stepping beautifully into the explosive release. Nelson seemed to be daydreaming, squinting at the clouds at that moment, and the ball caught him square in his mouth. The blood burst from his lips, leaping out in a perfect corolla of droplets.

The three of them just stood there for a second, Ray's eye peripherally catching Danielle back on the terrace. Then Nelson dropped to his knees, alert but stunned, his pale yellow sweatshirt, his chin and his teeth awash in blood.

Ray had no idea how Danielle could have made it from the third-floor terrace to her son on the grass faster than he himself from just a hundred feet away, but she did, skidding up to Nelson on her knees, sitting behind him in her bra, her formerly white pullover sweater pressed to his shattered mouth to stanch the flow.

"Stay there," he barked at her, then raced upstairs, emptied the ice compartment of the refrigerator into a bath towel and flew back down to the lawn.

"Put your sweater back on," he said, shoulder-butting her away.

There was enough ice in the towel to keep a corpse fresh, and he had to dump most of it out on the grass.

"Let's go." Ray and Danielle helped Nelson to his feet, the three of them race-walking to her car; it wasn't until they had almost cleared the parking lot that he remembered Ruby, who was still standing on the lawn.

The ER of the Dempsy Medical Center was miraculously quiet. Nelson and Danielle were sent to the trauma room after only a half-hour wait. Ray and Ruby were allowed to stand in the hallway directly outside the door.

Neither kid had said a word since the injury: Nelson seemingly too stunned, his eyes as wide and round as poker chips; Ruby's muteness having an air of melancholy defiance, which Ray was not prepared to breach.

The sting of the Betadine made Nelson cry out and fall backward off his stool, the exhausted-looking East Indian doctor who was working on him flinching as if someone had sneaked up from behind and shouted in her ear; not a good sign. And when she reached for the synthetic catgut and suturing needle, Ray signaled for Danielle to tell the doctor to hold off and then come out to the hallway.

"Listen, I don't think you should get him stitched up in here," he murmured. "Let me call this plastic surgeon I know."

"Plastic . . . Whoa." Danielle held up a staying hand.

"Listen to me, listen. When Ruby was three she fell off a swing, and her bottom teeth went right through her lip. We rushed her to an ER just like this, got her sewn up by some overworked resident, the guy did her up like he was basting a dress and she wound up looking like she had marbles inside her lip. She had to have two more surgeries just to repair the botch job of the first butcher. Remember that, Ruby?" Ray hated the false chirpiness in his voice but was still unable to confront the inappropriateness of his daughter's sullen coolness.

"Anyways, this guy who finally fixed her up? He said when it comes to a child's face you never, never get it done in a chop shop like this. I still have his card, he's just over in Gannon."

"The money." Danielle winced.

"Not your problem."

"Plastic surgeon," she said.

"Look, this doctor here? She's got the bleeding stopped, the cuts are disinfected. Just get him and we'll go."

Danielle returned to the trauma room and Ray began sorting through the business cards in his wallet.

"Dad?" Ruby said in a small, troubled voice.

"Yeah, Ruby." Ray wide open to her.

"We left the softball in the grass."

By the time they were on their way back to Little Venice from the office of the plastic surgeon, Nelson's lips were Sambo-sized, the tissue trauma converting them into rubbery tires so inflated that the kid couldn't open his mouth. It would be impossible for him to go to school for the next few days, Ray thought, unless he was immune to derision.

"I can't say enough how sorry I am," he addressed Danielle via the rearview mirror.

Sitting next to him in the shotgun seat, Ruby studied the passing scenery.

"Hey"—Danielle shrugged—"you're a man, he's a boy. Somebody's got to teach him how to catch and throw a ball, right?"

Until that moment it had never occurred to Ray that she assumed that he was the one who had done the damage.

By the time they got back to the apartment complex it was dark, but Ruby ran unerringly to the spot on the grass where the softball had last come to rest, as if she had been thinking of nothing but that from the moment they took off for the hospital.

Upstairs, she disappeared into Ray's bedroom as Danielle collected her schoolbooks from the terrace and replaced the portable phone in its cradle.

"Listen, I accepted three collect calls here while I was doing my homework."

"Three?" Ray said, assuming that they were from the County Correctional Center: inmates were allowed only to call out collect.

"Just tell me when the phone bill comes in."

"Don't worry about it." Still mainly focused on Ruby, Ray attempted to back-burner the fact that Danielle's husband had his phone number.

"Thank you." Danielle kissed him in front of Nelson, the kid spinning in place. "You're something else."

"C'mon," he demurred, then those phone calls came rushing back in on him; Ray once again telling himself, in a fleeting moment of clarity, Get out of this now. But then Ruby returned to the living room; his anxieties shifted and the moment passed.

"Nelson." Ray stopped him at the door and on impulse stuck his baseball glove between the kid's arm and ribs. "Put a ball in there and keep it under your mattress when you're not using it, OK? We're gonna make an all-star out of you yet."

The kid's lips had continued to rise like bread in an oven, even in the time that it took to go from the parking lot back up to the apartment, rising so high that his eyes had become slits and Ray was unable to tell how he felt about this last-minute consolation prize.

With the apartment to themselves now, Ruby and Ray stared blindly at MTV, the sound still off. Ray felt leaden, a little breathless, almost afraid to cross the room and turn off the television.

"Dad?" Ruby struggled for a normal tone of voice, her eyes fixed on the screen. "Not that I care, but why did you give him your glove? It's OK that you did, I'm not upset, but you just met her."

"Him. Look, I felt bad for the kid, plus his father's in jail, it's like not having a father. He doesn't even know how to . . ."

"It's OK." Her voice was starting to wobble. "I'm not upset, I'm just curious."

"I felt bad for him, Ruby," stopping there, not ready to go where he had to go now.

"Edward Bosco," she abruptly declared through clenched teeth.

"What?"

"I fucking *hate* him . . ." And the tears finally came, although her eyes were still on the screen. "I just want to . . . I say *anything,* he comes up behind me in the cafeteria, repeats everything I say, but like 'Nyeh nyeh nyeh nyeh,'" a viciously mincing singsong. "I just want to fucking *kill* him. Fucking *school.*"

"Ruby." Ray slid off the arm of the couch, tried to take her hand. "Ruby, do you want me to stop seeing her?"

"*What?*" she squawked, horrified, the question so inescapably blunt. "I don't care! Don't stop seeing her because of me!"

"No no no, honey, I didn't mean that." Ray going mind's-eye blind. "I would *never* do that. . . . Come here." He attempted to gather her up, but she surprised him with a straight-arm—Ray feeling in it, the barely suppressed yearning in her to do violence to him.

"I'm OK! I'm OK!" she snapped, then swiftly backstepped out of his reach.

"OK." Ray stepped off, his hands in the air. "Are you OK?"

"I said *yes.*"

Then, exhausted by the long and awful afternoon, she rubbed the tear-blotched skin beneath her eyes.

"Honey, let me ask you . . ." Ray speaking as delicately as possible, just wanting this to be over with. "Did you ever apologize to Nelson?"

"No." She finger-raked matted tendrils of brown-blond hair away from her face.

"Why not?"

She opened her eyes, threw him what for her was a hard look. "It's not *my* fault he catches like a bitch."

Chapter 27 >

Field Trips — February 26

Nerese and her son stood silently in a chilling fog outside the Dempsy County Correctional Center with roughly two hundred other visitors, women for the most part, and kids, lots of kids; the few young men waiting to get in looking like they could just as easily be the visited as the visitors, including one tall goof whose mouthful of gold tooth caps kept falling out in ones and twos whenever he attempted to speak.

Not having the written permission of the police commissioner to make this trip to see her nephew Eric, Nerese had left her gun, shield and ID at home, figuring as long as she wasn't recognized by any of the COs she'd be OK. And if, in fact, they did ID her, she could always try to plead ignorance of the rules, although with Antoine and Butchie racking up enough frequent-flyer miles in and out of this place for a free trip to the moon it would be a miracle if anyone bought it.

She had decided to risk this trip not so much for her nephew's sake as for Darren's. Having come home the night before earlier than expected, Nerese found herself walking into a living room adrift in malt liquor fumes, her son and three of his high school buddies playing at being players, sprawled on the couch, throwing back forties and clutching their nuts, a porno video playing on the TV.

None of that would have been worth more than the usual tongue-lashing and a grounding, although she also intended to call each kid's parents; but when one of the boys shakily struggled to his feet, a nickel-plated .22 fell out of his pocket and all bets were off.

She wouldn't go so far as to run him in; he wasn't a bad kid as far as she knew, none of them were—but she did personally drive him home to show his folks what he'd been packing, and heard the satisfying smack of flesh on flesh before she had made it back to her car.

But even that wouldn't have pushed her to make this dicey move here—the last straw was what Darren had said to her when she returned home and laced into him about his moron friend: "But Ma, it wasn't even loaded. The bullets were in his other pocket." So this visit was for his sake, a field trip to Christmas Future.

They passed the first checkpoint without much hassle—taking off their shoes and socks the worst of it—then got on the appropriate bus which would take them the three hundred yards to one of the eight residential pods that ringed the hub of the central intake center.

But coming into Eric's unit there was a second frisk and check, this one more intense; fingers roaming the waists of their pants and underwear, then harrowing scalp and hair; a flashlight check of their mouths and the lockering of all extraneous clothing, coats, sweaters, shirts, everything down to a thin turtleneck for Nerese, and the sleeveless T-shirt beneath his pullover for Darren; socks and shoes examined again, and then they were finally, finally steered into the visitors' hall forty-five minutes after getting on line. The space was a cafeteria-size room filled with narrow wooden tables long enough for fifty chairs on a side, the walls covered with inmate art: fantastical landscapes featuring unicorns, Conans and Xenas, interspersed with earnest portraits of Malcolm, Martin, Frederick Douglass and some Hispanic-looking men whom Nerese couldn't identify.

There were no topside barriers between the visitors and the inmates, but vertical planks of wood bisected the world of knees and furtive exchanges from the underside of the tables down to the floor.

Inmates in groups of six wearing gray Velcro-trimmed jumpsuits and loafer-style sneakers or flip-flops were periodically herded into the hall and one by one allowed to survey the sea of family and friends, point them out to the CO and then head across the room, closely watched.

Nerese and Darren were directed to two chairs alongside each other midway down a half-empty table and began the wait for Eric.

Short, dark and stocky like his mother, wide-eyed, bud-lipped and with a high smooth forehead beneath a medium-length crop like his father's, Darren sat straight-spined at the table, his hands clasped before him as if he were in a classroom lorded over by a fierce teacher.

Nerese, however, sat somewhat hunched over, covering her nose and mouth to fend off the sour stink of stress sweat and poor digestion that hung in the air of every prison she had ever had occasion to enter, over the course of her career and for a few years before that, during her adolescence, when she would grudgingly visit one of her brothers.

Many of the inmates and their visitors, especially if the visitors were women, slumped forward, sliding their upper bodies across the tables toward each other as they spoke, forearms pressed into forearms, faces inches apart.

Heads would drop for consoling caresses, thumbs digging into tension-knotted necks and shoulders.

Children scrambled across the tables to climb atop their fathers while low-key conversations took place between the parents; the predominant vibration in this vast room filled with hundreds of the most ruthlessly violent and unstable men in the four incorporated cities and towns of Dempsy County was seemingly one of intimate sobriety, as if they had all been given hard time for predicate tenderness.

Nerese watched her son absorb the world around him, his expression deteriorating from rigidly composed to slack and hangdog, his eyes jerking from tableau to tableau as if his head were mounted on a rusted turret.

Next to them a huge acne-scarred inmate—Nerese recognized him from the Roosevelt Houses, his left eyebrow, nostril and lower lip pierced with hoops—cuddled his three-year-old son with unabashed delight while completely ignoring the boy's slightly older sister, who sat next to her mother silently playing with a naked Barbie.

At the next table over, Darren focused briefly on a small Gypsy-looking gray-haired woman, her heart-shaped face held at an angle in the cup of her brown hands as she mournfully studied her toothless, tattooed son who was going on and on about something in a half-whispered rant, Nerese nearly able to smell the Crank boiling in his veins.

Turning his eyes to the newest group of six herded into the hall, Darren tracked one chunky inmate as he marched purposefully across the room to his seat and, without a word of greeting to the woman who had been waiting for him, turned his back on her and tilted his chin to the ceiling so she could get to work rebraiding his hair.

And then Darren caught sight of something that made him look as if he were losing his mind altogether: a woman seated across from her man at the very end of their table had sneaked her hand around the edge of the partition and was furtively yanking on his charcoal prick, which arched out of his open fly like the head of a turtle, both of them sitting there with their faces pressed into their forearms, as if as long as they appeared to be asleep they wouldn't be caught.

"OK, here's the thing," Nerese said softly, her son jumping nonetheless. "You and your friend there with his 'It ain't even loaded'? If you *ever* wound up in a place like this, Darren, not only wouldn't I help you out, but there is no way in hell that I would ever come to see you. Do you understand what I'm saying to you?"

These were the first words spoken by either of them since they'd gotten on line outside the visitors' entrance, Nerese as usual shaking her pup by the scruff, but she wasn't even sure that Darren had heard her. He was breathing through his mouth, almost panting, his head continuing its jerky circuit from inmate to inmate, his eyes devouring faces, hands, tattoos. Whatever does the trick, Nerese thought, backing off and letting the pictures tell the story.

But thirty minutes later, when Eric was finally herded into the visitors' hall at the tail end of a group of six, Nerese carefully studied her son's face as he got his first look at his recently minted thug-life cousin and realized that she had made a grievous error here. What she had interpreted as fear in her son's eyes was in fact, awe. What she had interpreted as revulsion was in fact, self-revulsion. Darren—she should have known this—so far from being the type of kid who would ever wind up in a place like this, had spent the last hour and a half surrounded by what his young music-video-molded mind imagined to be *real* men, hardcore to the bone; not constantly scolded mama's boys like himself; and it made him feel like a punk.

Right now, a sit-down with Eric, who would be under tremendous pressure to come off like cold steel to his aunt and cousin in the presence of all these other inmates, would only make it worse for Darren. Deciding to cut her losses, Nerese rose from the table, and with her son in tow got the hell out of there before Eric could spot them, stopping just long enough to deposit a check for seventy-five dollars in her nephew's general-store account, by way of apology.

• • •

Halfway home from County, with Darren mute and demoralized in the passenger seat and Nerese desperately trying to figure out how to salvage their disastrous field trip, her cell phone rang, and she wound up weaving across three lanes in her effort to locate the damn thing.

"This is Frederick Martinez." Frederick, not Freddy, the voice cool and formal. "My parole officer said you wanted to talk to me?"

"Yeah, I do. Thanks for calling back." Nerese whipped the car to the shoulder of the interstate, killed the radio. "Is there any way you and I can have a sit-down? I'd prefer explaining to you what's going on face to face."

"I know what's going on," Frederick not Freddy said, as a sixteen-wheeler ripped past them, its wind-wake buffeting the car.

"Can you meet me at the South Precinct sometime today? Anytime that's good for you."

"I'd rather not," he said.

"All right. How about at your PO's office? Same deal. At your convenience."

"No. I don't feel very comfortable there."

Nerese hesitated; she could have his PO compel him, but . . . "Well, where would you like to meet?"

Silence for a beat, then: "In New York."

"In New York?" Nerese sinking into herself, regretting having over-played the solicitous routine. "Well look, what I want to talk to you about, it's not that big a deal. Why go all the way to New York?"

"Because it gets a little close around here," he said.

Darren blew air out of his cheeks, still beating on himself for not being a bad-ass motherfucker, an O.G. or whatever.

"You know, Mr. Martinez, first of all, you crossing over to New York is a violation of your parole. Second of all, I really don't want to do this, but if I need to, I can have your PO compel you to come in and meet with me at her office."

"Well," he sighed, "I really don't want to do this either, but if I have to, I can lawyer up as soon as I get off this phone."

Nerese's turn to exhale like a blowfish.

"Where in New York did you have in mind?"

Three hours later, in the shadow of the Forty-second Street library's south lion, on a small plaza above the sidewalk and below the broad marble stairs leading to the entrance, were the immovables of a closed-for-the-season sidewalk café: six round metal picnic tables, each one pierced by the shaft of a collapsed umbrella, and an undulating chorus line of folded-up chairs run through with a heavy metal chain and secured to protruding iron rings in the low wall that bordered the terraced side gardens.

There were also a few chairs scattered about unsecured, and that was where Nerese found him, Freddy—no, Frederick—Martinez, sitting by himself in the deserted sidewalk café, one leg crossed over the other as he read the *New York Times.*

He was a trim, handsome man, a welterweight with short wavy blue-black hair, a goatee and a lean self-possessed face the color of old ivory. His wardrobe reflected his aura: crisp tan chinos, a maroon turtleneck beneath a black double-breasted leather car coat and unscuffed oxblood construction boots.

But the chair that he had unfolded for himself was positioned at some distance from any of the tables, and on Nerese's second take, there was something about how he had chosen to create an absolute island of space for himself facing this busiest of New York intersections that made her feel there was perhaps a little too much self-consciousness going into this vision of self-possession.

Frederick not Freddy; Nerese decided to play this one here by catering to his inflated sense of dignity, at least at first.

"Mr. Martinez?" Nerese stood over him in the empty plaza.

He carefully folded the newspaper in quarters before looking up at her, silent, waiting for more.

"I'm Detective Ammons?" Then, in her awkwardness, "We talked on the phone?"

"OK." He nodded then continued to sit there, calmly taking her measure.

She was starting to feel like an idiot now, standing before him as if he were behind a desk, the boss-man, Nerese having just been called on the carpet.

A thin four-inch whippet of scar tissue that wasn't visible in his mug shot ran horizontally across his forehead midway between brow and hairline; most likely, she guessed, the first strike of that gym-cage death match.

"Do you think we could go somewheres?" Nerese asked, hunching her shoulders against the cold.

"I thought we just did," he said.

Picking up one of the stranded folding chairs, Nerese brought it to the nearest table, then gestured for Freddy to sit opposite her. "Please."

"I'm assuming you know Ray Mitchell," she said, the collapsed umbrella like a cloth-draped spear between them.

"I've never met him, but I know of him," Freddy said, crossed arms over crossed legs.

"You know what happened to him?"

"I heard he was hospitalized after some kind of assault." Freddy took an unwrinkled twenty-dollar bill from his inside coat pocket, folded it and picked his teeth.

"How'd you come to know that?"

"How?" He slipped the twenty back in his pocket. "People talk."

"People . . ."

He looked off at the Fifth Avenue traffic, then came back. "I didn't do it. I know that's what you expect me to say, but it happens to be the truth."

Leaning one elbow on the table, Nerese waited for more.

"However." He coughed into his fist. "Let me also add that, frankly, I'm not too broken up about it."

"And why would that be."

Now it was Freddy's turn to stare.

"So I take it you're aware of the rumors."

"The rumors?" he said acidly.

Nerese held her peace.

"Yeah," he said, looking away again. "I'm aware of the rumors."

"So you can understand why we need to have this conversation now."

"I have my demons, no doubt, but you're talking to the wrong person."

A ruddy piss-bum staggered up to the table, his face a hairy blur. Apparently having abandoned human speech some time ago, he simply put out his hand. Nerese waved him off, but Freddy slipped him a dollar. The guy toddles off down Fifth Avenue with the bill sticking out of his fist like a flower.

"You know, Freddy . . . Can I call you Freddy?"

He shrugged.

"Freddy, you say you didn't do it, and to be honest, at this point in time I'm inclined to believe you," she said with as straight a face as she could manage. "I mean, I studied your sheet and other than"—she nodded to the scar on his forehead, which, she realized, looked just like the Nike logo—"other than that one incident, which I was told was a matter of self-defense, there's no violence there, no history." Nerese leaned forward, adding more intimately, "However, there are those who think differently. Unfortunately, they happen to be my superiors." Nerese wasn't even sure if she had any superiors in this limbo time. "And in order for me to move on, I have to get them off my back. Now, the only way I can *do* that, is to clear you, so . . ."

"Help me help you," he said dryly.

"More or less." Nerese stuck in the gambit. "Well, let me just ask you . . . You say you had nothing to do with it. OK. Do you maybe have any thoughts on who did?"

"Sorry."

"Anybody. Friends, business associates, guys in County who would've, you know, maybe given the rumors, have taken it upon themselves out of friendship or loyalty to you . . ."

"One." Freddy held up a finger. "You can stop calling them rumors. And two . . . Do you honestly think I would discuss with another man the subject of my wife's infidelity? I'm only here talking to you about it because being on parole you pretty much have me over a barrel."

"I'm just saying, you didn't even have to talk to anybody. Someone could've . . . Look, I'm trying to help you out here. Give me some names. Friends, business associates . . ."

"You want me to give you the names of my business associates?" Freddy smiled incredulously.

"OK. For starters, who'd you bunk with in County this last go-round. C'mon, you dragged me over to New York, don't make me do all the work here." Nerese doing Ol' Man River now, but also belatedly thinking, Who would be a better witness to Freddy's mental state in the days before his release?

"My bunkie in County? Some cretin couldn't figure out how to open and close his Velcro jumpsuit. A real arch-criminal. You know, now that I think of it? That's definitely the guy."

"OK. Let's go the other way. Give me somebody who can vouch for you."

Freddy shrugged, reversed knees.

Another bum came by, disconcertingly fine-boned under the scabs and dirt, his hair either in dreadlocks or just hopelessly matted.

Once again Nerese waved him off, but Freddy, trapped by his audience, grudgingly forked over another buck.

"All right." Nerese sighed, pulling out her notepad as if it weighed a ton. "Let's do this the ABC way. Where were you on February seventh."

"What day of the week was that?"

"Two Tuesdays back. Two days after you were released."

Freddy thought about it, then not too furtively studied some passing skirts.

"C'mon, Freddy. Stay with me."

A squirrel jumped on and off the table in the space of a heartbeat; the both of them jerking in shock, then covering it up.

"I was at home."

"All day? All night?"

"Tuesday mornings I go to see my PO. Cassandra Wiggins. You can verify it with her. After that I came home, most likely made myself some lunch, who the hell remembers from almost three weeks ago, but then I definitely went for a run."

"A run. A jog?" Nerese thinking that opened up the road to anywhere and anything.

"See, understand something. In County? You can lift weights, you can play basketball, you can work out on the bags. The one thing you can*not* do, is run. So the one thing that tells me I'm out of there is that I can run. So I do."

"You ran. By yourself?"

"Yes."

"From where to where?"

"If I knew that someday I'd be having this conversation, I would've had a camcorder strapped to my head."

"From where to where," Nerese repeated, her pen motionless above the pad.

"From my house to County and back. Six miles."

"You ran to the county jail?"

"You bet. Get there, take a long long look, give it my back and I'm gone."

The late winter sun began to dip behind the skyscrapers, the deserted plaza slipping into shadow.

"You went straight from your house to County and back. No detours, no doglegs?"

"What, you mean like to Little Venice?"

Freddy flinched as soon as he'd said it; too clever by half.

"Why would Little Venice come into this?" she asked, seeing the self-disgust in Freddy's face.

He pulled a pair of sheer leather driving gloves from his pocket, deliberately flexed them onto his hands.

"Hello?" Nerese stared at his profile.

"Look. If thoughts were deeds this would be a barren planet."

She contemplated the glistening horizontal scar above his brow.

"I have never laid eyes on that man in my life," he added.

"Ever talk to him?"

Freddy hesitated, then: "No."

"Had to think about it, huh?"

"Not really," a lingering wisp of self-reproach in his tone.

"Not really?" Nerese fished around in her purse, and pulled up Ray's phone records. "I have four collect calls from County going to his house the week before you got out. Three on the first of February and one on the third."

The foot traffic along Fifth Avenue began to build as the hour approached five; Freddy staring without appetite now at the homeward-bound ass.

"They were to my wife," he finally said, each word bitten bloody.

"No kidding." Nerese leaned forward, her shoulders rippling with cold. "How did you know she'd be there?"

Freddy's jaw locked, his face pulled askew.

"Freddy?"

"Because she wasn't at her mother's house and she wasn't at work."

"But how did you know that was the third option?" Nerese pushed. "Huh?"

"Like I said, people talk," he muttered.

"But these calls you made." Nerese squinted at the sheets in her hand. "She was over there on two separate days in the last week of your incarceration. That's two days that you *know* of, Jesus . . ."

Nerese then let the silence come down, wanting Freddy to use the quiet time to feed the flames.

"I'm just curious," she said, closing her notebook. "When you called his house? Who accepted the charges, Ray or your wife?"

He took a deep, deliberate breath, turned from the street to Nerese. "Look," fixing her with fiercely clear eyes, the white line of his mouth. "I deal drugs. You know that. I deal *weight*. You know that too. And with those two things, you know everything about me that's relevant from a police point of view. I had nothing to do with that assault. You catch me on the other? I'll come in like a baby. Catch me on the other, and I'm yours. But if you want to lock me up, it's going to have to be for that, because I did *not* do this assault and I will *not* go down for it."

He took another long fuming breath to keep himself in check, those eyes never leaving her face.

"Now . . . You're into my shit and there's nothing I can do about it. I have to accept that because of the life I chose. Rules of the game. But you tell me what I have to do in order to get you off my back on this other thing, and I will do it." He cocked his head. "Help me help you help me."

Nerese shrugged as if they were just shooting the breeze. "Come in and take a polygraph."

"No. No way. There's a twelve and a half percent margin of error on those things. Forget it."

"What if I said you could pick the questions?" Nerese just wanting to get him in the House.

"No. And don't ask me hypothetically what questions I'd pick if I went for it. That trick is older than the hills. No. No. No. What else. You want a list of everybody I had contact with in jail? You'd go insane. You want a list of my friends on the outside? I don't have any. You want a list of people I do business with? Giving that to you would be like slitting my own throat. You want to talk to people in my family? My guess is you did that already. However, if you want to be thorough about it, I'll give you my brother's address and phone number in Boston, my sister's in Bayonne, my mother's in Atlantic City and my father's in St. Raymond's Cemetery. What else . . ."

Nerese pondered threatening to expose him as a County informant, but that would be the last of all last resorts. Right now she just needed him lawyer-free and talking.

"So you came back from running," she said.

Freddy lifted and dropped his hands in exasperation, that blazingly succinct speech all for nothing. "I came home, took a shower and went online, did some day trading. I'd like to say I'm good enough at it to quit the other business, but I'm not quite there yet. If it was a typical day, which it most likely was, once again you're asking me about almost three weeks ago, my son came home at four, my wife from school at seven, we ate dinner at eight, stayed in all night and went to sleep. Once again, what can I do to get you off my back. All I ask is that you be reasonable in your requests."

"Freddy, you say 'Be reasonable' but you won't take a polygraph, you won't talk about the bad guys . . ."

"There is nothing there but wasted time for you and unnecessary jeopardy for me. Look, I know you talked to my mother-in-law, I know you talked to my wife. You probably talked to people in Hopewell. You probably talked to County Narcotics. Who's left that could account for my whereabouts. My son? Do you want to talk to my son? You do it in front of my wife or myself and I will invite you into my home." He was starting to calm down a little, enjoying the sound of his own righteous thoroughness.

"I'm just curious," Nerese said mildly. "When you called your wife at Ray's place? What did you talk about?"

"Ask her." Freddy's face stormed up again.

"You know, when Danielle went over there she usually brought him with her."

"Who."

"Your son."

A fat blue vein popped up, a worm of lightning shooting from the corner of his left eye straight back to his temple, Freddy's mouth clamping into a rictus of rage, Nerese thinking, There it is . . .

"Did you know that?"

Without losing her eye, he shifted his chair sideways until he sat completely to one side of the umbrella pole, giving him an unobstructed shot at her. Nerese responded by leaning a little farther back in her seat, her thumb casually wedged beneath the snap on her sidearm.

"Did you know that, Freddy?"

"Yes, I did," the words small and throttled as he struggled once again to rein himself in.

"Fine," she said. "How about tomorrow?"

"What?"

"I accept your offer. Let me talk to your son. See if his recollections jibe with yours. Is tomorrow good? Say about seven, seven-thirty?"

Without another word, Freddy got up and stalked off into the Fifth Avenue foot traffic, leaving Nerese alone in the near-frigid shadows beneath the south lion.

"OK then," she said to his empty chair. "Tomorrow it is."

‹ Chapter 28

Nelson — February 3

The moment Ray opened the door he saw the speech in Danielle's eyes, put it together with Nelson and Dante loitering behind her back and beat her to the punch.

"It's OK. Just leave them with me."

"Look, something came up. I'm so sorry, but . . ."

"I just said, leave them with me."

"Just leave them with you?"

"Absolutely."

"You know, because I trust you so much . . ."

"Good."

Nelson's lips were less swollen today, but bristled with the short stiff tips of blood-blackened stitches. And, amazingly to Ray, the kid was dutifully carrying the glove that had failed to prevent the damage.

"I'm under so much stress, you don't . . ."

"Danielle, do what you have to do."

At this point, Ray almost welcomed her asexual flattery, her chronic distraction.

He still couldn't bring himself to call it quits yet, but moments like this were helping him get there. And he damn well knew that if he didn't walk away from her in the next few days, coming events would take care of the situation in a way that could be dangerously beyond his control.

"And your mother, I don't really mind, but no way she can watch them?"

"Oh, me and her." Danielle held up her hands. "We're most definitely not talking right now."

Ray nodded sympathetically, thinking, Moms are like that when their kid marries a convict. Danielle was headed over to County this afternoon, he'd bet his life on it.

"I'll be like two hours," she said.

"Whatever."

"You're the best." She kissed him startlingly hard, almost painfully, on the mouth; once again, in front of Nelson, the kid putting his face in the glove and doing a pirouette.

"Yeah, well, so," Ray said meaninglessly, as the unpredictable and ardent violence in her made a shambles of his resolve to say what had to be said.

Dante streaked into the apartment, Danielle yelling after him, "You break anything I'm not coming back to pick you up."

Then, to Nelson, "You watch him like a hawk," and was gone.

In the living room Dante had turned on MTV and was moving effortlessly, brilliantly to the beat, all shuddering shoulders, flying elbows, and with the light crossover footwork of a young Ali; Halloween-faced Nelson watching him with a covetous helplessness. But the sunlight streaming in from the terrace completely bleached out the screen.

"C'mon, fellas, it's really nice out," Ray said. "Let's go to the mall."

Coming into the vast, aviarylike Gannon Commons, Ray experienced the familiar pattern of elation/deflation, the liberating spaciousness of the nearly deserted three-story atrium, the bright splash of water in the unseen fountain and the endless possibilities of things, things, things to buy, quickly giving way to a psychosomatic exhaustion as first he noticed the filthiness of the floor tiles, then the limp Muzak, then the lonely kiosks, each with its own one-product inanity—Metabolife, Fragrance Hut, Piercing Palace, Pager Pagoda, Astro Gems—the solitary vendors sitting hunched over on high stools and staring at air.

A greasy aroma drifted down from the third-floor food court—spare ribs and Cinnabons—and from the fourth level came the clamor of young schoolchildren on a class trip to one of the multiplex movies, their echoing squawks and yowls punctuated by the flat-toned blaring threats of the teachers.

Dante, being Dante, simply took off on his own, and Ray, lacking the requisite anxiety, just let him go and find his own trouble.

Alone with Nelson now, he began to wander past the ground-floor retail outlets, cutting loose with a monotone roll call to amuse both himself and the kid.

"Gap Men Gap Women Gap Kids, Gap Tooth, Foot Locker, Lady Foot Locker, Athlete's Foot, Big Foot, Trench Foot, Kay Bee, Kmart, K-Ration, K-Nine, Bed Bath and Beyond, Beyond Bed Bath and Beyond, Bed Bath and Beyond Beyond," the unendurable predictability of what stood before them making Ray stagger until they pulled up in front of the sole independent shop, Onyx Men, a clothing store. All the mannequins in the windows were sporting what looked like the castoff wardrobe from a Kid 'N Play *House Party* sequel; the colors of the day black, silver and burnt orange.

"This is where the *Soul Train* dancers come for back-to-school."

The kid grunted, his unblinking eyes staring straight ahead.

"*You* wouldn't wear any of this stuff, would you?"

Nelson shook his head, no. He was still lugging around the baseball glove; Ray wondered if perhaps he had been unwilling to leave it at the apartment, in case it was misconstrued as a gift return.

"Where do you usually go to buy your clothes?"

"I don't know." Nelson singsonged.

"Who takes you, your mom or your dad?" Ray unable to stop himself from asking.

"My grandmother."

"Your grandmother. You like your grandmother?"

Nelson nodded his head in vigorous affirmation.

"Yeah, I was crazy about mine too. Well, I told you about her and the baseball glove," eyeing the one he had given Nelson, in a possessive head-lock between the kid's elbow and ribs. "Let me ask you, can you imagine your grandmother as a teenager?"

"Nope."

"Yeah well, see, that's funny to me, because I'm still having a hard time seeing Carla as anything but."

Alongside Onyx Men stood a Victoria's Secret, and in the midst of putting together a few one-liners to toss off once they came in front of those windows, he spotted a Bookworms outlet down the hall and felt himself coming back to life.

"Admiral, sir, over here."

But once Ray steered Nelson inside, he saw right off that this place was a bust, too, the literary equivalent of all the other shit in the mall: a sea of discount tables stacked with endless piles of crappy pop-up books, *Star Wars* spin-offs, Disney spin-offs, sandy-assed bikini calendars, topless firemen calendars, massage manuals, astrology manuals, Idiots and Dummies Guides to everything from beer to cancer; Ray hot as a pistol, wheeling to Nelson, "How the *hell* can you fuck up a bookstore . . ."

Once again startled by Ray's language, Nelson reared back; and then Dante materialized between the aisles as if summoned.

His pants were soaked, there was a CD-size button pinned to his shirt proclaiming PUSSY POWER in bold red letters and he was carrying two books, a hardback biography of a professional wrestler named Krisis and something called *The Big Book of Explosions*.

"Buy this for me."

"No. Why are your pants wet?"

"From the fountain."

"And where'd you get that stupid button?"

"From the fountain. And *look* . . ." Dante thrust his hands into his bulging front pockets and pulled out two fistfuls of wet change. "I'm coming back here every *day*."

"Jeez," Nelson said under his breath, turning away from his cousin.

"Put these books back," Ray said. "Just go back there and, whatever, OK?"

Dante disappeared.

Nelson eyed the piled tables, but made no move to reach for anything, see what was inside.

"You like to read?" Ray asked.

The kid nodded yes.

"What kind of books?"

Nelson shrugged.

"In English, please?"

"Horror."

"You ever read Stephen King?"

He nodded yes.

"Which one . . ."

"All."

"All?" Ray didn't believe it. "You read *The Tommyknockers*?"

He shook his head no.

"You read *The Stand*?"

Another no.

"You read—" Ray cut himself off. What was he doing, busting the kid like this. "Who else do you like to read?"

"Michael Crichton?" Nelson rhyming it with bitch.

"Really. Which book. Or all."

"Two," Nelson said. He had yet to look Ray in the eye.

"*Jurassic Park*?"

Nelson nodded yes.

"What else?"

"*Star Wars*."

"No, I mean what other Michael Crichton."

"*The Andromeda Strain*?"

"For real?" Ray was mildly impressed. "Good for you. You ever read any of the old-time guys?"

Nelson shrugged, not knowing, Ray realized, who the old-time guys were.

"You know—Poe, Wells, Lovecraft, any of those?"

Another mute, eyes-averted no.

"Well we have to do something about that."

And experiencing a little rush of largesse, he steered Nelson to the wall opposite the cash register; this was the only shelving in the store that seemed to hold books that were actually books.

There were two smallish sections: Fiction and Literature, like a value judgment. Ray wondered who working here got to decide which book went where.

He reached for *Dracula* but then balked, fretting that the kid might not have the skill or the patience to get through the pre-electronic pacing and prose. Same for *Frankenstein*. And anxious to hit nothing but homers here, Ray simply blew off all the favorites of his own adolescence and gathered up *Jaws*, *The Silence of the Lambs* and an abridged *Tales of Mystery and Imagination*, the last making him fret in the opposite direction: that in his eagerness to avoid a boring reading experience maybe he wasn't giving Nelson enough credit.

"I was just like you when I was your age," Ray said. "Monsters, ghosts, vampires . . . But then I discovered girls." He plucked *Pet Sematary* from the rack, added it to the pile. "Sometimes I try to get Ruby into this stuff,"

Ray said, then faltered, wondering what, if anything, Nelson thought about Ruby these days, her and her rocket-ball.

"You know, get her to read, of course, but even just to watch the old horror movies with me. But she won't bite. She thinks they're boring. It's probably because they're not in color and everybody's talking with that perfect theater diction, you know, 'Hello, dear,' and 'Oh my darling, are you all right?' And it's funny because she's obsessed with *Buffy* and *Angel*, but she just doesn't connect them to a genre."

"What's a genre?" Nelson asked, finally looking directly at Ray.

"A category. Like humor, or mystery. By the way, Ruby wanted me to apologize to you for, you know."

Nelson shrugged, looked away again.

"She feels very bad about it."

On their way to the register, they passed the *Buffy* section: the novelizations, the calendars, the action figures, the fanzines, and feeling that slightly sentimental, slightly panicky yearning for his daughter—what the hell was he doing here with someone else's kids?—he grabbed an *Angel* pinup calendar and a *Buffy* shot glass, but then just as quickly dumped them both, suddenly seized with despair, wall-eyed with it. Crap, crap, everything crap—books, videos, clothes, money, all is boredom and waiting and doing it wrong over and over and over until the day you die.

"Hey, Nelson," saying his name with a certain rage-born zip. "Repeat after me. Thank . . ." A cutting singsong.

"Thank . . ." Nelson dutifully repeated, tone-perfect; but, sensing that the boy was oblivious to the courtesy infraction, and that his despair-fit had nothing to do with him in any event, Ray just let it slide.

The three of them sat at a crumb-strewn table in the skylighted food court, Dante and Nelson working on Whoppers, Ray ignoring a white lettuce and steel-gray tomato salad.

He had bought Dante a book of World Wrestling Federation centerfolds and was flipping through the photos himself, eyeing the impossibly inflated yet chiseled physiques.

Nelson was sunk in *Pet Sematary*, holding the book in his lap beneath the table, as if guarding a straight flush.

"Do you know who used to be a huge wrestling fan?" Ray was addressing both of them but Nelson wouldn't lift his eyes from the book. "My grandmother. Well, me too, but she was completely around the bend with it. Like back when I was little? Every chance I'd get, I'd go over to her apartment, they still lived on Tonawanda back then, and we'd watch it on TV, and she'd get so carried away she'd almost be down on the rug with them. She completely bought it. Loved the good guys, hated the villains . . ."

Ray began to drift, come back. "And she was not what you'd call a happy person. She was very heavy, like two hundred plus pounds, maybe five foot, five-one tops, kind of moved all stooped over, with this wild look in her eye like something was chasing her. And, my grandfather, he never came home half the time, kind of ignored her when he did . . ."

"Get me more fries," Dante said, his cousin cutting him a quick look then plunging back into Stephen King.

"Anyways, with wrestling?" Ray stared at Nelson but the kid wasn't picking up on it. "Back then, every once in a while they'd have a live card at the old Dempsy armory, maybe six, eight matches. Tag teams, women, midgets . . ."

"Mini-Me," Dante said.

"And she took me one time, I was maybe nine, ten years old . . ." He reached across the table and gently removed *Pet Sematary* from Nelson's lap, the kid not protesting, but unable for some reason to meet Ray's eye.

"And, my grandmother, all night she's going bughouse, yelling at the villains, the ref, you know, doing her thing, and, this match comes up, features this bad guy Fritz Von Hundt, had high black boots with iron crosses on the sides, a monocle, I guess he was supposed to be some kind of half-assed Nazi. I mean in real life he was probably some meathead from Jersey City, but they play this bogus-German marching music and here he comes, goose-stepping down to the ring, and my grandmother who's been yowling all night, all of a sudden she's quiet and I'm thinking, What the hell, she should be doing jumping jacks for this guy . . .

"But as he passes us, we're sitting right on the aisle, my grandmother takes a pin, a diaper pin or something, and *jabs* him right in the ass."

"YAH!" Dante popped in his seat.

Nelson was still avoiding Ray's eyes, but his own had grown big and he was fighting off a grin.

"Anyways, this Von Hundt grabs his own behind, shoots six feet in the air, wheels around." Ray left out the explosive "Cocksucker!," the first profanity he had ever heard from an adult. "He's looking, looking, but my grandmother, now she's staring straight ahead, no pin, and the guy goes into the ring.

"See, there was this type of wrestling fan back then called a Hatpin Mary, ladies who would do this type of thing, and man, I tell you, it scared the crap out of me, seeing her do that . . . Anyways, that match goes down, the next one's announced, and coming down our aisle now, is this villain that I know *personally* my grandmother hated like the plague. Nature Boy Bobby Bragg. This Nature Boy, he had long platinum-blond hair all slicked back, and he wore a leopardskin kind of one-shoulder Tarzan outfit and he was *built*."

"*Built*," Dante mimed.

"So this Nature Boy starts down our aisle towards the ring, and the whole place is booing, cursing him out. And this guy, he's just standing there like bathing in it, like, 'Yeah, that's right, that's right.'"

Dante hopped up and mimed what Ray was describing; puffing out his chest while bobbing his head, an imperious smirk on his mug and a beckoning challenge in the come-hither flex of his fingers. The little anarchist, Ray had to admit, a genius of body-talk.

Nelson turned to his cousin and clucked in annoyance, something protective of Ray in that.

"Anyways, Nature Boy, he's still a way aways from us, but I see that my grandmother has got the pin out again and that she's waiting. Me, she does that jabbing thing on this dude, I'm running like hell. But the crowd, they saw my grandmother stick Fritz Von Hundt and they want her to do it again. So as Nature Boy gets nearer to us, this chant starts up, '*Stick* 'im, *stick* 'im, *stick* 'im . . .'

"And it's *hot* in there, Nelson," Ray momentarily catching his eye. "August hot. No ventilation, full house, people sweating like pigs, '*Stick* 'im *stick* 'im *stick* 'im . . .' And Nature Boy, he hears this, looks around, sees my grandmother with the pin in her hand, and what he does is, he comes right up to her seat and just stands over her in like this hands on hips, he-man pose, just stands in front of her, *daring* her to do it.

"And she is paralyzed. She cannot move. The crowd's chanting, boiler-room heat, this blond god looking into her eyes and she, this poor overweight lonely lady, she just, she can't move.

"You know what he does?"

"What," Dante asked.

"He bends over, like, bows, takes my grandmother's hand with the hatpin in it, says, 'Ma-dame . . .' and kisses it. Kisses the back of her hand. Then moves on down to the ring.

"And my grandmother? She just sat very very quietly for the rest of the evening.

"And for *years* after that, whenever we watched wrestling on the TV? No more yelling at the screen, no more rolling around the carpet. And every once in a while she'd say in this kind of drifty-dreamy voice, 'I wonder how the Nature Boy is doing. He's such a nice man.'"

"Ma-dame," Dante said, eyes wandering. "I'm going back to the fountain."

"Just stay for a minute," Ray said.

Nelson stared at the table.

"Anyways, when I was eighteen? I had a big fight with her. I came back from college on Thanksgiving break and we got into an argument about I can't even remember what . . . Politics, civil rights, I marched out of her house, slammed the door and never talked to her again. I mean, I would have, but two months later when I was back at school she had an embolism or a blood clot and died in her TV chair so I never got a chance. I never, I never talked to her again."

"Ho *shit*!" Dante exploded, leaping from his seat and, bug-eyed with glee, pointing at Ray. "Nelson, look! Look! He's *crying*!"

"Shut up!" Nelson hissed, grabbing for his cousin. "Just shut the fuck up!"

Undeterred, Dante twirled out of reach.

"Ray! Ray! You know what Nelson said last night?" His voice now a sinuous taunt. "Nelson said he *luh-ves* you."

"What?" Nelson said, a stunned exhalation, more breath than voice.

"Oh yeah. Oh yeah," Dante sang triumphantly, hopping from foot to foot.

"What's wrong with you," Ray said as mildly as he could. "Don't tease people like that."

But Dante was already in the wind, halfway back to the money fountain, his steps as light and splashy as the sounds that drew him.

Disoriented by Dante's exposé, Nelson's sudden pallor, Ray picked up *Pet Sematary* off the table and made a big show of reading the back cover copy.

"Your cousin's a little shit. You know that, right?" Ray said conspiratorially to Nelson without raising his eyes from the book. But he might was well have been talking to the salad on his plate: the kid, still abuzz with mortification, had simply turned to stone.

. . .

Later that day, a few hours after Danielle, tense and distracted, had come back to his apartment and collected the boys, the ringing of the phone pulled Ray out of the shower.

At first, given the operator's brisk yet lifeless greeting, he took her for a telemarketer, but in fact, it was a collect call from Frederick Martinez at the Dempsy County Correctional Center.

Ray stood there, the receiver cradling his jawbone as he numbly pondered accepting the charges.

"Sir?" the operator said.

He could hear Freddy breathing in the wings.

"What?" Ray said, then, "Yes."

The two men breathed at each other for a long moment, Ray going into some kind of cerebral free fall, the smallish kitchen that enveloped him beginning to wobble and shine.

"Do you know who I am?" Freddy finally said, his voice sober, measured, but with a slight tremor.

"Do what?" Ray said, then, "Yes. Yes I do."

"Do you know why I'm calling you?"

Ray wanted to say "Yes," then "No," settled on, "I'm not really sure."

Freddy retreated into that tense breathing again, Ray hearing in the background a cacophony of bellows and shouts, the sound of perpetually wired men in an acoustically uncushioned environment.

"I'm getting out of here the day after tomorrow," Freddy finally said. "And as of this moment? I would very much like to resume my life with no outside complications."

"OK."

"I have no intention of ever having to come back to a place like this."

"Great," Ray said automatically.

"On the other hand." Freddy paused as if winded, Ray thinking, He's scared. He's fucking scared. Of *me*. "On the other hand, if a situation recommends itself? Then whatever has to happen *will* happen, irregardless of the consequences to me or anybody else."

The silence came down again, save for the brutal aviary in back of Freddy, Ray transfixed by the shimmering steel base of his dead mother's blender, the thing levitating a little; hovering above the counter.

"Do you understand why I'm telling you this?"

Ray stalled, a pulse of pride trying to muscle its way through the fear.

"Yes?" Freddy softly pressed.

"I think so," Ray said.

"I think you do too. Thank you for accepting my call."

But before he could hang up, Ray impulsively blurted, "I just want to say, you have a great kid."

"Excuse me?" Freddy's voice suddenly flat, devoid of all vibration.

"No, I'm just saying . . ." Ray fell silent.

And Freddy hung up.

Ray stood leaning into the kitchen wall, his head a bowl of sonic crackle as he numbly played and replayed, word for word, everything Freddy had said, backward, forward, then reenacted his own responses, assessing their tonal heft.

The thing about the phone call that frightened Ray the most was Freddy's nervousness, his assumption that Ray was in possession of some kind of formidableness, physical or otherwise, that might have to be dealt with head-on; his impulsive compliment about Nelson a taunt, a challenge, a twist of the knife.

The dead weight of his own fear and humiliation perversely forced Ray to resist reaching out to Danielle until the evening, as if he could convince himself that he wasn't really in a panic, and that he'd get around to breaking it off with her when he got around to it; but when he did finally put through a call to Carla's apartment, only to hear the preliminary white noise of an answering machine kicking in, he hung up and then began redialing. He called every ten minutes for hours until Danielle finally picked up.

"He *called* you?" she said in a tone of aggressive disbelief, Ray unable to tell whether she was joyous or outraged. "What did he say?"

"It doesn't make a difference what he said. The news is that you and I are over."

"He fucking *called* you?" Danielle not hearing him.

"Look . . ."

"I don't believe it," she said, more to herself than to Ray, then: "Stay right there."

Thirty minutes later, preceded by a storm cloud of vanilla musk, Danielle marched into his apartment.

"OK, here's the deal" was all Ray could get out before she peeled herself down to two strips of lace riding high over her hips and converging minutely between her legs.

"Whoa." Ray stepped back, his heart lurching in his chest, but grabbing his jeans by the belt buckle she pulled him out fully sprung, turned her face to the wall and put him in her ass, Ray just going along for the ride, feeling the slick cool lubricant already in place.

Thinking, Dead Man Anyhow, he gave it his all, pushing himself into the unfamiliar tightness. And as soon as he became self-motivated she unhanded him, slamming both of her palms flat to the wall now for traction as she thrust herself backward into his rhythm.

In a trance of ecstatic panic Ray ground it in there, slow and deliberate, the flat of his belly lifting her buttocks until, going up on her toes and locking her body into an outward thrust, she went off on trembling legs, babbling to herself in a low voice as she came, Ray helplessly going off right after her.

They stood there for a moment, matted belly to butt, Danielle's face pressed into the wall, her visible eye unblinking and already distant.

Popping out of her still erect, his belly and legs beaded with sweat and lubricant, Ray searched for the words. "Danielle . . ."

"Hey, no, I understand," she said, bunching up her thong in her fist and wiping herself clean of him.

As she stepped back into her jeans, stuffed her thong in her front pocket and walked out of his life, he was left staring at the oily palm prints shimmering on his living room wall like ectoplasm.

"You're just going to fucking tell him," he said to the empty room. "Aren't you . . . ," his erection coming down in rigid gradations like a descending car jack.

Chapter 29 >

Pitches — February 27

Ray arrived at Hopewell a half hour before he was to hook up with White Tom Potenza, parking near his old building again, the sight of Carla Powell's blank windows, despite everything that had transpired, jolting him with a touch of sweet anguish. What was going on here, he helplessly recognized, was the feverish sanctification of inanimate objects: houses, windows, doors, benches, rocks, street corners, anything that a teenaged boy chose to associate with his one-way crush.

A PATH train blasted past the building, drawing his eye to the overhead tracks. He was surprised to see how, at this particular moment in the day, those tracks had become the precise dividing line between sun and shadow; sun below, shadow above, this exactitude washing the bleak vista of Rocker Drive clean and suffusing it with a graceful loneliness so pure that he felt as if he was standing inside a painting.

As he began to walk up the Hopewell Hill, in a reflexive act of self-protection against the cruel ghosts of his adolescent friends, Ray furtively stuffed his stricken right hand in the front pocket of his jeans.

At the crest of the hill, taking the same path he'd taken with Ruby that first night, he cut into the heart of Hopewell, moving past the kiddie playground in which he had told her his old stories — that place was too now potent with association—and headed for Big Playground at the far end of the projects.

With the basketball courts in sight, he walked past a tattered neon-orange strip of crime-scene tape snagged in a bush outside the entrance of Eight Building, then saw the dry brown remnants of a floral cross that hung from the battered address plaque above the recessed lobby entrance.

In a wind-sheltered corner of the exterior vestibule, directly beneath the intercom, stood a small wooden table bearing three extinguished memorial candles, a few rain-blotched handwritten notes and, nesting inside a cloudy sandwich bag taped to the wall above the still-life, an Instamatic photograph of a young black woman holding a solemn toddler.

In the eighteen years he had lived here, Ray could only recall one murder, no motive other than insanity, the killer a fourteen-year-old boy who had stabbed his father in bed and then went screaming naked out to the cement kiddie sprinklers in the hot August sun.

In contrast to the rest of the projects, Big Playground was full to capacity, the chain-link fences that lined the perimeter hung with dozens of almost identical North Face puffy coats, like a rack of nylon pelts.

All four of the handball courts had been painted over as Memorialistas, each one featuring a big-eyed kid sporting either a stubbly shaved head or a military-style buzz cut, the faces themselves flanked with splashy images of birds, winged hearts, eternal flames and the names of the surviving friends who would miss them. But the courts were still in use, four doubles games going on, the blue or pink balls alternately swallowed up then spat out by the vividly spray-painted faces.

With a few minutes to kill before his get-together, Ray turned his attention to the basketball action—eight half-court games—and when it was finally time to move out, he was amazed at how few of the kids out there firing off three-pointers, driving to the hoop or banging under the boards were any good at all.

White Tom Potenza was waiting for him at the corner of Hurley and Rocker, directly across the street from the giraffe-high fence that bordered Big Playground.

In sunlight, Tom was even more blatantly a wreck, standing there slightly tilted forward on his cane, lips parted as if he were on the nod, his body both bloated and frail. His face was hidden behind shades, a Mets cap and that broad mustache, all of which, centered by his large strong nose, suggested a cheap one-piece novelty mask.

The bodega behind him, a candy store and soda fountain back in Ray's playground days, was now trimmed with one of the ubiquitous red-and-yellow metal awnings that punctuated the poorer street corners all over Dempsy.

"Tom," Ray said tentatively, the guy's name sounding false in his mouth.

White Tom reared back and lifted his cane like a peg-legged pirate.

"Man's as good as his word," he said, then opened his arms. Ray stepped into the pulpy embrace, then quickly stepped back.

"Listen, before I say another word I have to apologize to you for the other day."

"For what?" Ray said.

"For talking to you like that. Going in there telling you how to be with your daughter, deal with the darkness, all of that. It's none of my business. None of it."

"Don't worry about it."

"Me going into the Medical Center is like Daniel going into the lion's den except if God hated Daniel's guts. That place scares the shit out of me, and when I get scared I go motor-mouth."

"I said don't worry about it," Ray shrugged, thinking, *Just tell me who you are.*

"You're a good man, Charlie Brown." Tom opened his arms again, Ray having to step into another hug. "Come here, I want to show you something . . ."

Leading the way, White Tom pushed into the bodega. The reek of the boric acid in roach powder hit Ray between the eyes three steps in from the door.

The place was close and untidy, the aisles dark and narrow, the cash register almost obscured behind its Slim Jim– and pork rind–festooned cutout. Filmy Plexiglas food bins filled with yucca, plantain and other, hairier tubers that Ray had never seen before ran along the floor all the way to the rear wall.

Two Hopewell women, both in curlers and kerchiefs, were at the counter buying cigarettes and lottery tickets from the owner, a slight Latino sitting on a high stool behind the register with a three-year-old girl perched on his knee. The guy was doing his transactions with one hand, the other holding aloft a half-eaten FrozFruit.

White Tom gimped his way down the aisle farthest from the cash register to the back of the store. Before following him, Ray feigned a fist-to-mouth cough in order to pop a Vicodin, then saw that the owner was watching him. Apparently underwhelmed though, the guy soon returned his attention to the FrozFruit, alternating nibbles with his pudgy-fisted daughter.

Tom waited for Ray alongside a picture window that looked out at the handball and basketball courts across the street, his legs planted wide and both of his hands resting on the head of his cane as if he were about to make an announcement.

"You're getting to the point with those where you don't even need water?" White Tom said, nodding to the amber vial outlined in Ray's chest pocket.

"Change the subject," Ray said flatly.

Shrugging, White Tom took another step back and gestured for Ray to follow.

"You remember this place back in the day?" he said in a half-whisper. "Remember the Mope?"

"The Mope," Ray murmured, recalling the heavy-faced owner from the 1960s, early '70s; sour, slow, silent, the sleeves of his always immaculate white shirt carefully folded back to the elbows as if to purposely exhibit the tattooed numbers on the inside of one forearm. "I haven't thought about him in a thousand years."

"We gave that poor bastard hell, remember? Come running in here every day, 'Heil Hitler! Heil Hitler!' Big joke. Even the Jewish kids did it. *You* did it, right? We all did it."

"No way," Ray getting his ass up, then thinking, Maybe once or twice, thinking, Who *is* this guy . . .

"But the Mope wouldn't bite. We could never get a rise out of him. Come in an hour later, buy some baseball cards, a cherry Coke, the guy never said Boo. Am I right?"

"Yeah," Ray seeing him: gray skin, gray hair, the blurry blue digits; the seven with a European crossbar.

"Had those pictures of food up over the counter, hamburger platters, BLTs, ice-cream sodas . . . Never quite looked like that when it was in front of you, right?"

"Yeah, no." Ray recalled those photos, as color-doctored as old Mexican postcards.

Despite the Vicodin, that drilling localized skull ache began to announce itself again, and Ray found himself leaning into the shelves for support. "So what's up," he said quickly.

Picking up on Ray's sudden distress, White Tom hesitated, as if weighing whether to say something about it, then got back on course.

"This moke up front, Lazaro?" Tom full-bore whispering now. "It's a fucking drug bazaar in here—horse, coke, crack, weed, grams, decks, eight-balls, it's like Dope-Mart—but in a few days? He's going down. The place is getting raided and, you know, they'll offer him the usual, 'Help us with the bigger fish or we'll drop you down a hole,' but he's not stupid, Lazaro. Alive in jail is better than dead in the street, so he'll say 'Fuck yourselves,' and they'll padlock the joint."

A woman came into the store, young and pregnant, slipped behind the counter and took the kid off Lazaro's lap.

"How do I know this, right?"

But Ray had no reason to doubt that White Tom was speaking the truth, and now he just stared at the family behind the counter.

"I'll tell you anyway . . . Are you listening to me?"

"Yeah." Ray couldn't take his eyes off them.

"I'm sober since November '93, and I've been running a meeting in the basement of Immaculate Conception since '95, and, in that time, I must've sponsored over a dozen cops, saw each and every one of them through the night, night after night, OK? It started out one guy came in on his own, six months later another guy in his squad is looking for help. Guy One tells him, 'I'll hook you up with Tommy Potenza.' Guy Two says, 'Potenza? White Tom? That fucking lowlife?' Guy One says, 'Hey, that *low*life saved *my* life.' And what started out as a drop, Ray, became a stream, became a cascade, became Niagara. And now it's like they all know, if you hit the wall, White Tom's the guy. Shit, I get more cop calls from midnight to dawn than central dispatch. I even wound up sponsoring the last cop to lock me up. Partner comes to me, 'Tom, Eddie's got a problem with painkillers from when he almost broke his back chasing that Moulie down the stairs in Four Building.' Painkillers, he says. I never knew painkillers could be snorted, you know what I mean? These guys, Ray, they're out there dealing with the street around the clock yet they're so naive when it comes to one of their own. I even had one guy, three years in Narcotics, talking to me about his buddy in the squad, says, 'Tom, where would he *get* the stuff?'

"So, you know how it works in this city, favors beget favors, so I know what's gonna go down here. And I also know that once this place gets padlocked? It can be had for back taxes."

"Really," Ray said mildly, thinking, Here it comes . . .

"They got it all set up for me, it's a done deal."

"Last guy to lock you up . . ." Ray stalled. "Lock you up for what?"

"For *what?*" Tommy laughed. "I was a fiend, Ray. For everything. Are you kidding me? I don't just have a record, my man, I have a fucking album.

"But I stopped. I stopped. I had . . . I literally had some sense beat into me. October fifteen, nineteen hundred and ninety-three, me and Danny Ryan, the last two great white Hopewell heads, we're trying to get past some Yoms hanging on the stoop of Nine Building to go up and watch the Jets game in Danny's crib? They won't move, won't get out of the way. And Danny had that . . . No. No. *I* had the mouth, the, the *rage*, and, because at that moment I was feeling no pain? Feeling, *above* pain? I refused to do the smart thing, which was step off, go around the back of the building, come in from the super's entrance. Make a long story short, I go and open my mouth? Out comes a Louisville, and Danny goes into the black land for good. Me? Multiple skull fractures. Bone chips in the brain. Chronic cerebral edema. No offense, but what happened to you?" White Tom perfunctorily gestured to Ray's half-hidden hand, his burr-holed crown. "That's nothing. I'm talking twenty-one operations. Twenty, *one*. They went in and replaced part of my skull with a porcelain plug because it's porous and easy to remove." He took off his Mets cap and bowed low. "You want to feel it?"

"Fuck no." Ray stepped back, his stomach dipping.

"Some mornings I wake up with headaches so bad I start crying like a baby. I go in for CAT scans more than you go in to change the oil in your car. But you know what? It was all worth it because that beating saved my life. As soon as I got out of the hospital after the first operation I went straight into the Program. And I found my calling. *Yes*, I'm a drug addict. But now I'm also a healer. Me, who caused so much hurt and sadness in my life, to myself, to my family, to whoever crossed my path. I'm a healer. I have a gift for it, a *hunger* for it. And I remarried. A Howard Houses girl, Arletta Barnes . . . Black, beautiful, soulful strong woman. We met in the Program, and we have two boys, twins, Eric and Maceo, like God's gift twice over. I have a third boy, Tom Junior, but he's grown now. Lives in Cali. He might have . . . I might be a grandfather, we don't exactly talk. Well, one thing's for sure. He's never touched drugs. Growing up with me, I at least gave him an allergy to that, although as you well know it could have more likely gone the other way."

Tom took a break, staring out the window, Ray right then breathing deep and experiencing the all too familiar urge to give something—not money to buy this shithole, but something, some gift; the feeling, for the moment at least, lifting the drill bit from his skull.

"Anyways," Tommy forged on. "My big boy, Tom Junior? I'm hoping to get to know him again but I understand his position, I understand. I just hope he might someday be curious to meet his new, you know, his little brothers, but I understand . . ."

The three-year-old girl ran up the aisle to Tom and handed him the stick from her father's FrozFruit.

"Is this for me, sweetheart?" Tom patting her face and taking it. "Go back to your daddy." He watched her as she ran back to the front of the store.

Ray looked at the girl, then looked at Tom.

"Hey, if there was anything I could do for that kid I would, but there isn't. It's the parents. They chose the life they live. My hands are tied. Besides, Lazaro's got one of those big extended families. Half are scumbags so let's hope she winds up with one of the good ones."

"And if she doesn't?"

"Then she doesn't. This is the Boulevard of Broken Dreams around here, are you kidding me? It's all you can do to have a say in your *own* destiny, let alone anybody else's. I mean, wouldn't you agree?"

"Yeah, sure," Ray said just to keep this moving.

"In any event," Tom continued, "I guess I would have to say things are about as good for me now as they've ever been. I mean, my health is for shit, high blood pressure, diabetes, liver damage, need a hip replacement, but thank God I never bought the Package—HIV-negative all the way. Or so they tell me. Shit man, you don't know, what am I, forty-one? I had extreme unction said over me three times in the last twenty years. But I'm still here. And that's because there's a reason. God had a reason for not . . . See, when people talk to outsiders or new recruits about the Program, they always downplay the Higher Power thing, the God thing, they don't want to scare people away, and it's understandable. You have to let each individual come to terms with what it is they're surrendering to by themselves, right? But you know something? There *is* a God. There *is* a fucking God. People say the World Trade Center, the Holocaust, the, the Rwanda thing, the Bosnians, what kind of God is this? Well, I'll tell you. It's a God who watches. It's a God who gives us free will, foreknowledge of our mortality, kicks back and watches. It's up to us."

"You make him sound like a psychopath." Ray's eyes strayed to the front of the store again, to the little girl.

"Ray, understand something. Pain is the chisel with which we sculpt ourselves into who we become. Like, OK, off the top of my head? This is going to sound trivial, but Peter Garro . . . Remember Peter Garro? Built like a Greek god. Like a fucking Olympian. Never gave a shit about school. Didn't have to. Gonna be a ballplayer, gonna be a ballplayer. Gets a tryout with the Cardinals. Trips coming off the plane into spring training camp, breaks his ankle, never gets a second chance. What was God thinking there, right? But then you consider what was the guy looking at . . . Realistically we're talking three, four years of class D ball, C ball, B ball, then getting released.

"So what's Peter do? He goes back to school. Winds up with a master's in social work. Today he's running Health and Human Services for Dempsy County. Or with me. Opening my mouth that day. Twenty-one operations, but here I am. And what did I do with my life after that . . . Pain, is the chisel. We can make a mess or we can make something beautiful. It's up to us."

"How about Danny Ryan's pain?" Ray said, talk of God making him feel like he was among idiots and cavemen. "What can you sculpt when you're dead?"

"OK. OK." White Tom prepared for this. "Think of God as a blackjack dealer. Guy deals you nineteen, are you going to blame him if *you* say 'Hit me' and wind up going over? Free will, Ray. Danny had come to many a crossroad before that day, don't kid yourself. He had lots of hot tips from above. I mean if you *really* want to challenge me on this, I mean more to the point, you can say what about some home-battered three-year-old brought in DOA to the Medical Center, or, or some young pregnant secretary crushed in the Twin Towers, and my answer to you would be, I don't have all the answers, I just believe what I believe and I feel what I feel.

"Oh Ray, the shit I could tell you. My wife, Arletta? Ten years ago, beat up, fucked up, in and out of jail, hospitals, shelters, hittin' that glass dick 24/7.

"Been in the program, what, eight years? Now she's working over at the Homework Club in the Armstrong Houses, you know, the after-school program? She's got this project going on over there, to, to, well maybe 'cure' is the wrong word, to *save* these kids from the streets, from themselves, through the practice of, get this, of *manners*. Can you believe that? She gets them young over there in Armstrong, six, seven, eight, and she does her thing. Last year she had the kids put on a play called 'The Kourtesy Kids Kome Korrect.' Toured schools all over Dempsy, Jersey City, East Orange, and the kids, the teachers, they ate it up, wherever she went. She got so many thank-you letters she made a collage of them, framed it over our bed.

"Arletta, Ray, I'm so fucking proud of her. I mean talk about a vertical climb, you know what I'm saying? And if you think *I'm* lucky to duck the Package? It's God, Ray. He *knew* she had to put on that play. He *knew* she had to bring our twins into this world, to, to help *me* get where *I* had to go. Are you OK?"

"What?"

"Are you crying?"

"No," coughing into his fist, the flesh beneath his eyes feeling dense, as if packed with damp sand, Ray right then once again just wanting to *do* something—something clear-eyed and right and good, something selfless yet to the heart of him, to find that thing, that place, and stand fast; commitment, not flourish; commitment, not gesture. To stand fast, to stand fast, to stand fast—the ferocity of his yearnings reawakening that drilling ache—but with the pain this time came, uninvited, his memory of the assault, the shame of it; and then self-loathing began to rise in him like a watery acid.

"It's your heart, Ray. That big heart of yours."

"The fuck it is," he muttered, but Tom, starting to get all teary too, hadn't heard him.

"I want for you to meet Arletta, man. And I want you to meet the twins."

"Sure," Ray said hoarsely.

"My boys, you know what their middle names are? Sosa and McGwire. Eric Sosa, Maceo McGwire. Well, you remember me with baseball."

Ray nodded, it being way too late to say, I don't remember you at all.

"All right." Tom wiped his eyes. "Back to business. This place here?" swirling a hand to take in the bodega. "You know what I want to do? Rip all this shit out, the shelves, the counters, the cuchifritos, everything. Then I'm gonna put it back together like it was, like the Mope had it, like *we* had it. Lunch counter with stools, those Formica tables along the windows, you know, with those red vinyl banquettes, put back the soda pumps . . . I'm even going to sell comic books again . . . But you know what I'd really be selling with all this? I'd be selling a safe haven for those kids out there." He tilted his chin to the courts across the street, and finally Ray remembered him, remembered Tommy Potenza, last image first, a visit back to the old neighborhood about twenty years ago, after his parents and everybody else had moved out, coming upon Tommy, a guy from the opposite end of the projects, a guy he only knew by face, who at that moment on that day was sitting by himself on the low cement ledge bordering the handball courts, his back against the chain-link fence. Tommy had left no impression on Ray of being stoned that day, but he was definitely on the wrong side of eighteen to be still hanging there, the playground packed with the new generation of Hopewell kids; black, Dominican, Puerto Rican—Tommy sitting alone, still dressed like a thirteen-year-old in ill-fitting jeans, red high-tops and a wrinkled white T-shirt, just sitting there flaccid-faced, staring out at the action as if he were in a daze—as if he were stranded, so lost and stranded, Ray now imagined, that he had to be rechristened White Tom.

"And Ray, let me tell you," Tom brought him back, "those kids out there? I set this place up like I want? They will come. They'll come in here every day after school, get a Coke, a candy bar and two packs of base-ball cards. They'll sit at those tables and do their homework. And if they're a little light in the pocket? Depending on the kid? What's his home situation? If he's, you know, retrievable? That kid's got a tab with me."

Ray smiled, looked off. White Tom was starting to sound like George describing the rabbit farm to Lenny.

"And they'll come, Ray. They'll come in droves because the shit's so fucked out there, so utterly fucked . . .

"And along with every Coke, every Hershey bar, they'll get a free antidrug lecture. You want to hear my lecture?"

And before Ray could beg out, White Tom took a further step back, removed his sunglasses, removed his teeth, lifted then pinioned the hem of his shirt under his chin, and raised his arms from his sides, inviting Ray to see him: the swollen bluish gut, the caved-in chest, the caved-in mouth, the eyes steady enough, but cracked and starred like fried mar-bles; the picture as a whole a great antidrug visual but a disaster as a sales tool for bringing investors on board.

"Remember that song?" He put back his teeth, his shades. "'Every pic-ture tells a story, don't it' . . . ?"

"Right," Ray said faintly. This planned takeover would never happen. Whether the guy behind the register got arrested or not, whether the bodega got padlocked or not, White Tom Potenza taking ownership here would never come to pass; he was sure of it.

"So anyways, it's my understanding that it'll run me about ten, eleven thousand for the back taxes, another four, five to grease various wheels. Now, Daddy Warbucks I'm not. Obviously. Nonetheless that's OK, because to tell you the truth I have a few silent partners on board, a couple of housing cops if you can believe it, and these guys are coming in on this, putting their money where their mouth is, because they share my vision, my, my commitment . . .

"Plus, I got a guy in my meeting can hook me up for the fixtures and furniture, counter stools, chairs, tables, dishes glasses pumps spigots refrigerator dishwasher. Another guy in the meeting can wire me into meat, bread, produce, anything along that line. I mean it's not like it's *not* gonna cost, but I'm getting rock-bottom prices every step of the way."

It would never happen; Ray was both saddened and relieved.

"So, in addition to what it's gonna cost me to take title, from what I've been told, I'm looking at maybe between thirty and forty thousand to open the doors. But you know what, Ray? I know you're bracing yourself for the big touch here, but I'm not asking you for a dime. I'm going to First Dempsy and let *them* pay for it. All I'm asking *you* for, is to walk into that bank with me and cosign the loan. Now, I know you're thinking, Who the fuck does this guy think he is hitting on me . . ."

"Not at all," Ray said, then stalling for a graceful way out, "So whatever happened to the Mope. Did he die?"

"By now, I'd assume so, but no, he was just getting robbed every week, got sick of it and sold the place. I'm talking twenty years ago."

"Robbed. How do you know that won't happen to you?"

"How do I know? Because the Mope didn't have cops as partners and the Mope wasn't packing this."

White Tom turned his back to Ray, then lifted his shirt again, this time revealing a .25 automatic snugly tucked against the base of his spine.

"I'll tell you what," Ray said. "You pay the back taxes, take title, then come back at me and I'll do what I can."

Tommy cocked his head and studied Ray's eyes; a half-smile playing on his face.

"What," Ray said self-consciously.

"Come here." Tommy raised his arms, Ray stepping in for another hug. "You're wrong, you know," he said in Ray's ear. "This is most definitely gonna happen."

"The fuck, man . . ." Lazaro, the owner, his daughter riding his shoulders like a circus queen, came up on them. "What are you guys doing back here?"

"Lazaro, this is my boy Ray, from back in the day."

Ray extended his hand, Lazaro taking it, sizing him up.

"We just got caught up in catching up," Tommy said easily.

"You buying something or what. 'Cause in five minutes I'm putting a fuckin' meter back here."

"Hey, sweetheart." White Tom wiggled his fingers at the little girl up top, some vestigial junkie amorality in his false playfulness.

A moment later, as Ray followed Tom to the door, he took a last glance at Lazaro, his pregnant wife and his daughter, all now absorbed in a Spanish soap on a miniature TV behind the counter, the three of them as serene as if they were cruising down a highway, oblivious to the head-on that was waiting for them just a few miles down the road.

"Buckle your seat belts, huh?" White Tom Potenza said under his breath as he pushed through to the street.

Standing in front of the bodega, just as Ray was about to go his own way, White Tom startled and embarrassed him by reaching out and taking his limp right hand out of its pocket pouch and holding it in both of his own, gently turning it palm up and then down, before letting it retreat into its unnatural curl.

"You gots to do that physical therapy, my man. No joke."

"I know, I know." Ray turned his head away.

"And beware of *this* shit," flicking the Vicodin bottle in Ray's shirt with a fingernail.

"Here . . ." Ray impulsively tossed them in the general direction of a sewer grate, shame once again working its magic. "OK?"

"Can I ask you something?" White Tom said, ignoring Ray's invitation to applaud. "Not that it's any of my business, but how come you won't tell Neesy who gave you the tune-up?"

"How come?" Ray tasting that rising acid again. "I don't know. Maybe because I had it coming?"

To his surprise, White Tom simply nodded.

. . .

Ray stood alone outside the basketball fence, scanning the action as if he were looking for somebody. And when he finally got himself into gear, cutting through Big Playground again in order to get to his car, he became aware this time of the boy-girl thing; the sweet slow walk of the teenaged Hopewell girls, both languid and alert as they sashayed past the games; and in response to their presence, the self-conscious herky-jerk moves of the boys as they muscled their way to the baskets; this fenced-in arena still, as it was in his time, suffused with a nearly unbearable sexual longing.

As he came up on the smaller kiddie playground again, he spied Carla Powell leaving one of the projects' laundry rooms, lugging a shopping cart stuffed with four pillowcases' worth of wash.

She looked lumpy and tired, hauling the cart after her just like Ray's mother had back in the sixties; like her own mother had too.

Catching her in the midst of this eternal drudgery, he was struck with the weight of what it must feel like to have never left this place, or to have left but failed out there and had to return; to metamorphose from one of the tireless ever-burning kids to one who's now worn down by them, vexed by them.

On the other hand, Ray thought, despite the scars and traumas of her younger life, despite her current catalogue of ailments both physical and mental, Carla, much like White Tom and most likely his ex-dope-fiend wife, Arletta, had somehow emerged in middle age in possession of a certain battered presence; had emerged as a rock for others, a bulwark against her family's disintegration—picking up the ones that fall off the back of the truck, Danielle had said—had emerged as so much more than a mere survivor.

Yet despite their hard-fought victories, Ray often sensed an air of fragility around people like these, a distinct possibility that they could just as easily come apart again as not. Recalling White Tom's advice to never take his eye off the Darkness, he imagined that their only defense against this coming to pass was an acute awareness of their condition; Carla, Arletta, White Tom and all the others like them endlessly needing to itemize for themselves what and who would be lost if they ever gave in.

Watching Carla make her way through the projects, Ray initially had no intention of talking to her—she'd most likely freak, about the loan, her daughter, his assault—but finally, he just couldn't help himself and called out her name.

Either she didn't hear him or she recognized his voice and just kept walking. Ray watched her head down the hill, waiting for her to disappear into his old building before taking the same path to get to his car.

Once he was on the move again, he saw a tall elderly white woman coming up the hill toward him with a small bag of groceries, both of them slowing down as they closed the gap, hesitatingly checking each other out.

She was Dolores Rosen, chalk white and papery now, the mother of one of his childhood friends, another of the stranded ones; everybody coming out of the woodwork today. But not wanting to stop and talk, not wanting to be the kid again, Ray simply walked on without acknowledging her, but catching out of the corner of his eye, as he did, her tentatively outstretched hand.

Chapter 30 >

Interview — February 27

Pulling into the narrow driveway of the brick two-family house on Taylor Street, Nerese looked up and saw Freddy and Danielle waiting for her on the small porch outside their second-story apartment, the light streaming out of the living room window directly behind them casting their joined silhouettes monstrously large against the facades of the identically constructed brick two-families across the street.

As she trudged up the short flight of cement stairs they watched her, silently tracking her progress like cats.

"Whoo," she huffed, hand to chest, putting it on a little. "So . . ."

"Here's the deal," Freddy said, looking away from her. "You want to talk with him, fine. But we're both in there with you."

"No." Nerese shrugged. "Here's what my boss'll go for. Me and the boy alone. His mother could be in the next room listening in, but she's got to be out of his sight. And frankly, I would prefer for you to not even be in the house, OK?"

"Right." Freddy snorted. "Who do you think you're talking to with that 'And frankly' crap. Forget it. I'm there."

"Well, if you insist on being around then you have to be outside the room with your wife. Anything you hear me say rubs you the wrong way? You're free to come in and stop me. But, and here I'm using that 'And frankly' crap again, frankly, unless you have something to hide, I don't think you have anything to worry about."

Danielle nodded in agreement but Freddy shook his head in emphatic rejection.

"I'm in the room."

Nerese took five, studying the solid street of blue-collar houses, an unidentifiable waft of third-world dinner floating past her from up the block.

"Look." She slowly turned her eyes to him. "I need to clear you. You need to get cleared. Do you honestly think anything out of that boy's mouth is going to be worth a damn to me with you sitting right next to him?"

Freddy and Danielle's apartment was overstuffed, spotless and far too bright; two chandeliers in sight of each other going full blast; one suspended above a seven-piece living room ensemble, the other hanging over a dining table in the adjoining alcove, this L-shaped common room almost chased free of shadows.

Nelson sat dwarfed in the middle of a high-backed royal blue couch, beneath a painting of the Last Supper which was illuminated by two small bulbs, an electrical cord nakedly kinking down from the bottom of the picture frame until it disappeared behind the boy's head.

He seemed slack with dread, sitting there slouched down and gape-mouthed, staring at Nerese with bottomed-out eyes, his hands lying lifelessly, palms up, on either side of him.

Although they could both hear his parents shuffling restlessly in the kitchen beyond the dining nook, the boy seemed completely focused on Nerese, who sat facing him, perched on the edge of a coffee table, their knees almost touching.

"That's healing up nice," Nerese said, tapping her lower lip.

Nelson stared at her as if she hadn't spoken yet.

"I doubt you're even going to have a scar."

Again the nonreaction, the kid most likely bracing for the bad stuff, deaf to any small talk. Nonetheless Nerese kept it up, needing something, a smile, a blink, some tip-off as to how Nelson was put together.

"You a Steelers fan?" She nodded at his oversize black-and-yellow jersey.

"What?"

"Pittsburgh."

Nelson looked down at himself as if someone else had dressed him this morning.

"Nelson, my name's Nerese. Do you remember me? I was here two nights ago, we talked a little at the door?"

"Yes."

"Good." She smiled. "You know why I'm here?"

"Yes." Once again that clipped wariness, Nerese thinking, This kid has been prepped, has been warned, and is now terrified of fucking up.

She turned to look behind her, see if Freddy or Danielle had popped into his sight line, then angled herself on the coffee table so that she could keep an eye on the wall between the kitchen and dining alcove.

"I'm trying to find out what happened to Mr. Mitchell a few weeks back. Or Ray. What did you call him?"

He shrugged, said something that didn't quite make it past his lips.

"I didn't hear you, sweetie." Leaning in.

"I didn't call him anything," he said.

"But you heard about what happened to him, right? Somebody came into his house, hurt him bad enough to put him in the hospital. You know that, right?"

"Yes." His eyes briefly moved past her to the wall shielding his parents.

"Anyways"—Nerese touched his knee to get him back—"I have a hunch, Nelson, that you can help me find out who did this to the guy just by answering a few simple questions. Are you up for that?"

"OK." His mouth remained open after the response.

"And by the way," touching him again. "He's fine, Mr. Mitchell. Pretty much fully recovered, just doing his thing, so right now it's mainly just me being curious as to what happened, OK?"

"OK."

"All right then. Now. Before we start? I have to lay down some ground rules. Well, really just one. And that is, whatever I ask you? It's very important that you tell me the truth. But, telling me the truth means, other than saying what you know? It also means that if I ask you something and you don't know the answer? Then you say to me, 'I don't know,' or 'I don't remember.' The worst thing you can do is to make something up because it's what you think I want to hear, OK? Even if you're doing it because you're a great kid and you're trying to help me, that one little lie will make everything else you say sound like a lie and next thing you know I can't find my behind with two hands and a road map, OK?"

Freddy could be heard now, an indistinct complaint, rising and falling from the kitchen.

Nerese bowed her head until she could master herself.

"And here's something else you should keep in mind, Nelson. Whatever you tell me, as long as it's truthful? It can't hurt anyone." Nerese straight-out lied. "Because we can always fight the truth with the truth . . . ," shifting now into double-talk, "but we can't fight the truth with a lie."

The kid was all eyes, waiting.

"OK. Now. Your mom told me you came home from school sick one day about two, two and a half weeks ago. You remember that day?"

"Yes."

"When was that. Do you remember what day of the week? Maybe something special happened that day in school, maybe something you remember watching on TV that night. I mean obviously it wasn't on a Saturday or a Sunday but . . ."

"I don't remember," Nelson said. "I'm sorry."

"No problem, no problem." Nerese waved it away. "I probably couldn't've remembered either. But you *do* remember coming home sick one day back about then."

"Yes."

"What was wrong with you?"

"I was sick."

Again Freddy's muttered risings and fallings.

"What kind of sick."

"What?"

"Headache, nauseous, flu . . ."

Nelson just sat there open-mouthed for a moment, then said, "Headache," as if picking the word from a hat.

This stunk.

"Did you tell your teacher?"

"No."

"Did you leave school early?"

Nelson shook his head no.

"When you left school that day, where'd you go?"

He stared at her.

"Did you go home?"

"Yes."

"Just like any other day."

"Yes."

"So what time would that have been?"

"Four?"

"Four. OK. Four. Was anybody home when you got here?"

"I don't know." He shrugged. "I just went to bed."

"You just went to bed. You didn't look for your mom or dad to tell them how you felt?"

"My mom was in school. She goes to school until night."

"OK. That's an answer. How about your dad? Was your dad home?"

"I don't know. Maybe. I don't remember."

I don't know. Maybe. I don't remember—all better than Yes, he was home, which would at least give Nerese something to pick at, chip away at; and better than No, No being the magic word, No being catching Freddy in a lie. Any lie would do.

"So you don't know if your father was home."

"I guess so."

"You guess so. You guess so, Yes? Or you guess so, No?"

"I just went to my room."

Nerese must have been coming off angrier than she thought, because the boy then blurted almost pleadingly, "You said if I don't remember I should say I don't remember."

"He's doing what you asked," Freddy snapped, unable to resist, addressing her from his absurd hiding place behind the kitchen wall.

At the sound of his father's disembodied voice, Nelson flinched as if bitten. "I think I came home at five." Granting his dad an extra hour to come and go unobserved.

"At five," Nerese said heavily. "Not at four."

"Yeah. Yes."

"I thought you were sick."

"I *was*."

"And you didn't come right home?"

"I tried to but I missed my bus." The kid was begging now, reverse-blooming into a little old man before her eyes.

"Nelson, listen to me," Nerese said, struggling to keep the rage behind her teeth. "What I want to do . . . What . . . Nelson, I really want to get out of here. What I want more than anything in the world right now, is to get up, shake your hand and walk out that door, see you later, alligator."

Nerese let that hang for a bit, the boy downcast and wretched, his eyebrows arching with grief.

"But in order for me to do that, I need your help. I need for you to tell me who was or wasn't here when you came home from school on February seventh, that's a Tuesday two weeks and five days ago, the day that you got sick. I need to know what *time* you got home, who was in the house when you walked in, who wasn't, what time whoever wasn't here finally came in the door, if anybody *left* this house once you came home or did everyone stay put for the evening. I really need for you to think back and try your hardest to recall these things. But that's *all* I want from you, Nelson. Nothing more than that. Then our business is done, OK?"

"OK." Avoiding her eyes, but she wasn't feeling it yet, this kid being sold on the fact that it was OK to rat out his father, even indirectly; and in a further effort to get him to that place, she became counsel for the defense.

"You know, wait, hang on, before . . . I just, I just want to say to you, about Mr. Mitchell getting assaulted like he did?" She lowered her voice, hunkered forward. "Man, I have been doing this for twenty years and I can pretty much guarantee you that I am most definitely going to find out who did this to him."

She continued to inch forward, dropped her voice even lower.

"You know why?," waiting for his eyes. "Because whoever hurt him did it out of anger, and people who do things out of anger make mistakes.

"This wasn't the act of some criminal mastermind. Whoever did this, they didn't even take anything, steal anything. This was the act of someone who for a single heartbeat simply let their emotions get the best of them."

Nerese waited again; the boy was staring at his hands, but he was listening.

"In fact, the way I'm thinking about it? Mr. Mitchell, he must have done something to hurt this person *so* bad, that they just *lashed* out, probably didn't even know they had something in their hand, didn't even *mean* to hurt him."

Nelson slowly lifted his blurry eyes to her; Nerese, feeling him on the verge of buying it, prayed that Freddy couldn't pick up this change in vibrations. But even if he did, and busted up the interview, the crack in the door would still open a little wider: Nerese then needing to know what he was so afraid of.

"Now, like I said before, emotional people, they're not thinking with their heads, they're thinking with their hearts, and when something like this goes down, they make mistakes.

"We're going to find evidence, we're going to find witnesses, we're going to find something or someone that's going to give this person away . . .

"But I'm going to tell you something else, Nelson . . . Right here and now I'm willing to bet you"—Nerese emptied her pockets, counted bills, poked coins—"twelve dollars and sixty-two cents that when we catch up to this individual and I finally get a chance to sit down and hear their side of the story? I *guarantee* you that they're gonna say, 'I never meant to do it, I never meant to hurt him, but that guy, he just made me *so* angry, he just made me *so* mad, he made—' "

"He did," Nelson said in his swallowed voice, his eyebrows rising but his gaze fixed on his own clasped hands.

"What?"

"He *did*."

"*Who* did." Nerese unthinkingly rose to her feet, taking a half-step toward the kitchen, toward Freddy.

"I'm sorry," Nelson called out tearily to his father who appeared from around the wall as if to meet Nerese head on.

"*Stop*," Freddy bellowed, pointing a finger at his son. "You don't say another *word*."

Nerese and Freddy were face to face in the dining alcove now, her movements mirroring his, blocking his forward progress.

Although she was dying to clock him on the spot, Nerese couldn't quite get his attention, Freddy speaking over her shoulder to his son as if she were an inanimate barrier.

"Come here," he barked at the kid, hot-eyed.

"I'm *sorry*," Nelson said again, weeping openly now.

"You go *near* that kid, God as my witness," Nerese up on her toes, up in his face, her head twisted to bore into Freddy's eyes at some crazy jailhouse angle.

"Come here *now*." Freddy was ignoring Nerese and her homicide eyes, then, shifting gears, took a step back and reached for the wall phone; no doubt about to lawyer up right in front of her. Nerese scrambled for something to say that would convince him to put down that phone.

"He taught me catch," Nelson wailed from the couch. "He bought me books, he *showed* me stuff, he *told* me stuff and then he didn't want to see me anymore. What did I *do*?" Nelson began rocking, his eyes blistered with grief.

"What?" Nerese said faintly. She turned to face the kid, forgetting about Freddy, who hung up the phone mid-dial, then moved past her before she could stop him.

"You keep your mouth *shut*," he said, grabbing his son's wrist. But Nelson snatched his arm free with surprising speed and violence.

"Get away from me!" Nelson nearly shrieked then scrabbled to his feet. "What did I *do*! What did I *do*!" crying to Nerese, to his mother. Danielle stood in the dining alcove now, speechless, gripping the back of a chair with both hands.

Nelson.

Nerese stutter-stepped in place, a little dance of disorder, the information still hovering.

Nelson.

Did his parents know this all along?

No, Nerese decided. They were as poleaxed as she was. Freddy was just the first to grasp what was going on here, first to fly into action.

"I'm going to need for you to leave my home," he said, nearly chest-bumping her backward to the door.

"Hang on, hold on . . ."

"*Now*," his breath in her face.

Nerese abruptly dug in, so that he had to lurch to a stop.

"Yeah, you *lay* a hand on me. I'd *like* that."

Nelson was gone.

"Where'd he go . . ."

Danielle, still in a daze, still working things out, wordlessly tilted her chin to the rear of the apartment, and Nerese found herself on the move.

Although she had never set foot in this house before, somehow she was the one who wound up leading Danielle and Freddy to Nelson's room. It was narrow and fairly austere: two Eminem posters and a small plank-and-cinder-block bookcase half-filled with creased paperbacks and some extra-terrestrial action figures.

The boy was sitting on the edge of his bed, his shoulders slumped, his hands between his knees and his face to the wall.

The three of them stood in the doorway as if his misery had set up a force field.

"I don't get it," Nelson said, his face still averted. Then he turned to them, singling out Nerese and peering beseechingly into her eyes. "What did I do?" The boy as open-faced to her now as he had been closed off before.

At last, Danielle moved to her son. But as if animated by the threat of her touch, Nelson vehemently came to life, rearing away from her and swatting the air between them.

"Take him out of here," Freddy said to his wife as he once again reached for a phone, this one on Nelson's small desk.

"Hold on," Nerese said quickly. "Did you hear me read him his Mirandas? Because I don't believe I did, but if you're calling a lawyer right now? Reading him his rights is gonna be the next thing out of my mouth, and then everybody's got a problem."

Freddy hesitated, desperately trying to figure out Nerese's play.

"Just hang up the phone, Freddy." Nerese saying it as if the receiver were a gun. "Hang it up. You don't like what I'm about to say, you can get right back on the line."

Freddy stood there, the receiver tentatively feathering its way down to the desk.

"Just hang it up." Saying it as carefully as if she were talking to a jumper on a ledge. "Please."

Freddy's indecision pulled the room into a momentary silence, which was abruptly broken by his son.

"It's *your* fault!" Nelson exploded at his mother. Danielle flinched, then glared at her husband, passing it on; Nerese thinking, While you're at it, don't forget Ray.

"Nelson." Nerese knelt down before him on the edge of his bed, looking up into his eyes. "Nelson." Reaching up and clearing away the tears with the sides of her thumbs. "Nelson, listen to me. You tell me what happened that day. You tell me how this all came about. You be *truthful*, you make me a believer . . ."

Racked with nervous exhaustion, he unwittingly cut loose with a spectacular yawn, then rubbed his eyes, Nerese sensing that if they all decided to tiptoe out of there, he'd be unconscious in two minutes.

"You make me a believer, Nelson." Nerese squeezed his knee to keep him in the room, then looked at the parents. "And I think we can call it a day."

< Chapter 31

Nelson — February 7

The off-key blare of the intercom brought Ray in from the terrace, where, legal pad in hand, he had been thinking about a writing assignment for the kids. The class after this next one tomorrow would fall directly on Valentine's Day and some of the challenge titles bouncing around in his head were "Dating Game," "Blind Date" and "Prisoner of Love," although nothing as yet had made its way onto paper.

"Yeah?" He leaned into the speaker, the scratch pad tucked under his arm.

There was no answer, just the ambient sound of outside, scattered and lax.

"Yes?"

The caw of a careening gull, and faint open-mouthed breathing.

"Yes?" Ray thinking, Freddy. "Who is this." Thinking, 911. He turned to reach for the phone.

"It's Nelson." The kid's voice came through thin and plaintive, Ray envisioning him down there with Freddy's hand on the back of his neck.

Ray retrieved the portable phone, then returned to the intercom.

"Let me talk to your father, Nelson."

Again the noisy silence.

"Let me talk to your father," he repeated, then waited for some confirmation before he put through a false alarm and made a complete horse's ass out of himself: a basso murmur, a mutter, a heavy shuffling tread, anything.

"You tell him—"

"It's *Nelson!*" the boy's voice breaking high with frustration.

"Nelson, give me your phone number."

"What?"

"Give me the phone number of your home."

Freddy picked up on the second ring and Ray killed the call without a word.

A moment later, rising from the murk of the stairwell into the river light streaming into the hallway from Ray's open apartment door, Nelson's face appeared, vaguely swollen, his features both puffed and slitted with sullen determination.

And once again, he was carrying the baseball glove.

"What's up, Nelson?" Ray asked lightly, casually blocking access to the apartment.

"I want to stay here." The kid's voice was reedy but determined.

"What?" Ray blinked.

"I want to stay with you."

"Nelson, no, you can't." But then, absorbing the kid's misery, he took it down a peg, "You can't, Nelson, I'm sorry."

"I don't *want* him to be home," Nelson declared, clutching the doorknob and dipping into an emphatic crouch.

Unconsciously wincing, Ray reached out and lightly touched the boy's arms, nudging him upright again.

"What happened," he asked. "Did anything happen?"

"Stay out of my sight," Nelson said.

"What?" Ray took a step back into the apartment. Nelson followed him in.

"You go to school, you come home, you go to your room, you do your homework, you come out, you eat your dinner, you go back to your room. You *stay* out of my *sight*." Nelson aped his father as if possessed, then dropped onto one of the couches.

"*Why?*," Ray asked. The only reason he could imagine was that Nelson had been a witness to Freddy's being cheated on.

"I didn't *do* anything!" Nelson wailed, hitting his leg with the baseball glove.

Ray had never heard or seen him so nakedly expressive before, and it carried some of the slightly repulsive shock of seeing the puniness of a turtle extracted from its shell.

"Nelson, you have to go home," Ray said as gently as he could, easing himself down on the couch next to him.

Nelson sank deeper into the upholstery, his face clenched with resolution.

Ray anxiously batted the narrow gap between his own knees with the writing pad, then flipped it to the floor.

"You have to go home, Nelson," he said, laying a hand on the kid's shoulder as if it might be hot.

Nelson started to cry, a stingy high-pitched keen.

"Look," Ray began, then just faded. "How did you get here?" he asked. "Did you take a bus from school?"

But Nelson had gone off into some deeper permutation of his own blues and Ray might as well have been talking to himself. "Nelson . . ."

"Everybody *hates* me," he wailed abruptly through those ruined lips, Ray taken once again by how much this almost-thirteen-year-old boy was still so much a child.

"Nobody hates you, Nelson." Ray put a hand on his arm. "But you have to go home."

"I want to have a catch," he announced desperately, but with a knowing touch of hopelessness; the kid apparently not so immature that he didn't in some way understand the bottom line here.

"We can't, sweetheart."

"Why *not*," Nelson demanded of the far wall, still refusing to meet Ray's eye.

"Nelson, I'm sorry, but your parents are your parents." Then, "Does anybody know you came here?"

The kid refused to answer, his face bunching up again, blurry and red, as he mutely railed against the desolating unfairness of it all.

"I want to see your baseball cards again," he declared.

"My what?" Ray took his head out of his hands. "Hey, I'll do you one better."

He began to rise, ready to just give the kid one of his albums, but then sank back into the couch as he envisioned Nelson bringing this consolation prize home, Freddy asking him where he got it. Besides, that wasn't what Nelson was after.

Sitting side by side, both of them staring straight ahead at the far wall as if they were watching a tragic movie, Ray found himself burning with the desire to give this kid something both enduring and in some way consoling, but there was nothing that Nelson could leave this apartment with, absolutely nothing that couldn't in some way come back to snap Ray's neck.

"Can't I even see your baseball cards?" Nelson said brokenly.

Ray slid up to the edge of the couch and dropped his head beneath his hunched shoulders.

"Nelson," Ray began, intending to offer him a ride but, no, he couldn't even risk doing that. "Nelson, I'm going to call you a cab to take you home. I'm sorry, I wish I could . . ."

Ray rose to his feet and retrieved the portable phone from across the room, then went into the kitchen to get the phone number for Garden State Taxi taped to the side of the refrigerator. Returning to sit by Nelson on the couch, he began to dial, but he was overcome once again with that urge, near-irresistible, to just *give* the damn kid something, anything; and wound up killing the call before it rang through, opting instead to reach into his pocket and fish out two twenties, which he pressed into Nelson's hand.

"This is for the cab. Whatever's left over, that's yours. Buy yourself something stupid, whatever you want."

Nelson stared at the bills in his palm as if he'd never seen money before, his hand remaining open. Then his face darkened.

At first Ray thought the kid was silently demanding more, and for an instant he entertained the notion that this whole visit was a carefully scripted attempt at blackmail. But then he decided that the sudden rush of color was about confusion, Nelson having a hard time processing the significance of the forty dollars.

Pulsing with shame, Ray rose to his feet and with his back to Nelson on the couch, put the call through to Garden State.

"Yeah, how soon can you get a cab to Little Venice?"

"Where you going," the dispatcher said, chewing something as he spoke.

"Hang on." Ray turned to face Nelson and get his address.

The blow announced itself as an odor and as a sound—a singed-smelling, high-pitched whine, dog-whistle high, followed by a blind tumble to the floor, a cascade of Ray, images and words and limbs and then out.

Chapter 32 >

Nerese—February 28

Ray and Nerese stood at the railing of his terrace, staring out at the wind-ripped Hudson as if they were waiting for Neptune to rise from the deep and make an announcement.

"Well, I can't say I don't see where you were coming from on this," she said.

"So what did you do," Ray asked. It was cold as hell, but he made no move to head back inside.

"I did my job," she said.

"Meaning what."

"The Youth House."

"No," Ray hissed, gray-faced. "Oh please, you didn't."

Nerese cut him a long dry look.

"Jesus," he said, a hand on his heart. "Why'd you just fuck with me like that?"

"Oh, I'm sorry," Nerese said. "Did you just get fucked with?"

Ray looked away.

"I called Danielle this morning with the names of a few therapists I know through Family Services. That kid definitely needs to get himself an out-of-the-house ally."

"Good," Ray said, still avoiding her eyes. "That's a good idea."

"And I also suggested a few names for her, too, but I don't think that's going to go anywhere."

"You say anything else to her?"

A flatbed barge the size of a football field made its way toward the bay, Ray staring at it as if he would give anything just to be the cabin boy on that thing right now.

"You mean did I read her the riot act?" Nerese studied him. "That's not my job."

"OK."

"It's not appropriate."

"OK."

"Not that I didn't want to."

"I hear you," he said, finally venturing a quick glance her way.

Nerese inhaled the clammy low-tide stench from the bay and was momentarily saddened that this would be her last visit here.

"If I had spoke my mind? I would have most likely said something way too hot and uncalled for."

"Really."

"Because I have my own personal history with this stuff to contend with, and . . ." Nerese retreated, staring out at the water and silently sliding her hands over each other as if washing them in wind.

"What," Ray asked with as much dread as curiosity. And when she continued to hold back, he asked again, "What," the second time more emphatically, suddenly staring at her full on, offering himself up.

"Look, as a rule I don't ever talk about my son on the job. I just don't, but . . ."

Ray continued to stare at her as if afraid, now, to look away.

"It's like, his father? Darren's father?" Nerese eased back in. "He cut out a few months after Darren was born. It was drugs, a lot of it, but even if he had been clean, he still wasn't . . . He would've split sooner or later. And frankly, sooner was better. I mean, if you're gonna go, go."

"Absolutely."

"Ray, just shut up and listen," she said without rancor. "And it was hard for me, raising a child by myself, plus, you know, being a rookie cop and all. But I did it. And at first, when he was real little? I had a series of boyfriends. They'd sleep over the house, walk around morning noon night. None of them bad guys, mean to Darren or whatever, but it was a series of guys who wound up kind of half-living with me. Some were married, some not, about four maybe five guys since Darren's father had skipped.

"Now, all this was going on when my son was a crawler, a toddler, a runner, a put-together kid as far as I could tell, pretty happy . . .

"But when he was in first grade, he started acting up in school, fighting, crying, throwing things, wound up hitting another kid with a rock, no stitches thank God, but he drew blood. So I get called in for a conference by his teacher, Miss Hanley, nice, nice woman, asks me if anything's going on at home she should know about, you know, anything stressful, I say, 'Not, not really.'

"But Miss Hanley, she had apparently talked to Darren the day before, and now she calls him over, says, 'Honey? Do you want to tell your mommy what you told me?' Darren's like, 'Unh-uh. Nope. No way.' So she sends him back to the play yard.

"Once he's out of earshot, she tells me that Darren had said to her the day before that he didn't like the 'new daddy' he had now.

"Not *his* daddy. The *new* daddy.

"The woman asks me about the guy, who at the time was this cop Ernie Howard, decent man, a little gruff, drank a bit, but decent. She asks me how he is with Darren, et cetera, et cetera. But I thought she missed the point. It wasn't that this guy was a bad player. It was the fact that Darren had called him his new daddy. Had called him *any* kind of daddy.

"See, I had been oblivious to this, that my son saw these men in my life as a succession of fathers, each of which disappeared on him as soon as our romance went sour . . . That, that Darren, whose biological father had bailed on him and never looked back, needed a father in *any* kind of way.

"It was like, as a parent, I thought I was doing good. And my sex life was behind the bedroom door. Plus, I would never hook up with a man who was in any way unkind to children in general, let alone my own child.

"Now, I didn't know if Ernie had been short with Darren one time, expressed irritation with him, gave him a dirty look or if Darren just didn't like his face, but it didn't matter, because Ernie wasn't the problem. You see what I'm saying?

"Well, I went home that day and I swore that I would never bring any man into my house save for the one that would in fact *be* Darren's new daddy."

Nerese straightened up from her hunched-over stance at the terrace rail, a fist pressed into the small of her back.

"What was that, twelve years ago?" She snorted. "My son is approaching his eighteenth birthday and I have kept that promise. In the last twelve years he has never woken up *once* in his own home come morning to see some guy in boxer shorts raiding the refrigerator. In the last twelve years, he has never been told what to do *once* in his own home by some man whose only claim to authority would be that he was sleeping with his mother.

"I have kept that promise and I have suffered for it, but my son is *intact*.

"I didn't give up sex, didn't give up men, but my love life for the past twelve years has been largely a matter of motels, which are not really conducive to romance, or intimacy or even conversation. Once in a blue moon there's been the odd getaway weekend but not for a few years.

"Now, I'm not saying for sure that I would definitely be with a man today if things hadn't been the way they were, but who knows, you know?

"And the hell of it is, now that Darren's about to take off and I'm going to be a free agent again? I look in the mirror and what do I see . . . I see a forty-one-year-old woman whose weight fluctuates between a hundred and sixty and a hundred and seventy-five pounds . . . I see a woman whose hair is starting to streak up gray, I see . . ." Nerese took a fuming breath, scowled at her nails. "Who's gonna want me now . . ."

"Aw c'mon, Tweetie," Ray said weakly.

"Do *you*?" Just saying it.

"Do I what."

"Do you want to try and get something going with me? See where it takes us?"

She had never seen someone go literally speechless before, and it pained her to have made her point so easily.

"Anyways, that's what Florida's all about. My turn. I just hope to God it's not too late."

"Tweetie," Ray pleaded, still snagged in the brambles. But Nerese was past it.

"And if I look back on the last twelve or so years, you know, all the, the love, the possibilities for love that never came to pass, am I angry at my son? Probably. Did making that sacrifice mean I was a good parent? I don't know. Sometimes I feel like I fuck up with that kid every time I open my mouth. Say the wrong thing, do the wrong thing. He's definitely a mama's boy, but I guess given the other males in my family tree he could have turned out a hell of a lot worse . . . If I had to do it all over again, would I make the same sacrifice? I wouldn't be happy about it, but yeah, I would.

"My child was starved for a father so no way, once I understood that, would I torment him with a parade of boyfriends and that was that."

"Tweetie, I had no idea . . ."

"Of course you had no idea. Why would you have?"

"I'm just saying . . ." He trailed off.

"The point I'm trying to get at here is, given all this I just told you? With Nelson's mother yesterday, I had to be careful of what I said, otherwise it would've gotten way too personal, you know, judgmental. I mean what the hell was she doing dragging along that kid to your house like that. I mean fuck who you want, but that's a *child*."

Ray nodded, his face ruddy with shame.

"Which brings me to you," she said mildly, worried a little bit now about coming off self-righteous but no way after she had been put through the hoops on this one was she *not* going to have her say.

"Remember that day I got caught spray-painting that shit on Eleven Building? Those two cops had me bookended, walked me all the way through Hopewell to the management office, all those little shitheels following us, woofing me out, made me feel like Dumbo leading the circus into town . . . Hands down the worst moment of my life. Well, you were there for that part of things.

"Anyways, here's what you didn't see. They get me in the management office, one cop goes and calls my mother to come pick me up, then disappears to do the arrest report, right?

"The other cop? That white cop? He's sitting next to me on the lobby bench, we're waiting for my mother, people coming in and out of the office to pay their rent or whatnot, everybody's looking at me, knowing what I did.

"We're waiting, waiting . . . That white cop's reading the *Dispatch*, not talking all that much, but when he comes to the comics section, he folds it back and passes me the paper, although I was too far gone to get into Li'l Abner just then . . .

"Do you know how long I had to wait for my mother to come pick me up? Forty-five minutes. Forty-five motherfucking minutes to make it over from three buildings away. Forty-five minutes of me just sitting there with everybody staring at me like I was the lowest piece of shit on earth. And when she finally came in to get me? I'm talking three o'clock in the afternoon, now—she comes shuffling into the management office in a *house*-coat. A two-buttons-missing housecoat, got slippers on, her hair's up in rollers, got a pack of Larks in a vinyl cigarette case in one hand and a lit cigarette in the other. Comes into the office like that in the middle of the afternoon before, the *housing* manager . . ." Nerese began ticking off on her fingers, pinky first. "Before, the, the *clerks*, the *cops*, the *neighbors* . . .

"I just wanted to curl up and die right on that bench.

"But then something happened, Ray, something amazing. Something . . .

"That white cop sitting next to me? He took a long look at my mother when she came in, just like, absorbed her, and then without even turning to me, he just put his hand on my back, up between my neck and shoulder . . .

"And all he did was squeeze. Give me a little squeeze of sympathy, then kind of rubbed that same spot with his palm for maybe two, three seconds, and that was it.

"But I swear to you, nobody, in my entire life up to that point had *ever* touched me with that kind of tenderness. I had never experienced a sympathetic hand like that, and Ray, it felt like *lightning*.

"I mean, the guy did it without thinking, I'm sure. And when dinnertime rolled around he had probably forgotten all about it. Forgot about me, too, for that matter . . . But *I* didn't forget.

"I didn't walk around thinking about it nonstop either, but something like seven years later when I was at the community college? The recruiting officer for the PD came on campus for Career Day, and I didn't really like college all that much to begin with, so I took the test for the academy, scored high, quit school and never looked back.

"And usually when I tell people why I became a cop I say because it would keep Butchie and Antoine out of my life, and there's some truth in that.

"But I think the real reason was because that recruiting officer on campus that day reminded me, in some way, you know, conscious or not, of that housing cop who had sat on the bench with me when I was thirteen.

"In fact, I don't think it, I *know* it. As sure as I'm standing here, I *know* I became a cop because of him. *For* him. To *be* like him. God as my witness Ray, the man put his hand on my back for three seconds and it rerouted my life for the next twenty-nine years.

"It's the enormity of small things . . . Adults, grown-ups, *us*, we have so much power . . . And sometimes when we find ourselves coming into contact with certain kinds of kids? Needy kids? We have to be ever so careful . . ."

"Yup," Ray whispered.

"When I first saw you in the hospital and you didn't want to cooperate? I went through my checklist. He likes the boys, he likes the girls, he likes men, he's into the needle, the powder, the pipe. He's into loan sharks, he's a degenerate gambler, something humiliating like that, because I could smell the shame coming off you like body odor."

Ray slowly sucked air through clenched teeth as if he'd been waiting for her to lay into him like this from the first time they'd met.

"Nelson," she said. "What did you think, that kid would just stop thinking about you after he went home like you stopped thinking about him? You reach out in any way to a child like that, you can*not* be oblivious to what you might be unleashing.

"I mean, you're a good guy, Ray, you have good intentions and all, but you need too much to be liked and that's a bad weakness to have. It makes you reckless. And it makes you dangerous . . ."

Nerese then turned to him and smiled. "That's it. I'm done."

At first she thought Ray was just smothering a series of explosive sneezes, but then the tears came and he turned away.

Nerese studied the New York skyline across the river, a fortress inside a fortress inside a fortress, a deep thicket of spires, gleaming in the late winter light.

"Anyways," she said, "guess who's not a cop anymore."

He turned to her and waited for more.

"I used my accrued sick days to get out early. Put in my papers yesterday afternoon."

"What?" Ray came upright off the rail.

"I'm going down to Florida in a few days, oversee the guys rehabbing my house."

"So now it begins for you, huh?" he managed, his voice still clogged.

"Well, yes and no," she said, baring her teeth. "I'm kind of taking that ninety-seven-year-old man with me. There's nobody up here that I feel comfortable leaving him with. Besides, he doesn't have all that much time left, so I can't see him cramping my style down there for too long. The good news is I got my mother and uncle going into the same old-age home that I'm taking him out of, so it's like one way or another, everybody's covered."

"How about your son?" he asked, breathing through his mouth.

"Darren? Darren's in charge of the house up here until he graduates, and then we'll see.

"I got him applying to this community college about twenty miles from the new house down there? It isn't Harvard, but neither is he. He can live in the dorms if he gets accepted. Or . . . I mean I have a finished basement in the new place, but . . . I don't know, we'll see, we'll see."

"The new you's shaping up a lot like the old you."

Nerese shrugged, not wanting to think that one through, telling herself, I am blessed . . .

"Anyways," she said. "It's time for me to book."

"Actually, I'm kind of heading out of here myself," he said.

"Meaning . . ." She hauled her bag up on her shoulder.

His mouth and eyes began working in such a way that she knew whatever he was about to say would almost be as much of a news flash to him as to her.

"I'm going back to Los Angeles."

"Really . . ."

"Yeah," he said slowly, as if feeling his way. "I'll see, I'll see this writing class thing through to the end, but basically I don't know what the fuck I'm doing here. I mean, writing for some TV show is dopey but it's work, it's life. It's no worse than being a real estate lawyer or an advertising executive or whatever. Maybe it's not fighting the good fight, but . . . I just can't do this anymore. I just can't.

"I mean, I'll try my hardest not to leave anyone else in the lurch, but . . ."

Although his words were becoming increasingly lucid and thought out, their tone had become almost pleading.

"It's what you said, Tweetie. I don't have the discipline. I don't have . . . People like me"—he held his nerve-curled right hand against his chest, the gesture enhancing the aura of supplication—"I need to be beholden to something or someone up the ladder, no matter how stupid the finished product is. I'm just not strong enough for anything else."

"What about Ruby?" Nerese almost hating to bring up the kid's name in the face of Ray's pitch, his use of the word beholden.

"Tweetie, I'm not doing her any favors just hanging around here like this. I have to live," straight-out begging her. "I have to have a *life*."

"Hey, you do what you got to do," she said, hands in the air. "You don't have to sell me." Then: "How'd she take the news?"

Ray put all ten fingers to his temples and widened his eyes, as if to get more air around the sockets. "I haven't really figured out how to tell her yet."

"You will," Nerese said, just to say it, coming at him with bowed arms, embracing him. "I got to go."

At the door she turned to face him one last time.

"You know, Ray, in terms of what put you in the hospital, I'll tell you one thing that you might want to take as the silver lining on the cloud . . . You were very lucky that it was little Nelson who took that whack at you.

"Because if it was your boy Salim? That's a grown man, and he'd've taken your head clean off your shoulders. I mean, all due respect to what you said about not wanting to leave anybody else in the lurch around here? But if I were you, I'd cut that half-a-headcase loose today."

Chapter 33 >

Take Our Daughters to Work—March 5

Ray's first day back teaching since the assault coincided with Take Our Daughters to Work Day. Although the event was primarily designed for working mothers, Ruby had agreed to sit in on the class, and so despite the neurologist's warning against driving these days, he found himself behind the wheel again, heading into the city at the height of the morning crush in order to pick her up at St. Simon's and bring her back over to Dempsy.

Actually, the pickup wasn't necessary; with his right-side extremities still dragging, his head still singing and his stamina tentative at best, he had arranged for this, his comeback class, to be something of a half-assed field trip. Mrs. Bondo was taking the kids by bus to Little Venice, where they would have lunch and read their work out on his terrace. And Ruby made her own way from lower Manhattan to his place all the time. But, anxious about breaking the news to her of his fairly impending return to Los Angeles—in a month, he figured—he felt like he needed to see her as soon as possible.

Walking from his car to St. Simon's, he caught sight of Ruby from a block away, hanging with a bunch of kids her age, thirteen, fourteen, in front of a deli around the corner from the school.

There were roughly half a dozen of them goofing around before the eight a.m. bell, the boys slap-boxing, miming jump shots and honking like geese; the girls a little more in control of their physicality but as noisy as the boys.

A cigarette was being passed around, and Ray was transfixed by the sight of his daughter taking a deep drag—no coughing, no darting glances—then flicking the butt into the gutter.

Settling himself down on a car hood out of their sight lines, he continued to watch, as Ruby snatched a loose-knit Rasta cap off a blond boy's head, then took off in an evasive zigzag, the kid happily grabbing her from behind, Ruby squawking "What the fuck are you *doing*?" but not trying all that hard to get free. In fact, after a few token wriggles she more or less settled into the clinch, the boy, still hugging her from behind, placidly resting his chin on her shoulder.

Ruby took another drag on a fresh cigarette being passed around, then, with a languid feline ease that left Ray floored, raised it to the lips of the boy holding her, allowing him his taste before returning it to general circulation.

Smoking, cursing, public lewdness: Ray found himself thrilled by this kid of his, lifted by this other Ruby that he had never seen before, her secret vices, secret powers; the only queasiness was evoked by the notion that it was as if she had intuitively decided to leave him, to leave his idea of who she was, before he could literally leave her.

"So this guy White Tom?" Ray said as they entered the Holland Tunnel. "If and when they bust this grocery, he wants to buy it and make it into kind of a candy store–luncheonette for the Hopewell kids. Frankly I think he's talking air castles, he's a bit of a whack-job, but if he manages to pull this off? He's supposed to call me, because I would very much like to be a little part of that, you know? What do you think?"

Ruby shrugged noncommittally.

"What."

"Where are the people going to buy groceries then?"

"There's a supermarket a block away," Ray said. "Better stuff, half the price."

Ruby threw him another discomfited shrug; something still bothering her.

"What."

"I feel bad for the grocery store guy."

"He's a drug dealer."

"I know," she said halfheartedly; something else.

"Anyways," Ray mumbled as the car broke into Jersey-side sunlight, "it's probably all bullshit, so, whatever."

A burdened silence came down on them as he made a long slow arc around Jersey City, then ascended the ramp onto the southbound turn-pike.

Ruby, it's time for me to go back to . . .

Ruby, how would you feel if I . . .

Ruby, I need to work at a real job, I need . . .

Ruby . . .

Honey . . .

Sweetie . . .

There were two tentative offers out there already: one for a series gearing up about the Secret Service, the other about a detective agency in which all the gumshoes were certified, whatever that meant, psychics.

"So, did you bring a story with you?"

"I forgot," she said, looking out the window at a gaggle of waterfront derricks.

"You *forgot?*," Ray honestly upset. "I thought you were going to read some stuff today."

"I forgot. I'm sorry," a bit of an edge creeping into her voice.

"I can't believe you forgot. The kids would've loved it. *I* would have loved it."

"*Dad!*" The edge turning jagged. "I said I *forgot*, OK? I'm *sorry.*"

"OK. OK. No problem."

But once I get set up out there . . .

Ray exited the turnpike as the Statue of Liberty came into view.

"No, I think it's a good idea," she said faintly as if drained, breaking this second silence.

"What is."

"Helping White Tom."

"Oh yeah?" Ray eyed her. "Good."

She leaned her head into the passenger-side window, her face cinched tight as a purse.

Definitely something else.

. . .

The small school bus, squat as a concertina, was unable to enter the grounds of Little Venice—something about insurance restrictions regarding private property—so Ray and Ruby had to meet the class at the security gate and hoof it back to the apartment, a half-mile walk past the overgrown construction mounds and beneath the spiraling cruciform shadows of the gulls. The trudge was a happy one, though, the boys periodically popping straight up in the air for no reason he could discern save for the anarchy of being so far from school on a late Wednesday morning—that, and/or the presence of the girls.

"What grade are you in?" Altagracia asked Ruby, who lagged behind Ray just enough to be disaffiliated from him.

"They don't have grades in my school," Ruby said.

"What?"

Ray briefly glanced behind him, but too briefly, nothing registering.

"Then how do you get promoted?"

"They just promote us," Ruby said, Ray envisioning her shrugging. "What grade are you in?"

"Ninth," Altagracia said. Ray was dying to turn around.

"I like your hair," Ruby said. "How do you do that?"

"I don't have time enough to tell you."

"Hey Ruby." Ray wheeled, walking backward now, but the sunlight was a dagger in his left eye and he forgot whatever little piece of rehearsed banter he had in mind to justify his joining in.

Despite waving them in from the middle of the living room, the kids lingered in Ray's doorway as if the floor tiles were sewn with land mines; not until Rashaad caught sight of the TV—"Dag, a flat screen," the kid making a beeline for it—did the others tentatively file in after him, Mrs. Bondo and Ruby after-you-ing each other to death in order to be last.

"It's *broke*?" Rashaad reared back from his own question.

"Yeah," Ray said. "For today."

Shaking off the setback, Rashaad discovered the funhouse mirror, and within seconds the three boys were jockeying for center stage, throwing elbows and shouting incoherently.

The girls, blocked from viewing themselves, settled for inspecting the CDs and videos in the wall unit; Ruby and Mrs. Bondo standing side by side like edgy museum guards waiting for something bad to happen.

"Ruby, you OK?"

"Yeah," more of a yip than a word, Ray feeling her sense of invasion.

"*Boys!*" Mrs. Bondo snapped at the mirror crew.

"It's OK." Ray shrugged. "That's what it's there for."

But then Jamaal discovered the miniature basketball hoop that Ray had tacked up over the hallway entrance for Ruby right after he moved in. The kid whipped out his wallet for use as a ball, and a three-way game of one-on-one began, the floors now shaking like thunder.

"Guys, guys," Ray waded into them, handing Jamaal back his wallet. "My neighbors are like a thousand years old."

Three of the girls were in front of the funhouse mirror now, their turn to whoop it up, Altagracia begging Mrs. Bondo to come over and cast a freaky reflection—nothing doing—while Ruby and Myra wandered off in separate spheres, Myra checking out his book collection, Ruby holding up a wall, the poor kid striving for impassive but mainly coming off as overwhelmed.

Crossing the room, Ray took his daughter by the hand and dragged her over to the bookshelves.

Myra was studying his framed Emmy nomination now, open-mouthed, river light flashing off her glasses.

"That's an Oscar?" she asked.

"It's for TV."

"You have so many books. I'd love having books like this, you know, everywhere you looked, books, books."

"Well here," Ray, still holding Ruby's hand, impulsively plucked a collection of William Carlos Williams poems from a high shelf and gave it to her. "Here's one to grow on."

"What?" she said, meaning, Thank you, and immediately started reading.

Ruby jerked her hand free.

"Myra, did you meet my daughter, Ruby?"

"Hey," Myra said minutely.

"Hey," Ruby's voice even tinier.

"Myra's a killer writer," he said, then, "Ruby's a killer writer, too. She was supposed to bring stuff to read today, but . . ."

"*Dad,*" the word dripping with grief.

"Mr. Mitchell," Myra said, "would it be OK if I didn't read today either? I felt like I needed to give my mind a rest this week."

"Sure, absolutely," Ray even a little charmed by the phrasing of her excuses.

Mrs. Bondo caught his eye and tapped her wristwatch.

"OK," Ray announced. "Grab your lunches and come see the greatest view in New Jersey," sliding open the terrace door. "Mainly the view of New York."

The kids filed out, rushing to the railing in a way that made his gut flutter.

"Hang on, hang on," herding them back, then pointing to the Statue of Liberty. "Check it out."

"That's the Declaration of Independence?" Rashaad asked. The others blew up with laughter. "Naw naw naw, I mean . . ." Rashaad at least having the good humor to laugh too.

As the kids and Mrs. Bondo broke out their sandwiches and sodas, Ray looked back into the apartment and saw Ruby sitting by herself on the couch, poring over one of his baseball-card albums.

Stepping back into the living room, he eased himself down next to her. "What's up?"

"Nothing," she said in a near-whisper, eyes still on the cards.

"Why don't you come out?"

"It's too cold."

"Ruby, what's wrong." Ray felt a wave of sandy exhaustion in his joints, his skull humming like a hive.

"*Nothing*, I said."

"Ruby, I was so excited to have you here today," vindictively using the past tense. "Tell me what's wrong. It's not *fair*."

"I don't know," she said through near-motionless lips. "I'm embarrassed."

"About *what*. You're not reading anything. All's you got to do is sit there and listen. What's the big deal?"

Ruby shrugged and looked away, "embarrassed" a euphemism for God knows what.

He fleetingly wondered if perhaps she was feeling self-conscious about being the only white kid, but he wasn't really picking that up.

"Just come out. Please?"

> "When my uncle was in high school he beat up a kid who was beating up him and the kid had got a concussion from it and even though it wasn't his fault the judge said he had to go into the army where there was a war going on."

Ray eyed Ruby sitting against the railing behind the other kids. She looked open to the story, though, and he let her be.

"He spent a year in the war and was in a lot of firefights."

Rashaad looked up. "That's what he called it. Firefights.

"Even though a lot of people and soldiers got killed all around him, or wounded, he didn't even have a scratch on him when he finally came home and was even given an award for bravery."

Rashaad looked up again. "OK, here's where it gets . . . You'll see."

"Then two days after he came back to Dempsy, he went over to the public swimming pool that used to be on Liba- tore Street, dove into the water and broke his neck. Ever since he's been in a wheelchair."

Winces and "dag"s all around.
"Comments?"
"Can I read?" Efram raised his hand.
"No comments?"
"It was sad," said Jamaal, Ray surprised by that adjective coming out of a boy's mouth.

"OK," Efram grinned, "you're gonna like this," then,

"King Efram the First . . ."

And that was as far as he got, the class blowing up as usual. Ruby seemed intrigued but out of the loop.

"King Efram the First guided his laser beam refractor unit through the porthole of his warship at the planet Venus, which was populated by gorgeous ten-foot-tall women."

Another wave of chaos, Efram waiting it out.

"'Put down your arms,' he telepathically announced, 'or Venus will be reduced to a lump of coal.'

"The Venusian Queen telepathically returned his command: 'If you won't come to our planet and have our babies we just as soon be smoked because there are no men here and we're going crazy.'"

The kids were howling, Ruby finally cracking up too, shrugging help-lessly at Ray—What a maroon.

"OK. Stop, stop," Ray reared back, not sure who he was addressing.

"They're gonna make *him* pregnant?" Rashaad said.

"No, no." Efram fended him off.

"Yeah! You said, 'Come and have our babies!'"

"What?" Efram scanned his pages, then, "Oh, shit."

"*Hey!*" Ray and Bondo said together.

"He's a *bitch*," Rashaad crowed.

"Hey!" Another tandem bark, the terrace threatening to fall into the river.

"Aaah," Rashaad gurgled with glee.

After Felicia and Mercedes read, two painfully stiff recitations which as usual were interesting despite themselves, Ray scanned the terrace and saw that they were done.

"OK, usually Myra gives us a taste right about now, but apparently she's on a brain break this week, so . . ."

Ruby raised her hand.

"Yeah, Ruby," Ray on his toes.

"Can I . . ."

"Read?"

She nodded.

"But I thought . . ." he said, then, "Sure. Absolutely."

The other kids twisted around and wordlessly sized Ruby up as she extracted from her hip-slung fanny-pack two intensely wrinkled pages, looking as if they had been obsessively crumpled then flattened, crum-pled then flattened . . .

"I didn't know if there was an assignment for today?" Ruby addressed the Astroturf. "But I wrote something for the assignment you had where you were a dead person talking about his life."

She coughed, smoothed out the sheets.
"It's called 'In My Grave.'

"If I had just decided not to visit my wife and daughter that last time I would still be walking the earth. I would still be free, I would still be alive.

"But even before that, if I had decided years ago that drugs weren't my true love in life I would never even have *had* to visit them, because I would still be sharing a home with them, but that wasn't the case.

"Oh sure, I cared for them in some way, but even my own flesh and blood was no match for the white powder.

"It made me crazy for more and I couldn't ignore the demand no matter what.

"My wife kicked me out of the house when my daughter was little and she saw that I wouldn't stop, and although part of me was sad to say good-bye like that, there was another part of me that felt free, free at last.

"I wandered the Earth over the years, always looking for more and more white powder, and sometimes at night I would lie in my cheap bed in some hotel and think about my wife and child, think about divorcing myself from drugs instead of my family, but when the morning came, I always changed my mind.

"Even though I thought my wife was a real bitch she was still right to kick me out but I kept thinking of my kid growing up without me and it drove me crazy.

"What did she think of me? What did she look like now? How did she like school? Was she popular? I had no answers.

"Finally one day I returned to New York, snorted up a huge amount of the white powder and got my nerve up to go back, knock on the door and finally see them for better or worse.

"It was about midnight and although I banged on the door like a crazy man, no one answered. Then I realized I still had my key from when that bitch kicked me out years ago, so I let myself in.

"The house was dark and I couldn't find the lights so I

just bumped into everything calling out my daughter's name, which was Denise.

"Finally I saw someone standing in the doorway of my old bedroom. At the same time I found the light, which I turned on and saw in front of me a tall young woman I didn't know.

"Then it hit me. It was my daughter Denise who I hadn't seen since she was little.

"'Denise!' I yelled joyously as I came at her with open arms.

"I didn't see the gun in her hands until it went off, shooting me in the chest.

"As I lay dying on the floor, I realized that she didn't know who I was and shot me because she thought I was a burglar or a rapist.

"When my wife came home, although she recognized me, she didn't tell Denise that I was her father, just some criminal that had broken in.

"My wife called up her new boyfriend, who came over, rolled me up in a carpet and dumped me in the bottom of a river, which is where I lie now, talking to you. The end."

She had delivered the story in a thin yet determined monotone, her eyes never leaving the page.

Shattered, Ray numbly watched as the tremor in Ruby's hands traveled up her arms to her back and shoulders like electricity, culminating in a single fishtail ripple of the upper body, Ruby coming to rest after that, although her eyes were still fixed on the pages before her.

"I like that surprise ending," Altagracia said quietly.

"That was really good," Myra offered in her small voice, then added, nodding to Ray's framed one-fifth Emmy nomination, "That should be on TV."

Chapter 34 >

Nerese—March 5

Having surrendered her car for its annual inspection before driving it down to Florida, Nerese descended the stairs from the arcade level of the main PATH station in Dempsy to the tracks, where she immediately encountered a crouched-over piss-bum holding on to a pay phone stanchion and crooning to his shoes.

She walked to the far end of the platform in order to keep her distance and waited for the train that would take her home to Jersey City.

It was the dinner hour, the station deserted except for the drunk and herself, and she began drifting off into her worries: Darren taking over the house up here until his graduation—could he handle the responsibility, keep it presentable for prospective buyers? Although the type of people who at this point would be house shopping in a neighborhood like hers . . .

She didn't think he'd turn it into Bubble Hill in her absence, but for sure his girlfriend Patrice would be moving in the minute Nerese pulled away from the curb.

And how would Darren deal with Butchie and Antoine when they showed up without a reservation come the middle of the night?

Darren got along with Queen Toni pretty well, but Butchie, with his furrowed silences and lightless eyes, had always terrified him.

And telling either uncle to keep his distance was about as effective as pissing on a forest fire. Well, if things got out of hand she'd only be a long-distance phone call away.

"Yo, whoa, this right here."

The hissy communiqué snapped her back into the present, two hoodies having materialized twenty feet away while she was drifting in Darrensville, one of them eyeing her handbag through half-mast eyes, the other up on his toes checking out the drunk at the opposite end of the platform.

"Right here, right here," the first kid all but pointing at Nerese's bag.

"No him, him."

"He too close to the stair, this right here. Here." Still not looking at Nerese herself, just her bag.

"Hold on, hang on."

"*Hey*!" she exploded, both kids jumping. "Do I look fucking *deaf* to you?"

Exchanging glances, the two of them simply shrugged and walked away, leaving her standing there, trembling with insult.

They were most definitely going after the drunk now, Nerese groaning with the hassle of it all, obliged to follow them.

They traversed the platform at a leisurely pace for the first two-thirds of the journey, but when they came within a hundred feet of the vic, a disheveled young black man, they suddenly exploded forward, swooping like hawks; leaving Nerese standing there flatfooted.

But before she could get herself together, three plainclothes PATH cops materialized out of nowhere, the drunk himself whipping an arm around one kid's throat and twisting the hand—it now held a box cutter—behind the kid's back, that kid quickly going down in a flurry of police.

The other one though, was a little faster on his feet, wheeling and racing back toward Nerese, who, having no time to reach for her gun, braced herself to straighten him up with a forearm shiver.

But it never came to that: before he could get into striking range, he was taken down from behind by two of the cops.

Nerese stepped back as they pressed the side of his face into the litter-strewn platform and stripped him of his arsenal, a butter knife and a pair of homemade brass knuckles.

"You OK, miss?" one of the cops, flush-faced with victory, asked her from his kneeling position alongside the downed mugger.

"I'm good," she said mildly, refraining from identifying herself—not her table—and headed for the street, intending to spring for a cab.

But halfway up the stairs she stopped and came back down a few steps to watch these guys finish frisking and cuffing their grabs.

There were four of them including the decoy drunk; two white, two black, all young, fit and utterly alive to the Job.

Standing there observing the postaction mop-up, a ritual that she had partaken in hundreds of times, usually as part of a team but occasionally alone, she found herself pondering the fact that not once, on her many trips to Florida over the years, had she ever checked out the various law enforcement agencies, state, county or local, operating around where she would be settling.

And not for nothing; she still intended to finish up college and check out the social services job market down there, but just thinking the thought for now, any police force in the Florida panhandle would have to be out of its mind not to want a twenty-year veteran of the New York–New Jersey iron triangle on their team.

"Miss, you sure you're OK?" that same flush-faced cop asked her once he noticed that she hadn't left the scene after all.

"I'm fine," Nerese said, turning for good this time, and ascending to the street.

Chapter 35 >

Ghost Story — March 5

Unable to take the tension of spending the rest of the day alone in a room with his daughter, a few hours after the class had left the apartment Ray found himself driving her through the twilight streets of Dempsy, the two of them sitting next to each other like a pair of unexploded bombs.

It wasn't her night to stay with him, and he had to get her back to the city, but on impulse he decided to take a small detour past Hopewell, just to do a drive-by on White Tom's alleged future candy store, see what was happening.

Earlier, back in the apartment, in a desperate attempt to distract himself from thinking about what she had read to the class, he had the bright idea to call the guy rather than wait for his own phone to ring, and was not surprised to discover that the number for Thomas Potenza given to him by information was no longer in service.

"My guess is the bodega is still going full steam," he said, his throat dry with self-consciousness as they flew under the elevated PATH tracks along Rocker Drive.

"If he's selling drugs in there, don't get out of the car," Ruby said.

"I wasn't planning to," he said, touched by her protective fretfulness. "But do me a favor, if you're going in? Could you pick me up an eight-ball?"

Ruby stared at him as if slapped, Ray wondering what the fuck was wrong with him.

"It was a joke," he said weakly. "I was joking."

Slowing down as they approached Hopewell, Ray managed to cruise past his old building without turning his head, then slowed even further as they approached the far end of the projects, finally rolling to a double-parked stop in front of the bodega directly across the street from the Big Playground basketball courts.

It was barely six in the evening but to his astonishment, the store was dark.

Without thinking, he left the car, left Ruby and stepped under the red-and-yellow metal awning.

There was no padlock, but the door was sealed along the frame with multiple neon orange posters fairly shouting that the Del-Roy Mini-Mart had been shut down by order of the Dempsy County Prosecutor's Office.

"Ruby!" Inexplicably elated, he called back to the car, "It's closed!"

Ruby and Ray sat huddled side by side on the top slat of the bench in Little Playground. The cement seals and crawl-through barrels were bare of snow this time around, and near-phosphorescent in the climbing moonlight.

Ray wasn't quite sure what they were doing back here; it was at Ruby's request that they had walked over from the bodega. Nor could he say why the bodega being shut down as White Tom had foretold picked up his spirits so much. It still didn't mean that the guy was going to pull off buying the place, let alone transform it into a ghetto Candy Land. Maybe it was simply bearing witness to someone, anyone, being as good as his word, even partially.

"So who else lived here," Ruby asked, as she calmly tracked a rat or a mouse as it shot out of one of the striped play-barrels and disappeared through the mesh fence into the bushes.

"Who else, meaning kids I grew up with?"

"Yeah."

Ray opened his mouth to begin another roll call of two-bit legends, then, "Better yet, you want to hear a ghost story?"

"Sure," she said, briefly jackknifing against the cold.

"It has to do with your great-grandmother."

"The one who used to take you wrestling?"

Two kids with a boom box blasting Power 105.1 walked along the footpath that ran behind Little Playground. Ray had to wait for the DJ jabber to fade before answering, "Yeah, my grandma Ceil."

"OK."

He hunched forward, elbows on knees. "OK, when I was about eleven, twelve? She got very sick, my grandmother, very bad, and, at the time, she was living with my grandfather who you never met, and he just couldn't deal with it, so instead of going to a hospital like she should have, she moved here into Hopewell with us for about a week."

"They relocated me to the couch in the living room and she lay in my bed for seven days and seven nights with undiagnosed diabetes."

"Why didn't she go to the doctor?"

"Why? Because she thought doctors made you sick. That's how they got rich. But anyways, you know how crazy I was about her, right?"

"She took you to monster movies, too," Ruby said.

"What?" Ray faltered as he watched two young boys smack the crap out of each other in a low-story bedroom window of the building directly across the playground from them. "Yeah, exactly. So, every afternoon that week, I'd come running home from school and sit with her, talk to her, listen to the radio together, do my homework on the foot of the bed, whatever . . . And she was in bad shape, Ruby. Getting worse day by day, but she wouldn't let my mother anywhere near the phone to call for help."

"Why didn't she call anyhow?" Ruby said with heat. "*I* would have."

"Well, she could be pretty intimidating. I definitely got the impression that it was much better to be her grandchild than her child."

"Go on," Ruby said.

"So we're freaked, me and my parents, and one day, the last day actually, I'm in the bedroom with her, listening to the radio, she's going in and out of being awake, or conscious, and this song comes on, a jazzy kind of instrumental called 'Midnight in Moscow,' a clarinet thing, and my grandmother, she opens her eyes, says, 'I *love* this. What is this.' Then conks out again."

Ray became aware of three small kids watching them from a ground-floor window in that same line of bedroom windows, their heads in an unblinking pyramid.

"Well, I jump up like a jack-in-the-box and decide that I'm going to run out and buy her that record. I go downstairs, race over to a record store, find out 'Midnight in Moscow' is an oldie, they don't have it. I hit all three record stores in Dempsy, no dice. I wind up in Newark, a Sam

Goody's there, by the time I get back to the house with the damn thing it's three hours later and she's gone."

"*Dead?*"

"No. Taken to the hospital by ambulance. Just made it, too. Doctors said another day would've been too late. Ruby, look."

Ray pointed out the solemn pyramid of little kids. Ruby gave them a small wave and the heads vanished.

"What's the ghost part?" she asked.

"This record I bought? 'Midnight in Moscow'? I never got to play it for her. Obviously you can't play it in a hospital, and when she went home, she didn't have a record player in her house, so I pretty much forgot all about it.

"OK. Eight years later, I'm in college, my grandmother passes away, finally, and life goes on."

"That's sad," Ruby said.

"Wait. Twelve years after that, OK? Twenty years after she was sick and living with us? I'm thirty years old, driving a cab, and you're born."

"Me?" Ruby fought back a smile.

"I see you the morning you were born, Ruby, you were so . . ." Ray stumbled, remembering the cocaine funk, jumping out of his skin.

"You were so . . ." He tried again, sucker-punched by his own story. "But I have to get to work, drive, driving a cab; so I leave you . . ." He looked off. "I leave you at the hospital, with Mom, and . . ."

"What's wrong?"

"Nothing." Ray coughed. "So I leave you. All that day, all that night I'm driving, got the radio on low, driving and, at some point, I found myself talking to her, my grandmother, you know, in my imagination," Ray coughed again, "about you. I say, 'Grandma, you should see her, she's so beautiful, she's so . . .'" Ray palmed his face, hid his eyes. "'She's so precious, so . . . I wish you were here. I wish you could hold her, I wish . . .'"

"And I swear to God, Ruby, right then and there on the radio they played 'Midnight in Moscow.' I had not heard that fucking thing since I bought it twenty years earlier, but it was like she was reaching out to me, telling me she was still here, that she would always look out for you, that she would protect . . ."

Ray fell silent.

"Dad . . ."

"Ruby, I'm so . . ." He cut himself off.

That fucking story of hers . . .

"You're so *what* . . . " Ruby demanded.

"Nothing."

"*Tell* me." Ruby's voice was both angry and pleading. "You always make me tell *you*."

"I said, *nothing*."

"Are you leaving?" she asked, suddenly breathless.

"What?" Ray felt shock like a cream creeping along his scalp.

"Are you *leaving*," she repeated, her voice growing tremulous. "Are you going back to California."

"What?" he said again, then, "No."

"No?" Her voice still shaking as she searched his eyes.

"No," he said more calmly, then again, "No," just to hear himself say it.

She took another moment to anxiously scan his face, then said, "Good," in a tone of nearly muscular relief that sealed the deal for him.

"I'm staying right here," he said more to himself than to her. "Right here."

He'd sweat the details later.

"Hey, look . . ." And to change the subject, he pointed to the three small heads that had reappeared in the ground-floor window.

They sat in relative silence for a while, Ray feeling his daughter gradually subsiding into herself as ragged plastic whispered in the branches above their heads.

"Do you think she would have liked me?" Ruby finally said.

"Who."

"Your grandmother."

"Are you serious?" He bumped her with his shoulder. "She would have adored you."

"Good," she said once again, more softly this time, bobbing her head in satisfaction.

Ray leaned back and took in all the bedroom windows of the building facing them, all the various shadow plays, the sagas writ small; this place so never-ending.

"So go on," Ruby said.

"Go on where." He turned to her.

"Tell me another one."

CODA

Salim—March 12

When Ray got back from a job interview–dinner with the *Law & Order* people that night, the kid was waiting for him outside the apartment door, a scatter of cigarette butts at his feet.

"Hey, what's up?" Ray called out from halfway down the hall, where he had come to an abrupt stop at the first sight of him.

"Yeah, I was waiting for you," Salim said, his face studiously blank.

"OK." Ray held his ground.

"Can we go in?"

Ray was about to say "I was just leaving," then spent the next few seconds scrambling for a smoother walkaway. In the end, embarrassment as much as anything else had him reluctantly moving forward, digging in his pocket for the keys. And when the apartment door was finally opened, Salim was the first one through, gliding past Ray like he split the rent, immediately setting himself to pacing, smoking, his glance bouncing off surfaces like tracer fire.

Remaining in the open doorway, one foot still in the hall, Ray attempted to take Salim's measure; in addition to the raw agitation, there was something physically different about him tonight.

"So Salim, what's up?" he asked in a voice way too lively. "What's happening?"

"What's happening?" Salim repeated mindlessly, perching momentarily on the edge of the coffee table, then popping right up again and resuming patrol.

"What's shaking?" clutching the doorknob behind his back with both hands. "How's Omar?"

"Omar?" Salim moved to the window and peered out at the black river. "He's good."

"Michelle go to Atlanta?"

"Michelle?" Salim did an about-face back into the living room. "No."

"You two back together?" Ray starting to pay as little attention to his own questions as Salim now.

"No."

"OK," Ray said, tensely pondering this new Salim, simultaneously distracted and all business.

Pointedly leaving the front door ajar, he reluctantly came inside and took a seat on the corner of the couch as Salim moved to the glass again; and when he whirled back into the room this time, Ray was finally able to pinpoint the physical change in him: a uniform thickness around the rib cage, as if he were inflated.

"What did you do to yourself?" he asked.

"What?"

"You bulk up on steroids or something?"

"Nah, nah." Salim stopped short and briefly raised his sweatshirt to reveal a bulletproof vest.

"So what's up," Ray said quickly. "What can I do for you?" Just wanting now to speed the kid along to his cash money punch line and then, he hoped, the door.

"Yeah well, no, see, I couldn't get . . ." Salim took a deep breath, then forced himself to settle on the edge of the coffee table again, his knees pumping. "OK. See. I need a vendor's license, right?"

"I know. Five hundred dollars," Ray said, then just couldn't help adding, "That was already factored in."

"Yeah uh-huh but like, OK I went downtown to get one, right?" Salim's eyes were trained on a spot over Ray's left shoulder. "You have got to have . . . You have got to be a war veteran, see, 'cause they got like a five-year waiting list, and war veterans get top priority."

"War veterans. Not just veterans? You have to have been in actual combat?"

There was a paperback peeking out of Salim's sweatshirt muff, furled tight as a newspaper. Ray couldn't catch the title.

"Well, I don't know about the combat part, per se . . ." Salim addressed the skyline across the water now. "But they got a five-year waiting list and the veterans come first."

"Well, that sucks," Ray said brightly, a chagrined anger in him briefly boiling over.

Salim sat up straighter for a moment in response to Ray's edgy tone but then simply forged on.

"OK, the thing is? I got this cousin, right? He's gonna hook me up with this dude in the, the license bureau? He says if I slip this guy an *extra* five hundred? Like, under the table? He can jump me up on the list, get me my license in about six months."

"No kidding," Ray said, thinking, Is he asking for five hundred, then? Or a thousand . . .

The six months' wait after the bribe was a nice realistic touch, though.

"Because I'm getting rousted wherever I go, so . . ." Salim trailed off, as if exhausted by his own saga, his mouth hanging open in expectation.

They were seated facing each other barely a foot apart, and from this close up Salim's skin looked bad, ashy; his short, tight, normally fastidious crop was a little unkempt, too, individual corkscrews sprouting up here and there like the first tendrils of spring. And then Ray noticed, for the first time, that Salim's hair was starting to go gray; the kid twenty-nine, thirty years old tops, still looking to get on base any way he could.

"So, Ray . . ." His pitch apparently done, he became nearly motionless.

But, overcome by an embarrassed surliness as he found himself recalling the semi-euphoric flush of altruism that he had experienced in lessening degrees on each of the kid's previous cash-themed visits, Ray refused to bite.

"Yeah, so . . ." Salim still waiting.

And then Ray finally caught the title of that paperback peeking out of the sweatshirt: *Samurai Sense: A Bushido Primer for the 21st-Century Businessman.* And in a red rush of pity and anger, the words were out of his mouth before he could shut himself down. "Hey Salim, I'm not a fucking cash machine."

At first, they just stared at each other, mutually astonished; then Salim levitated from the edge of the coffee table into a half-crouch. "You're not *what?*" His mouth fish-round, his face clouding with blood. "Why you got to say something like that?" the words exploding out of him in a choleric gobble.

Ray felt stop-time dreamy, the clock a Popsicle stick lost somewhere in the back of a freezer.

"It came out wrong," he said evenly, not sure he could rise to his feet without provoking something physical. "I'm a little off today."

"Oh yeah? Why's *that,*" the question not really a question, Salim's mouth remaining locked in that spittle-flecked ring, his unblinking eyes aping the shape.

Ray said nothing.

"You're not a fuckin' *cash* machine?"

"Look, no disrespect. I didn't mean it the way it sounded," hating the phony nonchalance of his own voice.

"Did I *ask* you for money?" Salim's voice getting dangerously wobbly.

"I guess I misunderstood," Ray said carefully, trying to maintain eye contact. "So how can I help you . . ."

But, finessed by his own disclaimer, Salim remained locked in that outraged crouch. "What, you *scared* of me now?"

"No."

"Why you got to talk to me like that, huh?" Salim was almost shouting now. "*Why.*"

"I told you," Ray said, then froze as he spied the upright steel shaft of an eight-inch screwdriver tilting out of the back pocket of Salim's jeans like a miniature lance.

"Ah, Coley," he heard himself say huskily. "What the hell are you doing, you have *so* much to live for."

"I *what?*" Salim's face twisted chaotically.

At first, Ray felt half-moved by his own earnest tone; then repulsed by it, repulsed by the fact that even now he was automatically reviewing himself, his words; Ray once again brought face to face with the narcissism that propelled so much of his largesse, alive to how it brought him to this room, this jam; and as he came out of shock into a low state of self-disgust, his voice, for the first time since he'd come through the door, became truly his own.

"Well," he passed a trembling hand across his mouth as he rigidly refused to lower his gaze to Salim's back pocket again. "The fact of the matter is, whether you came here for money or not, I'm completely tapped out."

And then, spurred by an overwhelming desire to speed things along to their natural conclusion one way or the other, he finally rose to his feet. "And I think I need to ask you to leave."

Thank You — March 12–March 13

At five minutes before midnight, a filthy orange cab sat with its left front tire up on the curb of JFK Boulevard, exhaust fumes curling upward from the tailpipe into the crisp March night. In the sporadic headlights of oncoming cars, Pete Heinz, stopped at the intersection directly across the street, could see the drama within unfold; the passenger leaning forward from the rear seat, an arm hooked around the turbaned driver's throat, his free hand pressing a knife against this poor bastard's gullet.

Despite the direness of the tableau, Heinz, on the groovy side of drunk, absolutely knew that everything was going to turn out OK, and as he parked his own homeward-bound sedan and gingerly picked his way across the broad two-way street, he found himself scrambling for a memorable one-liner with which to dismantle the play.

Coming up from behind the cab and resting his forearms on the open front passenger-side window as if it were a backyard fence, he saw that the passenger was a youngish black man and that the weapon half-buried in the Sikh driver's beard was, in fact, a screwdriver.

"No, no, no," he addressed the kid in the backseat. "You see the turban? You got to use a Phillips head."

For an endless off-balance moment, both the driver and the jail-bound kid stared at him with a look of deep embarrassment, as if there was sex involved. The driver recovered first, abruptly swatting the screwdriver upward and away, accidentally slashing his own cheek in the process, then rolling out of his door onto the boulevard, instantly popping upright and hop-dancing away from his cab, one hand to his freshly bloody face, the other pointed accusingly at the backseat.

The kid, still holding his weapon, just sat there, slumped and distant.

Heinz leaned into the window a little more in order to study this bone-head: coffee-skinned, delicate in both frame and face, tiny turned-down ears and a small pursed mouth. He was dressed in spotless Timberland from sweatshirt to work boots.

Without ever looking at Heinz, the kid disgustedly tossed the screw-driver into the front passenger seat.

"Stinks in here," he muttered, sulkily rolling down his rear-seat window.

"Are you wearing a vest?" Heinz asked. "Please tell me you're not wearing a Kevlar vest."

The kid shrugged and looked away.

"What the hell's wrong with you," Heinz said evenly.

"I'm arrested, right?"

"Right."

"I get my phone call, right?"

Enjoying himself, Heinz tossed his county-owned cell phone in the kid's lap. "On me."

"Where'm I going, South Precinct?"

"Central Booking on Allerton. And don't forget to dial one before the area code."

The kid moved his lips as he punched in the numbers, Heinz grunt-ing, prone to the same dopey habit himself.

"Yeah, Ray . . ." The kid closed his eyes as he spoke. "It's me, Salim."

But before he could continue, the driver reappeared, thrusting a fist through the open rear window of the cab and socking Salim clumsily but squarely on the temple.

At three a.m., Heinz awoke from a ninety-minute sober-up in a disused jail cell, came out, washed his face, tucked in his shirt, then began the three-flight trudge from the lowest level of Central Booking to the street.

One flight up, he passed the nearly deserted bullpen, saw his collar, Salim El-Amin, sitting there behind the bars, lips silently moving as if he were still trying to punch in that phone number. On the bench facing him was the only other detainee, some disheveled but not poorly dressed white kid furiously attempting to blink himself back into a state of sobriety.

When he finally made it up to the street-level lobby, Heinz turned to the twenty-four-hour bail window, intending to throw a wave to the clerk, but was caught up short by the sight of the lone customer there, the guy quacking like a duck to the retired cop on duty behind the grille.

"He said five hundred!" the guy sputtered, not quite hostile, more distressed, unsure of how to deal here.

"Well then, he was blowing smoke," the clerk said, "because bail hasn't even been set yet. It's a felony charge. It's got to go before a judge in the morning, at which point you deal with the bail unit at the courthouse. But frankly, between you and me and the apple tree, my guess is you're gonna have to pony up more like five thousand than five hundred, come up with a security for the rest."

"Five thousand," the guy repeated softly.

He was wearing a knit watch cap beneath which the perimeter of a recently shaved patch of scalp was peeking out; this, combined with a pronounced right-side dragginess, suggested to Heinz either a stroke or a serious tune-up at the hands of another.

"Gene," he said to the bail clerk, "five thousand for who, the drunk kid? He looks like he couldn't boost a Mars Bar."

"No, Pete," the clerk said. "The other, your guy."

"Abdul Ben Fazool?"

"Salim El-Amin," the civilian corrected him self-consciously, Heinz looking at him with new eyes now; white man, early forties, possibly assaulted in the not too long ago, bailing out a Young Brother at four in the morning . . .

But although there seemed to be a strong vibration of embarrassment coming off the guy, it didn't feel quite outwardly focused; more like an internal audit going on than anything concerning judgment by others.

"I'm Pete Heinz." He offered his hand. "Maybe I can help."

The four a.m. diner was like all diners: gray Formica, dull raspberry padding, either Mylar wallpaper or marble-veined mirrors on every vertical surface. The comatose waiters in mock semiformal wear stood dead-eyed by the cash register, one or two holding Ten Commandment–sized menus and all slightly listing on their heels at this voidish hour.

"You don't understand." Ray spoke to the sugar canister between himself and this red-eyed detective. "This is a very good kid."

"Good," the cop said lightly, then clammed up, his eyes slightly bulging as if he were trying to contain one hell of a guffaw.

Ray was pretty sure the guy thought his relationship with Salim was sexual, but he didn't know how to disabuse him of that notion without being the first to bring up the subject.

"Look. His wife just left him, took the kid, trashed the apartment, his mother's in the hospital, his father's wherever, whoever, and Salim, Salim is hanging by a thread."

"It's armed robbery," the cop said. "The thread snapped."

"It wasn't his fault."

"You were there?"

Ray looked off, tried to regroup.

"What happened to you," the cop demanded, tilting his chin to Ray's watch cap.

"Nothing with him. Listen to me," holding up both hands, fingers splayed. "I'm not saying he didn't do time but he's killing himself out there trying to do the right thing, and he's an incredibly talented individual. An artist." Ray flinched as soon as the word was out of his mouth.

"An artist," the cop marveled, having a grand old time, his lower face moving now as if he had a mouse in his mouth.

"Graphic, commercial, illustrative," Ray forged on, trying to come off vocational rather than bleeding-heart sentimental, but still hating the naive dipshit tone of his own words. "He's got a portfolio that would knock your eyes out. I mean you should see . . ."

Ray faded, done in by his own earnestness. "Look, this kid, whatever kind of . . . Whatever I sound like to you, and I can imagine, you know, from your vantage point what that is . . . All I'm saying is this. Salim? If he gets lost in the system, if he falls through the cracks . . . You have no idea of what you'd be burying here."

"No doubt," the cop said evenly, sipping his grayish coffee.

"OK. Just . . ." Ray scrambled. "He's got this three-year-old son, Omar, right? I've never seen a connection between a father and a child like this. I mean, he's more a mother to that kid than the real one. And c'mon, you know, coming from where he's coming from? I mean how many young—"

"No doubt," the cop said again.

"Look, like I said, I know what I sound like . . ."

"So what's he to you, you help him out?"

"I . . . When I can."

"You're his what, mentor?"

"Fuck you," Ray said wearily.

"Excuse me?" The cop finally swallowed the mouse.

"There's nothing sexual about it. I'd say I'm as straight as you are, but I really don't know you."

The cop stared.

"I used to be his teacher."

"No kidding," the cop said coldly. "What did you teach him?"

"Most likely not a damn thing, but the subject was language arts."

"English? Huh. I always wanted to be a writer."

"Back at the bail window, you said maybe you could help."

"Yeah, well, technically you could spring the kid tonight if you call a judge at home, get him to set bail over the phone. It's not unheard of, but I just don't think this kid's worth it."

"If I say he is . . ."

"What's he got over you? You say no sex but then . . ." The cop's eyes traveled back up to Ray's damaged crown, Ray reflexively readjusting his watch cap.

"He came at you too, tonight, didn't he . . ."

"Actually," Ray said, "he didn't."

"You say that like he could have."

Ray closed his eyes, took a power nap.

"Yes?"

Ray glanced out the diner window at the immobile street.

"Look." The cop slowly came forward, elbows on the table. "You say the kid's got all this talent, all this potential, and I have no reason to disbelieve you. But I have to say . . . If Leonardo da Fucking Vinci came at me with a screwdriver, there's no way I'm posting his bail."

"But he *didn't*." Ray stared at him with ragged determined eyes. "So can you help me here, or not?"

Two hours later Salim El-Amin was released from the subbasement bullpen of Central Booking, Pete Heinz hanging in to see what would pass between this nitwit and his savior.

The kid looked calm, made eye contact with this Ray Mitchell, curtly nodding in thanks, but there was also something congested in his expression, something unlearned, and it made Heinz instantly regret his decision to help.

Mitchell steered the kid across the lobby to introduce him to his arresting officer, the guy at least savvy enough to do that.

"Salim? This is Detective Heinz. He's the one that called the judge for you."

Salim nodded, not offering his hand. Heinz extended his own, though, the kid having no choice but to take it. Heinz squeezed.

"Something happens to your godfather here, you know who I'm gonna look for first, right?"

"Uh-huh," the kid said neutrally, avoiding eye contact.

Well, he couldn't squeeze this kid's hand forever. And the fact of the matter was, if this Salim here was intent on doing mayhem on Mitchell, there was almost nothing Heinz or anybody else could do to stop him, really.

"And you best show up for your court date," Heinz said. "Because if they have to issue a bench warrant? I'm gonna execute it myself."

More bullshit, the kid lighting a cigarette.

"When do I get my vest back," he said.

"Never. It's illegal."

Salim hissed like a leaking tire.

"Thanks." Mitchell shook Heinz's hand. "Thank you for your help."

Heinz, standing just inside the doorway, watched the two of them step to the street, the kid getting into the guy's car without a word, as if the ride was a given.

Mitchell walked around to the driver's side, hesitated, then, using the car roof as a desk, wrote something on a scrap of paper.

He came back into the building.

"Listen, I don't know you, you don't know me. But if there's anything I can do for you—and I mean *any*thing . . . Here's my name and number. Please."

"All right," Heinz said, shaking his hand. "Thanks."

He could tell the guy really meant it. In fact, he intuited that if he were to take him up on it, called him for say, a loan, a piano, a year's supply of Pampers for his son, it would put him over the moon. Not that Heinz ever would call—the night was fucked enough as is.

If anything should happen to this Mitchell . . .

He had really put himself in a potential jackpot tonight, would remain in that precarious state for who knew how long, all because of his Seagram's-fueled impulse to "help out"; to see what would happen.

At the very least, he had squandered a valuable favor chit with the judge.

He watched as Mitchell finally took off, the kid in the shotgun seat lighting himself another cigarette and staring straight ahead.

Fucked.

It was definitely that time again. Heinz took out his wallet, shuffling through credit cards, business cards, PBA courtesy cards, looking for White Tom Potenza's phone number.

Ray and Salim sat parked in front of Salim's mother's building on Tonawanda Avenue as the sun began to climb above the defeated block of six-story walkups and unfenced lots, two mini-marts posted at opposite ends of the street like lookouts.

Ray's grandparents had lived in this very same building for nearly a quarter of a century, from the late 1940s through the early 1970s, but he didn't share this information with Salim because he didn't think his protégé here would give a shit.

They had been sitting in silence like this for slightly more than an hour, Ray deciding to take Salim's disinclination to leave the car as some half-assed form of apology.

Last night, despite whatever pressures were driving him, Salim had been unable to bring himself to do more than squawk and sputter, had in fact, simply marched out of the apartment when asked to. Ray, once first his fear then his self-disgust had subsided, had been moved by that and so felt reasonably unembarrassed to be here now.

"So what did you really need the money for," he asked almost apathetically.

"I told you," Salim said.

"Give me a break . . ."

Salim exhaled. "Michelle's cousin Busy? I told you how she had got him on my ass after we had that fight? Nigger comes up to me yesterday, says he wants a thousand dollars or he's gonna take my life."

Ray had no idea whether this scenario held any more truth than last night's vendor's license story.

"You believe him?"

"I did when he said it to me, yeah, but I don't really know. It's like, people say they're gonna do shit, but . . ." Salim shrugged, and Ray took his cue from that.

"Maybe you should have said something about it to that cop."

Salim just stared at him.

"So what are you going to do?"

"I got to raise the money," Salim said blandly.

Ray stared straight ahead. Don't you do it . . .

"Well, you have the T-shirts, right?"

Salim hesitated for a beat. "Yup."

"Well then, there you go."

They sat there and pondered the crusty-eyed street slowly coming to life around them.

"Can I ask you something personal?" Salim said. "How much was my bail."

"Twenty-five hundred."

"Yeah, see." Salim clucked his tongue. "I'm really sorry about last night, I was in fear for my life and I really din't have no choice but to come to you, but if you had lent me the thousand? You'd've saved yourself fifteen hundred dollars, you know what I'm saying?"

Ray laughed. "Always looking out for me, huh?"

"Nah, I'm just sayin'." Salim shrugged, and the car returned to silence.

It had been a raw and freaky evening, though, and as the sun continued to climb, striking first the rooftops then slowly working its way down brick by brick to the street, a fatigue headache or possibly something else began to set up house in Ray at the same incremental pace.

"I need to go home," he finally said.

Salim exhaled long and slow, then nodded in acceptance. "All right," the words as hushed as the hour.

Eyes narrowed against the growing brightness, Ray stared straight ahead.

Salim opened the car door and stepped out onto the street. But then, as if belatedly struck by an unspoken demand, unspoken plea, he abruptly ducked back into the car and extended his hand.

"Yo, Mr. Mitchell, *thank* you."

And Ray was happy.

Richard Price is the author of six previous novels, including the national best-sellers *Freedomland* and *Clockers*, which was nominated for the National Book Critics Circle Award. In 1999 he received a Literature Award from the American Academy of Arts and Letters. His fiction, articles and essays have appeared in *Best American Essays 2002*, the *New York Times*, the *New York Times Book Review*, *The New Yorker*, *Esquire*, *The Village Voice*, and *Rolling Stone*. He has also written numerous screenplays, including *Sea of Love*, *Ransom*, and *The Color of Money*. He lives in New York City with his wife, the painter Judith Hudson, and his two daughters.

A NOTE ABOUT THE TYPE

The text of this book was set in Electra, a typeface designed by W. A. Dwiggins (1880–1956). This face cannot be classified as either modern or old style. It is not based on any historical model, nor does it echo any particular period or style. It avoids the extreme contrasts between thick and thin elements that mark most modern faces, and it attempts to give a feeling of fluidity, power, and speed.

Composed by Stratford Publishing Services,
Brattleboro, Vermont
Printed and bound by Berryville Graphics,
Berryville, Virginia
Designed by Virginia Tan